BROTHERHOOD OF FOREVER
BAND IN THE WIND, BOOK 3 - THE FINAL CHAPTER

Cover Design and Interior Format

BROTHERHOOD
OF
FOREVER

BAND IN THE WIND
THE FINAL CHAPTER

William John Rostron

WORKS BY

WILLIAM JOHN ROSTRON

Band in the Wind Trilogy
Band in the Wind — A Novel
Sound of Redemption - Band in the Wind - Book 2
Brotherhood of Forever — Band in the Wind — The Final Chapter

Video Productions of Written Work from New York Stage
"Pretty Flamingo"
"In the Garden of Eden"
"Ava's Bubble"

Viewed on website - www.williamjohnrostron.com

DEDICATED

To My Children:
Justin (and Heather)
Jarrod (and Erin)
Brittany (and Michael)

&

To My Children's Children:
William M. Rostron
Samantha S. Rostron
Bella–Capri Rostron
Ava Marie Brunjes

CAST OF CHARACTERS
From
Band in the Wind **and** *Sound of Redemption*
As of October 1967

Those Born Free Band

James (Jimmy Mac) McAvoy *(Drums) – 1949 to 1967 – murdered in store robbery.*

Joseph (Joey Tinman) Tinley, Jr. *(Keyboards) – 1949 to 1967- poisoned.*

Rocco (Bracko) Brackowski *(Lead Guitar) – 1949 to 1967- died in a suspicious fire.*

Giovanni (Gio) DeAngelis *(Rhythm Guitar) – 1949 to 1967- murdered but assumed missing.*

John (Johnny Cipp) Cippitelli, Jr. *(Bass) – 1949 - hiding in Key West, Florida.*

Family

Noel McAvoy *– (father of Jimmy Mac) murdered during the robbery of his store.*

Adele McAvoy *– (mother of Jimmy Mac) – trying to run Mac and Son Candy Store and raise three daughters.*

Aylin McAvoy (16), Sioban McAvoy (14), Maggie McAvoy (12) *– sisters of Jimmy Mac.*

John Cippitelli, Sr. and **Anna Cippitelli** *– (parents of Johnny) - confused and depressed about missing son.*

Joseph Tinley, Sr. and **Margaret Tinley** *- (parents of Joey) killed in a suspicious car accident.*

Stan Brackowski *– (father of Bracko) killed in a house fire that also took his son's life.*

Giuseppe (Gyp) DeAngelis and **Rosalie DeAngelis** *– (parents of Gio) – upset by their son's departure and the note he left* *behind.*

Friends

Maria Romano *(girlfriend of Johnny Cipp)* – *confused by the sudden disappearance of her boyfriend.*

Diane Montgomery *(girlfriend of Jimmy Mac)* – *best friend of Maria Romano, murdered in the same robbery that killed her boyfriend, Jimmy Mac.*

Riet Carver *(girlfriend of Gio DeAngelis)* – *upset by the sudden disappearance of her boyfriend, Gio. Pregnant with his son* – *Giovanni (Van) DeAngelis, Jr.*

DJ Spinelli – *Johnny's best friend from Bishop McCarthy High School. Songwriter for Those Born Free. Now a student at Queens College.*

Br. Christian – *religious brother and teacher who was a mentor and music teacher to Johnny Cipp. He inspired Johnny, Joey, and DJ to write songs and perform during lunch breaks. A skilled musician with an unknown past.*

Tony Provenzano – *brother of Guy Provenzano. Mentally disabled by mistakenly huffing too much glue.*

Enemies

Gaetano (Mad Guy) Provenzano – *assistant to his father's workings in organized crime. He was limited in his advancement opportunities because of his mistakes during the Driftwood Club/Those Born Free fiasco.*

Richie Shea – *a corrupt police detective and cousin of Guy Provenzano. He has been tasked with tracking down Johnny Cipp by his cousin Guy.*

Sal Timpani – *One of two hitmen responsible for the murder of Jimmy McAvoy, Noel McAvoy, and Diane Montgomery. He also was involved in the killing of Gio DeAngelis.*

Sammy Crespo – *Sal Timpani's partner in crime and actual gunman who shot Jimmy McAvoy.*

Nicky Toto – *cousin of Guy Provenzano. Arsonist and murderer of Bracko Brackowski.*

United States Army

Greg "Chinx" Cincotta – *formerly a member of the Provenzano gang. He intervened when a drunk harassed Maria Romano and Tony Provenzano. As a result, he was charged with assault and joined the army as an alternative to jail.*

Jack "Leo" Leonardo – *formerly handball partner of Guy Provenzano. Provenzano disgraced him because he spoke up against racist attack on two black handball opponents.*

John "Goody" Barlow – *saved Johnny Cipp from a black gang attack. Labeled as an "Uncle Tom," he was shunned by his black community.*

Davis "Junior" Jones - *a black youth who suffered an attack by the O'Neil brothers while playing basketball. He fended off one brother with his martial arts skills before suffering an injury in a fight with the other brother.*

Others

Neil Connaughton – *known as "Neil the Squeal," he was a victim of bullying in high school by his white peers. A case of mistaken identity led to a vicious attack by a black gang. However, Neil was saved by the intervention of Bracko Brackowski.*

Mary Lou Casali – *abandoned and pregnant at 16-years-old.*

Freddy Resch – *father of Mary Lou's child. In his anger at the news of her pregnancy, he has an altercation that causes the death of a young black boy, Willie Calder. In the process, he is wounded.*

Larry Kimski – *Carvel owner.*

Thad Carver – *uncle of Riet Carver.*

1990

Padre – *Iconic priest who attempts to physically and spiritually save the "Key-wasted" of Key West.*

Cal Fremont – *Johnny/Jack's AA sponsor.*

Giovanni "Van" DeAngelis – *son of Gio DeAngelis and Riet Carver*

"Life is what happens to you while you're busy making other plans."

– *John Lennon*

PROLOGUE

"Walking in the Sand"
- Shangri-Las
Key West, Florida

February 15, 2013

JOHNNY CIPP HAD LIED IN his journal. He had written that he had not been to New York since 1990. However, he had returned—only a few weeks before for Riet's funeral. It was almost as if by lying to an inanimate object, it would somehow change reality—it would somehow insulate him from the sheer stupidity of what he had done.

All the events that happened twenty-three years ago were in the past. Johnny had told himself that no one would notice his presence. There was no reason for anyone *up there* to care about his visit. He was wrong. Someone did notice. Someone definitely did care.

◆

On September 9, 1967, Johnny Cipp fled his home in Queens. On that day, he had witnessed the death of his best friend, Gio DeAngelis, at the hands of mob leader Mad Guy Provenzano. Johnny was now the sole survivor of the band Those Born Free, a group whose success would have been his route to fame and fortune. However, on the night of the band's greatest achievement, their hopes came crashing down—and it had all been Johnny's fault.

As underage performers at Mad Guy Provenzano's Driftwood

Club, a police raid led to both the band's arrest and the wrath of its owner. Disgraced in front of *his* bosses, Mad Guy vowed a lifelong vendetta against Those Born Free. With the death of Gio, Johnny saw the writing on the wall. He fled.

Johnny's escape saved his life, but not his sanity. He had left behind his family, friends, and the love of his life, Maria Romano, all without any explanation. However, as Johnny descended into a two-decade period of drug and alcohol abuse, another burden of shame fell upon him.

After saving Johnny's life, Gio DeAngelis had made one dying request to his friend—to give a message to Riet Carver. Johnny was the only person in the world who knew of Gio's secret love of the young black woman. Gio had died while he was on his way to tell Riet that he was running away, but that he would return for her. Because of his cowardice, Johnny never passed on the message, and Riet never knew what had happened to the love of her life. However, Gio *had* left a short note to his parents telling them he was leaving. With Gio's body hidden by Provenzano, and Johnny missing, the world assumed they had escaped together.

Johnny's destructive path eventually led to a suicide attempt in 1990. After being saved by a local priest named Padre, he started anew. On the road to sobriety, Johnny helped coach the college baseball team of his AA sponsor, only to find one of the players had a familiar name. Giovanni "Van" DeAngelis, Jr., was now 22 years old and heading for a major league baseball career in Queens, New York—home of the still vengeful Mad Guy Provenzano. The madman had vowed to kill not only the band but all those related to them. By 1990, he had taken eleven lives, and Johnny realized that Van and Riet would be next.

Johnny's rescue mission resulted in the death of Mad Guy. However, in the process, he had been left critically wounded and still on the run. It had been Riet who hid Johnny and secretly nursed him back to health. What Riet did not know was the fact that it was Richie Shea, Mad Guy's cousin, and heir to his throne, who had left Johnny at her doorstep. For his own reasons, Shea helped Johnny hide from both the police and the rest of the Provenzano gang. But there was one caveat.

Shea spared Johnny's life on the condition that he *never* return to New York. Johnny Cipp made a pact with the devil, and it saved his life. In February of 2013, Johnny broke that pact.

Johnny had wanted to go to Riet's funeral. He needed to go even though, in 1990, he had given away the right to ever return to the Heights. Still, this was Riet. Riet, who had done so much for him despite his failures to her. He needed to comfort her son Van and his family and to pay his respects to a wonderful woman. He had to be there for his departed friend Gio.

Throwing caution to the wind, he packed up his rickety old car and drove straight through the night, pausing only for brief catnaps. Hidden in the shadows during the ceremony, he only revealed himself to the family at the cemetery. No one else at the funeral would even know who he was—at least, that was what he had thought. After the last few mourners started to drift away, Johnny came out of the shadows to console Riet's family. Johnny refused offers to stay. He had been tempting fate by even being there. He needed to remove himself as soon as possible. He remembered Shea's words as clearly as the night they were spoken to him 23 years ago.

"Let's get this straight. I'm not letting you go because I'm a nice guy. Your disappearance helps me, but if you ever step foot in New York again, you *are* dead. Just in case you ever think of reneging on our deal, I want you to remember this simple equation: return equals death. I'm in deep shit if you ever show up, and if it comes down to you or me, you lose."

Johnny remembered the warning, but he had come back anyway. He hoped everything would work out. It didn't.

———◆———

Johnny began the long trek back to Key West. Unknown to him, the occupants of a black Lincoln Navigator had noted his presence and the numbers of his Florida license plate. Car registration information was readily available if you had connections to a police department. To double-check on the identity of the mystery man from Florida, Van DeAngelis was surveilled after he returned home to Miami. Three weeks later, as Van and Johnny met at the Those Born Free Club in Key West, a spy at a nearby table watched and listened. From his observations, he had attained all the information necessary to prove Johnny's identity. It was just a question of finding the right time for his boss to act.

Johnny Cipp had built a life in Key West, Florida. He owned the Those Born Free Club, a music venue that catered to the music-loving, but sober clientele of the area. After his club emptied each night, he found his way to the beach. He enjoyed the peace and solitude these moments brought to him. However, on this night, as Johnny saw visions of friends in the clouds and heard mumblings in his ear from the Music Doctor, he realized that he was not alone. He heard footsteps walking in the sand. Despite lying in his journal, he had expected this visit would happen since his return from New York.

Richie Shea had come to Key West.

PART
1

"Dancing on the Other Side of the Wind"

We were drifting on the wind,
Living for the day.
We kept asking each other,
Who knows the way?

We were dancing,
We were dancing.
On the other side of the wind.

- Chris Delaney and the Brotherhood Blues Band

1

"All Those Years Ago"
- *George Harrison*

Diary of DJ Spinelli

Entry #1 – October 6, 1967

JOHNNY, ARE YOU DEAD? THAT'S one explanation for what the hell happened to you? Nobody knows—not even your parents. We had long talks in July when Bracko died, and again in August when Jimmy Mac was killed during the robbery. But after we talked on Labor Day about how we would start Queens College together, I heard nothing!

I called over and over, but your parents said that you wouldn't talk to anyone. Fear? Anger? Depression? I don't know. We'd always been open with each other, sharing our inner thoughts and feelings. It had helped us develop some great songs. But now it is more than a month later and nothing.

Today is my birthday. I turned 18. (Thanks for the birthday card I never got!) I decided that on this historic day I'd do two things. I would start to chronicle my life—my struggles, my thoughts, my feelings—all my shit. What I'll do with it, I don't know. Perhaps, it will help me to find direction in my life. I'll try to get around to personal stuff at some point, but for now, I'm just going to deal with my current quest to find you!

Because I live in goddamned NYC, I couldn't drive until

today even though I had already passed the tests and had a junior license. And where is the first place I chose to drive? Was there any doubt? My second birthday task was to go to your house and confront you, you inconsiderate prick.

When I got there, your parents told me that you weren't at home. The fact that they seemed on the verge of tears said to me that there was more to it. All of a sudden, they hugged me and invited me to your room.

The stairs to your attic hideaway remained as cluttered as ever—you're a damn slob! We made our way through the debris of your life—through your obstacle course. When we finally made it to the top of the stairs, they motioned for me to sit. After moving dirty clothes from the chair by your desk, I sat down (dirty clothes on the chair—like I said, *a damn slob.*). Your mom spoke first.

"Look around you."

"Typical Johnny," I joked.

"It's been exactly like this for a month—since he left."

"What do you mean left?"

"We think that maybe Johnny and Gio ran away. But we just don't know." I could see the tears starting to form in her brown eyes, and your dad hugged her tightly.

"The deaths did something to him." Your dad continued the story.

Deaths? Johnny, I knew that you were having a hard time dealing with the loss of Bracko and Jimmy Mac. I told your parents that you seemed to be doing OK when we talked on the phone.

"Yeah, but he didn't take Tinman's death nearly as well."

"What the f . . ." I started but remembered who I was talking too. "What are you saying?"

"Yeah, Gio and Johnny are the only ones left," lamented your father.

"How sad that they all are gone in a few short months," answered your mom, halfheartedly.

Your dad got angry.

"It's more than sad!" His expression told me that he was not buying into the whole coincidence scenario. "Johnny found out about Tinman's death, and he went to blow off steam.

He took a *spaldeen* and his glove and went to the yard. A little while later, Gio came looking for Johnny, and we told him where he was. That was the last time we saw Johnny."

They told me that Gio had left a note to his parents explaining that he was running away. However, you hadn't even done that. I think that hurt them as much as anything. Johnny, don't you care?

I decided that talking about this right now was very emotional for both of them. I decided it best to leave them alone. I went to the stairs. "I know the way out," was my stupid way of saying goodbye.

"Come back some time, DJ. Johnny always talked about you and what you meant to him. I can still hear the two of you up here—writing songs." She burst into tears, unable to hold in her feelings any longer. After promising to visit, I left.

I'll keep that promise. It wasn't the only promise I made today. I vowed that I would find you, even if it takes forever. Johnny, I'm going to keep writing these entries *to you*. Someday I'm going to stick this diary up your damn ass. I'm going to let you know what you did to the feelings of the people who love you, including me. At least, that is what I hope to do. However, my gut tells me that the Johnny I know could never hurt his parents like this. So, I ask again—Johnny, are you dead?

Entry # 2 - October 7, 1967

Johnny, you're a selfish bastard. Sure, you use me to write song lyrics for your band, but when there is no more band—bye, bye DJ. But maybe I'm wrong. Maybe there's something else going on.

I guess that perhaps I'm the one being selfish. I always envied you Heights guys. Yeah, I know that you lived in a tough neighborhood. I mean, you all knew how to use the word "fuck" as all seven parts of speech. In fact, on one occasion. I could swear that I heard Gio do precisely that in one *single* sentence!

Yet, you always seemed so close. Was it because of that toughness—or despite it? I wanted to be there with you instead of my safe place in Floral Park. No beatings for me—no fun either. I would've given anything to be there for that "Night of the Pretty Flamingos." I mean, I care about the life and liberty of plastic wildlife as much as the next man.

It's just that our lives seemed set. You, Maria, and I were going to go to Queens College together. That might have been true if the band had succeeded. Johnny, you always were one to hedge your bets.

You would get your driver's license in June, and I would get mine the following October. Then I could be part of that life I'd only briefly tasted. I could be with the band regularly as musicians and as friends. They had made it clear that I would always be welcomed into your group as a songwriter, but more importantly, as a friend. Now I go to school alone. I write my lyrics alone. I have no dreams for the future.

I know that Maria is here at Queens College, but so are over twenty thousand other people. I liked Maria from the day you introduced us. I spent endless hours listening to you talk about her. I only hope that someday I'll feel as deeply for someone as you felt for her.

Entry #3 - October 8, 1967

So far, so good. I promised myself that I would start keeping a diary of my daily events. I don't care that you told me that diaries are something that little girls do.

"Oh, are you going to write about whether you like John, Paul, George, or Ringo best?" you once rebuked me in your best sarcastic voice.

I disagreed. I pulled out the old Webster's and read you the definition of a diary—*a daily record of personal activities, reflections, or feelings.*

"That's what I want to do. I want to keep a record of things— to remember things—to make sense of the universe somehow," I argued.

"OK, but I'll ask one favor of you," you obnoxiously countered, "Call it a journal instead of a diary. It sounds more manly!"

I just rolled my eyes and didn't answer you. You waited a few minutes and then spat, "Well?"

"Well, what?" I answered annoyed.

"John, Paul, George, or Ringo?"

"Screw you," was my answer that day—and it is my answer now. You lost all rights when you took off. When you, Johnny Cipp, write something, you can call it a journal, or a diary, or whatever the hell you want, you bastard. But I know you never will. There will never be a Journal of Johnny Cipp or a Johnny Cipp Diary. Therefore, you don't get to have an opinion on what I call mine. You ran away. Screw you. This is the "Diary of DJ Spinelli."

Entry #4 – October 10, 1967

I calmed myself down since writing last time. I realized that if I'm going to tell the story right, I've got to be more objective and distance myself from what occurred. So here goes.

You and I met freshman year at Bishop McCarthy High School. You were from Cambria Heights, and I was from the city section of Floral Park. Though I could say I was from the city, my life and yours were very different. Your area was violently changing. I'm a big believer in integration, but it just wasn't working very well in Cambria Heights. I don't know who was instigating the violence, and I may never know.

You always told me about the fights that you had seen (or, in some cases, been in). It all seemed so senseless, yet no one could stop it. I know that you wanted out, and you saw your way to do that by playing in the band. I think that it went beyond *wanting* to get out—you *needed* to get out.

But Johnny, what about all of us who cared about you? It wasn't just me. There was Maria—you loved her. And your parents. And our teacher and mentor, Brother Christian, who took pity on you because of the hand injury that left you unable to play the guitar? He spent an unbelievable time teaching you the bass. Don't care what happened to him—to any of us?

2

"Nowhere Man"
- The Beatles

THOSE BORN FREE Tape #17 – (May 4, 1967)

"...I'm gonna love you, gonna love you in my own sweet way." (singing – Gio)

"Cut!" (Jimmy Mac)

"That was good." (Tinman)

"Good? That was fucking goddam great!" (Gio)

"To quote my mom, 'The mouth on you, Gio DeAngelis!'" (Aylin McAvoy)

"Well, Aylin, then it's a good thing she isn't home." (Jimmy Mac)

"You know that a Spencer W. Kimball once wrote, 'Profanity is the product of a feeble mind trying to express itself forcefully.'" (Tinman)

"Who you calling feeble-minded, Tinman?" (Gio)

"Oh, Tinman, you are such a weirdo." (Aylin)

"I prefer nerd, if you don't mind." (Tinman)

"What egghead came up with that word?" (Gio)

"Dr. Seuss—in his 1950 classic book, If I Ran the Zoo." (Tinman)

"Hey, Tinman, you think you'll ever get any of this—talking like that?" (Aylin)

"Aylin, keep your damn tits in your blouse, please!" (Jimmy Mac)

"As much as I am enjoying Aylin's sideshow, can we get back to business?" (Johnny)

"Aylin, get the hell outta here." (Jimmy Mac)

"Anyone else got anything important to say before we get back to practice?" (Gio)

"Yeah, Jimmy Mac, can I have that tape to give to Brother Christian?" (Johnny)

"Good idea." (Tinman)

"I wouldn't be here without his help. Hey, maybe we all wouldn't be here if it weren't for him. He taught me to play the bass." (Johnny)

"Well, that's open to debate." (Gio)

"Asshole!" (Johnny)

"I think that Johnny plays extremely well." (Tinman)

"It was a joke, Tinman, a joke. Do you have any sense of humor?" (Gio)

"No, but that's the difference between you and me. I don't have a sense of humor, and I know it. You don't have a sense of humor, but you think you do." (Tinman)

"Snag, he got you." (Jimmy Mac)

"And Brother Christian gave Tinman balls. Balls to stand up to his father so he could play with us. And balls to stand up to Gio." (Johnny)

"For that alone, he deserves to get this tape. Give it to him with our compliments." (Jimmy Mac)

"Thanks." (Johnny)

"OK, if you punks are done being sappy, we can move on." (Gio)

"Bracko, start us off with some 'Spoonful.'" (Johnny)

"OK." (Bracko)

"Tinman's still a weirdo—and a nerd." (Aylin from the top of the stairs)

<hr/>

November 22, 1967

He removed the stiff white collar for the last time. Today was the day that he moved on to the next chapter of his life. From now on, he would be Christian, not Brother Christian. He still had a deep abiding love of God, and he still loved to see the wonder in the eyes of students when he taught. However, he could not stomach the archaic attitudes of his superiors and the sheer self-righteousness of the administration. He convinced himself that these were good enough reasons to enter the real world again. He had made his decision without knowing where he would go or what he would do. Something had stirred in him almost two years before.

It was those boys and their unbridled love of music. Johnny Cipp, DJ Spinelli, and Joey Tinley and their little makeshift band had graduated from McCarthy High. He understood that they were following the natural progression of life. Students always moved on. Yet when they moved on, the music had also moved on, and he missed it. He rationalized that teachers always felt a little left behind by graduating students. However, the new school year had not brought the usual bonding with his students. He just could not make the connection. And then he found the tape.

Johnny had given him a tape of the band playing a few of their numbers. It had been his way of thanking his teacher and showing how far he had come.

Damn, thought Christian, *they were great.* They had nailed Ten Years After's "Spoonful." Not just Johnny on the bass, but that guitarist—unbelievable! They all could play—really play. He listened to the tape frequently that summer and fall, and old feelings rekindled in his soul. It made him remember the joy of making music that had once been a part of *his* life.

With Thanksgiving vacation coming, Christian considered it a good time to make a change. He had given the school enough warning so that they could replace him. It was obvious that the administrators were glad to see him go.

Upon leaving McCarthy High, he should probably have gone home to his family in Connecticut. They would welcome him, but he was not ready to see them yet. Christian had not been able to face any of them since *that* day. The day he killed his brother.

November 23, 1967 – Thanksgiving Day

The soup was hot, but the bread was stale. The company was not very friendly, but that was to be expected from the down-and-outers who crammed the charity kitchen in New York's Greenwich Village. Christian had better options. He had some cash to his name and could have found shelter in a mid-range hotel for the cold winter months. His choice of accommodations was more a statement of self-punishment. He had failed as a *brother*—in every sense of the word. He had been unable to maintain his commitments as a religious brother. More importantly, he had failed in the genuine sense of a flesh and blood brother.

After finishing his dinner, he left the warmth of the church basement. On the way out, he dropped enough money in a donation basket to pay for at least three meals. He needed to get out and breathe the air of the city. He wandered aimlessly, all the while considering his future. It was then that he saw the exterior of the Café Wha. It was closed for the holiday, and nothing about the exterior of the venue gave a hint to its dramatic history.

In the summer of 1966, superstar Jimi Hendrix had been discovered playing in the bowels of this converted folk music club. A month later, a group named Those Born Free had also played there. Yet it was not the still-rising star of Hendrix or the doomed band that drove his memory. Christian thought instead of the spectacular rise of *his* band from its humble beginnings on that very same stage. Their success had preceded the others, and so had their devastating fall from grace.

3

"Over, Under, Sideways, Down"
- The Yardbirds

Diary of DJ Spinelli

Entry #5 - December 23, 1967

JOHNNY, I'VE KEPT MY PROMISE to see your parents today. But it's a hard promise to keep because it's so damn depressing to be around them. You sure did screw them up. I brought them a little box of Italian cookies for Christmas, and they were grateful. I realized that there would be no celebrating in your home this year. Yet I remember how much you used to tell me how your family enjoyed the holidays.

No, I just can't dwell on this anymore. I haven't been consistent writing in this book because it always ends up being about grief. My life is moving along great, but somehow, I feel guilty writing that. No more! Johnny, screw you!

I finished my first semester of college last week, and my grades were fantastic. I'm on my way to a career as a writer. I just don't know if I will write fiction, or non-fiction, or maybe even poetry. Scratch that, no money in that poetry shit.

I'm going to be more positive about life and not dwell on dead or missing friends. For all I know, you and Gio are somewhere laughing and having a good time.

Entry #6 - January 9, 1968

I figured that I would get one last visit in with your parents before the spring semester starts, and I get too busy. When I was about to leave, they handed me a little bag with something in it. I don't think that it was a present. After they told me not to open it until I got home, I noticed that there were tears in their eyes.

I left immediately and didn't look *in* the bag until I was home and safely locked away in my bedroom. Yet as I drove, the mystery played out in my mind. This was a Wetson hamburger bag, and your parents had not given me some greasy almost-meat patties. Even before I reached my house, I understood why this had been such an emotional experience. On the old receipt stapled to the top of the bag was the notation "For DJ." Johnny, I immediately recognized that these words were in your handwriting. I looked at the date - June 19. You had set this aside for me just before you and the band went to the big audition— before your life got so damn confusing. Were you going to give it to me the next time you saw me?

In the bag was a tape from band practice. It was labeled "Words of Doubt." I had written the lyrics to that song, and you and Joey had added the music. I knew that Those Born Free had decided to do it, but I had never heard the finished product. I put it in my cassette recorder and listened. I couldn't help but wonder what happened to the rest of the tapes.

——◆——

THOSE BORN FREE Tape –
"Words of Doubt" – Tape # 63 – (June 1967)

"Understand,
Take my hand,
Stop and see what's inside of me,
I love you."

"We nailed it." (Johnny)
"That makes ten original songs for the album—we're set" (Jimmy Mac)

"Yeah, Vinnie the Cat told my father that the winner of the audition has a record deal with Red Bird Records." (Tinman)

"Sweet!" (Johnny)

"Then, I guess millions will hear this song." (Gio)

"And you tell DJ that he wrote some damn good lyrics" (Jimmy Mac)

"Amen." (Tinman)

"I will. How about we give him this tape." (Johnny)

"Sounds good. Tell him that we seriously owe him." (Jimmy Mac)

"Yeah, DJ really is a wordsmith." (Tinman)

"What the hell does that mean—wordsmith?" (Gio)

"He knows how to craft words and create emotion." (Tinman)

"Yeah, Yeah, Yeah. All I know is that there are a lot of guys who are going to be happy to dance to this slow sexy song." (Gio)

"What are you talking about?" (Tinman)

"What he is saying—if I can read my buddy's mind—is that there is going to be some sexual tension and . . ." (Johnny)

"Yeah, some guys are going to have their things ping." (Gio)

"You're gross! (Tinman)

"Oh yeah, even Bracko agrees with me." (Gio)

"What are you saying?" (Tinman)

"He's playing the Stones . . . 'Let's Spend the Night Together.'" (Johnny)

Entry #6 – December 23, 1967 (continued)

The band's words have made me think that music, maybe even songwriting, would be in my future. The tape has me thinking.

4

"Lost Little Girl"
- *The Doors*

November 1967

" SHE'S NOT HERE, MA."

"But I need her to watch you two. Do you have any idea where she is, Siobhan?"

"No."

"Maggie? How about you? Any idea where your sister Aylin is? I need her."

"Sorry, Ma. No idea."

"She is going to be the death of me."

The three of them stared at each other and then moved in for a group hug. The mother and her two youngest children were surviving. The same could not be said for Aylin McAvoy, eldest of the surviving McAvoy siblings. Since the tragedy that had taken her father, Noel, and brother Jimmy Mac, she had changed. There were too many of the wrong kind of guys hanging around. There were too many late nights. Sometimes, Adele McAvoy could smell the faint odor of smoke on her daughter's clothes, and it was *not* tobacco.

Aylin had always been a spirited, adventurous young girl. Her green eyes sparkled with a mischievous glint that was accented by long luxurious layers of auburn hair. Everything about her said beauty. At sixteen, she was already a stunner, and her brother

Jimmy Mac had always known he would spend an excessive amount of his time protecting her honor. The entire Those Born Free band had unofficially adopted her (and her younger sisters). Not only would none of them date Aylin (though she was less than two years younger than them), but anyone caught assaulting her virtue would have to deal with all five of them.

But they were all gone now. There were no knights in shining armor to protect her from the vultures that descended upon the impressionable young maiden. Worse yet, the beautiful Aylin did not seem to want protection. She seemed to throw herself into trouble. She seemed to care about nothing and no one.

Aylin had a secret. It was a secret so deeply ensconced in her subconscious that even she could not remember it. Yet it was there. It had wormed its way into her mind like cancer metastasizing in her brain. It changed the person that Aylin had been in ways that even she could not understand. She was destroying herself, and she had no protectors now that her father, brother, and Those Born Free were all gone.

5

"Sad Little Girl"
- *Beau Brummels*

Diary of DJ Spinelli

Entry #7 – January 23, 1968

FIRST DAY OF CLASSES IN the spring semester. Amazing surprise. Maria and I are in the same history class. What are the odds of that happening? She was sitting close to the door, and I was by the window when I noticed her. Johnny, she is more beautiful than ever! You really should come back before she meets someone else.

When the professor finished up the lesson, she was gone before I could catch up to her. I'll see her in two days when we have the class again.

I like all my courses, especially the writing ones. I believe that the best way to become a better writer is to write often. That means that this diary and my school papers are simply not enough. I decided to join the staff of the school paper.

Entry #8 – January 25, 1968

I talked to Maria today. I guess that she was trying to forget about you, but then she saw me, and that reminded her of the past. She cried, and I didn't know what to do.

"I'm just going through the motions. I'm getting nothing out of this school," she admitted. Johnny, I remembered you telling me how hard she worked to get into college—the endless hours of extra work for an academic diploma. Now, she was a mere shell of the girl that I'd known—another one of your victims.

"He'll be back," was my weak reply, and even I knew that was probably not true. I took Maria for coffee to try and cheer her up. Johnny, she needs you. As much as my anger seethed at you for leaving, I figured I owed it to you to console Maria. She wasn't buying it.

"Thanks, DJ, for trying."

She just hugged me and left.

Entry #9 – February 4, 1968

Maria wasn't in class today—third straight time. Her name was not even read when the Prof took attendance, which means she is not registered in the class anymore.

After school, I got Maria's phone number from your parents, and I called her. Her parents had always been assholes. You always told me that. However, the woman who answered the phone was distressed. Maria was gone. She had left ten days ago—the day we had talked. For some strange reason, my reaction was to think of one of your weird quirks. You were always putting song titles or lyrics to events that took place. All I could think of were the words to the Beau Brummels' song "Sad Little Girl."

"He went away, didn't say goodbye,
He went away and made her cry."

Entry #10 - February 13, 1968

Holy Shit! A blizzard has paralyzed the city. After four days, there still is not even a hint of snowplows arriving at the fringes of the city. Meanwhile, in the part of Floral Park that is in Nassau County, people are driving around as if nothing happened. The news is reporting that forty-two people have died, and most of them are in Queens. They are not even thinking of opening the college until next Monday. After helping Mom and Dad shovel for the first few days, I've decided to do a lot of writing. Not much else to do. I'm looking forward to working on the school paper.

I called over to your house to see if your parents were OK. I would've asked if I could help them out, but I'd have as much chance of getting to Siberia as I would getting over to your house. Nothing is moving in this city.

In case you are wondering, they are doing well. At least that is what they said. I'll see them again when the roads are clear. That could be the Fourth of July at the rate things are going.

6

"Tonight, I Just Need My Guitar"
- Jimmy Buffet

February 9, 1968

SNOW RAVAGED THE NORTHEAST AS Christian peered out the window of his tiny Greenwich Village apartment. The massive amounts of white he saw would ensure two very distinct outcomes. First, the grimy metropolis would appear to be a place of pristine beauty as the thick layers of snow covered a multitude of visual sins. The other outcome of the storm was the entire mechanism of America's most populated area would grind to complete and lengthy standstill.

The view of virgin whiteness from his window reminded him of his own fresh start—the epiphany had come to him three months ago on Thanksgiving Day when he had stood outside the Café Wha. He loved music. Though the young musicians he had molded were gone, did music have to be gone also?

He would go it alone. He had been an excellent musician on many instruments and an exceptional singer. Why not make a go of it as a solo artist? Though the charts were cluttered with mostly four and five-man groups, there was a place for someone like him. And if stardom did not come knocking on his door, maybe he would be satisfied with eking out an existence playing local clubs for a small fee and tips.

A band might be an easier route to success, but he just was not ready to play with others. He had had a group once. Christian had been the lead guitar and lead singer of a band which had been rounded out by his brothers Kevin and Tommy on bass and drums, respectively, and his cousin Walt on rhythm guitar. That band was his family, and right now, he could not face them.

As New York City ground to a halt in the great blizzard of 1968, Christian hardly noticed. Armed with the used Gibson guitar that he bought in a pawnshop, he continued to spend almost every waking moment working on his playing and singing, hoping that he would somehow create a musical act worthy of audience acceptance.

7

"Hero"

"He never wondered what was right or wrong—he just knew."
- David Crosby

February 9, 1968

D EEP SWEAT COVERED HIS ENTIRE body. The continuous repetitions with the barbells had done their job on the muscles of his toned torso. His goals were clear, and his methods correct, but there was no guarantee that he would succeed. When would the damn letter arrive?

Neil Connaughton had a plan. The germ had been planted in him almost two years prior. He had been the victim of every bully who walked the halls of Andrew Jackson High School. "Neil the Squeal" was what they had called him, and he had bought into what they believed about him. A skinny red-headed little turd was all that he would ever be. Until . . .

Until a hero came along. This hero had saved him from a beating by some black kids who had mistaken him for someone else and were going to make him pay for a crime that he had not committed. He knew his savior only by the unlikely name of "Bracko" and owed his life to this strong silent giant.

However, Bracko had done more than save his life; he had changed it. Neil was no longer satisfied with being "The Squeal," as in someone who squealed like a pig when hit. He wanted to be a hero too. This goal seemed like a long shot two years ago when he first came upon the idea. However, a late growth spurt had added six inches to his height and left him a hair under six-foot tall. The rest had been sheer effort. Self-defense courses, weight-lifting, and an extensive running program had turned Neil Connaughton into the type of person that someone would think twice about picking on. But it was not enough. Neil still had the dream of being a hero. And so, he waited for the letter. It was due any day.

February 15, 1968

Again, there was no postal delivery due to the accumulated snow. Yet, the view out his front window produced an interesting sight—two impeccably dressed soldiers exiting the house across the street, the Leonardo residence. His parents had told him Leo Leonardo was home on a brief leave from the army following his completion of basic training.

Though Leo was five years older than Neil, they had both played in city games that included all the kids from the block. Whether it was hide-go-seek, red light-green light, red rover, or numerous other games, the younger kids were never left out.

Impulsively, Neil ran out the door and called out, "Good luck, Leo."

"Hey, Neil. How ya doin'? Damn, have you changed? You been working out?"

"Yeah, and so have you."

"The army sort of makes you do that."

"No one's going to mess with Leo now," babbled Neil, and he almost immediately regretted it.

Everyone in the Heights knew Leo's story. He had angered Mad Guy Provenzano by interfering with the bully's attack on two black kids who had defeated Leo and Guy in handball. As revenge for his disrespect, Guy taunted Leo in front of the entire schoolyard crowd. The bully had placed a gun to Leo's forehead and pulled the trigger. The realization that it was only a water gun came too late for Leo as he had already pissed in his pants—in front of most of the cool kids. Disgraced in front of everyone he knew, he stopped going out. Eventually, he decided to join the army to regain his dignity. Would anyone mess with him now? Or would he always be "Pisser" Leonardo on the streets of the Heights?

"Neil, this is my buddy Chinx. . .er. . .Greg," started Leo.

"Cincotta," slipped out unconsciously from Neil's unguarded mouth. Everyone knew Greg Cincotta. He had been one of Mad Guy Provenzano's in-crowd until he was arrested for assault. He had taken Guy's brother, Tony, to listen to a band at a Rosedale church dance. He had pummeled some unfortunate guy after overhearing him called the younger Provenzano a "retard." After he was found guilty, the judge offered him a choice of jail or enlisting in the army. No one in the world knew that Greg "Chinx" Cincotta had been offered a third choice by Mad Guy Provenzano—and turned it down.

"So, where are you two going now?"

"A little place you might have heard about on the news. It's called Vietnam."

February 17, 1968

Neither snow nor rain nor heat nor gloom of night stays these couriers from the swift completion of their appointed rounds. "Bullshit," muttered Neil as he looked out his window and waited for the mailman to hopefully make his first delivery since the snow had fallen more than a week ago. He had once seen this motto chiseled in the gray granite over the entrance to the New York City Post Office on 8th Avenue. *You think that being etched in stone would mean that it was, well, etched in stone,* he thought to himself.

Just as he had reached his breaking point, he spied Jerry, his regular postman down the street. Not willing to wait one extra moment, he ran into the snow with only his slippers on to intercept the carrier.

"Here ya go," said Jerry with a smile. He knew Neil had been waiting so long that he felt a tingle of joy just handing him the official-looking letter. "I hope it's good news." Neil tore it open right there on the snow-encrusted sidewalk.

"The New York City Police Department officially welcomes Neil Connaughton to the Cadet Class beginning March 1,

1968." The letter contained all the pertinent details about his assignment. Neil was so happy that he threw a bear hug around the mailman, and ran home to tell his parents.

March 1, 1968

He caught the F train into the city. Today was to be the most important day of his life. Today Neil Connaughton would be joining the New York City Police Department. Though he would start the academy this very morning, he understood that he could not be sworn in as a full-fledged officer until his 21st birthday. New York had a unique program that allowed candidates to take all the qualifying tests at the young age of eighteen. If a person could prove worthy after a barrage of physical, mental, and psychological tests, he or she would be taken on the force as a probationary cadet. At age 21, the appointment would be automatic.

Neil Connaughton knew that this was the city's way of getting up to three years of cheap manpower on the force. Paid next to nothing, cadets handled all the menial tasks so that the "real cops" were free to handle the critical job of fighting crime.

Neil was using these years to prepare himself. Right out of high school, he had started John Jay College of Criminal Justice. The college courses were geared to those who wanted advancement with the police force. More importantly, the uniquely rotating classes served the ever-changing schedules of active-duty officers. With any luck, Cadet Connaughton would graduate from John Jay less than a year after becoming Officer Connaughton. He was on his way. He would make a difference.

8

"Expecting to Fly"
- Buffalo Springfield

Diary of DJ Spinelli

Entry #11 - March 2, 1968

ICAN'T BELIEVE THOSE SELF-CENTERED PRICKS. I applied to work on the Queens College newspaper, and they turned me down. Their excuse was that I was a freshman. It's a lie. There are freshmen on the paper, but it's the *who-you-know game*—I didn't count on that. While I was waiting to be accepted, I wanted to knock their socks off with an exciting bit of exclusive writing.

When the snowstorm last month closed down the college, I scooped everyone with a view of the campus. I took a long walk through deep snow out to the LIRR station in Nassau County. I then took the train into Flushing. I walked a few more miles in the deep snow that still hadn't been plowed.

I took pictures and wrote notes about my journey. When I finally got to the campus, it was locked down tight behind the ten-foot-high chain-link fence. No one was there. Efforts to clear the snow hadn't even begun—and this was four days into the shutdown! I had expected this and had come prepared.

From my knapsack, I withdrew the bolt cutter that I had pilfered from my father's work area. I found a portion of the fence that was obscured on both sides by overgrown forsythia bushes. I cut an opening large enough to give me entry onto the silent, white campus. There I snapped an entire roll of film and took pages of notes. Even as I retraced my arduous trip home, I was composing the article I'd submit to the paper.

They accepted my article and my pictures, and it became the headlines of the school paper. However, the bastards didn't accept me. I'd been used, and I learned a valuable lesson when the byline of the article read "guest contributor." What they didn't realize is that they had validated me as a writer. I now knew that I had the skills to write, even if their closed club would block my path.

I think that I will start an alternative paper. It will take a while to figure out how and I'll probably have to use most of the money I saved last summer caddying to fund it. But, I am committed to this path. Watch out world, DJ Spinelli is on his way.

Entry # 12 – March 10, 1968

My plan to create an alternate paper is starting to take form. I'll do most of my distribution and sales on the Queens College campus, and it will be an alternative, underground newspaper. I think that I have come up with the perfect irreverent name— *The Queens Undies?*

I can't decide if I'll try to deal with everything that the "other" paper covers and maybe give it an outsider's take. On the other hand, perhaps I'll focus on one area. News? Politics? Campus Life? The social scene? Or the number one contender—music.

Entry #13 – March 11, 1968

I visited your parents today. I think they are concluding that they will never see you again. This was a bit depressing for me, and I hope if you ever read this, that you feel like shit. I think that my visits cheer them up a bit. However, it got me to think-ing. If you had stayed, we would all be getting near to the end of our first year of college. Perhaps you, Maria, and I would be working on my alternative newspaper together. I know that you both liked to write, and it would have been so much fun taking on this challenge together.

It was just about a year ago that we were putting in our college applications and thinking about our futures. I know that Those Born Free was the path that you wanted to take. Only I knew that you were also preparing to get an education.

What a difference a year makes. We had such high expectations for the future.

THOSE BORN FREE Tape - (March 12, 1967)

"That's why I'm crying, yeah, I'm crying, hear me cry, hear me cry." (singing - Jimmy Mac)

"Yowser, that was good." (Johnny)

"Fuckin' A" (Gio)

"Let's break. Jimmy Mac, got the tape off?" (Johnny)

"In a minute. I'm tightening up my snare." (Jimmy Mac)

"So, Joey, you get those college apps done?" (Johnny)

"Yeah, got most done." (Tinman)

"How many places you put in for?" (Johnny)

"Ten." (Tinman)

"What?" (Johnny)

"Yeah, half the Ivy League schools, and of course, Juilliard." (Tinman)

"Oh yeah, of course, Juilliard." (Johnny - sarcastically)

"And some safe schools like NYU and Duke." (Tinman)

"Yeah, those safe schools." (Johnny—again sarcastically)

"How about you? You know, if this whole thing doesn't work out?" (Tinman)

"If I do end up going to college instead of just running away with Maria, it will end up being a CUNY school." (Johnny)

"Huh, oh yeah, the City University of New York." (Tinman)

"Is that what CUNY stands for? I thought it was Cash Unneeded if New Yorker— ya know because it's free if you live in the city." (Johnny - laughing)

(laugh) (Gio, Tinman, and Jimmy Mac)

"How about you, Jimmy Mac? Ya know—what are you going to do

if this whole thing doesn't pan out?" (Tinman)

"McAvoy State." (Jimmy Mac)

"Huh?" (Tinman)

"He means that he will end up working with our dad in the candy store for the rest of his life." (Aylin)

"Aylin, get lost, and take the other two with you. This is band time." (Jimmy Mac)

"Aylin, Siobhan, Maggie, up here now." (voice from a distance)

"Thanks, Ma." (Jimmy Mac)

"Sore spot?" (Tinman)

"Yeah, it fucking scares the shit out of me—the thought of makin' egg creams the rest of my life." (Jimmy Mac)

"Don't worry. We'll make it." (Tinman)

"Hey, Bracko, where are you going if this all falls apart?" (Gio)

"F. U." (Bracko)

"Hey, hey. No reason to get nasty." (Gio)

"Fender University." (Bracko)

(laughing - Tinman, Johnny, Jimmy Mac)

"He's smiling. Holy shit, that was a joke—a real joke from Bracko!" (Gio)

(more laughing)

"The big guy made a joke—the big guy made a joke." (Gio)

"F.U." (Bracko)

"Yeah, I know, Fender University. I get it—your Fender guitar." (Gio)

"No . . . F. U. This time. fuck you." (Bracko)

9

"Heroes in the Night"
- Chris Delaney and the Brotherhood Blues Band

THOSE BORN FREE Tape – (recorded November 23, 1966)

"Earth to Johnny! We're recording now." (Jimmy Mac)

"Yeah, OK. Just thinking." (Johnny)

"You want a medal or a chest to pin it on?" (Gio)

"No, seriously. It was three years ago today that Kennedy got assassinated. Remember that day?" (Johnny)

"Yeah . . . unfortunately." (Gio)

"Mmm." (Bracko)

"Bummer." (Jimmy Mac)

"I think the whole world changed that day. It changed the way I looked at things." (Johnny)

"I think we all might agree with you on that." (Gio)

"Ha," (Johnny)

"What are you looking at, Johnny? I can have serious thoughts sometimes." (Gio)

"In what universe is that, Gio?" (Tinman)

"Shut the fuck up, Joseph." (Gio)

"Well, at least, that will probably never happen again. You know, someone important getting assassinated." (Johnny)

"Dream on." (Tinman)

April 4, 1968 – 6 p.m.

It had once been a factory. This was evident by the high ceiling and wide-open space that filled the center of the building. It now served as housing for six struggling young men. Its cavernous walls were filled with six inexpensively built ten by ten cubicles that served as windowless residences. Indeed, the entire structure received its only natural light from a pair of ancient windows that had probably had their last washing during the Truman presidency. The shared kitchen and living room area were adequate for the men's social interaction, but no one would be inviting their family for Thanksgiving in this depressing location.

However, the "Grand Lispenard Hotel," as its inhabitants had mockingly dubbed it, had three features that ingratiated it to them. First, it was cheap by New York City standards. Second, it had location. Lispenard Street was a mere hundred feet south of Canal Street, a position that put it within striking distance of Chinatown, Little Italy, and most importantly, Greenwich Village. The intersection of Broadway and Canal was a world-famous crossroad, and Lispenard was a literal stone's throw from that corner. The street itself was only a few hundred yards long and would go unnoticed by most New York residents. Yet, it was home to Christian, and five others who took advantage of the third unique feature of the Grand Lispenard—the soundproof studios embedded in its rear walls.

The building's landlord had once been a minor success with a doo-wop band in the fifties. His grandiose plans of a musical empire had fizzled after his group's records were relegated to the economy bins of record stores. The only tangible remnant of his success was this building and the rental income it generated. The two recording studios he had invested in had been stripped of their equipment. However, they still served as acoustically desirable venues for the six creative individuals whose bedrooms lined the walls.

Christian did not know much about his fellow boarders besides Trip Grimes. He knew their first names and that most of them, like him, were trying to break into the Village music scene. Occasionally, he would spend a few hours jamming with some of them. Eventually, he might get to know them better if they all lived long enough in this fire trap. The only real friendship that Christian had developed had been with Trip, a young black filmmaker who had moved into the city after graduating with a film degree from Syracuse University.

Trip had been born in the less than wealthy suburb of Gordon Heights, way out on Long Island. He liked to joke that he was "no city nigger," yet even the joking bothered both friends. It was not the concept of Trip being from a semi-rural area that was the problem, but rather the use of the "n" word itself. These were changing times, and almost anything could set off the flames of racial hatred on both sides.

In reality, Trip Grimes was an intelligent, educated young man looking for a career in documentary filmmaking. As such, he looked for the truth in situations and often found it by pressing the issue. His rough exterior was just that, a facade meant to attain a reaction from those he interacted with at any level. Christian saw through this false layer and merely responded to Trip's description by calling him a "country bumpkin," even referring to him as "Bump" instead of "Trip" on occasion.

Both knew that they would grow together as roommates, professionals, and friends.

———◆———

"Christian, what time tonight?" yelled Trip across the vast abyss that was the center of the living complex.

"Well, I finish playing at midnight, and then by the time I take the train here to this hellhole, I guess it will be about 12:30 or so," replied Christian.

"I'll see if any of the Grand Lispenard crew want to hit the bar with us."

"Good idea, Trip."

"Yeah, Christian, living here, we all need to drink heavily and often. If those religious guys could only see you now."

"Trip, I'm not a religious brother anymore. I'm just plain old Christian Andrews, and to be honest, I don't even really drink—anymore. It's just good to get out with the guys."

"Well, excuse me, *Mr. Andrews*."

"That's right, Reginald Edmund Grimes."

"Please, don't go there. You know if I were a white guy, I would be Reginald Edmund Grimes—the third. Or if I might have one of those waspy nicknames like 'Trey.'"

"Oh, is Trip so different?"

"I'm Reginald Edmund Grimes—triple cool."

"OK, Triple Cool, why don't you come down to the show tonight?"

"Gotta finish up some footage in the studio. Going in right now and probably won't even stick my head out until you get home."

"OK, catch you later, *Bump*."

Christian left for his regular gig as a singer-guitarist at the Vision Club. It did not pay a great deal, but it kept him going while he planned for bigger things. He could sing, and he could play. What he needed was a song—a song that would set him apart from all the others like him who were trying to make it.

April 4, 1968 – 10:53 p.m.

Christian had heard the news about four hours after it had happened. The night's performance had been going very well, and he was looking forward to his last set when a man ran in from the street shouting. The club had almost immediately emptied. After packing up his equipment, the singer had joined them on the street. He needed to get home. Was it because he needed to see Trip? Or was he simply seeking the shelter the Grand Lispenard provided?

The streets of New York were electric. People were hustling in every direction. Some were crying. Some were simply stunned. And some displayed deep abiding anger. All that he knew for sure was that Martin Luther King had been shot and killed around 6 p.m. that night. As he walked rapidly toward home, he heard bits and pieces of conversation. *Riots!* But was that here in New York? How had this happened? Why had it happened?

As he turned the corner onto Lispenard Street, Christian felt relief. A few more steps and he would be home. It was then that he heard the raised voices and pounding feet of an angry mob approaching. He bolted for the door of his building. What had moments before seemed so close, now seemed miles away.

The first blow came from behind and sent him crashing to the asphalt only a few feet in front of his home. It was then that the relentless kicking began. Christian heard the screaming of his attackers.

"Fuck him up!"

"No more shit. Fuck him up! Fuck them all up!"

"Respect? We'll take it! I'm not waiting for you cocksuckers to give it!"

"But . . ." Christian looked up through a veil of blood that covered his eyes. If his swollen mouth could speak, he did not even know what he would say to stop the beating. In the distance, he saw a lone figure. A savior? But what could one person do against the four outraged individuals who stood over his body?

———◆———

Desperate times called for extreme measures. Seeing the violence that was consuming other cities across the nation, Mayor John Lindsay decided that he would go up to Harlem and enlist black leaders' aid. He would appeal to their inherent devotion to the late Reverend King. The mayor and the leaders knew the violence descending on New York, and every other major city in the country would have shaken the now martyred leader. However, these measures would take time, and right now, the city's safety called for immediate action.

The mayor called on the police to hit the streets in full force, including emptying the police academy of raw recruits and putting them into the line of fire. Numbers mattered if you were going to intimidate the rising crowds of angry black men who were beginning to flood the streets. He needed time to unite the government with the black community's leaders to quell the rising violence. It was time that everyone knew was limited.

The commandeered school buses that ferried the expanded police force around the city were scenes of chaos. Calling in every available officer and cadet augmented police presence on the streets, yet there was no way to expand leadership. The result was a massive manpower presence on the streets of New York with very little supervision. This was how Neil Connaughton, and his one-month of training, found himself alone to confront four angry young men.

Not yet twenty years old, Cadet Connaughton status limited him to merely carrying a wooden baton. He knew that this would not be much help in confronting the four assailants who were armed with tire irons and baseball bats. He could have ignored the situation, turned his back, and convinced himself that he had seen nothing. There would be no one to call him to task for declining to throw himself into an impossible situation. No one except *Bracko*.

Neil judged all actions in his life by the standard of the mythological hero who had saved him two years prior. He had been the victim of mistaken identity and was suffering a beating from a group of black teens bent on revenge for an act that he had not committed. It was then that a big white kid that he only knew as Bracko had come to his rescue. But not just *his* rescue. When the same black teens found themselves trapped by a larger group of angry white kids, he also defended them. There was no hate in Bracko. It seemed as if he just did what was right no matter the consequences.

In the situation that he now found himself, Neil knew *what was right*. Armed with only his NYPD issued baton, he entered the fray. As he charged toward the injured victim and his four attackers, he blew his whistle—a signal to his unit that he needed help. Realistically, Neil did not expect anyone to answer his call. Sergeant Wishansky had made it extremely clear that he considered the cadets a nuisance. He had told them all to get lost—which was why this cadet found himself in this situation. As he closed in on the fallen body, he blustered with a false bravado that belied the fact that he was near unconscious with fear.

"OK, step back from the . . ." Neil's voice caught in his throat as he observed the actual damage to Christian's body that lay on the asphalt. He choked for a second, tempted to run far away from this situation. But then his mind cleared.

That could have been me if it had not been for Bracko.

"You're fucking kidding me . . . right? A meter maid wants to tell me what to do," barked the leader of the attackers. Neil realized that his cadet uniform, in all its bland gray, did not strike fear into the hearts of any criminal. Yet he kept up his air of authority.

"You're all under arrest."

"If I weren't laughing so hard, I'd fucking take your fucking head off," began the leader. He could not contain his amusement. "Ronald, you take care of him."

"Stop now before you get yourselves in more trouble," spoke Neil bravely, but he knew he was the one in trouble. Though Neil stood almost six-foot, the one called Ronald had him by at least five inches. The tire iron in his right hand was already in motion as he moved toward the cadet. Yet the overconfidence of the attacker played against him as much as Neil's agility and training. Even as the downward swing of the weapon missed the cadet by inches, Neil's baton caught his opponent in the ribs. Howling in pain, Ronald moved away.

"Fuck him up bad," screamed the leader as all three remaining rioters moved in. Christian, barely conscious on the floor, looked up at Neil's valiant, but futile effort. In the end, the number and size of the attackers resulted in the cadet also lying in a pool of blood. Neil, however, had inflicted damage on another of the mob. Now, this was no longer about civil rights, but rather anger and revenge. The four men stood over the bloodied bodies of Christian and Neil. Christian's injuries made it impossible for him even to lift his head, but the cadet was again rising from the ground to do battle.

"Let me," insisted Ronald as he held his broken rib with one hand and raised the tire iron with the other.

"Do it," replied the leader with a smirk, and Ronald moved in for his payback.

———◆———

Trip Grimes gave no warning. He had heard the commotion outside his door and immediately assessed what was happening. Trip had not spent all of his time at Syracuse University studying film. He had also been an exceptional linebacker on the Orangemen football team. His flying tackle sent Ronald crashing to the ground with the wind knocked out of him. Trip immediately seized the tire iron that he had knocked free and faced the remaining three attackers.

"You want some of this," yelled Trip as he brandished the weapon in front of him.

"What are you, a fuckin' Uncle Tom?" sneered the leader as all three moved a bit closer and raised their assorted weapons. "Don't you know what these white bastards did to Dr. King?"

"No," mumbled Trip, now confused. He had been in a sound-proof studio for the last five hours and had no contact with the outside world.

"Around six o'clock, they fuckin' killed him in Memphis— and you're going to let these fuckin' bastards get away with it?"

"You're doing this in the name of King? You goddamn hypocrites. This is the exact opposite of his message," shouted Trip.

"But we got to get them back for what they did in Memphis."

"Christian," started Trip as he pointed to his fallen friend, "was with me at 6 p.m." He then looked down at Neil and hissed, "And I'm pretty sure he wasn't in Memphis."

"You fuckin' don't get it," spat the leader and started to move belligerently toward Trip.

"No, you don't fuckin' get it, or what Dr. King was saying about violence," answered Trip.

"How about we show you what we think about violence. Let's see what Mr. Brave Uncle Tom can do against three of us."

"Three against one, I guess you like the odds," jabbed Trip, trying to sound brave.

"That's three against two," spoke the forgotten Cadet Neil Connaughton, struggling to rise to his feet with only one good leg. With Christian and the monstrous Ronald lying in the street, the two sides stared at each other.

"Help Ronald up and let's get out of here," spoke the leader begrudgingly as they turned and walked away and out of sight. His brave front not needed anymore, Neil allowed himself to sink to the ground. Trip looked at the two injured men on the floor and grew both angry and sad. Martin Luther King was dead, and his message had probably died with him.

"I'll go call an ambulance, so you two can . . ." Trip never got to finish the sentence. Sergeant Wishansky and reinforcements brought on by Neil's whistle were just turning the corner from Sixth Avenue. Trip stood with a bloody tire iron in his hand and two white men on the floor.

Trip hoped that the oncoming police squad would see the situation as it had happened. However, he had been a black man in America too long to expect this. He didn't need to be treated like a hero. All he cared about was that the two injured men receive aid and that the real attackers be pursued. He was hoping for too much. Not a word was spoken before the first blow landed on him. He staggered but did not fall as another nightstick jabbed into in ribs.

"No, no . . . you've got it all wrong," beseeched Neil. Christian, clinging barely to consciousness, mumbled much the same through his damaged mouth. But Wishansky was not listening. Trip dropped the tire iron and stood as submissive as he possibly could. He had once been trained as a freedom rider and gone down to Alabama. He had been through this before. Unfortunately, this New York police sergeant was acting much like the infamous Bull Connor had in Birmingham.

"Teach him a lesson," ordered the sergeant to his two subordinates. Trip stood ready to suffer the pain and indignity of a beating without giving these officers any justification to fall back on later. As he stared into the eyes of Wishansky, he stood tall and proud.

"I did nothing wrong. I came out to help my friend and this other guy. That's all."

"Bullshit," answered the sergeant and nodded his head. Trip doubled over as a nightstick found its target in his solar plexus.

"Stop, stop now," begged Neil as he painfully rose to his feet. Trip looked on in confusion.

"Shut up, cadet! Learn how we enforce justice in the streets," fired back Wishansky.

"This isn't justice. This is just plain wrong. This guy saved us." Trip understood the dilemma of this young cadet. He was going up against a superior officer, and he was not yet even out of the academy.

"Back off," ordered the sergeant. "Know your place."

"I know my place. I always stand for what is right. Someone taught me that." Trip was amazed but confused by this young kid.

"What kind of corny shit is that?" chuckled one of the officers.

Wishansky was not even listening to his pleas and was moving in for another strike on Trip Grimes.

Standing on his one good leg, Neil propelled himself into the midsection of his superior officer, taking him down to the ground. As the two other officers pulled the cadet off their sergeant, they pounded him with body blows that would hurt but not be visible to the naked eye when the incident report was written. They were interrupted by the sounds of an awakening neighborhood that had found its way out on to Lispenard Street. Through the crowd pushed a police captain who looked incredulously upon the scene.

"Does someone want to explain this whole situation?" Captain Charlie Walls looked at the three police officers, the cadet, an injured white man, and a barely standing black man. Christian looked up from the asphalt of Lispenard Street. He looked at the crowd and police. He looked at the young cadet who risked everything to save his life and that of his friend Trip. He would never forget this night. Ever. His consciousness started to fade, his injuries finally taking their toll. His final vision was of Trip smiling. Was it because they were finally out of danger? Everything went black.

Trip Grimes tried to subdue his emotions. He had learned in Birmingham all those years ago that any facial expression could be misconstrued by authorities looking for an excuse to blame a black victim for white violence. Yet Trip could not contain his smile completely, and so he turned his head away from the action and toward his friend. Yes, he was happy that this ordeal appeared to be over. Yet, Trip knew there was something more than that. He stole a look at the bloodied cadet. He had not only stood up beside him against the black rioters but had also taken on his superiors. What was it he had yelled at his sergeant, "I know my place, I always stand for what is right. Someone taught me that." *I would like to meet that someone* thought Trip. He realized that this one cadet had renewed his faith in humanity, especially *white* humanity.

He peered over at the cadet's hat, which lay on the floor next to his now fading friend. He noticed a piece of tape inside the interior of the cap. It had one word written, "Bracko."

What the hell did that mean?

10

"Helter-Skelter"
- *The Beatles*

Diary of DJ Spinelli

Entry #14 - April 11, 1968

JOHNNY, INSANITY HAS TAKEN OVER America. There have been riots in many places. However, I hadn't seen it first-hand until today.

The college had seemed to return to normality a week after the assassination. Because of *Queens Undies*, I'd fallen behind on my assignments. It was around noon when I left the cafeteria for an afternoon of music. It was not the kind of music that I liked, but it was OK. I had to catch up on a few symphonies for a required music appreciation course. I decided to devote the rest of the day to sitting in a soundproof room with some heavy-duty earphones and an awful lot of Bach.

On the way over there, I met a "friend" of mine named Dougie Wilk. I use the term "friend" loosely because he was one of those guys that you hang out with in college, but with whom you don't form any long-term attachments. Dougie is an idiot. He is 24 years old and probably has fewer credits to his name than I do. This isn't because he started college late or he is stupid. It is just the opposite. Dougie goes to most classes because he wants to expand his mind. However, he always drops most of them just before he qualifies for credits. This sounds weird, but Dougie has a plan.

Queens College is free to city residents; therefore, his five-year stay has cost him nothing. He isn't going to graduate, and that is the key. Dougie knows that as soon as he graduates, Uncle Sam is going to send him to Vietnam. If he stays in school, he can keep his student deferment, at least until the Selective Service figures out his scam. By then, he will probably have figured out some new scheme to avoid the draft.

Meanwhile, Dougie has developed into an interesting yet quirky person. His longevity has made him a master of campus stories, and he can entertain people for hours while relaxing in the grassy commons. This is especially true at the end of each semester when he has a great deal of free time. I particularly like listening to him because I go home at the end of the day and record his stories for future writing. Someday they'll be the color that fleshes out a novel I write. I might even give him his own section of the *Queens Undies* called "Dougie Tales." Yet today was different. Today I was one of the lead characters in a story none of us will ever forget. As I entered the hallway that contained the soundproof six-by-six listening rooms, I ran into him.

"Hey DJ, what's happening?" He looked distracted.

"A little Bach, maybe a little Beethoven," I responded, thinking I was witty. "How about you?"

"A little cutie," he sniggered with a sly smile and pointed to inside one of the rooms. I have to mention here that Dougie had probably screwed every underclass female on the campus. He was tall and good looking. He wore his long hair in a Rod Stewart–like style that made him look very hip. Either some sort of physical regimen or the extensive use of drugs has made his body slender in the vein of popular modern rockers. And on top of all that, he has a great deal of free time.

"Is there anyone new for you left on this campus?"

"Ya know, this is the dawning of the Age of Aquarius—free love and such," he responded, quoting an overdone song by the Fifth Dimension. I felt like saying to him that nothing in life is free. However, I caught myself before I sounded like my parents. I wondered who the "lucky" girl was, and I write that with a great deal of sarcasm.

"You're a dog," I glowered, and I didn't smile because I have more respect for women than he displayed with his constant "love'em and leave'em" attitude.

"This one isn't even a student here. She comes on campus just to see me. Today we are going to 'hang-out' in one of these little rooms—if you get my drift."

I did, and I felt sorry for his latest conquest. I sadly shook my head and went into my sealed room where I could take solace in classical music for the next two hours. When I emerged later from enveloping myself in Bach's "Jesu, Joy of Man's Desiring," I was mellow and smirking at the irony of the title that I'd chosen unconsciously. Down the hall stood Dougie and a stunning young girl. She looked vaguely familiar, but the coating of sexy makeup on the youthful face made it hard to ferret out her real features. Ah, the *Joy of Man's Desiring*. Yet it was not a look of requited desiring that filled their faces, but fear.

"Something's going on out there," he screamed, "And it's not good!"

"What are you talking about?" He didn't answer and simply led me outside. The campus seemed totally and completely deserted. It was eerie, and I realized that Dougie was right. *Something was going on—but what?* There was only one way to find out, and that was to explore. It was then that we saw the disaster waiting to happen.

What appeared to be hundreds of police officers were marching onto the campus in rows of four. I estimated the amount based on the fact that the lines stretched from the Cafeteria to the northernmost gate of the fenced campus. They reminded me of a military unit rather than the police. But what was their purpose? Police weren't allowed on campus without permission and a very good reason. I soon saw that very good reason.

About three hundred yards away stood hundreds of angry students. Though mostly black, there were a significant number of white sympathizers interspersed with the group. The windows of the cafeteria had been shattered—many still held the plastic chairs that had been thrown through them. Though the group taunted the police from a distance, they seemed propelled by leadership that wanted a confrontation. As a police bullhorn screeched orders, I understood the severity of our dilemma.

"This campus is officially closed. Anyone who does not exit immediately will be persecuted to the full extent of the law." The attitude given off by the voice didn't give me the impression that "full extent" meant a ticket. The protesting crowd seemed not to care, but the three of us did. In the silence of the music rooms, we had missed the initial confrontation, the violence, and the orders to close the campus. While everyone else not involved in the protest was quietly exiting the campus hours before, we had been ignorant. Somehow, I didn't think that the police would believe our story. We were in violation as much as the hundreds who were belatedly reacting to the assassination of Dr. King.

"We're trapped," Dougie's latest girl started to cry hysterically. A ten-foot-high fence surrounded the campus, and we considered our options for exit. The north gate still had police streaming through it. To get to the west gate would mean passing in front of the advancing troops. The rioters seemed to move toward the occupation of the Goodman Building—this choice had indicated that the eastern gate of the campus was now off-limits.

Dougie must have read my mind because he started to move toward the one unencumbered exit, the south entrance. The three of us moved together, stealthily avoiding the police who were now panning out to create a web to catch stragglers like us. We finally arrived at the south gate only to find it locked. When officials decided that anyone still on the campus was guilty of something, they bolted any escape route. They hadn't counted anyone being hidden away in a soundproof corner of the college.

"We're screwed," stammered Dougie, and the girl cried even more.

"No," I replied. Dougie and I could scale this fence, but the girl, because of her emotional state, probably could not. I motioned them to follow me. I weaved my way along the fence line that was mostly just chain link. Occasionally, the straight vision of the fence would be interrupted by sections lined with trees and bushes—forsythia bushes! If I could only find the section that I had cut open on that wintery day, we could make our escape. But now everything looked so different.

"What the fuck are we doing," yelled Dougie as I plodded forward. I didn't know where it was, and I didn't know if they had fixed it. Not wishing to get up their hopes, I said nothing. The bullhorns blared, and it seemed as if time was running out. Then, I saw it. The bushes had bloomed, creating an undergrowth was so thick that it wouldn't be easy getting to the opening. Because of this, Dougie went first to clear the way. The girl followed. I held back. I needed to see more of the event to report it in my paper.

"You go ahead. I'm going to stay a little to see what happens."

"You're fuckin' nuts," blurted Dougie.

"Someone has to tell the story," I insisted. Dougie smiled at me as he went through the hole in the fence. The girl followed but then turned to face me. She spoke for the first time in the whole incident.

"Thanks, DJ," I was shocked when she smiled and called from the other side of the fence. I didn't know how she knew my name. And then she spoke again.

"Aylin . . . Aylin McAvoy . . . Jimmy Mac's sister."

Holy Shit! How had I not recognized her?

Entry #15- April 12, 1968

I made a brief and unsuccessful attempt to investigate the confrontation, but I didn't follow through. Was it that I was afraid of the violence, or had Aylin McAvoy thrown off my game? I'd gotten to know Aylin at your practices. I hadn't recognized her, but she had known me right away. Her quiet, even sad demeanor had been her unwitting disguise. The Aylin I remembered was a cheerful, exciting person. She had been full of life. I guess having your brother and father murdered will do that to you. I tried to understand the depth of her grief.

And fuckin' Dougie! Aylin was two years younger than Jimmy, which made her 17 now. Didn't Dougie know that it was wrong to take advantage of this young, fragile girl? Hell, she was even jailbait! Next time I see that bastard, I'm going to say or do something that I might regret. Screw that. I won't regret it a bit.

Entry #16 - April 13, 1968

It's after midnight, and I'm tired. However, so much happened today that I have to write it down, so I don't forget. The *Queens Undies* came out a few days ago, and it is a great success. Johnny, you would get a kick out of it. I skewered the school paper for its elitist and closed attitudes. Those thoughts struck a chord with the students. Nothing is sacred anymore. These are new times, and I'm glad to be living in them. Well, most of the time I am.

My paper did go into a long and thoughtful eulogy about Dr. King, and I meant every word of it. However, I find that writing about the real world and all that it encompasses is not fun. Politics is not fun. War is not fun. So what is fun? My answer is increasingly tending to be music. I know that sounds shallow, but if I can't enjoy writing about what I want to, then what is the use? I have some serious thinking to do.

Speaking of music makes me realize, Johnny, that I need to get over and see your parents. No, take that back. I want to go over and see them. How about you, Johnny? Want to join me?

Aylin keeps popping up in my mind. What's that all about?

Entry #17 - April 14, 1968

Your mom (she likes me to call her Mrs. C.) asked me why I never took up guitar. I had no right answer for her. You guys started playing when you were 14. I guess I thought I was too old—that I had missed the boat.

"I'll be almost 19 if I started to play now," I responded.

"How old will you be if you *don't* start playing?" she quickly shot back.

"19," and then I realized what she was saying. Maybe I'll pick up a guitar. Something to think about. OK, life goals. 1) become a writer 2) solve the mystery of Johnny Cipp 3) play guitar? 4) Aylin?????

Entry #18 – April 15

Today I went to see Aylin. While talking to your parents, I just happened to mention running into her and that I didn't like the fact that she was with Dougie "Douchebag" Wilk, but that I didn't know what to do about it. I didn't know her well enough to just knock on her door. Your sneaky mom came up with a fabricated story about needing to get something to Adele McAvoy. Because I had a car and was passing by, I would be the errand boy. I didn't know if we tricked anyone, but I did find myself at the McAvoy house.

Mrs. Mac talked to me for a while, but I think that she found it too emotional to continue to talk with anyone who had known her son. She probably knew I'd come to talk to Aylin. She soon made an excuse and left the two of us alone.

"Thanks for getting me out of the jam at the college the other day," said Aylin with a broad, endearing smile, "And thanks for not mentioning it to my mom. She worries about me."

"She should. . .Dougie's a jerk." I blurted out.

"Watch it. That's my boyfriend you're talking about," she answered, and her beautiful smile was gone.

"You may think that he's your boyfriend, but he's a selfish prick who could care less about you."

"Who are you to tell me what to do? Just because you knew my brother, you think that you can waltz in here and tell me what to do, like. . .like he used to do." With that, the anger stopped, and the tears rolled from her eyes. Her body quivered. I was at a loss.

"Aylin, it will be OK." I knew it was a weak response.

"It fucking won't ever be OK again. I miss Jimmy, my dad—all of them."

She fell into my arms, and I hugged her tightly as she lost control of her emotions, a cry long overdue. After a while, she pulled away and looked in my eyes.

"Thanks."

"You ever need anything, you call me. You know how the guys always said Brian Epstein was the fifth Beatle—well, I was sort of like the sixth member of Those Born Free."

What a stupid thing to say. Johnny, please come back. I need a wingman.

———◆———

THOSE BORN FREE Tape – April 10, 1967

"DJ fuckin' Spinelli, what the hell are you staring at?" (Jimmy Mac)
"Nothing, Jimmy Mac, nothing." (DJ)
"Now, you're calling my sister Aylin's ass nothing?" (Jimmy Mac)
"Er, no, I mean, I wasn't looking at nothing." (DJ).
"Anything." (Tinman)
"What?" (DJ and Jimmy Mac)
"'I wasn't looking at nothing' is a double negative. It's supposed to be 'I wasn't looking at anything.'" (Tinman)
"Shut the hell up, Tinman. He's looking at my kid sister's ass, and you're giving us a lesson in grammar?" (Jimmy Mac)
"You're right, Joey. If I intend to make a career of writing, I must be more careful." (DJ)
"My little sister's honor is at stake, and you two nerds are still talking grammar." (Jimmy Mac)
"DJ, you really should tell Jimmy Mac that you are interested in his sister." (Johnny whispered to DJ)
"Are you nuts? I like living." (DJ whispered to Johnny)
"You don't deny the feelings then?" (Johnny whispered to DJ)
"No, I got it bad for her." (DJ whispered to Johnny)
"You do realize that we are being taped." (Johnny)
"Oh, shit! How about I show you all some new lyrics to 'Words of Doubt.'" (DJ loudly to entire band)

11

"He Ain't Heavy, He's My Brother"
- *The Hollies*

CHRISTIAN LAY IN HIS HOSPITAL bed, recovering from the massive damage inflicted on him. His one eye was swollen shut, as was the area around his mouth, making it impossible to speak. Three ribs were broken, and a full-length cast covered his left leg from the tip of his toe to mid-thigh. His other injuries were becoming less visible with time. Trip sat by his side. There was a great deal of eye contact between the two, but only one of them could speak.

"Doctors say that you will make a complete recovery. Before you know it, you'll be playing and singing again." He was at a loss on how to continue the conversation when Christian motioned for him to hand him the pad and pen that lay on the table next to his bed.

Thanks for saving my life, he scribbled.

"It wasn't me. I helped, but it was a rookie cop who jumped in at the right time," answered Trip.

I know, saw everything, still thank you.

"But I hear he got screwed for what he did. What do they say? No good deed goes unpunished." Christian frowned at Trip's comment.

Tell me everything again from your point of view. But Christian's scribbling now reflected profound exhaustion caused by the healing process. Trip saw his friend fading fast.

"Next time," he whispered, and he went to pull the blanket up to Christian's neck. He was surprised when Christian grabbed his wrist, and his friend again wrote on the pad.

Bring my guitar here. I want to tell the story—my way.   He
attempted to smile as Trip read the note and headed toward the
door.

Trip had one other stop to make at the hospital. As he entered
the room, he noticed that Neil Connaughton was unconscious.
He didn't want to disturb him. He only wanted to thank him
for having the courage to stand up for Christian and him. He
thought he might also want to ask him what "Bracko" meant.

April 17, 1968

Trip sat by Christian's bed and waited for him to wake. Trip
would be taking him home if Plan A didn't work out.

"Hey, Trip, aren't you supposed to be working on that documentary that you started?" The bleary eyes of Christian were
just beginning to focus on his friend, and the swelling around
his mouth had subsided enough for him to speak.

"Soon," was all Trip could think to respond. He was stalling
for time. Maybe he could slip out to see the Connaughton kid
before, or perhaps he should wait until after they arrived.

"So, there's our long-lost brother," boomed a boisterous voice
from the doorway.

"Kevin? Tommy?" Christian looked at his two younger
brothers in total disbelief. "How the hell did you know I was
here?"

"Him," said Kevin pointing to the sheepish looking Trip.

"He looked us up and called to tell us what had happened to
you. Did you think that we wouldn't be here for you?" chimed
in Tommy.

"Besides, Chris, we never had a problem with . . . well, you
know," softly added Kevin.

"You left us, but we never left you."

"Yes, you did," spoke Christian in a combination of anger and
embarrassment.

"I can see that you guys have a lot of catching up, so I'll just
take a walk," interrupted Trip as he stood up to leave. He felt
like an interloper. With that, both Kevin and Tommy embraced

him in an unexpected bear hug.

"Thanks for giving us back our big brother," said the two in unison. Trip was still confused as he left the room and bid his goodbyes. He felt like asking what had happened. What were these three keeping from him? He thought again. *If Christian wants me to know, he will tell me.*

As Trip Grimes walked out of the room, he looked back one final time. The two brothers approached the bed. "Irish Twins" is what Christian had called them because they were only eleven months apart in age. Kevin was the taller of the two at about six-two with longish black hair that framed his light skin and blue eyes. Tommy's curly brown hair encircled a face full of brown freckles and an all-consuming smile. The three brothers hugged, and he saw tears rolling down all three of their faces.

He had done the right thing.

12

"Better Man Than I"
- The Yardbirds

Diary of DJ Spinelli

Entry #19 – May 3, 1968

THE CAMPUS HAS REGAINED ENOUGH normalcy to host a concert in Colden Auditorium last night. The Yardbirds killed it. I was so pumped through the whole show that I couldn't sit for a moment. I was blown away by the music, and yet trying to plan my review article.

Today, in the light of day, I realize why it was such an emotional experience. Those Born Free, your group, did quite a few of the group's songs. I remember you and Bracko met by playing "I'm a Man" in some garden near your house. Then you and Bracko had impressed Gio and Jimmy with a "Heart Full of Soul" and "Train Kept a Rollin'."

Yet on a deeper level, I remember sitting with you in physics class. You had an earplug stuck in your left ear, listening to the radio and intensely writing down the words to one of the group's more obscure songs. I remember you turning to me and out of nowhere, saying, "Can you tell a wise man by the way he speaks or spells? Is this more important than the stories that he tells?" I looked at you like you had gone bonkers. You pointed to your ear. I believe it was then that our not amused teacher whacked you upside your head with his right palm. At lunch later, you got serious.

"You know, in my neighborhood, it's all about hating the black kids. But I don't feel like that. I never could put words to why until today." I asked you what you meant.

"Can you condemn a man if your faith he doesn't hold? Say the color of his skin is the color of his soul?" That was all you responded.

"Let me guess—Yardbirds?"

You nodded. "Songs can say so much about life. They can tell you the real truth."

And last night I saw and heard them live. *Johnny, you would've loved it. But you missed it and, goddammit, I miss having you as a friend."*

And so today I'm writing my article about The Yardbirds, and thinking of you and Those Born Free—and music's effect on the world. I can't deny it anymore; my future lies in writing about music. The *Queens Undies* is about to become a music newspaper.

Entry #20 – May 4, 1968

There is no turning back; music will be my life. I hope I'm not sorry, Johnny. I found the perfect way to tie my old and new writing together. There is a little-known story floating around from the riots last month. A struggling musician named Christian Andrews got caught up in the violence on the way home from a gig that night. His beating at the hands of angry rioters was only prevented by a black friend and a white cop's joint effort. Musician, white cop, black friend—sounds like a great story. Tomorrow I'm going to investigate and try to interview all three of the principles.

Entry # 21 – May 6, 1968

I took the train to St Vincent's Hospital. I talked briefly with the white cop, a guy named Neil Connaughton. I arranged to interview him in-depth when he is home from the hospital. The cop told me that the primary victim had already been released to his family. I can't find an address for him, or the black friend who I'm told is named Trip.

Entry # 22– May 9, 1968

Neil Connaughton called me up late yesterday and told me that he would meet with me today. In an amazing coincidence, he lives in Cambria Heights on 223rd street—only about six blocks from where you live. Or is it lived?

We started talking about the incident. Neil and the victim, a guy named Christian Andrews, have still never met. He had left the hospital with his brothers and has gone home to recuperate in Connecticut.

When I got there, Neil was very quiet. He had just gotten a call from his supervisor and had been told that he had been suspended for six months, pending a possible dismissal on the grounds of insubordination. This was not good news for Neil, but possibly a scoop for the *Queens Undies*. I had started out looking for a story of a struggling musician who suffered in the MLK riots. Now I have an account of a young man's career ruined because he did something righteous.

"Maybe I shouldn't say anything while they are making up their minds about me. All I ever wanted to do in life since I was sixteen was to be a cop." Neil was torn about his future. I mean, this was a great story. I could make my name as a writer even though still in college. Should I be selfish and urge him to speak up? I decided to wait until I knew the whole tale before I screwed up this kid for my own reasons.

"I did the right thing—just not the smart thing. I stood up for that guy, and I stood up for Trip. Yeah, Trip Grimes and I are now close enough for me to call him that. I still haven't spoken to his friend, but he wrote me a letter thanking me and telling me that we would meet once he recovered."

"I still don't know how you got the balls to take on four thugs who were beating on a perfect stranger. You could have just waited for help. You're only a cadet."

"The way they were hauling ass on that guy, he may not have

made it while I waited."

I was in awe of his courage and wondered if I could ever be that brave. I could never betray this guy. If he didn't want the story told, I had to honor his wishes. And then my mind exploded with what he said next.

"That's what Bracko would want," he murmured in a low, almost reverent tone.

"What did you say?" I screeched, not very professionally.

"Oh, nothing," he whispered. "You wouldn't understand."

"Bracko Brackowski of Those Born Free?"

"I only know the name Bracko, and I don't know what Those Born Free means."

"The band. . .Those Born Free?" I mean, how many guys named Bracko can there be in this world? He has no idea what I was talking about.

"Where do you live?"

"Here in Cambria. Why?"

"Tell me about Bracko," I insisted.

"When I was sixteen, I was a short, skinny kid who got bullied a lot in high school. They gave me wedgies and threw me in lockers. They called me "Neil the . . ."

"The Squeal," I finished his sentence, and he looked perplexed.

"How?"

"I know your story. Johnny told me."

"Who?"

"Johnny Cipp. He was—I mean, is a friend of mine."

"I never heard of him." A look of confusion overtook his face. I guess, Johnny, that you weren't as famous as you thought.

"You were mistaken for someone who had severely injured a black kid and were being beaten by a black gang when Bracko stepped in and saved you."

"And then he saved the black kids when a gang of white kids showed up . . . "

"The White Devils," I interrupted.

"Yeah, how did you know?"

"Johnny . . . Johnny Cipp and I were friends. Johnny and Bracko were friends and were in a band, Those Born Free."

"Why do you say 'were friends'?"

I realized that he had no idea who you were. He had no idea even who Bracko was. All he knew was that Bracko was the hero who had saved him. He sat before me a strong, confident man. Yet when he spoke now, he was that weak, timid kid again. And I had to be the one who shattered his world.

"Bracko is dead."

Neil became very silent, and I didn't interrupt his thoughts. After a while, we talked. We talked of Bracko, and Those Born Free, and the fire, and the deaths. In the end, I knew that I wouldn't tell Neil's story to the public until he was ready. I also knew that Neil and I would be friends—brothers in the quest to find you and to find the truth of what happened.

Entry #23 - June 1, 1968

So now, my first year of college is over. It wasn't what I expected when I began, but in many ways, it was good. I'm on the right track with my life. Yet there are so many, many questions.

I put out the last issue of the year of *Queens Undies* a couple of weeks ago. I did pretty well as an alternative paper on the college campus. It was worth all those nights of typing, taking it to the printer, and then hawking it on the campus. I learned a great deal about layouts, editing, and writing. Still, when school resumes, the paper will be back with a new theme: the music scene on campus and around the metropolitan area.

Meanwhile, Johnny, I will never stop searching for you.

PART 2

"Brothers in Arms"

*"Though you did not desert me,
my brothers in arms."*

- Dire Straits

July 1968

13

"My Brother"
-Justin Hayward and John Lodge

THOSE BORN FREE Tape – Undated

"Tape Rolling." (Jimmy Mac)
"Let's do the Everly Brothers' 'Dream' next." (Gio)
"Are they actually brothers?" (Jimmy Mac)
"Who?" (Johnny)
"The Everly Brothers." (Jimmy Mac)
"Of course!" (Johnny)
"Well, the Righteous Brothers aren't." (Jimmy Mac)
"Yeah . . . but." (Johnny)
"So, what makes them call themselves brothers then?" (Jimmy Mac)
"I guess you don't always have to be of the same blood to feel—or be a brother." (Tinman)
"You ever realize that none of us have a brother? I mean, I have those three punky little sisters." (Jimmy Mac)
"Hey, watch that!" (from a distance—Aylin)
"You're right—no brothers." (Johnny)
"Wrong!" (Bracko)
"What do you mean, Bracko?" (Johnny)
"Just look around this room. You have brothers." (Bracko)

July 4, 1968

Trip sat on the train as it worked its way from the city out to Southington, Connecticut. It was not a long trip as the crow flies. However, no trip made from an urban area to a suburban area on a holiday was ever like any living crow had ever flown. There were delays at almost every stop en route to this little enclave in the center of what Christian had told Trip was "the whitest state that you have ever been in."

Though they had talked often on the phone, Trip had not seen Christian since early May. Except for the slight limp in his stride, Christian looked well. As Kevin and Tommy held back, Christian walked up to his friend and welcomed him with a hug.

"Thanks for coming," mumbled Christian.

"Hey, I wouldn't miss a chance to see how you white people barbecue."

"C'mon," chuckled Kevin as he shook Trip's hand, "Who can mess up hamburgers and hot dogs on a grill?"

"Well, I've tasted your brother's attempt at spaghetti and meatballs," answered Trip holding his stomach in an obvious statement about the quality of the food.

"Huh-oh," sniggered Tommy. "He's our best cook, and spaghetti is his best dish." They all laughed and jumped in Kevin's rusty old Ford for the trip to their home. The conversation flowed smoothly since all of the brothers were outgoing. Why hadn't Christian talked about them more often? The final part of the journey was on a lonely country road that seemed populated by no more than a handful of houses.

"Geez, I thought that I grew up in the country out on Long Island, but where I'm from is a metropolis compared to this."

"It is what it is," responded Christian without a positive or a negative tone to his voice.

"What the hell did you do for fun?" Trip had been amazed by the miles and miles of beautiful, but unused land. And then, as if on cue, an ancient building with a large dirt parking lot appeared outside on the passenger side of the car. Even though it was still early afternoon, the neon sign was brightly lit, announcing the venue as Fred's Place. By the volume of cars already parked on the dirt, it was evident that Fred was not doing badly.

"You should see it at the end of the month," offered Kevin as if reading Trip's mind.

"What? Why is that?"

"Connecticut State Horseshoe Championship is held there," exclaimed Tommy pointing to twenty pits that were now coming into view. "Big-time crowds."

"Yeah, not to mention the home of our debut," added Kevin. Christian bit his lip at that comment, but Trip would not let the comment slide.

"Whose debut?"

"Why the . . ." started Kevin, but was quickly cut off by Christian.

"Give it a rest."

"Why? I'm proud of what we did. Aren't you, Chris?"

"We had a band," spoke Christian reluctantly to Trip, "We played there."

"We didn't just play there—we filled the place every night. And then it was Lake Compounce Amusement Park to crowds of thousands." Kevin was finding it hard to control his enthusiasm. "And then our tour—the Village—the Hamptons."

"Remember, Kevin," interrupted Tommy, "the weekends at The Barge in Hampton Bays on Long Island opening for The Young Rascals?"

"Yeah, and then Cape Cod? We played. . ." Kevin stopped.

"Oh shit," mumbled Tommy.

Christian just looked with daggers at his brothers.

"What just happened?" questioned Trip, but Christian's gaze stopped him in his tracks.

"The band isn't together anymore!" Christian emphatically ended the conversation.

———◆———

When they reached their destination, Christian told his brothers to give him and Trip some time alone.

"So, they call you 'Chris' instead of 'Christian' I notice," questioned Trip smiling.

"It's the name I always used to use—until I didn't."

"What the hell does that mean?"

"I brought you here to tell you the truth. By the end of the day, you will have it all. Just give me time."

"OK, that's fair."

"My name isn't Christian Andrews. It's Chris Delaney."

"No shit. The hospital had your correct name, you idiot. I just thought that you were using Christian Andrews as a stage name for Christian Delaney. I wondered why you kept that from me. Wait. . ."

"Yup, I'm that Chris Delaney."

"Lead singer of the Delaney Brothers Band?"

"Yup."

"You guys were famous in the Tri-State area in the early sixties and then nothing?"

"I promise you by the end of the day you'll know it all. Now let's get inside. My parents are waiting to meet you, their hero."

———————

The hamburgers weren't half bad. Trip was starving by the time the food was spread out on the picnic table in the backyard. Trip surveyed the feast and assumed there were bound to be cultural differences between what he was used at home.

"You don't happen to have collard greens, do you?" asked the visitor.

"Sure, right over there," said Chris pointing to the end of the table. Trip started to reach over until he realized that he didn't see any of his favorite side dish.

"I only see baked potatoes," he blurted, looking confused. All three Delaney brothers started to laugh.

"Baked potatoes *are* the Irish collard greens. Potatoes are the Irish everything. You're lucky there is meat in your hamburger," With that even Trip laughed, and they knew he was alright with their ribbing.

Chris's mom and dad were as outgoing as their offspring. Kevin and Tommy's wives were more subdued, but still smiled often and joined in the conversations. The day passed into night as they all laughed and ate, and ate and laughed. Yet Trip noticed there was no beer or any other kind of alcohol. He didn't want to stereotype, but wasn't an occasional beer at least as Irish as potatoes?

As the sun started to set, they all headed down to Lake Compounce to watch the fireworks display. Only a few miles down the road from their home, all of the boys had worked at one of America's oldest amusement parks during their summer breaks. Even today, they were allowed to enter the park for free as one the perks of being alumni workers.

"Remember when Tommy had a crush Natalie Meacham, and she got stuck up on the top of the roller coaster?" Chris just shook his head as Kevin spoke.

"Yeah," interrupted Danny, the father of the clan, "They called me up and said I had to come and get my boy because he got halfway up and froze. Couldn't go up and couldn't go down. I told them to leave him there until he got the balls to do something."

"I guess love could only take you so far," interjected Trip.

"Bullshit, love? She was putting out." Chris and Kevin laughed, but Tommy's wife gave him a look that hinted at the fact that she never knew about Tommy and Natalie.

After the fireworks ended, the group found its way down the lakeside beach and sat in the sand. The conversation flowed, and it seemed as if every sentence started with the words,

"Remember the time?" Chris, Kevin, and Tommy had been so full of mischief that Trip commented that someone should have authored a book, *The Adventures of the Three Insane Delaney Brothers.*"

"Yeah, the missus and I had our hands full," agreed Danny.

"I would think so—with three sons," added Trip.

Their mother's face instantly turned somber, and she spoke softly, "Four, four sons."

———◆———

No further words were spoken, but it seemed as if the party had ended by mutual consent at that very moment.

"We're heading back home," said Danny Delaney, "Your mom and I are tired."

"Yeah, us too," agreed Kevin and Tommy, almost in unison.

They each put their arms around their wives and started down the road to home. After they had walked a few feet, Kevin turned back to Chris and Trip, who still sat on the beach. He walked back and bent down to Chris' level and spoke in a whisper.

"She didn't mean anything by that." He then rose and rejoined his wife and brother for the walk home.

What was all that? Trip wanted to say, but he respected his friend's privacy enough not to ask the question that hung over them as they sat alone on the sand. Neither spoke as they skimmed rocks along the lake for a few minutes. Suddenly Chris stopped, throwing down the stones that he still had in his hand.

"I guess I should tell you the story."

14

"Fountain of Sorrow"
- Jackson Browne

WE WERE GOOD, DAMN GOOD. Tommy played drums, Kevin bass, and I rotated between keyboards and lead guitar. Sometimes, our cousin Walt would join us and sometimes not. He always understood that someday our youngest brother would join the band. But that was years in the future. I was 22. Kevin and Tommy were 20 and 19.

We started in our garage. When we thought we were ready, we auditioned at Fred's Place down the road. It was a blue-collar, after-work-get-drunk place that heavily favored country music, or as they called it "cowboy music." Knowing your audience, we learned quite a few crossover songs, especially by the Everly Brothers. I guess that was when we realized that we could produce great three-part harmonies.

Because Southington was such a small, tight-knit community, Fred's Place was where the owner of Lake Compounce Amusement Park hung out. After hearing us, he built a small stage for us to play at the park. We immediately went from earning our keep by running the rides and hawking cotton candy to performing six days a week. I was already a college graduate who was teaching in a local school, so this was the cherry on top as far as extra money at night.

By the next summer of 1964, we had a manager and had exploded onto the club scene. We now moved out of our comfort zone in the middle of Connecticut. Our big break came when we were booked into The Barge in the Hamptons on Long Island. At first, we opened for

The Young Rascals. It was amazing to hear them do "Good Lovin',"
a song that had gone nowhere for The Olympics, the original group that
had recorded it. It taught us that you could make big bucks recording
cover songs.

Felix Cavaliere, the leader of The Rascals, would have long talks
with me about what we needed to do to succeed. He told me that it didn't
matter what songs we did if we had our own style. Yet he also said to
me that there was a great deal more money to be made in writing origi-
nal songs. Originals brought residuals and all kinds of perks that lasted
long after the music had fallen off the charts. We had a new direction
and purpose. That summer was our peak—before it all came tumbling
down.

By mid-August, we were flying high. Our manager parlayed the
Barge gig into a headlining job on Cape Cod and all kinds of work
that would bring us gobs of money. There was also mention of a record
contract. Yet all this success meant that we had to make some personal
decisions that were risky. We all had to quit our full-time jobs. Kevin
and Tommy were working in construction, and the work was spotty at
best, and so they were all in. It was a little tougher for me to quit my
teaching job and all the security that it offered. Hey, nothing ventured,
nothing gained. I turned in my papers.

Our cousin Walt was another story. He had a great civil service job
with the town, and more than that, he and his wife had a baby on the
way. He left the band. Now Walt was no superstar. He played decent
rhythm guitar and sang some harmony, but we were not going to suffer
significantly in the quality department. It did, however, leave us with
a less powerful sound. This was not the way to launch The Delaney
Brothers into stardom., I had an answer, and it changed all our lives
forever.

There was a fourth Delaney brother—Andrew. Drew, as we all called
him, was just fifteen. However, that was his only downside. He could
sing as well, if not better than the three of us, and his guitar playing was
out of sight. But how could we put him in the band? We knew that his
age would limit our playing venues. More than that, what would it do
to him personally? It was me who fought with my parents to give it a try
just for the two-week engagement on the Cape. He could return in time
for the fall semester, and it would give us time to find a replacement for
Walt. Reluctantly, my parents gave in, with my mother's final words

being, "Promise me you will take care of him."

Within two days, we had worked Drew into the act and were ready to start playing at an outdoor beach venue at Nauset Beach. Because we were performing on the beach and not in a club, there were no problems with Drew's age. In reality, much of the audience was not quite eighteen. Each night was a promotion night for some product or business so the only alcohol involved was brought in from the surrounding bars.

Drew crushed it. By the end of the first set of the first night, we knew he was just that little spark that put us over the top. At first, we thought it was his youth that was appealing to the young crowd that night. It didn't take us long to realize it was only a small part of it. Musically, we had grown astronomically. When I played guitar, we fed off each other with solos that interwove with a dramatic effect. When I played the organ, his guitar slipped right into the spot where mine had been for so many years, therefore, giving us another dimension.

However, the most significant improvement could be heard in our vocals. We always had very good vocals, but now they were great. I sang some leads, and Kevin, Tommy, and Drew joined in exceptional harmony. Sometimes Drew sang lead, and I took a back seat. Other times we joined together and sang harmony leads. We were now producing a diversity of sounds like we never had before. We were great for that one night—the only night that the four of us ever performed together.

Chris bowed his head and sobbed uncontrollably. It was not the first time that he had grieved his brother's death, but it was the first time he had talked about it out loud to anyone. All of the emotions that had been pent up for four years came out. Yet in only minutes, he got control of himself. He had to finish telling Trip quickly, or never.

We left the stage pumped up on adrenaline and the high that only success can create. We walked along the beach—four brothers as close as we had ever been. Eventually, we found a secluded little cove and built a fire out of driftwood. Tommy and Kevin brought a case of beer, and Drew and I brought some acoustic guitars. We all started to sing and play by the light of the fire.

However, shortly after we arrived, we were interrupted by the fact that Kevin and Tommy's girlfriends showed up unexpectedly. Given the opportunity to have some unscheduled pre-marital sex, they left us flat on the beach. Because of our age difference, Drew and I had never really been close. That night our world changed. We talked and played guitar. I got to know my youngest brother for the first time.

Drew showed me ideas he had for songs, and they were fantastic. We worked on them together a bit longer before he stopped playing and looked at me. I'll never forget the conversation that changed my life.

"You know my friend, Jonathan Roth?"

"Yeah, he's the Jewish kid whose father owns the deli in town," I answered, not knowing where this was going.

"Well, when he turned thirteen, he had a bar-mitzvah. He stood up in front of everyone and said, 'Today I am a man.'"

"Yeah, so?"

"Well, I'm fifteen. Am I a man?"

"Why? You want a bar-mitzvah?" I thought I was funny. Drew wasn't laughing.

"No . . . I want a beer!"

I thought about it for a while. Maybe it was the excitement of the evening. Perhaps, it was my arrogance. I guess I'll never know. I didn't give him a beer. I gave many, many beers. I justified this to myself by saying. Hey, we're Irish. We drink beer. As his oldest brother, it was my responsibility to teach him our culture—to break him in right? This was my Gaelic version of a bar-mitzvah.

As the night wore on, the two of us put a big dent in the case of beer. The songs sounded even better as we lost all sense of judgment. I had passed my limit, and with no previous experience in drinking at all, Drew was totally and completely gone.

The last thing I remember was Drew saying something about a midnight swim, and then I passed out with my guitar in hand.

They found Drew's body washed up on the shore the next morning. The coroner ruled that he had drowned after becoming unconscious in the water. My mother's final words haunted me. "Promise me that you will take care of him."

I hadn't.

15

"War"
- Edwin Starr

Diary of DJ Spinelli

Entry # 24 – July 18, 1968

THOUGH I KNOW IT IS crucial to understand the world around me, I find it hard to get enthusiastic about events taking place in far off places. Everyone is becoming radical about the Vietnam War, and I'm apathetic. However, I believe that the music associated with the anti-war movement is fantastic. But did the music cause the anti-war feelings—or did the anti-war sentiments influence the music? Because the *Queens Undies* is now a music newspaper these are issues that I must consider. Politics itself is so mind-boggling. Are we *supposed* to go into every country where dictatorships take over? I'm just asking the question. I don't know the answer.

I picked up a paper, and the headlines were all about some guy who had just taken over his country today as a totalitarian ruler. Isn't that happening every day of the year in some country or another? Isn't that why we are fighting in Vietnam? The next thing you know is we'll be fighting in *that* guy's country. I mean, who will ever care about this guy Saddam Hussein?

———◆———

THOSE BORN FREE Tape - May 26, 1967

"Break time." (Jimmy Mac)

"Man, Johnny, you seem out of it today." (Gio)

"Just thinking. A month from today, I turn 18." (Johnny)

"Big Whoop. I'm right there three weeks later—and then we are legal to drive, and to drink, and to play in clubs—legally that is." (Gio)

"And to get drafted into the army. One month from today, I've got to fill out the papers at the Selective Service Board." (Johnny)

"Yeah, I know." (Gio)

"I've been thinking." (Johnny)

"You think too much." (Gio)

"Remember when Greg Cincotta punched out that idiot while we were playing in St Clare's last year. The judge agreed to put him on probation if he joined the army, and now he is in Vietnam." (Jimmy Mac)

"All because he came to see us play and decked that asshole who was hassling Tony and Maria. It could have been me if I could've gotten off the stage faster." (Johnny)

"You couldn't punch hard enough to get into trouble." (Gio)

(laughs- Jimmy Mac, Tinman, Bracko)

"Besides, I've never heard of anyone punching as hard as Greg did that night." (Jimmy Mac)

"Oh yeah? Tell that to the black kid who attacked Neil 'The Squeal' Connaughton and took one from him." (Gio)

"Gio, you jerk, that was just a story that the White Devils spread. Bracko could've knocked the kid into next Tuesday, and instead, he just pushed him down." (Jimmy Mac)

(Sound of footsteps on stairs)

"Bracko, don't leave! Look what you did, Gio. Dammit, you embarrassed him." (Johnny)

"I thought it was a compliment. I'll go get him." (Gio)

"I'll go with you" (Jimmy Mac)

(footsteps going up the stairs)

"Johnny, I think about the draft and going to Vietnam—and maybe dying." (Tinman)

"Yeah, I know, and we are the only two who are thinking of going to college, which would give us a deferment." (Johnny)

"If the band makes it or doesn't, the other three are going to be draft bait real soon." (Tinman)

"I know. We have an out, but because of the band, we may not take it. Is it a gamble that we are willing to take?" (Johnny)

"Yeah" (Tinman)

"Fuck, yeah." (Johnny)

"I hope Greg makes it back alive." (Tinman)

"Yeah, me too. He was a good friend when we were kids. And he was a good friend when he saved Maria. I don't pray a lot, but I pray for him." (Johnny)

(Footsteps coming down the stairs)

"My brother says I should turn off the tape recorder. None of you jerks ever remember to!" (Aylin)

16

"Brothers in Arms" (Reprise)
"Through these fields of destruction,
Baptisms of fire."
- Dire Straits

August 1968 - Vietnam

THE CIVIL WAR HAD ENDED 103 years before the hot August night in 1968 when Sergeant Dirk Connor had ordered four soldiers under his command to their certain deaths. Connor would not even agree with that timeline. There had never been a "Civil War," but rather, a "War Against Northern Aggression," and that war did *not* end when Grant and Lee sat down at Appomattox. That war would never end as long as those damn Yankees kept interfering in the affairs of the upstanding Southern folk who lived on the right side of the Mason-Dixon Line.

He hated the outsiders who had "riled up" the *darkies* in his hometown of Birmingham, Alabama. He was very proud to be the first cousin to Theophilus "Bull" Connor, the Director of Public Safety of his hometown. Good old Bull had had the balls to sick the dogs on the Negro troublemakers who were trying to turn Birmingham into a city like those pinko liberal places up North.

No reasonable person could miss observing that Dirk Connor was a bigot. Yet few people realized that he hated (in varying degrees) almost anyone who was not a native of Alabama (and most definitely white). Connor reserved a unique brand of hatred for white northerners who consorted with blacks and even treated them as friends. Therefore, he considered the four New Yorkers as the most expendable assets in his command when a suicidal mission arose.

———◆———

Their friendship seemed unlikely. It was quite unusual that four recruits from the same small section of New York City would end up in the same outfit. However, The Tet Offensive in January of 1968 had sent shock waves throughout the American military. This massive attack by hundreds of thousands of Viet Cong had forced a rapid and chaotic troop buildup. As a result, four young men from Cambria Heights ended up deployed together to Vietnam.

It would seem that this would be an ideal situation for four men to bond themselves into the type of tight-knit friendship that combat usually fosters. However, the Heights was a different place for Leo Leonardo and Chinx Cincotta, who were white, and Goody Barlow and Junior Jones, who were black. They came in the army from different backgrounds—ones that had taught them that the color of their skins should have made them more enemies to each other than to the Viet Cong. Throughout boot camp, they eyed each other with suspicion. Eventually, it was only the mutual hatred for Sergeant Connor that drove them together. The bigoted redneck had united them with his contempt.

Leo Leonardo had been Mad Guy Provenzano's handball partner until the day that he had been embarrassed beyond redemption by his former friend. His life spiraled downward from that dreaded day. Leo enlisted in the United States Army to win back his honor.

Chinx Cincotta had plenty of self-pride before entering the armed forces. What he also had was a conviction for assault. Ironically, the actions that led to that conviction were on behalf of Maria Romano and Mad Guy's brother Tony. A judge offered him the option of jail or the army. So now it was Private Chinx Cincotta at your service.

Goody Barlow had had a very bland life for a black teen in the Heights. He worked hard in school and minded his own business most of the time. All that he had wanted was to get an education. Unfortunately, the one time he had *not* minded his own business had been to save the skin of a white boy named Johnny Cipp. He rushed into the midst of five black boys just as they were beating the white boy senseless. He wasn't a great fighter, and his arrival on the scene was more helpful as a distraction for the white boy to escape. For his trouble, he got trouble. He now was an outcast among his own kind, branded an "Uncle Tom" merely for doing what he thought was right.

Mockingly, his enemies dubbed him "Goody" as in "Goody Two Shoes." In a moment of misguided friendship, Barlow had made the mistake of telling Junior Jones this story. He soon became "Goody" to the entire platoon—especially to the guys who liked him. Life had not been particularly pleasant for Goody since that day in the Heights. After talking to a recruiter, he realized that the G.I. Bill would pay for college if he put in his time. Private Goody Barlow at your service.

Junior Jones was different from the other Heights' soldiers in many ways. First, he had always known that he would be joining the army. His father had been career military and had even put in his time in Vietnam. He had come home to a respectable job at the armory in South Jamaica. He had also started teaching his son some fighting skills that he had learned in the service. Unfortunately, this was the second reason that Junior was different from Goody. Junior hated the white race.

It all stemmed back to the same schoolyard that had seen the demise of Leo Leonardo. Davis had been the brunt of a brutal white bullying incident. Surrounded by a group of whites while playing basketball, he had restrained himself at first. However, when Sean O'Neill had taken out a knife and threatened to cut him, Junior had used his defensive skills to disarm his attacker and knock him to the floor. He would have left at that point, but the bully's brother did not agree. Junior only got out of the yard after suffering bruises and lost teeth. All he'd wanted to do was to play basketball. Now he wanted to be a fighter that no one else would dare to take on.

They were an odd group, and after almost nine months of

service together, they'd developed some facsimile of friendship. Indeed, the same Cambria Heights that had kept them apart had brought them together in the hot sticky jungles of Southeast Asia. How long the friendship would have lasted is anyone's guess. No one will ever know because Sergeant Dirk Conner sent them out to die on August 15, 1968.

◆

"They're calling it the 'Mini-Tet Offensive' as compared to last January's massive assault." Sergeant Conner listened as his superior officer spoke. "And just like then, we just don't know what is going on out there."

"We'll fucking beat their asses back again, sir . . . pardon my language," offered Conner.

"Sergeant, we technically won the battle, but you think for a minute that it was a victory. At home, they're talking about us not being able to win this damn thing. But I don't care about any of that shit. I just want us to perform well and do our share, and I can't do that unless I know what's going on."

"What are your orders, sir?"

"Get me intelligence on where the enemy is—and do it quickly."

"Yes, sir," responded Sergeant Conner as he saluted and left his commander's tent.

◆

"So, what are we going to do?" asked Corporal Justus Elliot, as they walked back to their staging area.

"You and I know that the Cong are everywhere. It would be suicide to take my entire platoon out there. I'm not going to have the record show that I lost a whole platoon? For what?"

"So, what are you gonna do, Sarge?"

"Maybe a small scouting party would be better. What do you think?"

"You mean like a small expendable scouting party of nig-gers and nigger-lovers?" The corporal looked to his sergeant for affirmation.

"I never said that!" Conner smiled and winked as he spoke the words.

"You mean like Yankees . . . New York Yankees?"

"That's a baseball team, but I think you get the idea."

"Give them the orders. God rest their souls."

And so, it was that four young men from the Heights were sent on a mission from which they were never expected to return.

17

"Highway to Hell"
- AC/DC

"WHAT ARE WE LISTENING TO, Chinx?" asked his buddy Leo.

"A group called Those Born Free. One of my neighbors, Johnny Cipp gave this tape to my mom while I was waiting to go on trial. It's really good music," answered Chinx.

"Maybe, we'll go see them when we get back to the Heights," offered Leo.

"Well, if it ain't Motown, I ain't going," chimed in Junior.

"Junior, unless things have changed, they ain't letting our two black faces on that side of the line to see this group anyway," rebuked Goody.

"They're not around anymore, so don't worry about it," lamented Chinx. He knew what had happened to them. He knew *more* than anyone else on the whole damn planet. He took the tape out of its player and placed it safely in its case. He loved the music, but it was the conversation before the music that choked him up even more. *You pray for me, Johnny. I'm doing the same for you.*

"Get your asses up. Time to earn your keep, you fuckin' Yankee pricks," announced Private Elliot. "Report to Sgt. Connor immediately for your orders."

"And so, this screwed up situation continues," mumbled Chinx.

————

Though it was only the middle of the afternoon, the dense canopy of the jungle made it seem as if nightfall was imminent. The four soldiers felt lost and alone. Weariness consumed their bodies. The only consolation was that their loyalty to each other seemed to give them a particular shield against the dangerous situation around them.

"Why the fuck are we here?" Junior looked at his comrades as they sat in a small clearing and took a well-deserved rest after spending hours scouting for an enemy that they knew was out there somewhere.

"Because the United States government has deemed this country as a strategic area of the world to be defended against the rapid dispersion of communism," answered Goody.

"Goody, what the fuck are you talking about?" Junior just shook his head.

"Well, you asked why we were here?"

"Nigger, I said, why are *we* here?" At that, the two white members of the group, Chinx and Leo, almost choked on their dried-out rations.

"Calm down," offered Leo.

"I can say that word to another brother. You can't."

"Fuck you, I've probably said that word more times than I've said my own name," teased Chinx with a slight smirk forming on his lips.

"Not to me, you didn't," replied Junior, yet he too was smiling.

"Not yet, but I was there when someone else did and then kicked your ass," said Chinx, and looked to Junior for some recognition of what he had revealed.

"You were there when those fucking assholes attacked me with a knife and tried to kill me?"

"The only thing that got killed was your basketball when O'Neil stabbed it to death. But, you fuckin' impressed the shit out of me when you took away that knife with your fancy karate moves."

"Yeah, but it cost me two teeth when the bastard's brother stepped in," grimaced Junior as he pointed to the gap in the top right section of his mouth.

"I don't like it," interrupted Goody retracing the conversation.

"What the fuck are you talking about, Goody?"

"Junior, I don't think that anyone, white or black, should be using *that* word."

"And that is why you were called *Goody* back in the old neighborhood—Mr. Goody Two-Shoes."

"Just because I stood up for what I thought was right and saved some white kid, I'm some kind of an outcast in the Heights. It's not fair!" Goody offered a rare show of emotion.

"You saved a white kid and got screwed?" Now it was Leo's turn to interrupt. "I saved a black kid, and Guy Provenzano made my life a living hell." Leo's serious expression turned into a partial smile and he added, "Ironic isn't it?"

"Boo-hoo to you two," cracked Chinx. "I saved a fucking retard and ended up in jail. Yeah, but I would do it again. I liked at least one of the Provenzanos."

"And there's your answer. We're all here because it was all screwed up back there—and in one way or another, it all came back to the Provenzanos." Leo raised his canteen in a mock toast to the Heights and the madman who had screwed it up.

"Yes, but if you want to know *why we are here in this very location, at this very time,* I'll tell you. It's that red-neck bastard, Connor. He thinks we are expendable—both us niggers and nigger-lovers." Goody brought the conversation full circle.

"Holy shit, I never heard him speak like that." Shocked, Junior laughed. "They going to let you be a lawyer with a mouth like that?"

Goody had a stunned look—realizing he had used a word he never thought he'd use.

"You're going to be a lawyer?" Leo looked at him with a new admiration.

"Yes, I'm going to use the GI Bill to finance my education."

"He's going to be a damn fine lawyer too," added Junior.

"How do you know?" questioned Leo.

"He's got to be because I'm going to need him. When I get out of here, I'm going to do some nasty shit!"

They all laughed and raised their canteens in a final toast.

"And on that note, I've gotta drain the lizard," declared Junior as he put down his canteen and trudged off into the woods.

"Can't hold your water," commented Goody.

———◆———

Less than a minute later, a grenade landed in their midst. The dull thud sounded equidistant from the three circled soldiers. Because Goody and Leo were looking over their shoulders taunting Junior, they hadn't seen it land. Only Chinx eyed the object that lay at their feet.

"Grenade," Chinx frantically warned but realized that there was not enough time for anyone but him to act. As he seized the explosive sphere, his only thoughts were to get it as far away as possible. Even as it left his hand, he knew he was too late. Only a few feet from his fingers, it detonated.

Seconds later, three Viet Cong soldiers swarmed into the clearing, smiles on their faces as they assessed the damage they had done. Three mangled Americans lay splayed in a mixture of dirt and blood—still alive. It was time to move in for the kill.

Junior heard the explosion and ran back to the clearing. He saw what had happened and realized that he had the option of staying tucked away in the undergrowth. He could survive this clusterfuck, but that was not how Junior had been raised. You stuck up for your buddies. It took him only seconds to realize that all of his friends' rifles lay scattered on the floor. Chinx looked bad—half his right arm was missing. Blood covered Leo's face, and Goody had a massive gash in one of his legs. But they all were alive—barely.

Junior found himself parallel to an enemy who had not noticed his presence. He tried to plan his actions carefully. However, when they raised their guns to finish off his friends, all thought ended. Instinct took over. He grabbed his knife, his only available weapon, and sprinted the few yards separating him from the three attackers. He plunged his blade into the neck of the closest foe. His right leg almost simultaneously swung backward with a roundhouse kick that caught another enemy in the jaw and sent him back to the ground unconscious. The third defender fired, and the bullet caught Junior in his left shoulder just as his right palm was landing a fatal blow to the shooter.

Junior's vicious strike would push the rigid bone in his enemy's nose through his brain.

Junior fell to his knees. His wound was severe, but not fatal. He looked at his three buddies, who lay fifteen feet away at the opposite end of the clearing. He saw that Goody and Leo were moving. Chinx was alive but in bad shape.

"Saved, your motherfucking asses." Junior panted with a broad smile on his face. The smile turned to a dark look of surprise as a bullet tore through his stomach. "There's more of them coming," he yelled to his wounded comrades. Yet even as he warned them, he realized that he was probably the only one who could do anything about the problem. He got to his feet and slowly staggered toward the rifles that lay near his friends.

Leo was blind—shrapnel had taken his eyesight. He yelled to Chinx and Goody to help him, or at least tell him what was going on. Chinx was in shock and barely conscious, but Goody answered, "My leg's fucked up, and I can't move. Leo, the guns are all near you. You gotta do something."

"Goody, I can't see!"

"Shit! OK, move your left hand out to ten o'clock position. You gotta get a gun to me," Leo reached out but felt nothing.

Junior continued to stagger across the clearing toward them in a valiant attempt to get to the weapons. Goody was the first to notice the two enemies approaching.

"Where, Goody, where?" screamed Leo—his blind hands reaching out in search of the weapons.

"Six inches more," urged Goody calmly, but panic was building inside of him. Junior was not going to make it to the rifles in time.

"Got it," exclaimed Leo triumphantly, finally grabbing hold of the rifle.

"Throw it to me. Six feet to your left."

Goody received the weapon quickly and readied it to fire, but it was too late to save Junior. Two of the enemy had entered the clearing and immediately aimed at Junior, the only soldier still standing. A bullet hit his left thigh, and another found the middle of the chest. His forward motion carried him to the feet of Goody, who only looked briefly at his friend before letting off two rounds that caught both attackers in their heads. There was silence in the jungle.

Leo crawled toward the sound of the now fallen body, and Goody moved closer to his friend's head. Junior was dying. They leaned in close to hear his final words.

"Tell my dad that I did him proud," whispered the barely audible Junior.

"Very proud," was all that the choked-up Goody could get out.

"We'll tell your daddy. We'll tell the army. We'll tell anyone who will goddamn listen. You're a fuckin' hero, man," cried Leo.

Junior smiled at them and died.

———◆———

"We're screwed, Leo."

"Goody, I can't see a thing, so tell me why we're screwed."

"Leo, you not seeing anything is part of why we're screwed. Junior's dead and Chinx looks like he is on his way—and you can't fuckin' see."

"And how about you, Goody.?"

"My leg's bad."

"How about the gooks who did this to us?

"Four dead and one unconscious over there."

"The first thing you do is put a damn bullet in the last one's head."

"OK. . ."

"Now I'm coming over to you, so make some noise."

A single discharge from a rifle echoed in the jungle, and then there was silence. Leo crawled toward the sound, feeling his way along the blood-soaked turf. Upon reaching his friends, he immediately took charge.

"Now cut up Junior's jacket and shirt. I'm going to put a tourniquet on your leg, and then when you can move, you're going to put them on Chinx wherever he needs them."

"Leo, he needs a lot of them. He's missing . . .er. . .parts."

"OK, but stick with me. We gotta get out of here—and soon. There's got to be more of those bastards around."

"But what about Chinx and Junior?"

"Goody, they come with us. No soldier gets left behind, especially no Heights soldier. Understand?"

"How are you staying so calm, Leo?"

"I once pissed in my pants in front of a whole schoolyard of guys because I was scared. Once you've done that, this is easy shit. Besides, I'm blind. I can't see how bad things are!"

"I can't believe you are joking at a time like this."

"I'd cry, but I think that my actual tear ducts got blown off."

"Again, you're fucking unbelievable."

"I think all my other parts are intact. You see any other injuries on me?"

"No, Leo, just your ugly face."

"Hey, don't pick on the blind guy. I can joke about my face, but you can't."

"Sorry."

"That's a joke, Goody. They'll be plenty of time to cry after this is over. For now, we laugh so we don't cry. You've got to get the hang of this handicap humor thing."

"No, I guess it's a good thing that I'm not handicapped." Yet as he looked down, he realized that Leo had no way to see that he was lying. The muscles of his calf lay outside of the leg itself, and a few bones were out there with them. It was only the tight wrapping of Junior's jacket that held the pieces together.

"Think you can walk?"

"Yeah," lied Goody.

"Put Chinx over my shoulder, and let's get going." With that, he rose to his full six-foot height and stood ready to carry his wounded friend back to camp. "A little help here with a direction before I walk halfway to North Vietnam."

"Yeah, I'm coming—just lifting Junior onto my shoulders."

"Are you fucking kidding me? I was worried about needing to carry you too, and you're going to carry Junior's body on your bad leg."

"No soldier left behind, Leo. No *Heights* soldier left behind—ever."

And they moved out. Goody led the way with his rifle supporting the weight that his injured leg could not. Junior's body hung over his other shoulder, and Leo clung to their dead friend's outstretched arm, so he knew where he had to go. Goody's loyalty to his friends would cost him his leg.

———◆———

Every inch of the jungle they traveled was paid for in blood and pain. Neither Goody nor Leo remembered much of the ordeal except for hours of excruciating pain. When a patrol found them, they were all near death from dehydration and blood loss. A forward medical squad did miracles to keep the three of them alive while they waited for a helicopter to take them to a secure hospital. There they were given emergency care that kept the three survivors alive for the time being. With the facility tight for space, they found themselves in three adjoining beds.

"Goody, you there?" Leo was conscious most of the time. The same could not be said for Goody and Chinx. Finally, he received an answer.

"Yeah, I'm here, Leo."

"Eh. What about Chinx?"

"Believe it or not, he's still hanging in there. He's a tough bastard."

"Holy shit, Leo. You see that female doctor that was working on us?"

"Goody, I can't see anything—remember?"

"Oh, yeah."

"Why don't you come over here closer and we can talk without screaming."

"I can't."

"Why, Goody? Too busy flirting with that doctor?"

"I can't walk. They took my left leg."

"Oh shit, I'm sorry."

"Yeah, otherwise, I'd be asking that doc to go dancing with me."

"Wow, it took losing a leg for you to understand my gimp humor finally."

"A small price to make you laugh, asshole." Goody looked sadly down at his missing limb. They both knew that their humor was part false bravado and part a heavy dose of painkillers.

"What about Chinx?"

"I don't think he's going to make it. No matter how much that pretty doc works on him."

"Goody, tell that piece of ass to work harder on Chinx."

"That *piece of ass*, as you described me, is standing right here," snapped the attractive female doctor entering the room.

"Oops, Goody, you've got to be my eyes around here."

"Private Leonardo, you are addressing an officer," commanded the doctor, "And Chinx is a derogatory term for a Chinese person."

"No, it isn't, sir. I mean, at least not in this case. It is just short for Cincotta."

"Sir, yes, sir," relented Goody, who could see that the doctor was not taking this as seriously as Leo thought she was.

"So, what do you say now, Leonardo?"

"Sorry, sir."

"That's *Sir Piece of Ass* to you, private," answered the doctor, unable to hold back her laughter. On that note, she left the tent and moved on to the next area of patients.

"So, what does she look like, Goody?"

"An Angel. The face of an angel—long black hair, maybe five-foot-six. Skin—probably halfway in color between you and me. She's probably a spic."

"I can hear you. These are only tents," the doctor called from the next tent.

"Oh shit," whispered Goody.

"I ever hear the word 'spic' come out of your mouth again, I'll take my forceps and stick them up your ass until I can pull your balls out of your rear end. Do you hear me? And I'm five-foot-seven, Private Prick."

"She's tough," interjected Leo.

"You fuckin' bet I am," said the doctor re-entering their tent.

"Goody, is she back?"

"Shit, yeah."

"Should I be afraid?"

"Shit, yeah," answered the doctor as she walked toward them.

"Now, Private Barlow, who are you calling a spic?"

"He didn't mean anything," interrupted Leo.

"When I want your opinion, Stevie Wonder, I'll ask for it."

"Can she say that to me?" said Leo.

"What's the matter? Can't take a little 'gimp' humor as you called it?" With that, a big smile came across her face, and she laughed a loud, warm laugh. She took Leo's hand and smiled at Goody.

"She's smiling, Leo," announced Goody.

"I wanted you two to realize that not everyone is going to be nice to you two out there because of your handicaps. Back in the States, they're starting to treat all veterans like we did something wrong. The war isn't popular, and neither are we."

"Doc, will I see again?"

"Private Leonardo, you lost your right eye. Your left eye is damaged pretty severely. Experts with a great deal more skill than me will see what they can do for you. All I can do is my best and tell it to you straight."

"What about me?" Goody somberly looked down at the remains of his leg.

"No, your leg won't grow back."

"I know that . . . oh yeah, more gimp humor."

"Seriously, though, they have come a long way with prosthetics, but it won't be easy."

"Thanks for being honest, doc," mumbled Leo. "Let's start over. Private Leonardo reporting for duty. But my friends call me Leo."

"Private John Barlow reporting for duty. But my friends call me Goody." They both saluted her.

"I'm Major Piece of Ass," said the doctor, and then she laughed. "You don't get it, do you? I don't stand on formalities. You have enough bullshit to deal with, and I don't need you to be worrying about the bureaucratic army shit. Except when the brass is around, you two can call me by my nickname—Shylo."

"Does she have a smile or a serious look on her face?" questioned Leo.

"I think she means it, Leo," offered Goody.

"Of course, I mean it, and if you two ever salute me again, I'm going to cut off your right hands and give both of you another handicap."

"Yes, Shylo, sir," they both answered but kept their hands at their sides.

On the fourth day after they arrived at the hospital, Greg "Chinx" Cincotta regained consciousness. Leo, Goody, and Shylo were immediately by his side. He had lost his right arm, his right leg, part of an ear, and had a large wound on the right side of his chest. His first sight was of Goody on crutches and Leo with his eyes bandaged.

"You guys don't look so good," whispered the hoarse voice of Chinx.

"Hey, Chinx," Goody said weakly. He knew Chinx did not truly understand his own situation yet.

"You, on the other hand, look fantastic." Chinx chuckled, looking at Shylo and giving his best flirty smile.

"Soldier, you are speaking to an officer," she offered sternly. Chinx looked quizzically at his friends.

"Sorry, sir," started Chinx but was cut off by the laughter of the three of them.

"She does that, Chinx," interrupted Leo.

"Just call her Shylo, and she actually *is* an officer and a doctor," affirmed Leo.

"If I knew doctors looked liked this, I would have gotten injured sooner," Chinx said with a slight smile, but he knew the small talk and introductions were over. All humor left the conversation.

"I have to examine you," said Shylo.

"Doc . . ."

"Shylo," corrected the examining physician.

"Shylo, it hurts a lot."

"Where?"

"Everywhere."

"I've given you as much morphine as I can. I'm afraid you have a massive infection besides all your injuries."

"Will I make it?" Chinx asked. Goody and Leo listened carefully. She had promised to be honest with them.

"Maybe, if we could get you to a better hospital, your chances would be better. But the Mini-Tet Offensive is limiting flights and ."

"So that's a no," said Chinx looking her right in the eyes.

"There's a chance—if I can get you out of here."

"But that isn't going to happen, is it?"

"No, I don't think so."

"Could the three of you leave me alone? I need to think."

———◆———

Hours later, Chinx's condition worsened, and he knew the end was near. He asked Shylo to send for a priest. When he arrived, he was left alone with him so that he could confess his sins and die in peace.

"Bless me, father, for I have sinned. My last confession was a lifetime ago."

"Go on, son."

"I guess that I should start with the fact that I knocked out a priest," said Chinx humbly hoping that the priest wouldn't hold that against him. He seemed to notice that Father Thomas was looking at his missing limbs when Chinx added, "You don't have to worry. I won't be doing that anymore."

The priest and the dying soldier talked at length about many things, and Fr. Thomas provided solace during Chinx's final moments. When they had finished, the priest offered him the final absolution. Yet as he was about to leave, Fr. Thomas turned to Chinx and spoke one last time.

"You know that I'm bound by God's laws not to speak about all that you have told me, and I never will. But I think that maybe you might want to tell someone else what you confided in me. I may be wrong, but I think that is what you really want. You don't want your secrets to die with you."

"You're right, Father Thomas. Could you ask Leo and Goody to come back into the room when you leave?"

"You got it," replied the priest.

Moments later, Leo was at his bedside.

"Where's Goody?"

"He's down for the count. Doc Shylo gave him some pain-killers."

"I . . . I wanted to get something off my chest, and I wanted both of you to hear it."

"Well, I'll have to do for now."

"Leo, I only have now."

"Who sez?"

"She does," answered Chinx as Shylo walked through the door.

"I've got to check your vitals and see what's going on," said Shylo.

"What's going on is that I'm dying, and I need to tell Leo something important before I do!"

"I'm your doctor, and don't you ever forget that."

"Fine. Stay, but you're going to hear some heavy shit."

Leo and Doc Shylo heard Chinx's deathbed secret. He told them something about Johnny Cipp that no one else in this world knew.

———◆———

All four of the Heights soldiers were home in the United States by the end of September. Leo and Goody would spend the next six months rehabbing at Walter Reed Hospital. Davis "Junior" Jones and Greg "Chinx" Cincotta would make their journey home in caskets.

They all received the Army's Distinguished Service Medal for the bravery displayed on the field of combat. Most who knew their story believed that they should have received a higher honor, possibly the Congressional Medal of Honor for Valor for Junior and Chinx. That, however, could never happen. The army was too embarrassed by the back story of the four heroes. What were four privates doing alone in one of the most dangerous combat zones of the war? Where was a lieutenant or sergeant or any form of a leader on this suicide mission?

Once the chain of command uncovered the actions of Sergeant Dirk Connor, he was promptly busted in rank, and his career in the army came to an end. Yet no one wanted the story to get out, and Medal of Honor winners were always big news, especially posthumously. And so, the whole affair lived on only in the minds and hearts of Leo Leonardo and Goody Barlow, who bonded together to become life-long friends. They would never forget their fallen comrades, especially Chinx, whose death bed confession changed their lives forever.

18

"Turn the Page"
– *Bob Seger and the Silver Bullet Band*

Diary of DJ Spinelli

Entry # 25 – August 29, 1968

I'M ABOUT TO START MY second year of college, and so much has changed since you left. Maria is gone. Do you understand? She's out there doing who knows what, who knows where, because of you. Are you happy now?

I started the *Queens Undies* and gave my life some direction. I've some new friendships with Neil and Aylin. We all agree that the world is going to hell in a handbag. The Vietnam War is raging. Martin Luther King and Bobby Kennedy have been assassinated. Campuses all over the country are closing down in protests about the war and civil rights. Yet, all I care about is writing about music.

I don't mean to minimize the deaths of those great men, but there are signs that this is the end of western civilization. I just heard there is a company offering a fast-food hamburger for $.49. Are they nuts? Who would spend money like that when you can have Wetson's for $.15 and White Castle for $.08? I mean, who are these McDonald people and what the hell is a Big Mac?

Entry #26 - August 31, 1968

Johnny, I heard that Greg Cincotta died.

Entry #27 - Sept 2, 1968

I know that time will be tight once I start my classes, so I went to see your parents today. Your dad doesn't look very well. In the middle of my visit, he excused himself to take a nap. I don't know what's wrong, but I guess that they don't want to tell me.

"It's time for us to downsize," your mother whispered to me. I didn't know what she meant until she continued. "He's not well, and I think we should get rid of a lot of stuff and lead a simpler life. You know, just in case."

At first, I wasn't following, and then I realized that she was preparing mentally and physically to be alone. How would she ever be able to empty this house on her own? She had no one— she thought.

"I'll help," I volunteered, and I gave her a big hug. Nineteen years old and it was going to fall on me to help your mother dismantle her life. I would find the time. Somehow.

Johnny, you're an even bigger ass now!

Entry #28 - September 24, 1968

Time to catch up with what's going on. Classes are a bit harder this semester, but also more enjoyable. We have a small group of guys who hang out at the Student Center during our free time. We talk about music, politics, and girls. I don't have much time for actual dating, but I do get to talk about it. (Does that count as a social life?)

The *Queens Undies* issue with an interview of Neil has made me a campus sensation. The editors at the school paper now asked me to join the staff, and I politely told them where they could stick it. It felt so good. Neil is going to meet Christian Andrews when he comes back to town in a few weeks. He says that he's going to bring me along to record the historic meeting.

Neil and I have become close friends. You would like him, Johnny. He is a great guy who is getting railroaded by the police department because he did a good thing. However, he remains calm while he waits to see if his suspension is permanent. I didn't write any of that in the article.

Meanwhile, he has a great deal of free time and so he is helping me pack up your house. It's tough on me. Every time I put away one of your personal items, I think of you—our days in class together—our "band" with Tinman and Brother Christian—our songwriting in this very room.

Neil gets a kick out of your "Hall of Monsters," and occasionally, we stop to rest and read one of your comics. After a few hours of this, we go out to pick up a sack of White Castle hamburgers and bring them back and have a very "formal" dinner with your parents. As I downed my fifth "burger," I looked around at my dinner company—three good people whose lives had been screwed up by the world around them.

Entry #29 - Sept 25, 1968

My big break in life! Neil got a call, and he is going down to the Café Wha to meet Christian Andrews. Neil asked if it was OK if he brought a friend along, and so on October 1, I'm going see, hear, and talk with the elusive Christian Andrews. But his name isn't Christian Andrews. That was a stage name, and his real name is Chris Delaney. I knew that it sounded familiar, and I did some research and found out that he had a band and had some success a few years ago. I wonder if he had any other secret identities? I wonder how he chose the name Andrews?

I don't want to overwhelm Delaney with questions. Neil just told Chris Andrews/Delaney that he was bringing a friend—not specifically me, a reporter trying to get a scoop. Maybe, I'll just sit in awe of this guy and listen. Afterward, I'll ask if it is OK to write his story down for my paper. Yeah, October 1 will be my big break, an interview with someone that no one has been able to get to know.

Entry #30 – Sept 30, 1968

Tomorrow is the big day for the *Queens Undies*. I will have
all three of the principles in the story of the Lispenard Attack
in one place and at one time. Of course, the fact that Chris
Delaney is a musician will ease the transition of my paper from
general topics to a music-themed success.

No one knows anything about this Delaney guy. It's like
he came out of nowhere. Even before being attacked, he was
becoming well known around the Village for his performances.
Now I will reveal the man behind the victim—the man behind
the music. I can't wait.

Entry #31 – September 30, 1968

We found a cassette tape sitting in one of your drawers. After
we listened to it, Neil asked if he could have it. I think that Neil
feels that the tape confirms his *What-would-Bracko-do?* moral
code.

THOSE BORN FREE Tape – May 28, 1967

"Before the rest of the guys get here, I want to ask you something."
(Jimmy Mac)
"Then stop fiddling with that damn tape recorder and speak."
(Johnny)
"You think that Bracko's all there?" (Jimmy Mac)
"What do you mean?"
*"I mean, most guys would have been proud to be considered a hero.
He saved that Neil Connaughton kid, and when we complimented him
about it—he just walked out of practice." (Jimmy Mac)*
*"We didn't compliment him on saving the kid; we made a big deal out
of how tough he was." (Johnny)*
"Yeah, so?" (Jimmy Mac)
*"Bracko doesn't think of his ability to hurt someone as a good thing.
Remember, he has been on the opposite end of a fist most of his life."*
(Johnny)

"His prick of a father?" (Jimmy Mac)

"Yup. And if I know Bracko, he only knocked the kid down as a last resort. Bracko always does what's right—whatever it takes. But he's never proud of hurting someone else—ever." (Johnny)

Entry #32 - Oct. 2, 1968

Bracko spoke very little at band practices, and so I never got to know him very well. However, my friendship with Neil has made him a genuine influence on *my* life. Neil's mantra is always, *what would Bracko do?* I made that a part of my article. I guess hearing it said often enough has rubbed off on me. Last night I had to make one of the toughest decisions of my life. I found myself asking, *what would Bracko do?*

After I had already shit, shaved, showered and put on my coolest outfit, I was minutes away from leaving for the Café Wha. Once out the door, it would be less than an hour before I would be sitting with Neil, Trip, and the elusive Chris Delaney. The music would be great, the company would be great, and the opportunity would be great. Just minutes away. And then the phone rang.

Your mom was hysterical. Your dad had collapsed, and an ambulance was just about to take him away. She needed someone to be with her. I'd like to think that I made my decision instantaneously, but I know that's not true. For a split second, I envisioned myself at the Café Wha and all that it meant to me. For a split second, my future stood before me. I wavered in my compassion for another and thought only of my selfish needs. And then I could hear Neil's voice, *what would Bracko do?*

Johnny, this should be you. I was with your mom all night and just left her off at her door. I'll take her back to the hospital later today, and the doctors will have a better idea of what is going on. I'll call Neil then and apologize for leaving him hanging. He'll understand. He'll agree I did the right thing.

Entry #33 - Oct 2, 1968 (again)

About noon, I hung up the phone with Neil. He was so

excited about the night before that he didn't bother to ask why I wasn't there. I cut him off. I told him about your dad and what had happened. He told me to do what I had to do, and he would catch up with me later. I didn't know that I'd find him waiting for us at the hospital. He hugged your mom and just gave me a shrug of the shoulders.

The three of us waited all afternoon, but the doctors couldn't tell us anything. When we left your mom off that night, we went to dinner. As much as I tried to get details about last night, he held back. I did most of the talking while he seemed obsessed with the clock on the wall. At precisely seven p.m., he took me over to a payphone and dialed a number. He didn't say a word and just handed me the phone. I looked at him like he was insane—until I heard the voice.

"This is Chris Delaney. I just wanted to tell you that I'm sorry I didn't meet you last night. Neil explained the whole situation," The voice sounded vaguely familiar, but I couldn't hear well in the noisy diner.

"Sorry," I said and then found myself quoting my father, who often quoted old cheesy westerns, "A man's got to do what a man's got to do." Holy shit! Did I actually say that to him?

"I agree," was his answer. "I think you're a stand-up guy, and I'd be proud to meet anywhere at any time." (Damn, that voice was familiar. Maybe like one of my college teachers?)

"Thank you," was all I could think to say.

"You know, I never got your name." As I went to answer, I heard a loud voice on his side of the phone overwhelm my attempt to answer.

"Chris, the train is leaving the station—literally. If you want to perform tomorrow in Philly, then we gotta go now," yelled a voice in the background—barely heard over a passing train.

"Sorry, catch you later," shouted Delaney over the sound of an incoming train, and a dial tone buzzed in my ear.

I turned to Neil with a big smile and a thumbs-up sign.

"Now, can you tell me about last night?"

"DJ, I wish you could have been there."

19

"We Could Be Heroes"
- *David Bowie*

NEIL CONNAUGHTON DROVE TO HILLSIDE Avenue in Jamaica and parked his car. He caught the F train into Manhattan and then transferred to a downtown subway that took him to the Village. Outside the Café Wha, Trip Grimes met Neil and showed him to the table where the two of them would sit for Chris Delaney's performance. Though almost six months had passed, Delaney had still not met the man who had saved his life. His recovery had been long and slow and had taken place miles away from the city.

Now he was back, and he intended to finally thank the young police cadet. He had heard through Trip about the kid's suspension and was as furious with the bureaucrats as he was grateful to Neil. Hopefully, he had a solution. If he did his job well, those assholes would have to reinstate the hero of Lispenard.

"Not enough time to come out now, but Chris will hang out with us the rest of the night after he performs," offered Trip.

"That's fine. He has other things to worry about besides entertaining me."

"You're wrong. Tonight is all about you." With that, Trip lifted a camera from his side and placed it on a tripod. Neil looked at him quizzically. It was not the latest in equipment, but it would have to do. Trip was still a struggling filmmaker. The house lights dimmed, and Chris Delaney walked out on stage. As usual, the Wha crowd was subdued with a show-me-what-you-got attitude.

Chris Delaney ambled on to the stage. This was not for effect, but rather from the pain of injuries. When he found his spot, he studiously did one last tuning of his ancient Gibson acoustic guitar. He hit one C chord and then looked straight out into the audience.

"It's great to be here. It's great to be anywhere," he started. He knew that this sounded like a corny comedian's joke, but it was true in his case. He was happy to be alive and performing. A little over a year ago, he had been a religious brother teaching in a Catholic school. In the ensuing time, he had left and found a new life—and almost died. All the months of rehabilitation had been filled with thoughtful contemplation of the meaning of life. His every action would have a purpose. This became obvious when he introduced his first number.

"Less than two months ago, Dion released this song. It is a tribute to leaders who were slain in the cause of human rights." He looked down at his guitar as if deciding if he should say more.

"I'm insignificant compared to them, yet events in my life have made me feel a bond with them." The crowd knew how Chris Delaney had almost died. Indeed, many knew nothing of his music but had come out of curiosity to see the famous victim. "I hope my rendering of this song does justice to Dion's thoughts and the memory of Abraham, Martin, and John."

The silence that filled the Café Wha was overwhelming. Had he turned them off or reached into their hearts? His answer came moments later. It started with a single pair of clapping hands somewhere in the farthest reaches of the room. Trip Grimes' camera panned to the location, though he could not pinpoint any specific person. Soon it did not matter as the entire audience was standing and applauding. Chris Delaney had not played a single chord, yet he had struck a note with the crowd. The world had been mourning, and now it was ready for healing, and the man on stage had told them that music would be a part of the process.

Anybody here seen my old friend Abraham?
Can you tell me where he's gone?
He freed a lot of people, but it seems the good die young,
I just turned around, and he's gone.

Though initially scheduled for only four songs, Chris played for over an hour. Most songs consciously followed a theme of forgiveness and joining together. Most were covers of hits by stars like Simon and Garfunkel, The Beatles, and some unknowns. With no backing band, the singer had to be creative and original with the use of his acoustic guitar and arrangement of the songs. The crowd had gradually settled into a mood of mellow enjoyment. Even songs that Chris had created in the cold months of the previous winter received acceptance.

The night progressed well, but Neil noticed Trip had a concerned look on his face.

"He doesn't have the stamina to go on much longer." Trip said. "I'm worried about him."

"Why does he do it?"

"He's always loved this stuff, but now he is obsessed with it—with getting a message across."

"Can't you stop him before he goes too far—I mean physically?"

"He told me that he would give me a signal when he has one last song in him, and he wants me to film every second of his introduction and performance. It's something new. He wouldn't tell me much more. And there is the signal now."

"Thank you for welcoming me to the Café Wha. Years ago, I played here with my brothers, and you warmly welcomed us then. That is why this place means so much to me." A scattering of applause sprinkled the room.

"Where's he going with this?" whispered Neil. Trip shrugged ignorance.

"As most of you know by now, I almost died last April 4. The papers all talked about my experience and how two men rescued me—one a friend, one a stranger. . .one white, one black. By the end of the month, the story was gone from the headlines, but not for me."

"Where's he. . .?" started Neil, but Trip held his finger to his lips to quiet him and pointed to the camera.

"My good friend Trip Grimes is a struggling filmmaker, and he is spending his time filming me and trying to tell the whole story of that night and its aftermath. And why is that important, you might ask?"

"Yeah, why is it important?" yelled a patron who thought he was funny answering the rhetorical question. Chris ignored the clod and continued.

"Being a hero is not easy. Lord knows I probably am not brave enough to do what my two saviors did. But one of them is having his dream taken away from him for doing just that—being a hero."

"No way," someone yelled, and scattered boos filled the room. Neil flushed with embarrassment but did not make a sound.

"The young cadet who risked everything for me faces a permanent loss of his career for doing the right thing. But I'm going to fight that with the only weapon that I possess—music. I've written a song about that night, and I hope that you like it. But even if you don't like the way I sing or the melody I have created, take these lyrics and spread them to your friends. Write letters to the mayor and the police commissioner! Demand justice! If you don't do all these things, I have wasted my time."

A loud murmur drowned out his last few words. As arranged previously, waiters distributed printed copies of Delaney's lyrics to the boisterous crowd even as he held up his hands to quiet the noise.

"It's my fault that six months have gone by and I still have not met Neil. I want to correct that right now." He pointed to the back of the room and said authoritatively, "House lights up, please." Once the audience was bathed in glaring white light, Chris shielded his eyes enough to focus.

"Stand up, Trip," ordered the singer, and Trip stood next to his chair. "Now come up here to the stage." Trip obeyed but was not happy. As much as he liked to be behind the camera, he disdained any time in front of one. He knew that thanks to the tripod, the moment continued to be recorded.

"I'm gonna kill you for this," said Trip as he mounted the

stage.

"And now *I* would like to meet—and I would like *you* to meet and welcome Cadet Neil Connaughton—truly New York's Finest." The crowd roared as Neil took the stage next to Trip and Chris, welcomed by a heartfelt hug from the singer. As Trip and Neil attempted to return to their seats, Chris stopped them. "Stay here for the song," he whispered away from the mic.

"I'm embarrassed," said Neil to Trip.

"Yeah, me too, but it feels damn good."

The first chords caught the crowd's attention. The sheer force and tempo of the strings drove home the notion that this ode to Neil and Trip was not going to be a ballad. There was righteous anger flowing from the acoustic guitar as Chris Delaney stepped forward. While still in the throes of his musical introduction, his demeanor changed to one of serious resolve. "Remember that there is power in music!"

Heroes in the Night
-Chris Delaney

There was anger and rage,
A peacemaker's death set the stage,
The night I almost died on Lispenard.

Some chose to pray in quiet,
While others' choice was riot,
I found myself a victim of the latter.

(Chorus)
There were heroes that night,
One black and one white,
The night I almost died on Lispenard.

There was a crowd of four,
Stopping me inches from my door,
And beat me till my body broke in pieces.

There was no hope in sight,

My crime was being white,
Taking blame for something I hadn't known happened.

(Chorus)
There were heroes that night,
One black and one white,
The night I almost died on Lispenard.

"Stop in the name of the law,"
Said a white cop before a blow to the jaw,
And the two of us lay helpless on the ground.,

Though injured and in pain,
The policeman rose again,
"It's the right thing to do," he would say later.

(Chorus)
There were heroes that night,
One black and one white,
The night I almost died on Lispenard.

"Stop," yelled a black voice aloud,
Dr. King would not be proud,
Of what you are doing in his name.

The cop rose from the floor,
And stood with the black man to endure,
The violence that was coming from the mob.

(Chorus)
There were heroes that night,
One black and one white,
The night I almost died on Lispenard.

Together black and white stood,
Hoping the outside world would,
Understand they were doing the right thing together.

The white cop squad arrived,
Black and white heroes survived,
But only until racism raised its head.

(Alternate Chorus)
There were villains that night,
Some black and some white,
The night I almost died on Lispenard.

The racist sergeant said,
"You wished these white people dead?
You will now pay a price for your crimes."

On the black man blows did fall,
Again, the young cop rose tall,
"He did nothing wrong, he saved our lives."

(Alternate Chorus)
There were villains that night,
Some black and some white,
The night I almost died on Lispenard.

He acted to make it right,
He attacked the sergeant white to white,
And saved the black man from more harm.

Crowds of people arrived,
The white and black heroes survived,
But would there be a price for their good deeds?

(Chorus)
There were heroes that night,
One black and one white,
The night I almost died on Lispenard.

(Alternate Chorus)
There were villains that night,
Some black and some white,

The night I almost died on Lispenard.

(Chorus)
There were heroes that night,
One black and one white,
The night I almost died on Lispenard.

20

"A Hard Rain's Gonna Fall"
- *Bob Dylan*

Diary of DJ Spinelli

Entry # 35 - Oct 7, 1968

NEIL TOLD ME YESTERDAY ABOUT his night at the Wha and meeting Chris Delaney, yet I didn't understand the full impact until today. I'd read the powerful lyrics to the song. However, all this was nothing compared to hearing them on the radio. Tapes of the song had been rushed to all the local FM radio stations. Not all of them would play it, but those that did received spontaneous requests to replay the song. As the song and its story took on the designation of "A Happening," there became a clamor for more information about Neil, Trip, Chris, and the whole Lispenard incident.

This hunger for info spread like wildfire as Trip provided the film of the event to local news reporters. Excerpts of "Heroes in the Night" appeared on two of the three network affiliate channels. The bad news is that now I've no chance of scooping anyone with this story—a minor setback for my paper. However, what is bad for my journalistic career is good for my friend Neil.

Neil was told unofficially he would be reinstated. This source didn't hesitate to tell him that the commissioner wasn't happy about being forced to take back "an insubordinate little prick." However, the pressure created by "the" song had forced his hand. He wanted to know if Neil "could behave himself." Neil, of course, said yes. However, I have my doubts that he can keep that promise. I mean, what happens the next time he is faced with a *what-would-Bracko-do* moment?

He needs to complete the academy and then wait until he turns 21. However, I wonder if the powers that be will try to screw him behind the scenes. He will get the official word on October 31—Halloween. Will his future in the police department be trick or a treat?

Entry #36- October 12,1968

Columbus Day. It is more than thirteen months since you disappeared. I'm off from school, and Neil still isn't working. We went over to pack up *your* house. Your mom was on her way to church. She goes every morning now. Did your mother always do that, or is about your father's illness—and you?

Johnny, your dad has cancer, and it doesn't look hopeful. I don't understand the medical explanations, but what he has is very rare and unusual. Because of this, the prognosis is a bit sketchy. Your mom asked Neil and me to go up and see him in his room.

"You kids know anything about history?" was his weird opening line.

"I love the stuff," gushed Neil. I was a little less enthusiastic.

"What do they teach you, DJ, about Hiroshima?"

Now that was a hard question to answer. I knew that your dad was a veteran of World War II and had been in the Pacific Ocean during the war. My problem was that this was 1968, and every professor that I had was anti-war—any war. Therefore, any class I took elaborated on the "evil" American empire that had demolished a city with an atomic bomb. I knew that the alternative was that over a million American servicemen could have been lost in the invasion. I told him that I knew nothing.

"I was there."

"Where?" questioned Neil.

"On a ship heading toward the invasion of Japan." I knew on which side of the debate your dad stood.

"Then I guess the dropping of the bomb might have saved your life," I maintained smugly.

"Yes and no," he answered. Both Neil and I were confused.

"Very few people talk about what happened after the bomb was dropped. Everybody was celebrating. The troops were coming home. The war was over, but not for all of us."

"What do you mean?" Neil asked.

"Some of us stayed and took care of the sick and dying—the Japanese sick and dying."

"Where?"

"There, in Hiroshima."

"But it was radioactive, and radiation causes. . ."

"Cancer," he said as an ironic smile formed on his mouth. He was a teacher who had just schooled us in a little-known sidebar of history.

"Oh shit," slipped from my mouth.

"She goes to church every day to pray for me, but I don't think she understands how bad it is. I know that you are both young, but I was hoping you guys could get her through this. You. . .and God."

Neil and I did a lot of growing up this morning.

21

"Talk, Talk"
- *The Music Machine*

SHE MADE SURE THAT HER husband had had his breakfast and was safely tucked in bed before she ventured out into the fresh morning air. As usual, her destination was Sacred Heart Church. She would sit quietly in the first row and say her rosary while Monsignor Hanratty performed the mass. It was now in English by virtue of the Second Vatican Council. However, this did not change the way that Anna Cippitelli worshipped. Her traditions had been developed during a time mass had been performed in Latin, a language she could not understand.

After mass, the pastor always invited her back to his office and offered her words of comfort. He gave her tea. He often tried to take her mind off of her problems by telling her some story about bingo night, or perhaps a slip up one of the other priests made in his homily. He never told her any of the many humorous stories that happened at the teenage dances the parish held. These, he knew, would bring her back to the other tragedy in her life—her missing son Johnny.

"But Monsignor, I seem to pray and not get an answer."

"Anna, you might be getting an answer. It's just not one you like."

"Then what am I to do?"

"I just read about a nun. I think her name is something like Sister or Mother Theresa. She helps the poor somewhere in Asia. They asked her about prayer. Her answer was quite profound."

"What did she say?"

"She said, 'I used to pray for change in the world, and nothing happened. Now I pray for myself to change so that I can change the world.'"

Anna had no time to respond when, suddenly, the door to the pastor's office flew open.

"I tried to stop them," announced his harried secretary Joanne Carmichael.

"My door is always open, Joanne. However, ladies, courtesy demands that you respect others," scolded the monsignor.

"It's that whoo-a," Helen Murphy blurted out, ignoring the comments of the very calm priest.

"And she's again sleeping on church grounds," yelled Angela Marotti with venom and spittle exiting her mouth."

"Yeah, I know. I've been trying to get her to sleep in a church building instead of outside."

"You, you can't do that," gasped Helen in a way that the monsignor thought she might be bringing a heart attack upon herself.

"First, the correct pronunciation is 'whore,' at least in the Bible and to the rest of the world. Second, that poor girl is not one. And third, the Bible says, 'Judge not, lest you be judged.'"

"I think that you ladies should leave now," whispered Joanne to the two intruders, "Before you make even bigger fools out of yourselves." As his secretary nudged the two ladies out the door, the monsignor looked over at Anna, who was deep into pawing the rosary beads on her lap and mouthing the words to the "Hail Mary."

"Take a walk with me, Anna." They left the church by the side door and walked behind the parish school. There he led her to an area known as The Pit. In reality, The Pit was merely an outdoor stairwell that led to the basement of the school. It had gotten its name because the eighth-graders in the school would initiate the sixth-graders into the upper-grade schoolyard by trapping them at the bottom and throwing objects at them. The school was already in session for the day, and this yard was not in use. After lunch, The Pit would see action. The principal had tried to stop this whole scene, but traditions died hard.

"Where are we going?" asked Anna.

"You'll see," responded the priest.

As they approached the stairwell, Anna looked quizzically at the man leading her on this wild goose chase. Her son Johnny had once told her about this place from both the perspective of the victim and the perpetrator. However, it was now about 9:30 a.m. and The Pit, and the entire schoolyard should be empty. It wasn't.

"Mary Lou, it's time to come in for breakfast," pleaded the monsignor. Slowly Anna watched the body of a young girl, maybe eighteen at most, uncurl from a protective position at the bottom of the concrete stairs. As she stood, she revealed a very young child that she had sheltered beneath her. They ascended toward the yard.

"I've tried to get her to sleep in the convent, or at least with Joanne in the rectory. She just won't do it, and so she sleeps here each night. I keep telling her that it is getting too cold for her and her son."

"The poor dear."

"The best I can do is get her to come in for breakfast and dinner. Maybe you can convince her woman to woman, or mother to mother."

"I'll do more than that. I didn't know God could work so fast."

"What do you mean, Anna?"

"I've been praying to God like you said," She pointed down at the rosary beads that had been in her hands since they spoke in his office. "I asked him to change me so that I could change the world. I gotta say, He's quick."

Diary of DJ Spinelli

Entry # 36 – Oct 21, 1968

Chris Delaney's song is moving up the charts, especially in the New York area. He is on a tour of the entire country to try and build interest everywhere. However, if his main goal in writing the song was to get Neil reinstated on the police force, the song was already hit. Neil has been meeting with police brass almost every day for the last two weeks. Because of that, neither one of us has been over your house in a while. I hope it has not been hard on your mom without us.

Entry #37 – Oct 21, 1968 (again)

As Neil and I arrived at your house, your mom was rushing out the door to go to church. She gave us a quick welcoming hug, and then made an unusual request that we stick to the basement with our volunteer work. We both assumed that her request had something to do with your dad. We were wrong. We decided to clear the basement wall of all of its hideous decorations. No offense, Johnny, but your parents decorating taste is hideous. Neil and I just stared at the neon signs that your dad had gotten from the stores he serviced with his bread deliveries.

"What's that noise?" whispered Neil.

"Probably Mr. C," I answered.

"No, that was running. He's not doing much of that."

"Doesn't matter, Mrs. C asked us not to go up there, and I'm not." I turned back and lifted a particularly ugly neon Reingold Beer clock from the wall and readied it for storage.

"What's that?" It wasn't Neil speaking.

I turned and saw a very young child halfway down the stairs. I guessed that he was between two and three. Always awkward with little kids, I didn't answer right away.

"It's a really ugly clock. And who might you be, little man?" mimicked Neil in his best imitation of a Saturday morning cartoon character.

"Alex," the boy answered, which told us his name, but not *who* he was.

"I'm Neil, and that's DJ."

"Neil and Deegee." I never thought that my name was a tongue-twister, but then again, I don't remember being two or three.

"Alex, where'd you go to?" A female voice called out from the kitchen.

"Down here with Neil, Deegee, and an ugly cock."

"That's Clllllllock, Alex, clock," I shouted as I had visions of the vice police descending upon us. With that, a young woman walked down the stairs. Her long brown hair was parted in the middle and framed a pretty, but not sexy face. I say that because her delicate features were not usually the type to attract the bad boys.

Yes, I found myself already judging her. She could be our age, but my best guess was that she was younger, maybe seventeen or eighteen, and had a child who was old enough to speak to us. While I scolded myself for being so damn judgmental, Neil was making a friend.

"Alex was just supervising our work down here," offered Neil.

"Yeah, with this big ugly c-llll-ock," I repeated, emphasizing the letter that Alex had left of his description.

"I'm Mary Lou," she murmured and offered her hand out in friendship.

"I'm DJ," I responded and then looked at Alex as if to challenge him to say it wrong. He stuck his tongue out at me, but then smiled.

"I'm N . . ."

"Neil Connaughton," interrupted Mary Lou. "I had a crush on you when I was in sixth grade, and you were in the eighth."

"What?"

"I was younger and much fatter then. It's amazing what living on the streets will do for a weight problem."

"I got nothing," relented Neil.

"Mary Lou Casali."

"Holy shit," exclaimed Neil and then followed it quickly with "Sugar." Not quick enough.

"Mommy, he said a bad word. Are you going to wash his mouth out?"

"I might have to," teased Mary Lou with a smile on her face.

"I'm sorry," apologized Neil. "It's just you've changed so much."

"In so many ways. In so many ways."

We talked a bit longer before she excused herself. She had an appointment with the monsignor and your mom after the

9 o'clock mass ended. When she and Alex had left, I turned to Neil. He just had a sad look on his face. I didn't understand.

"I wonder what her story is?" I asked innocently.

"I don't. I know what happened to her—at least the basic facts. A few years ago, she was the talk of everyone in the Heights."

"Sorry, I'm not officially a Heights guy. There was some speculation about honorary Heights citizenship by Johnny, but he's not here."

"I don't know the whole story, but I do know that she got pregnant at 15-years-old by a scumbag named Freddy Resch. Beyond that, who knows."

22

"She's Not There"
- The Zombies

MARY LOU CASALI HAD GROWN up on 217th Street, only half a block from the Cippitelli family. However, Johnny Cipp hadn't known her. Johnny and his friends did not pay much attention to girls who were two years younger than them. Indeed, Mary Lou's social life was severely limited by her strict parents and her overly endowed girth. Her first (and last) boyfriend had been Freddy Resch.

Freddy worked in a local garage and hoped someday to be a mechanic. In the meantime, the twenty-year-old drifted through life, never caring about much besides his 1962 candy apple red Chevy Impala. All of his money went into the machine. This did not leave him much cash left to live his real life. His dream was to use his car to lure beautiful young women into bed with him. Unfortunately, the beautiful women wanted to go *some-where* in the car before putting out for Freddy.

Freddy pounced on the naïve young Mary Lou. She had come in with her father who needed an oil change. It took him all of five minutes to get her phone number and another five minutes to kiss up to her father and convince him that he was the nicest, most ambitious young man his daughter ever met.

Freddy had given up on the hot, sexy girls. He had given up on the beautiful girls, and he never had a chance with the intelligent girls. Therefore, he chose a needy, desperate girl who would do anything for him. He took her virginity before he ever took her out. In reality, he never took her out. Though there was a certain prettiness to her face, her weight made her an embarrassment to him.

Freddy came over a few nights a week. In her small attached house, there were only two bedrooms, her parents took one, and her brother took the other. When Mary Lou got old enough that her parents deemed it improper to share a room with her brother, Mr. Casali finished the basement to provide sleeping quarters for his daughter. That room had an exit out onto the street. It did not take long for Freddy and Mary Lou to realize that he could enter her room, stay the night, and leave the next day. This situation was just too good for the lecherous Freddy to give up. He had sex quite often and was free to spend all of his money on his true love—his car.

The morning after one of these trysts, Mary Lou told Freddy that she was pregnant. Though he had seduced an underage girl, he sought only to blame her. Not considering the child that he would father, he thought only about how the cost of an abortion would affect his car's customization. This inconvenience could prevent the purchase of the new set of rims he wanted for his Impala. From his point of view, this was a disaster even before she told him that she wanted him to marry her. No way that was happening! Next thing you know, he'd be driving a station wagon. However, he soon realized that she was underage, and he could be arrested for statutory rape.

All these thoughts crossed Freddy's mind as he left Mary Lou's home on a gray April morning. Stealing her brother's bat, he created havoc on garbage cans and assorted house decorations as he rambled down the street, letting off steam.

At the same time, Willie Calder, an angry young black man, approached the same corner. He carried a gun.

The day did not end the way either Freddy Resch or Willie Calder expected. Their unplanned collision at the corner of 217th Street and 115th Road was facilitated by an untrimmed hedge that blocked their view of each other. By the time they both assessed the situation, Willie had shot his gun, and Freddy struck with his bat. Having lost his weapon to the swing of the Louisville Slugger, Willie took off for the safety of his side of the racial line. Knowing that an angry white man now had his gun, he fled without giving any thought to the traffic on Springfield Boulevard.

Willie was pronounced dead less than half an hour after the Dugan's Cake truck struck him. He would never know that Freddy had no intention of pursuing him. A bullet lay lodged in his abdomen.

Freddy exited the scene and staggered home. His parents took him in and did the best they could until they realized that their son would die without professional help. Going to a hospital would mean police involvement and an arrest on manslaughter charges. Theodore and Regina Resch, though good law-abiding citizens, saw only one answer. The Provenzano crime family knew doctors who would treat wounds and never tell the police. They would sell their souls to these people for the sake of their son. Freddy Resch disappeared from the Heights for a very long recuperation period.

And so, it was that Alex Casali was born on a cold December morning with only his mother and grandmother at the hospital. His grandfather would not even acknowledge the boy's existence beyond calling him a bastard. For a year and a half, Mary Lou's parents fought over the future of their child and grandchild. Lou Casali wanted his daughter and grandson gone. Mary Lou's only chance of remaining was to put her son up for adoption. While Laura Casali fought her husband every day of her life, she too felt the shame and embarrassment of their unwed daughter and bastard grandson. The fighting became so intense that Mary Lou left.

After six months of living on the streets, Mary Lou now begged for food. She snuck into friends' houses for a night or two while parents were away. When she stole food, it always went to Alex first. Mary Lou only ate after he was full. She was weakening rapidly, and the cold weather was approaching.

Freddy had returned to the Heights when Alex was six months old. He had not made any effort to contact Mary Lou. When she mentioned approaching him to her parents, they questioned her sanity. Freddy was now tied to the Provenzano family. If he wanted nothing to do with her, there was nothing she was going to do about it. Mary Lou had meekly agreed. Now that she was on the streets alone with Alex, she tried to get the nerve to seek out Freddy, but she was still unable to face him. Freddy was happy with the situation. He cared nothing for Mary Lou or Alex.

23

"Monster Mash"
- *Bobby Pickett*

Diary of DJ Spinelli

Entry #38 - November 1, 1968

JOHNNY, IS IT WEIRD I'M still writing these diary entries *to you*? Lots of things going on:

Item #1: "Heroes in the Night" just broke into the top ten of the New York area songs. Countrywide, it is in the top twenty-five. This is great news for Chris Delaney and bad news for DJ Spinelli. His tour has been extended through next summer! Will I ever get to meet this guy?

Item #2: I changed my name. Well, not really. Everybody I know will still call me DJ. I was born Dennis James Spinelli, Jr. To differentiate me from my father, the family always called me DJ. Now to distinguish the real me from the professional me, I'm going to write under the byline Denny Spin. "DJ" in today's world, more and more, refers to someone who plays records on the radio. That's not me. I *write* about music. Put my spin on it. Get it?

Item #3: I'm going to play music. I didn't make that decision lightly. I'm going on 20 years old, and most musicians I know started in their early teens or younger. I've been thinking about it for a while. I always felt it was too late, but your mom has been pushing me. And then today, she took away my final obstacle. When I write my autobiography, this will be recalled as the moment it all began, the seminal awakening of the greatest singer/songwriter of all time. OK, a bit carried away with myself.

Neil and I were back to cleaning Johnny's room, though now it had become Mary Lou and Alex's room. The work went quickly, and we liked being around her. I don't mean that any romantic sparks were going on between us—*meaning Mary Lou and me*. There does seem to be something happening between Neil and her. It is too early for me to tell, and he clams up when I ask about it.

We had almost finished cleaning and organizing your room when we realized that all that remained was your "private corner." There lay your guitar and amp and your Hall of Monsters. To be honest, none of us wanted to touch that area. It was like sacred ground.

"DJ, take that guitar and amp," insisted your mom.

"Sorry, Mrs. C, you have to call him Denny Spin now," interrupted Neil. Mary Lou and Neil chuckled, and your mom looked confused.

"What?"

"His new professional name," added Neil.

"Take the guitar, Dizzy-Spin, or whatever you call yourself, and play it like I've been telling you since we met."

"I can't," I answered, looking away.

"You can, and you will. Do I have to play the *Johnny-would-want-you-to-have-it* card?"

Johnny, would you?

"No," I meekly answered, and she walked over, picked it up, and shoved it into my arms.

"Thanks," was all I could say.

"And you, Neil, I want you to have something, but I can't think what."

"The Monsters," laughed Neil. Your mom and I both looked at him like he was crazy.

"OK," was all she responded and walked over, picked up the box that Mary Lou was in the middle of packing, and went to hand it to him. Neil, in turn, took the box and gave it to Alex.

"These are for you."

"They scare me," mumbled the young boy and clung to his mother's leg.

What now, Neil?

"Wait. Mrs. C, where are Johnny's 45's?"

"How would I know? You guys packed them." With that, Mary Lou opened a box that contained hundreds of single records.

"I hope that Johnny had a sense of humor with at least one purchase," said Neil as he pawed through the records with reckless abandon looking for one particular title. A simple "Yes" signified his success as he went to the small record player with a disk in hand.

> *While working in my lab late one night,*
> *My eyes beheld an eerie sight.*

I immediately recognized the words to "Monster Mash." Yet, it was not enough to merely play the song, Neil meticulously acted out each line with the help of the plastic creatures that you had so long ago put together and painted. Soon we were all dancing around the bedroom and singing the chorus of the song.

> *We did the Mash,*
> *The Monster Mash.*

Alex, at first smiled, and soon broke into hysterical laughter. When the song ended, Neil took each of the monsters and held them in his hands.

"Frankenstein, Dracula, and Wolfman, do you promise to protect Alex from the dark or anything else that bothers him?" Neil's own falsetto voice answered, "Yes, we do." Alex smiled and took the monsters in his arms.

24

"Alexander the Great"
- Iron Maiden

AFTER DINNER THAT NIGHT, NEIL arrived home to find the long-awaited letter about his reinstatement in the New York City Police Cadet Program. He would start on November 8, back at the academy. Since his first tenure as a cadet, a new program had been instituted. In response to an uptick in crime, cadets were now required to spend three afternoons patrolling dangerous neighborhoods. These two-hour shifts were in addition to the regular eight-hour day on-site in the academy. Neil did not complain but was in awe that his post had ironically been chosen to be Cambria Heights. He was still taking in all the implications of his assignment when he heard the phone ring downstairs. His mother yelled up to him to pick up, with the added comment, "It's a girl."

"Hi, Neil? It's Mary Lou, you know Mary Lou Casali."

"Yeah, Mary Lou. I know who you are," he laughed.

"I just wanted to thank you for being so good with Alex today."

"Oh, that wasn't me. That was Frankenstein and his friends."

"Are you sticking to that story?"

"Yup." The conversation flowed as if they had known each other for years. They talked about nothing particular, but each knew that they didn't want the conversation to end. After an hour of flirtatious byplay, Mary Lou took a serious tone.

"Do you know why. . ." She started to cry, and Neil felt helpless to ease her emotions.

"Mary Lou, stay calm. Nothing is worth being so upset."

"Do you want to know how Alex got his name?"

"Sure, if you want to tell me."

"American History was the last class I went to in high school before my parents hid me away for my entire pregnancy. The teacher talked about the founding fathers and the formation of our country."

"I understand," consoled Neil.

"No, you don't," interrupted Mary. "All these men had accomplished greatness, and I only remembered one part of the lecture—Alexander Hamilton."

"The ten-dollar bill guy, right?"

"Alexander Hamilton, chief of staff to George Washington during the war, first Secretary of Treasury, founder of the Federalist Party, founder of the United States Coast Guard."

"Whoa, I get it—an accomplished man," interrupted Neil.

"And a bastard," replied Mary.

"Well, I didn't know him personally, but if you say so."

"Neil, you don't get it. All that he achieved and almost two centuries later the history books still feel the need to mention that he was bastard."

"Oh, and you think your son is going to carry that stigma with him?"

"What chance does he have if the ten-dollar bill guy couldn't shake the label?"

"Because the people who love him won't care about labels."

"You really think so? I mean, my immature mind at the time figured he would have another bastard to use as a role model."

"Mary Lou, I wouldn't tell him that story."

"No, you're right."

"How about Alexander the Great? He did conquer the civilized world."

"Yeah, but did he have a father?"

"Yup, Philip of Macedonia. He inherited the throne from him."

"Well, good for him." Mary Lou laughed, unmistakably feeling in a better mood.

"Yeah, and legend has it that he inherited it *after he killed his old man!*"

"I like this Alex even more now."

"Goodnight, Mary Lou."

"Goodnight, Neil."

"Sleep tight, and don't let the bed bugs bite."

"Bed bugs—not such a bad thing."

"Now you're talking crazy, Mary Lou."

"Bed bugs means you have a bed! Not always a given in my recent history."

"You'll never be without a bed again."

25

"Thief of My Forever"
- *Those Born Free*

AFTER HANGING UP THE PHONE, Mary Lou decided to clean up the room. Alex was already asleep. There was an unexplainable excitement in her thoughts—Neil? A slight smile came across her face as she looked at the trio of monsters Neil had made come to life for Alex just a few hours ago. She found the box they had been in before their song and dance act and went to place them back in it. However, the box itself was cluttered with remnants of Johnny Cipp's life.

Mary Lou pushed the items around to make space for the monsters. As she did so, she came upon a cassette tape. The plastic exterior box read very simply, *"The Thief of My Forever" Those Born Free - June 16, 1967.* Would anyone mind if she opened it and listened?

No, somehow, this seemed something private—intimate. Mary Lou would have to share it with Mr. and Mrs. C, DJ, and Neil. They might not even know that this existed. Who was she to be the first to hear it?

———◆———

Mr. and Mrs. Cippitelli sat on their son's bed. DJ sat cross-legged on the floor, and Neil sat with Alex on his lap on an old wooden chair near the desk. Mary Lou stood in front of them and had their rapt attention as she spoke.

"I found this tape last night while cleaning. I don't know why, but I think that it is important enough for us all to hear." She pressed the play button.

THOSE BORN FREE Tape – recorded June 16, 1967

"Tape running, Jimmy?" (Gio)
"Sure is." (Jimmy Mac)
"OK, this tape is being made for prosperity." (Gio)
"You mean 'posterity' which means future generations." (Tinman)
"Yeah that's what I said, 'prosperity'" (Gio)
"No, you said 'prosperity' which means 'wealth and fortune' instead of 'posterity'" (Tinman)
"Well, that works for me too." (Gio)
(Laughter on tape)

Laughter in the room listening to the tape.
"That's so Gio," said DJ.
"Good catch, Gio. Way to cover a mistake." (Johnny)

"That's Johnny, that's my Johnny," whispered Mrs. C, and she started to weep. Her husband held her close, and his body also quivered with emotion. Mary Lou stopped the tape.

"Oh," said Mary Lou. "I just didn't realize . . ."

"John, I can't do this right now."

"I'm so sorry, I didn't mean to upset you after you have been so good to me," sobbed Mary Lou, rushing over to hug Mr. and Mrs. C.

"It's OK, you couldn't know what was on the tape," said Mrs. C, as she turned to her husband and continued, "Let's get you back to bed." He nodded agreement, and they were soon finding their way down the winding stairs, almost slipping on a pile of papers that lay on the third step from the bottom.

"Anna, when are you going to move that sheet music from these bottom steps?"

"John, I will soon. It's just that Johnny's last words to me that last day were that he would put them away when he returned from the yard. I guess moving them will mean I accept that he is never coming home."

"Anna, it's over a year."

"I know—and I don't want Alex or Mary Lou slipping on them as they climb the steps. I know. I'll get to it."

As Anna and John's voices faded, DJ., Mary Lou, and Neil stared at each other. Alex found his way to the monsters and started to make them dance as Neil had done the day before.

"There is so much I don't understand," murmured a distraught Mary Lou.

"Me too," added Neil.

"Let me tell you the story of Those Born Free—at least as much as I know of it," DJ said softly.

—————

"Johnny was my best friend. We met in high school. To make a long story short, he had a band, a good band—no make that a great band. He had brought together guys from different backgrounds, yet they all lived in the Heights."

"How come I never heard of them?" interrupted Mary Lou.

"Yeah, me either," added Neil.

"It's a long story but let me just say that you would have, if . . ."

"If what?"

"If some or all of them didn't die!"

"Die?"

"Murdered? Wait, you're telling me that Mr. and Mrs. C's son was killed?" screamed Mary Lou. DJ motioned for them to be very hushed in this discussion for fear of Johnny's parents hearing.

"No, he is one of the two I'm not sure about, and neither are the Cipps. That's why I want to keep this soft. I've been investigating this story for about a year, and I still don't know what's going on. But I will tell you what I do know.

"Johnny and the band were together a little over a year when they had a crucial audition. It was probably the day after this tape was made. On that day, they could win a steady gig in a system of clubs and a record contract. They won the job only to have the police raid the place because they were all underage. The losing band made the call. At least, that is what Johnny assumed.

"Ironically, because of some mix-up, Johnny wasn't arrested with the others. Unnoticed by the police, he had slipped out of their view. The other four were taken into custody. We'll never know what would have happened to them because one by one, they started to die in 'accidental' deaths."

"Why?" interrupted Mary.

"Because Mad Guy Provenzano owned the club."

"And where were the police while this was going on?" asked Cadet Neil.

"I hate to break it to you, but quite a few of them were bought and paid for by Provenzanos. Remember that when you take up your new position in this same precinct. Keep your mouth shut. You don't know who you can trust."

"I'll remember that."

"Anyway, after Bracko died . . ."

"Wait, Bracko was one of the guys in Those Born Free, and that is how he died?"

"Oh yeah, I forgot your history with Bracko. He died in a very suspicious house fire."

"And nobody did anything?" Neil looked at DJ with questioning eyes.

"Are you listening to what he said about the police, Neil?" added Mary Lou in frustration.

"And then?" spat Neil.

"I don't know. After Bracko's death, Johnny was less open. He may have said more to his girlfriend, Maria. But now she's gone too."

"She must have gone with him. How romantic," offered Mary Lou.

"No, I saw Maria in college, and she was upset. So upset that she quit school and ran away from home. She was either the best goddam actress in the world, or she had no idea what happened to Johnny."

"Then?"

"Then, nothing. Jimmy Mac and Joey Tinman died under equally suspicious circumstances. The only two remaining were Johnny and Gio. Gio left a note for his parents telling them that he was leaving. Everyone assumed that Johnny went with him."

"Assumed by whom," yelled an emotional Mary Lou.

"The police—the same police who saw no connection in the deaths of Bracko, Jimmy Mac, and Joey."

"Surely, the Cippitellis don't buy that story?"

"No, but they want to believe that their son is out there somewhere instead of the alternative."

"This is a shitty situation all around," offered Neil.

"Yeah, and that's why over a year ago, I swore that I would get to the bottom of this even if it took me the rest of my life."

"Count me in," announced Neil.

"Me too," added Mary Lou. "And now, let's finish that tape." She pressed play.

THOSE BORN FREE Tape - June 16, 1967
(continued)

"OK, this tape is the final cut of Thief of My Forever, which will be our first release once we sign that contract with Red Bird Records." (Gio)

(Assorted cheers from other members of the band.)

"Seriously, guys, we all know what this song means to us—especially Bracko."

"Why did he say that?" interrupted Neil as he pressed the pause button on the tape recorder.

"Well, I guess that I'm not protecting anyone anymore. I used to go to the band's practices quite often. Sometimes they asked me to give an opinion on the lyrics to a song. For 'Thief of My Forever,' I told them it was perfect as it was. However, we talked long and hard about its meaning.

"The song is about where each of them was coming from, and where each hoped to go. It was about all the pressures they put upon themselves to succeed. Reading between the lines, you could find the specifics—if you knew their stories. The song was very personal to all of them, but especially to Bracko. It was Bracko who had brought the idea of the song to the rest of the band. It was about the abuse that he suffered at the hands of his father. Yet you never met a gentler and giving person—despite where he came from."

"Bracko was a good person," mumbled Neil.

"And you don't know the half of hit. You don't know what Bracko did for Tony, Mad Guy's mentally challenged brother."

"But I know what he did for me," whispered Neil.

"Huh," grunted Mary Lou.

"He saved my life. It was the one, and only time I met him." And then, Neil told Mary Lou the story of how Bracko had rescued him.

"Rocco 'Bracko' Brackowski was his name, and now he only exists in our memories and this song. Press play, Mary Lou, I need to hear Those Born Free one more time."

Bracko's guitar notes started the song and cast a spell over the bedroom. And then the lyrics began.

Suddenly I turn around,
And all of it is lost.
There is no going back now,
Once that line's been crossed.

I no longer look at the world,
Huge eyes filled with wonder.
Now I have them closed,
My dreams torn asunder.

Sometimes I sit for hours,
Thinking of times past.
All those years of innocence,
That abandoned me so fast.

He keeps taking it away from me,
A little more each year.
With each part of mind and body,
So grows my fear.

Fear of things that have gone,
And who I've always been.
Fear of what I'll never be,

Fear I'll never win.

He pushes me too far, too fast,
Before I feel I'm ready,
Sometimes I walk a confident path,
Sometimes doubt leaves me unsteady.

I sorely miss how it used to be,
Before he took it all away.
When I looked not to the future,
But lived life day by day.

I stand here today, I condemn him,
For all that he has done.
I no longer laugh or smile,
In this, he has truly won.

In time, Time takes everything,
As memories fade to never,
How long will he steal from me?
This thief of my forever.

There was nothing left to say when the song ended. It had been a long and emotional night, and each of them was spent. They took turns hugging each other, and then Neil and DJ left.

Mary Lou did not go to sleep. The words of this song could have been the story of her life. No! They *were* the story of her life. She played the tape over and over again until she finally could no longer keep her eyes open.

26

"Listen to the Music"
- Doobie Brothers

"ARE YOU SURE YOU JUST don't want to stop for a few minutes, Rook?"

"With all respect, sir, I'm not even a rookie," answered Neil.

"Well, you're out here on the streets with me puttin' your life on the line, so you're a cop to me," argued Cliff Collins, the officer assigned to babysit the young cadet.

"Yeah, I'm protecting the streets with my trusty club and nothing else."

"You want a gun and a uniform before you are twenty-one then join the army. You even get a vacation in Vietnam."

"No, thanks. The Heights is good enough for me."

"Yeah, and your girl just happens to be here too."

"She's not my girl. She's just a friend."

"A friend that you want to check up on at least three times a tour."

"Well, yeah. Mary Lou's had a lot of problems."

"Tell me about it," said Collins, just a little too interested.

"Nothing I can't handle."

"OK, my big shot, but I still think you should stop and tell her how you feel."

"I don't know what I feel."

"You're getting there. You're getting there. But we've got to do more than just pass by the house."

———◆———

She didn't know why, but Mary Lou couldn't stop listening to the "Thief of My Forever" tape. The song awakened feelings she had never had before. She analyzed every word and what it meant in her life. What did DJ say, "It's about where each of them was coming from, and where each of them was going to." Where had *she* come from? Where was *she* going to? What would she do next? Yet one overriding fact was undeniable— the identity of her personal "Thief of Forever."

She needed to confront Freddy. She needed to tell him what she thought. He had abused and abandoned her. In reality, she didn't care about the abandonment. After listening to the song and talking with her new friends, she had grown. She knew she was better off without him. However, she sure could use some financial help with *his* son. And she needed to tell him he was the bastard, not Alex.

The more she listened to the tape, the more her course became obvious.

November 15, 1968 – (9:42 a.m.)

She went to church that morning with Mrs. C. While the older woman silently prayed for the strength to deal with her husband's illness, Mary Lou prayed for guidance in her life. A good homily by the priest convinced her to calmly approach Freddy about the place that Alex should have in his life. This *was* her plan—until they left the church.

"They've got nerve bringing that little bastard into a house of worship," opinioned Helen Murphy loud enough for Mrs. C and Mary Lou to hear.

"The least you two hypocrites could do is say that to our faces," replied Mrs. C in a tone that she struggled very hard to control.

"OK, you shouldn't bring sinners into our church," added Angela Marotti, Helen's constant companion.

"Well . . ." started Mrs. C before Mary Lou cut her off.

"First of all, it's not *your* church. It's God's church, and it belongs to any person who wants to worship here. Second, God and the church forgive people who seek forgiveness from

Him—not you. And third, this is my son Alex. He has never done anything wrong in God's eyes or anyone else's eyes. So, who are you to judge? Are you more important, or more knowing than God?"

"Well, I never . . ." started Angela Marotti.

"That's right. You never had an intelligent or charitable thought in your life," said Mrs. C as she took Alex's hand and walked away from the church. Mary Lou stared at the bigoted duo and dared them to say another word. When no answer was forthcoming, she broke into a short jog to catch up to Mrs. C and her son.

"You go on home and look in on Mr. C. Meanwhile, Alex and I have something to take care of."

"OK, but don't be long. You know that Alex is due for a nap," cautioned Mrs. C.

"Yes, Mom," responded Mary Lou in an affectionate yet sarcastic tone. The two of them had laughed the first time Mary Lou had accidentally used that title when speaking to the person who had given her love and shelter. Mrs. C had told Mary Lou that she would be proud to have a daughter like her. Mary Lou responded she wished she had a mother like Anna Cippitelli.

As they walked away, Alex pulled on her pant leg and looked in his mother's eyes.

"What is it, honey?"

"Mommy, what's a *bashert*? Am I one?"

"No, honey, you're not a bastard. But you are about to meet one." Mary Lou hugged Alex tightly, then let go and took his hand firmly in hers. They walked the mile distance to where Freddy Resch was working.

How long will you steal from me, the thief of my forever?

10:36 a.m.

"What the hell do you want?" Freddy was surprised to see Mary Lou. He had not thought of her since he left her house the morning he had his run-in with Willie Calder. The self-centered Freddy had put everything out of his mind from before the altercation.

"Freddy, this is your son," commanded Mary Lou, calmer than even she thought possible.

"Fuck, it is," Freddy screamed at her. This outcry drew the attention of his boss and fellow workers.

"His name is Alex, and I really could use some help with . . ."

"I don't give a flying fuck about what you could use. Get your ass out of here now, you goddamn skank." The intensity with which he spoke took her back, and she momentarily lost some of her nerve. However, she did not back away. Her hands were strategically held over Alex's ears so that he would be protected from the verbal onslaught.

"What's going on out here?" yelled a voice from inside the garage's office. A middle-aged woman with a pencil stuck behind her ear stepped out of the office. Patty Yellen was the wife and partner of Freddy's boss Mike Yellen. "You know what I said about that language, Freddy."

"Fuckin' whores all stick together," mumbled Freddy under his breath, assuming no one heard him. However, Mike Yellen had been approaching from Freddy's blindside and picked up part of the slur directed at his wife.

"What did you say?"

"Oh, nothing, boss. Just having some trouble with this oil filter sticking together with, ah, something here."

"Freddy, you've been warned. What the heck is going on here? I told you no socializing while you're working."

"I wish you had that rule a few years ago when I met this nice gentleman here while he was supposed to be working," snapped Mary Lou with sarcasm dripping from her lips.

"And who might you be?" asked Mike Yellen.

"Mary Lou Casali, and this is Alex Casali. Though it should be Alex Resch."

"You mean . . ." started Mike Yellen.

"She's fu. . .I mean, she's freaking lying. The kid's not mine." He looked over at Patty Yellen to see if he had caught himself fast enough.

"*She's* lying? One look at that's boy's face, and the truth is kind of obvious," chided Patty.

"You give that girl part of your salary, or you won't have any salary. Get my drift,' warned Mike, and then he leaned in a little closer so only Freddy could hear him, "You fuckin' little prick."

"Mary Lou, you give us your address, and we'll make sure we send you something from each paycheck—*before he ever gets it*," said Patty.

"Right, Freddy?" snapped Mike.

Mary Lou held back the smile she knew would enrage Freddy even further. However, he caught a slight glimpse of it just before she walked away.

27

"Showdown"
- Doobie Brothers

November 15, 1968 - 4:36 p.m.

THE DOLCE FAMILY WHO LIVED on the fifth house from the corner on 217th Street, prided themselves on their rock collection. Every Sunday, they took the forty-mile trip out to a Bayville beach on Long Island's north shore to swim, they would return with a box full of rocks. Eventually, their entire ten-by-ten lawn was covered in the signature Long Island Sound stones. Freddy Resch lifted a stone about the size of a softball from the Dolce yard and hurled through the front window of the Cippitelli home.

Around noon, Mike Yellen had realized Freddy was too angry to complete even the most menial work task and sent him home. Instead, Freddy planted himself atop a barstool at the Linden Terrace bar. After eight boilermakers and some prodding from other drinkers, his fury at Mary Lou grew. The other patrons of the bar, all misogynistic drunks, agreed Freddy should not put up with "bullshit from the whore." And so, Freddy found his way to the address he had overheard Mary Lou give to the Yellens.

———◆———

"Call the police," Anna Cippitelli yelled to her husband, who lay in bed on the second floor. Mary Lou and Alex sat in the attic, playing with the monsters, not realizing that there was a real monster outside on the street.

"Where's the fuckin' skank whore who wants to ruin my life," screamed Freddy as he approached the house. Anna met him at the door, making the mistake of opening it to speak to him.

"Freddy, the police are on the way. I think you should leave."

"Fuck you, bitch!" Freddy was no longer sober or rational. He was obsessed with getting to Mary Lou. "I'm coming in whether you like it or not."

"Over my dead body," hissed Anna.

"OK, I'm good with that," slurred Freddy as he pulled Anna from the door and threw her off the three-step brick stoop. Her left arm took the main force of the fall onto the concrete alley that lay beside her house. She felt the bone crack and puncture the skin below her elbow. As pain coursed through her body, she merely focused on staying conscious.

Two blocks away, Officer Cliff Collins and the young cadet assigned to him received the call of a disturbance at 115-61 217th Street. Both immediately recognized the address as the Cippitelli home. With sirens blaring and lights flashing, they hurried to the scene as fast as humanly possible. As they turned the corner and viewed their destination, they couldn't know that Freddy was already bounding up the stairs to the second floor. They couldn't see that they did not have enough time to reach Mary Lou before he did.

John Cippitelli struggled to leave his bed. Routine tasks like this had become more difficult for him to accomplish. Yet, he'd heard his wife's screams and the verbal ranting of Freddy. After he had called the police, he immediately guessed what was happening. He knew that Freddy would reach Mary Lou before help arrived. He had to stall the insane onslaught of the intruder somehow. With great difficulty, he placed himself at the bottom of the staircase that led to the attic.

Struggling to even stand on his own, Mr. C absorbed Freddy's blow to the stomach. He knew he could never best this vicious punk who meant to harm his beloved Mary Lou and Alex. However, he heard the sirens and knew that help was near, but not near enough. He had to hold off Freddy with every last bit of his strength. As he fell to the ground, his two arms reached out and grabbed Freddy's right leg. He clung to it with every ounce of being, knowing that every second he delayed his attacker gave the police a better chance of getting there in time. As Freddy pounded on the top of John Cippitelli's head, his grip loosened. His weakened arms released their hold on Freddy's leg. John Cippitelli fell to the floor.

As they arrived on the scene, Officer Cliff Collins picked up the radio and called for an ambulance for Anna. By the time he finished, he noticed that Neil Connaughton was already at Anna's side.

"Go . . . go now," said the quivering voice of Anna to Neil as neighbors were quickly coming to her aide. Reluctant to leave her, the cadet needed the assurance that she would be taken care of before advancing into the house.

"Mrs. C, talk to me."

"It's Freddy, Alex's father. He'll kill her."

<hr />

"I'm gonna fuck you up, Mary Lou," bellowed Freddy as he bounded up the stairs. Thinking of her son first, Mary Lou placed her crying boy in a closet and looked around for something to use to defend herself. Everything had been packed except an old broken hockey stick that Johnny Cipp had years before pretended to be a guitar. She heard the madman open the attic door and hit the first step of eighteen-step path to her room. She was on her own.

Mary Lou then heard a loud thud and a stream of obscenities. She looked over the railing of the stairway that switch-backed its way to the attic. There lay Freddy, blood pouring from his chin. His journey up the steps had been interrupted by a slip on the third step. He had fallen forward hard, his face taking the brunt of his awkward landing. She noticed sheet music scattered all over the steps below the sprawled-out villain. *Johnny*, she thought. *Johnny Cipp to my rescue.* Mrs. C's sentimental refusal to move her son's sheet music had given her time.

In the distance, she heard Neil's voice scream her name. Help was on the way. However, the footsteps now resumed their path to her. She took one more look over the railing. Freddy, dripping blood and more furious than before, was now taking the steps two at a time.

Neil had been reluctant to leave Mrs. C, but he knew she would live. He was not sure about Mary Lou. What was that maniac capable of doing? He threw open the front door and yelled Mary Lou's name.

"You goddam little whore, you're ruining my life." Freddy was breathless and bleeding as he faced Mary Lou.

"Screw you! Stay back." Mary Lou had fire in her eyes and a broken hockey stick in her hands.

"You're dead, Motherfucker," screamed Freddy as he rushed her. Mary Lou swung the stick and caught him above his left eye, opening a two-inch gash. Still, he reached out and placed both hands around her neck. Breathing became difficult for Mary Lou as she struggled to maintain consciousness. She thought she heard Neil's voice in the distance. The oxygen remaining in her lungs would not sustain her much longer.

Tears in his eyes and monsters in his hands, Alex emerged from the closet.

"The monsters will save Mommy!" He threw first Frankenstein and then Dracula at Freddy, causing him to release his grip on Mary Lou. Freddy briefly turned to see Alex swing Wolfman at his kneecap. The distraction did not harm Freddy but did buy a few precious minutes for Mary Lou. Despite a few moments of *look-how-tough-my-kid-is* pride, Freddy threw the young boy into a wall with one hand—leaving him dazed and confused. He regained his grip on Mary Lou's throat.

"Mary Lou, I'm coming," Neil yelled, not knowing that she had already slipped into unconsciousness. Cliff Collins was not far behind him, but Neil knew he could not wait for his help. He hoped it was not too late. Yet, his mind raced as he saw the frail, collapsed body of Mr. C. *Do I have enough time?* Mr. C opened his eyes just long enough to see Neil and waved his arm toward the stairs.

Neil understood. He heard only one voice in the attic—Freddy's ranting insults. There were no replies, no sounds of struggle. *Was he too late?* As he started to scale the attic stairs, he was careful to avoid the scattered sheet music. Though he focused on getting to Mary Lou, his mind still wandered.

If Mrs. C had not delayed him at the door. If Mr. C had not sacrificed his fragile body. If Johnny Cipp's sheet music had not caused the bloodstain on the steps in front of him—Mary Lou would not even have had a chance.

———————◆———————

"You fuckin' little bitch," ranted Freddy as he took the last breaths from Mary Lou. His body filled with anger and alcohol, his grip held tight around her neck. There was no conscious thought or intent to kill Mary. There was no thought at all—just blind rage. Because of this, Freddy had no warning when Neil tackled him with all the power of a professional football player. Neil's fist then pummeled the face of the reeling assailant. Neil struck Freddy's chin and opened the already present gash wider. His left and right hands took turns blistering the helpless Freddy. Soon Cliff Collins was pulling the young cadet from the near unconscious intruder.

Neil immediately switched his attention to Mary Lou. He did not see her chest moving or any other sign of life coming from her. He immediately started to give her artificial respiration.

"Move over," said Cliff Collins, who was more experienced. He took over the massaging of the heart muscle. Neil, in turn, switched over to mouth to mouth resuscitation. The two of them worked in tandem in hopes of saving Mary Lou. It seemed like hours to Neil, but less than thirty seconds later, Mary Lou's body started to pulse. Collins noticed her revival first and ceased his rescue efforts. Neil, however, continued to breathe into Mary Lou's mouth. At that moment, Freddy started to sit up, and both the officer and his cadet looked at him. Cliff Collins did not move a muscle except his left arm, which shot out and knocked the madman unconscious with one blow. When Neil looked back at Mary Lou, her eyes were wide open and staring at him.

"Wow, our first kiss," whispered the raspy voice of Mary Lou.

———◆———

Three separate ambulances arrived for Mr. and Mrs. Cippitelli and Mary Lou, but they all arrived at Terrace Heights Hospital around the same time. As each of them was wheeled into the emergency room, they each questioned the health of the others.

On the pretense of gathering more information for their incident report, Neil and Cliff Collins drove to the hospital. In reality, the officer was doing the cadet a favor. He knew that Neil was worried about all three of the victims, especially the young girl.

"That was a great collar *you* made," said Neil soon after they sat in the patrol car.

"All I did was put the cuffs on the guy. You took him down," answered Collins.

"Sir, with all respect, I want to stay under the radar. I was suspended six months ago for doing what I thought was the right thing. The brass was not happy with having to reinstate me."

"But this was a clean, legitimate bust, and you deserve credit for it."

"You know that I would have done what I did even if I wasn't on duty."

"But you were on duty."

"Mary Lou and I may have a thing."

"You *do* have a thing even if you haven't realized it yet."

"Well, what if someone is out to get me . . ."

"They are."

"If they are out to get me and want to make it look like I attacked Freddy for personal reasons? Wouldn't a defense lawyer try and pull that crap?"

"Yeah, then how would he explain Mr. and Mrs. Cippitelli?"

"That wouldn't make me less screwed. I took down Freddy from behind. He was so out of it he won't be able to say who hit him. And you did give him that last shot. By the way, thank you very much."

"Are you sure about this?"

"Yes, sir."

"Neil, you're going to be a great cop."

"Thank you, sir."

"And call me Cliff when there's no brass around."

———◆———

Mary Lou was given a battery of tests and required to stay overnight for observation. Anna Cippitelli immediately went into surgery for the compound fracture of her arm. After insertion of several pins in the elbow area, a plaster cast was placed on her arm. However, before she even entered the operating room, the doctors had approached her about her husband.

"We think we should ship him over to St. Albans Naval Hospital. His head injuries are extensive. We could treat them here. However, we would like the doctors treating his cancer to be able to coordinate with the surgeons who will be working on him."

"So, what's the problem?" answered Anna.

"He doesn't want to leave you."

"Tell him I'll break the rest of his skull if he doesn't go."

"Can I quote you?"

"Damn right. And also tell my husband that when I get out of here tomorrow, he will be a lot closer to visit over there. That hospital is only three miles from our house."

———◆———

After Cliff Collins left off Neil at the hospital, he returned to the precinct to write up the partially falsified report of events. Alone in the waiting room, Neil called DJ and told him everything that had happened.

"Neil, maybe I should go over to St. Albans Naval Hospital and wait with Mr. C. What do you think? That way, you can stay here for Mrs. C and Mary Lou," DJ quickly interrupted.

"Thanks for thinking of me, DJ, but they told me they will be working on him most of the night and that he is already heavily sedated. They won't even allow visitors before tomorrow afternoon."

"You know what? I'll go over there early tomorrow and check out what is going on so I can come and tell Mrs. C how he is doing."

"Great, see you tomorrow."

28

"In Dreams"
- Roy Orbison

November 16, 1968 – 12:07 a.m.

JOHN CIPPITELLI HAD ONLY A vague idea of what had happened after he took numerous blows to his head. He remembered directing Neil to the attic. He remembered a ride in an ambulance—a hospital—another ride in an ambulance—another hospital. Then his world went dark. He went in and out of consciousness. It could have been a dream, but he could swear all that happened that night was real.

There had been a party going on around him for much of the evening. He knew he should open his eyes, but was afraid of what he might see. In reality, he had no pain. He felt pretty damn good, an illusion created by massive doses of Demerol. When the noise died down a bit, he got up the nerve to look around.

The bright white, immaculately clean walls surrounded four hospital beds. Though the bed next to John Cippitelli lay empty, the two facing him were occupied by two other patients, one black and one white. They were awake and holding a boisterous conversation that Mr. C did not want to interrupt.

"Hey, he lives," shouted the black patient

"Who?" said the much calmer white one.

"The guy across from us."

"What guy?"

"Him."

"And how would I know there is a guy across from us?"

"Where am I?" Mr. C asked in a weak voice.

"Uh, St. Albans Naval Hospital," answered the black soldier.

"Yeah, in Queens, New York," added the other.

"I know that. I only live a few miles from here. I didn't take that bad a shot to the head. Or did I?"

"Hey, the doctors didn't tell us anything about you, but they all seemed in a pretty good mood after seeing you. So, I'm guessing that you're going to be OK."

"That's good to know. What are you guys in for?"

"Hey, this isn't a prison. It's a hospital, and we're lucky to be here. We're on our way to Walter Reed Hospital in D.C. for months of rehab, and some strings were pulled to get us an overnight stay here."

"Hey, Leo, we're going to have to thank Shylo for this when we get a chance."

"Goody, we don't even know her real name. How are we going ever to find her to thank her?"

"What the hell are you two talking about? You want to clue me in. I'm John, formerly Chief Petty Officer Cippitelli, United States Navy. And who might you two be?"

"Corporal John Barlow, United States Army. But don't say that too loud. This is a Naval Hospital after all, and we're here on the QT."

"Corporal Leo Leonardo." Mr. C noticed Leo was not looking at him. He blankly stared into space. Goody saw the perplexed look on Mr. C's face.

"Yup, my friend's as blind as a bat."

"That was blunt," said Leo. "Yeah, but I'm hoping to get some sight back in one eye at Reed. My friend *will walk you through* his problem." He laughed. Mr. C looked confused until Goody threw back his blanket to reveal that he was missing a leg.

"Gimp humor," said Goody. "We've been practicing our stand-up act since that day in August in Vietnam."

"Yeah, a hand grenade," added Leo, suddenly getting serious.

"Was it my imagination, or was there a party going on before?" said Mr. C trying to regain the light mood.

"Oh yeah, that's why Shylo got us sent here. We both grew up near here," boasted Goody.

"We leave early in the morning for D.C. We had a great night with family and friends. It was well worth the risk."

"What risk?" interrupted Mr. C.

"Well, being army, not navy, breaks rule one," whispered Goody.

"And having no legitimate reason to be routed here breaks rule two," finished Leo. "There will be no paperwork to show we were ever here."

"Thank military bureaucracy for that." Goody laughed. He then looked across the room at Mr. C. "Please don't ever mention this to anyone. It's not just us, but Shylo who could get into trouble."

"John Cippitelli can keep a secret," said Mr. C with a salute.

"Wait, what did you say your name was?" asked Leo.

"John Cippitelli."

"Holy shit! Did anyone ever call you 'Johnny Cipp,'" continued Leo. His blindness made him unable to see the tears that had started to fall down the older man's cheeks.

"That's what they called my son. He's missing and probably dead."

"He's not dead," said Goody.

"Thanks for the hope, but we haven't heard from him in over a year."

"He's alive!" blurted out Goody, unwilling to see the old man suffer anymore.

"What are you talking about?"

"It's a long story, and I'm guessing that none of us are going anywhere before tomorrow morning. Leo can tell the story best because he was the only one who was there at the end."

"No, Goody. You may have been drugged out at the time, but Shylo was there."

"Leo, we'll never find her to verify the story."

"Why would you need someone else to verify a story about my son?"

"Because the story is about murder, and it was told to me by my friend on his death bed."

"I thought you said you knew my son was alive?"

"It wasn't his murder. Let Leo tell it."

"OK."

"There were four of us—all from Cambria Heights," started Leo.

"I'm from Cambria," blurted out Mr. C.

"I know that's why I'm telling you the story. We just made the connection—Johnny Cipp—Cambria Heights. Somehow, Chinx knew we would find you and pass on what happened that night."

"Who's Chinx?"

"Patience, John, let Leo tell you the whole story. Then everything will make sense."

"What kind of damn name is *Chinx*?"

"Oh, we all gave each other nicknames over there—Goody, Leo, Junior, and Chinx. Chinx was a takeoff on his real name— Greg Cincotta."

"Little Gregory, who lived a few doors away from us?"

"Uh, yeah, except he wasn't little anymore, and he's. . ."

"Dead is what you're telling me. Poor little Greg. Now tell me about my son."

———◆———

There were four of us from the Heights—two white and two black. That in and of itself was either an impossibility or a miracle. At first, we hated each other, but what's that old saying, "the enemy of my enemy is my friend"? A redneck sergeant hated all of us so much that he bonded us together in hatred for him. He then sent us on a suicide mission from which none of us returned in one piece.

Junior died saving our lives, but Chinx lingered on long enough to give us a death bed confession. Well, actually, not us, just me. Goody was unconscious at the time, so it fell on me to hear our friend's final words and now pass them on to you.

Chinx had worked for a mob boss named Guy Provenzano. While protecting this guy's brother, he had assaulted a couple of people—one of them a priest. He pleaded out with the condition that he join the army. However, before he left for boot camp, his boss offered him one last job— to kill your son and one other guy named Gio. If Chinx did the job, Provenzano would pull some strings, and there would be no jail or army.

Chinx considered the proposition for a split second, and for that, he felt guilty for the rest of his life. He had never killed anyone, and he wasn't about to start then, especially with two guys he knew and liked. His boss wasn't happy, and Chinx joined us on the road to Vietnam. He had done the right thing, but it still didn't sit right with his conscience. You see, Chinx knew that Mad Guy had already killed three members of a band called Those Born Free. Yet he had said nothing.

This prick Provenzano came in one night and bragged to his inner circle about just killing a kid named Gio. However, he was furious he hadn't been able to get the kid to tell him more about your son.

He gave Chinx one final job—find Johnny. If Chinx found him, that would be enough for Mad Guy to use his connections to keep him from the army. Chinx took the offer. He went out into the night to search for your son. However, unlike Mad Guy's other henchmen, Chinx knew of Johnny's love of his family. He knew that Johnny would stop home first.

He got that partially right. As he waited in the dark, Johnny approached your house, but instead of going in, your son just stared at you and your wife through the windows for a short time, and then abruptly walked away. Chinx followed him as Johnny walked out of the neighborhood. Once he made it to the Belt Parkway entrance in Rosedale, he stuck out his thumb. Chinx knew this was a bad idea. Mad Guy would soon widen his search to this area. When Chinx realized he was rooting against that happening, he knew he had to do something to help Johnny.

He approached some doo-wop singers on a corner and quickly negotiated a financial deal with one of them. Making believe he was a Good Samaritan, the guy picked up Johnny and drove him away from the Heights.

A week after the murder, Johnny had still not been found by the gang. Chinx couldn't even face his boss, so he asked to have his induction pushed up. He never returned to the Heights until after boot camp. He never spoke to Provenzano again.

While home on leave, Chinx wanted to tell you that Johnny had escaped. However, every time he approached your house, he noticed Mad Guy's henchmen were observing your every move. And then he was sent to Vietnam.

With his dying breath, this was his one regret. He never got to tell you that Johnny was alive.

———◆———

"Johnny's alive," whispered Mr. C as a small smile spread across his face.

"Yes, Johnny's alive, as far as we know," answered Leo.

"So, you both heard this?"

"No, maybe I wasn't clear. Goody was unconscious. When I say 'we,' I mean a doctor named Shylo and me. She is the only other witness to Chinx's death bed confession."

"I believe you, and that's enough," said Mr. C, his voice strengthening and smile broadening.

"Yeah, but Chinx also wanted us to bring this to the police, and my word is not enough. You see, Guy and I have history. It would appear to the authorities that I was out to get him with this story."

"But this other person?"

"As I said, don't know her real name. Don't know where she is. She sent a note saying she had arranged this little stopover. As you can see, we are in no shape to play detectives—yet. Someday we will figure this all out and what to do. Meanwhile, we completed our most important task—we told you."

"Johnny's alive," mumbled Mr. C as the narcotics he was taking began to make him drowsy. "Johnny's al . . ." He gave in to deep sleep.

———◆———

"I hope we did the right thing, Goody."

"I think we did. I'm just finally trying to put all the pieces together of Chinx's story."

"What do you mean?"

"I know that Chinx was a good guy, but what made him risk turning on his boss, who was a mean and vindictive bastard?"

"I don't know if we'll ever know that. But. . ."

"But what?"

"Goody, I think it has something to do with that tape that Chinx was always listening to."

"Yeah, might be. Chinx would always smile after listening to it. He said it gave him hope."

"Hope for what?"

"I don't know. He wouldn't answer me when I asked."

"Rest in peace, Chinx."

"Yeah, rest in peace."

———◆———

Before the morning shift ever entered the hospital, Leo and Goody were on their way to Walter Reed Hospital in Washington, their clandestine stay in St. Albans Naval Hospital never recorded in any official records.

———◆———

THOSE BORN FREE Tape – February 28, 1967
(Tape for Greg Cincotta)

"Greg, this tape is from all of us in Those Born Free, especially me." (Johnny)

"Of course, he knows who it's from, asshole. It's written on the damn cassette tape." (Gio)

"Hey, Jerk, I'm trying to do this right—with some class." (Johnny)

"We're a good band, but no one is ever going to accuse us of having any fucking class." (Gio)

"Especially you, Gio. Case in point—who else could use 'fucking' and 'class' together?" (Johnny)

"Yeah, it's an oxymoron." (Tinman)

"Who you calling a 'moron?'" (Gio)

"If the shoe fits. . ." (Tinman)

"Let's get back on track. Go ahead, Johnny." (Jimmy Mac)

"We understand what you did that night. You stood up for Tony and my Maria. We know you paid the price for that. We won't forget. The band, all of us, decided to dedicate this song to you whenever we perform it. It's how we feel." (Johnny)

"Bracko, start it off." (Jimmy Mac)

"So, did we decide on the Otis Redding version or The Vagrants' version?" (Johnny)

"Yeah, I hear even Aretha Franklin is coming out with a version of this song in a few months, but this is the Those Born Free version. And Gio, when you get to the part of the song where you spell it, it's R-e-s-p-e-c-t." (Jimmy Mac)

"I'm not an ox-moron." (Gio)

"Cool it, Gio. Greg, the title of this song says it all—'Respect.' Hit it, Bracko." (Johnny)

29

"Magical Mystery Tour"
- *The Beatles*

Diary of DJ Spinelli

Entry #39 - November 16, 1968

JOHNNY, I HAVE AN INCREDIBLE story to tell. I use the word incredible in every sense of the word, including that I don't believe part of it even happened.

This guy named Freddy broke into your house. He was drunk and trying to hurt Mary Lou. However, your parents blocked his path just long enough for Neil and his partner to save the day. Mary Lou and your parents are in the hospital. They will all recover from their injuries. That's the gist of what happened. But there are many side stories to this that I need to write down.

Neil's partner Cliff Collins pulled me aside and told me that Neil was a hero. He had fought off Freddy and saved Mary Lou. However, Neil begged Cliff to take the credit. I'm disappointed that the brass won't hail Neil as the hero, but I understand why. What a story this would have been for the *Queens Undies*, "The Continuing Adventures of the Hero Cop of Lispenard." Oh well, friendship has its costs.

A second side story is a bit more personal. If Mary Lou, your parents, and Neil are all on the way to the hospital, what happens to little Alex? Neil took the time to give me a call, and

I immediately got in my speedy Renault (note sarcasm here) and started over there. I knew that Neil couldn't leave until someone was there for Alex. "Uncle Deegee" to the rescue. However, on a good day, I'm a twenty-minute drive away, and I knew Neil was impatient. Your mom had the strength and wits to give Adele McAvoy's number to the police. Aylin went over to babysit. When I got there, Alex was safely napping in her arms.

Ah yes, Aylin. She remains a mystery to me. Her beauty and her wit beguile me (expanding my vocabulary). Yet there is a sadness and darkness that seem to overwhelm her soul. I know her father and brother were murdered, but it seems to go deeper than that. There is something else going on, and I need to know what it is.

Do I have feelings for Aylin? Do I want to be involved with a troubled, possibly drug-addicted girl/woman? I think that my answer is yes. But right now, she is with that scumbag Dougie. Does she care for him? Or are his company and his drugs just an escape from whatever is eating her up inside?

When I saw her holding Alex in her arms, I didn't see all the baggage. I saw someone full of love. I saw a warm, giving person that I wanted to wrap my arms around and be with forever. I wanted to solve her problems. I wanted to be her knight in shining armor. But she doesn't want that—at least not yet.

My final side story is fantastic, if true. However, I doubt the veracity of this part of the story. Neil went to Terrace Heights Hospital this morning to see Mary Lou and Mrs. C. In turn, I went to the Naval Hospital to visit your dad. As I entered the room, he was just waking up. His head was bandaged heavily, but his eyes seemed alert as they focused on me.

"Johnny's alive," were the first words that came from his mouth. Had he been hallucinating? They must have given him potent drugs.

"I hope so," I replied.

"No. The night he went missing, Gio was murdered, and Johnny got away."

"What are you talking about?"

"They killed Gio, but they still couldn't find Johnny."

"Who killed Gio? Who couldn't find Johnny?"

"Mad Guy Provenzano," he answered. Well, that fact was undeniable. I understood that whatever happened to Gio involved the madman. However, where was your father getting these conclusions?

"Mr. C, how do you know this?"

"Chinx told them." OK, now he was making up gibberish names.

"Chinx who?"

"Chinx who died in Vietnam told them."

"Who's them?"

"Them!" he screamed and pointed across the room. I looked and saw only two empty beds.

"Mr. C, no one's there."

"Yes, they said that they were never really here and that I should keep their secret. But Johnny's alive. I know that now." He must have hallucinated the whole thing. I mean, a person named Chinx told two guys who were not there that they knew Johnny was alive, and Gio was dead. What next?

"If you don't believe me, find Halo."

"Someone with a halo."

So now I'm looking for an angel to confirm his story. Damn hallucination. Damn drugs. But yet, I better check this out. I told him to rest easy and went to the nurses' station and inquired about his roommates the night before.

"According to this, he didn't have any," said the extremely efficient head nurse. "This is the official record. He was the only one in that room last night."

I returned to Mr. C's room. I found it hard to tell him that he had imagined the whole incident. I just couldn't break his heart, and why should I? Yet if it were true, I would have more pieces to the puzzle. They would not be good pieces for the DeAngelis family, but I would be further along in my quest to find you.

This wasn't a story of two buddies leaving to form a new band somewhere. This was Gio murdered and you running as far and fast as you could. You weren't selfish. This was a story I could understand.

30

"Instant Karma"

"Instant Karma's gonna get you,
Gonna look you right in the face."
- John Lennon

"OK," MARY LOU WHISPERED AS she gathered up Alex and left the house. She was fully recovered from her attack by Freddy but had been busy taking care of Mr. and Mrs. Cippitelli. Neil and DJ came over to relieve her—and give her some news. After leaving them, she went to church and prayed.

Freddy Resch had died in jail. According to Neil's sources in the police department, he had been running off his mouth while confined. He stupidly told everyone that he was a "made-man," so no one was going to touch him. He grew so brazen he bragged about causing Willie Calder's death.

Freddy couldn't know that one of his fellow detainees, Thad Carver, had been a friend of Willie's. Filled with rage at Freddy's revelation, he plunged a shiv into the braggart's neck, killing him instantly. Mary Lou would never know that his last thoughts were not of her or their child, but rather of his 1962 candy apple red Chevy Impala.

Angry with the disrespect shown one of his men, Mad Guy Provenzano had Carver murdered in his cell. He briefly contemplated doing away with some of his family as a lesson to anyone who dared touch one of his men. However, he didn't consider it long enough to find out that Thad Carver's niece

was Riet Carver, or that his great-nephew was named Gio
DeAngelis, Jr.

31

"Under Pressure"
- *David Bowie*

December 3, 1968

"THIS REALLY SHOULD BE YOU," whispered Officer Cliff Collins as he straightened the tie on his dress uniform. "You're the one who saved Mary Lou."

"This is the way I want it to be," answered Neil. He, too, was in his dress uniform, though the cadet grays were much less impressive than his friend's dress blues. They sat in Collins' '68 Chevy and waited for the ceremony that would place a medal on the officer's uniform, a medal that he knew he didn't deserve.

"Neil, you don't know everything that's going on." Collins thought long and hard about whether he could trust his young cadet friend.

"Yeah, that's why I'm only a cadet, and you're the big shot officer getting a medal today." Neil laughed, but Collins' demeanor remained serious.

"I'm doing this to protect you."

"I don't get it." The smile left Neil's face and zoned in on what Collins was saying.

"The wrong people are interested in you."

"What's that mean?"

"If I were smart, I wouldn't be telling you this."

"You're not telling me anything yet."

"The day they assigned me to you, a detective named Shea approached me. He told me in no uncertain terms that he wanted me to keep an eye on you, especially when we stopped by the Cippitelli house."

"Son of a bitch. Why would he do that? Are they under suspicion for anything?"

"No, you dumb ass. The word is that Shea's dirty."

"What makes you say that?"

"Why do you think he got assigned the deaths of the Brackowskis, the McAvoys, and the Tinleys?"

"Because they were all members of Those Born Free?"

"Yes, but there is no police report that even mentions the band by name. Nothing official makes any connection at all—except that the investigating officer is the same in each and. . ."

"And what?"

"You know who else was in the band? Johnny Cipp!"

"So Shea is trying to use me to spy on the family? Why?"

"In case Johnny contacts them."

"Couldn't it just be a coincidence?"

"You don't get it. No one detective gets an arson, a robbery, and out-of-state alcohol poisoning, not to mention the Tinley parents' vehicular death. Those are different specialties. They shouldn't be on one person's caseload."

"So, what are you saying?"

"I said it already. Shea is a fucking dirty cop, and he isn't the only one. Someone assigned him these cases. Someone's protecting him while he goes about his business."

"But who does he work for?"

"I've already said too much."

"C'mon, who does he work for?"

"A good guess would be his cousin—Guy Provenzano."

"What the hell?"

"Yeah, that's why you don't want to know too much."

"Cliff, are you. . .?"

"Dirty? No, but I want you to remember this phrase: *You don't have to play the game to know the score.* It's a phrase that those of us on the outs use to recognize each other."

"You don't have to play the game to know the score."

"Now, let's go in and watch this racist police chief have to shake my black hand and pin a medal on my chest."

"Is he. . .you know. . .dirty?"

"Not as far as I know. Just racist."

32

"New Kid in Town"
- The Eagles

Diary of DJ Spinelli

Entry #40 – December 10, 1968

SINCE YOUR MOM GAVE ME your electric guitar and amp, I've practiced every moment that I can. But to be honest, I was going nowhere fast—until I met Bobby Bright Eyes. That's not his real name, but it is what he insists I call him. Bobby is teaching me the guitar, but that was not how our friendship started.

Johnny, you would like this kid. I ran into him while I was distributing the *Queens Undies*. He asked if he could write for the paper. Just one drawback—English is his second language. I have no problem with that on general principle, but I'm talking about writing an English language newspaper. Still, there was something about the kid that I liked. I wanted to give him a chance.

It was then that you intervened. Yes, you, Johnny Cipp, missing well over a year now, influenced my decision. I was back in physics class in McCarthy High, and you were secretly listening to music through an earplug attached to a hidden transistor radio. You wrote down the words from a Yardbirds' tune that exploded in my mind.

Can you tell a wise man,
By the way he speaks or spells?
Is this more important,
Than the stories that he tells?

"What's your name, kid?"

"Bobby Bright Eyes!"

"No, your real name."

"That's the name I use."

"OK, at least tell me the story of how you got that moniker."

"What's a moniker?" I began to see the language problem.

"Your name, kid, your name."

"Do I have to?"

"You do if you want this impressive, lousy-paying job on the *Queens Undies.*"

"Roberto Weissman."

"What?"

"And that reaction is exactly why I've become Bobby Bright Eyes."

"Well, it isn't like Bobby Bright Eyes isn't going get a reaction, but I gotta hear this."

I thought of you, Johnny, and that long-ago day in Physics when you quoted The Yardbirds to me. *Is this more important than the stories that he tells?* I had my answer.

"Kid, tell me your story."

His story knocked the shit out of me!

———◆———

I was born in Cuba in 1950. My parents worked for the cruise lines that brought the tourists to Havana. They worked hard, and the generous tips that the Americans gave them raised us above the class of our neighbors. Perhaps that was what created our problem—when Fidel Castro's revolution proved successful.

Through the years, one particular old American couple came down annually. They became friends with my family. My mother did tailoring for them, and my father drove them around in his taxi. But more than that, the families shared a love of music. They would come to our house. Mr. Weissman would sing and laugh as my father played the flamenco guitar and they both harmonized. Meanwhile, my mother would teach

Mrs.Weissman how to make Cuban delicacies for us all to eat.

I would sit and watch both the music and the cooking—wanting to know everything about everything. My father joked that my eyes never stopped moving—never stopped learning. Mr. Weissman called them "bright eyes." I emulated everything that my parents did and was starting to learn the guitar myself when the world I knew ended.

I was nine years old when the Bautista government fell and Fidel Castro's troops marched into town. A family friend notified us that we were on a list of "collaborators" who would be imprisoned. There was no hope for my parents, and the Weissmans were far from their soon departing ship—the last one out of Cuba! As my father drove them through every traffic jam and roadblock, we all could see the terror on the faces of Havana's citizens.

When we arrived at the dock, the Weissmans begged my family to come with them, but we all knew that was impossible. Because of all the chaos, the American ship was turning away masses of fleeing Cubans. However, would they notice one little boy?

"Take him, David. Give him a chance at life," said my father, and my mother nodded agreement.

"Are you sure? We would be proud to, but won't you miss him?"

"We will think of him every day, but we will know he is in good hands. 'Adios, nuestros pequeños ojos brillantes.'"

I never saw my parents again. Months later, an aunt smuggled out a message that they had died in prison. "Goodbye, our little bright eyes," were the last words I would ever hear them speak.

It wasn't easy, but with the help of a great lawyer, David and Lucy Weissman adopted me. When they asked me what I wanted my new American name to be, I answered quickly. On my official records, I became Roberto Ojos Brillantes Weissman.

Now I'm telling you this whole story in English, but at the time, I spoke little or none. That changed thanks to one man, my ESL teacher Robert Primavera. Kids were making fun of me. I mean, what was I? One kid called me a "Jewban" in mocking confusion. I ran with it. I was proud of both my Cuban heritage and my Jewish family. From then on, when people asked what the hell I was, I simply said, a "Jewban."

At that point, all I wanted to do was play the guitar my father had given me. I wanted nothing to do with the kids at school. That is until Mr. Primavera intervened. I think he was great with all the kids, but he took particular notice of the fact that I was needy. After all, how many Jewbans could he have had in his ESL class? He encouraged me to bring my guitar to school, and in time he brought in one of his own. I learned more English playing Beatles songs than I thought possible. He worked with me every day to improve my English. He even introduced me to guys who were looking for a guitarist to play in their band.

When it came time to apply for college, I was hesitant. I was feeling sorry for myself and thought that the odds were against me. Mr. P. tried as hard as he could. Yet I resisted. However, it was one night with Zayde and Bubbe (What I called the Weissmans—Yiddish for grandparents) that pushed me in the right direction.

"Everything is against me," I said. They merely shook their heads.
"Everything?" said Zayde.
"Yes, everything, and everyone."
Solemnly, both Zayde and Bubbe started to roll up their sleeves.
"What are you doing?"
"Everything? Everyone? Do you see these?" They both pointed to the numbered tattoos with which the Nazis had branded them at Auschwitz Concentration Camp. They told me their story. When they finished, they simply asked me, "Is your life so tough?"
I didn't answer. I never questioned my opportunities or obstacles again.

Johnny, can you judge a man by the stories that he tells? Sure as shit can, when it's a story like that. Bobby became a part of the *Queens Undies.*

———◆———

I had pretty much been a one-man show: writing, typing, printing, and distributing. For all that, I probably made the same money as if I worked in a burger joint. However, there were perks. As the paper caught on, I started to get complimentary tickets to concerts and free albums for me to review. These little extras made the job well worthwhile.

Bobby wanted to write, and he wanted to be around music. How could I turn him down? He was a man after my own heart. Though I would much rather take a girl to these free concerts, I soon found that Bobby got wrapped up in the whole scene. When writing, we fed off each other's ideas in our reviews and opinions.

One day I walked in on him playing the guitar. Johnny, did I say playing the guitar? I mean crushing it. He was playing riffs and chords in a style reminiscent of some of my favorites like Clapton or Alvin Lee, yet he still put his personal signature into every note. I was ashamed to tell him that I, too, played. In reality, the comparison of our abilities could only be described by saying I was a baby taking my first steps compared to an Olympic sprinter. Gradually, he started to show me methods to improve my skills. I once remarked that it must be painfully frustrating to work with someone who was such a novice. He laughed and explained that I was doing much the same thing for him when it came to writing for the magazine.

Under Bobby's tutelage, my playing is rapidly improving. I don't know if I will ever be much more than an adequate rhythm guitarist, but that's OK. I just want to be able to put music to the words rolling around in my head. I want back what I lost—when I lost you as my songwriting partner.

33

"The Needle and the Damage Done"
- Neil Young

Diary of DJ Spinelli

Entry #41 – January 10, 1969

I'M GOING OVER TO YOUR parents' house to help out. OK, I have to be honest. There is not much for me to do there. Your dad is back in bed full time with the cancer that continues to ravage him. Your mom just got the cast off her arm, but we now take turns taking her to rehab. Of course, Mary Lou is still there. Aylin visits her often.

Neil and I stop by frequently. I think maybe I'm there to see Aylin and I know that Neil is there to see Mary Lou. Enough said about that situation.

Sometimes, Aylin will offer to watch Alex so that Neil and Mary Lou can have some alone time. Such was the case today while I was there. It seemed kind of right being in a room with Aylin and a kid. It was sort of like a foreshadowing of family life. But then the real world intruded.

Aylin held Alex in her arms. Unfortunately, Uncle DJ had spoiled the kid with a lot of junk food, and his dozing off was interrupted by a violent upchuck of Bonomo's Turkish Taffy. The once sweet treats covered Aylin's arm. She asked me to hold Alex while she removed her long-sleeve man-tailored outer shirt and stripped down to the red tank top she wore beneath. It was then that I noticed the tracks down her arm.

I don't know what I should do now. She's made it clear to me in the past that I'm not her older brother. What she does is her business. Yet, should I tell her mother? That is probably the right thing, but I know she'll never forgive me.

Entry # 42 – February 14, 1969

Valentine's Day. Day for love. I guess that is what made me realize that if I truly care for Aylin, I have to do the right thing. I guess maybe that is what love is all about.

I told Mrs. Mac about what I saw on Aylin's arm. She already knew. She cried in my arms and told me she had lost control of her eighteen-year-old daughter. I confronted Aylin about the problem. It didn't go well. Aylin threw a pillow, a clock, and a shoe at me.

No valentine for me this year. Maybe never. She's not even talking to me now.

I practiced guitar for about five hours today. It takes my mind off Aylin. Emotions are deep right now. I feel some lyrics floating in my head. I'll try to get them down on paper. This is my first song in a long time. Maybe the more I experience life, the more intense my writing will get. I remember you writing a song called "Gypsy Rose" after you befriended Tony Provenzano, a guy who had damaged his brain sniffing glue. As I experience the helplessness of Aylin's addiction, I can feel the words to a song coming from my heart—just like you did a long time ago.

If You Live, I Could Love You
(Aylin's Song)
By Denny Spin (DJ Spinelli)

If you live,
I could love you.
But that doesn't seem to be.

Monkey got a hold.
Of your damn soul,
Chokin' at my heart too, you see.

I could love you,
I know it.
If only you could break free.

Lines down your arm
Are doin' you harm.
They're killin' you and me.

(Chorus)
If you live,
I could love you.
But that doesn't seem to be.

I'm beat. I'm going to sleep. Work on this song tomorrow.

Entry #43– February 21, 1969

I saw Aylin's boyfriend, Dougie, today. He couldn't wait to mention that he was going to meet her later in the day. I wanted so much to wipe the shit-eating-grin off of his face. He's just using Aylin. He knows it. I know it. Only Aylin doesn't see what is going on. In her sadness and drug-induced condition, she's blind. I thought of another line for the song. I don't know if this piece is going anywhere, but it's therapy for me.

It's fryin' your brain,
Drivin' me insane.
And you're too blind to see.

Too much rhyme? Too immature? I'll look at it again tomorrow.

34

"Here, There, and Everywhere"
- *The Beatles*

Diary of DJ Spinelli

Entry #44 - March 20, 1969

IT'S BEEN FIVE MONTHS AND I still haven't mentioned your dad's delusions in the hospital to anyone. He's doing poorly, and I don't want people thinking he's crazy too. However, he continues to talk about it. Your mom humors him, but I think she likes what he is saying so much that she lets him ramble on. When I asked her if she really believed that someone with a halo told two people who didn't exist that Johnny was alive, she told me at least someone was giving her hope.

Entry #45 – April 4, 1969

The *Queens Undies* story about Chris Delaney was such a success I'm getting feelers from music magazines. They want me to write for them part-time. I gave some thought to quitting school so that I could follow music full time. That could be a mistake. I don't know.

Bobby's coming over later, and we're going to jam a little, then I'm going to your parents. Aylin is there a lot. Am I hoping to see her?

Entry #46 - May 4, 1969

I spoke again to Chris Delaney. Neil told me he would be expecting a call from Denny Spin. Was it smart to pick a pen name? I have to make so many decisions, and I have no one to advise me.

This time the hotel was in Bismarck, North Dakota. I'm worried this obscure venue meant Chris is on a downward spiral. The city is the sunflower capital of the world, but not particularly known as the mainline of rock and roll.

Again, he only had a few minutes. He felt bad our in-person meeting was now delayed almost a year. However, he was going to make it up to me by giving me a big music scoop. He has been approached to perform in a music festival in upstate New York this summer. His "Heroes in the Night" would fit right in with the theme of this event—three days of music and peace.

I feel bad for Chris. I mean, the guy is now going to play on a dairy farm owned by some guy named Max Yasgur. How low has he sunk? I mean, how many people are going to walk around in cow shit for three days? A thousand? And where the hell is Woodstock?

I'll write about it in the *Queens Undies*, but will anyone care?

Entry #47 – May 20, 1969

The spring semester is over. I stop by your parents' place a few times a week. Very often, Neil is there with Mary Lou and Alex. Yeah, they are a thing now. Mary Lou is sort of settling in and giving your mom help. But more than that, she has become like family. She is the daughter they never had, and Alex is the grandchild they *will* never have. That is unless the angel with a halo and the invisible duo are real—and you are still out there, Johnny. Are you?

Entry #48 – May 26, 1969

I went over to see your parents. No, that's a lie. I went there to Aylin, who was helping out while Mary Lou and Neil went on an actual date.

It was very awkward. Aylin still hasn't forgiven me for getting on her case for the drugs. We tried to talk, but whenever she mentioned Dougie, I wanted to puke. She told me that he was in summer school. I didn't understand that because his whole philosophy was not to graduate. She was hesitant to tell me the truth, perhaps thinking I would snitch to someone.

Dougie's getting grief from Selective Service. His little scheme to evade the draft by prolonging his college career hasn't gone unnoticed. He hoped that if he made a real effort to get some credits, they would let him slide. I already knew too much. I wanted to call the draft board myself and tell them what a sneaky prick he was. I don't think that will gain me any brownie points with Aylin.

Entry #49 – June 1, 1969

Neil got a call from Trip Grimes. He's filming every moment of the tour with Chris Delaney in hopes of creating an excellent documentary. Trip told Neil that this upstate New York thing is coming together. More importantly, Trip says he is setting aside two comp tickets for Neil and me. OK, maybe I can get a great story out of three days on a dairy farm. At least I'll finally get to meet Chris Delaney.

35

"I Am a Child"
- Buffalo Springfield

THOSE BORN FREE Tape - undated

"THE TAPE IS ON." (JIMMY Mac)

"Happy Ides of March, guys" (Tinman)

"He learned that in Latin class today." (Johnny)

"Et tu? See us public school guys know stuff too. Today is the day that Julius Caesar was stabbed to death in front of the Senate. (Jimmy Mac)

"Yeah, et tu means even you. It's what Caesar said when his friend Brutus stabbed him last." (Tinman)

"I can't imagine stabbing your best friend." (Gio)

"Well, I can—if it was you." (Johnny - laughs in background)

"Thanks, pal." (Gio)

"Could you imagine one of your friends dying in front of you?" (Johnny)

"Never." (Gio)

"Yeah, me neither. I can't even imagine an enemy dying in front of me." (Johnny)

"Yeah, Life is important." (Bracko)

"Bracko, you going to have kids someday?" (Tinman)

"How?" (Bracko)

"I sure hope that question meant he wants to know how to meet someone and not that he doesn't know how kids are made." (Gio)

"Asshole!" (Bracko)

"Well, I hope Maria and I have at least three kids." (Johnny)

"How about you, Gio?" (Jimmy Mac)

"With the right woman, yeah, I could see a lot of DeAngelis kids running around." (Gio)

"Think you'll ever find that woman, huh?" (Johnny)

"Watch it, Johnny. I'll go all Brutus on you if you don't watch what you say." (Gio)

"What got him all excited?" (Jimmy Mac)

"I haven't the faintest idea. . . do I, Gio?" (Johnny)

"What is Bracko playing now?" (Tinman)

"'I Am a Child' by Buffalo Springfield." (Jimmy Mac)

———————

June 26, 1969

Riet Carver liked to take Van to the Carvel ice cream store once a week. She enjoyed the big smile that filled his face when he saw his vanilla cone. True, it would melt down his hands faster than his little mouth could devour it. It was worth all the mess and bother for the joy she felt seeing him so happy.

As much as the ice cream excited her son, Riet looked forward to the interaction with Larry Kimski, the owner of the store. She had worked for him three years before. It was the summer that she and Gio DeAngelis had met and fallen in love. Riet and Gio's love affair had been a secret from everyone except Johnny Cipp. After Gio and Johnny had disappeared, she had no one to talk about her feelings.

She was three months pregnant when Gio disappeared. But did he leave? Or had he been murdered as rumored? As a black girl, there was no one in the white community she could reach out to except for Larry Kimski. Though he could not answer her questions about Gio's whereabouts, he did offer her sympathy. She realized this old white man had always known about them and had understood her sorrow.

Now three years later, she enjoyed his company and conversation every week. No matter how crowded his store, he always took a break when he saw Riet and Van approaching. Kimski had to personally prepare Van's small cone and hand it to him. No matter how many times Riet offered to pay for it, the old man just smiled and told her that he would take it out of her pay. Not having worked there since she was a sixteen-year-old, they both laughed at the same stale joke, until today.

As Riet and Van approached the Carvel, there was no bright smile waiting. Their eyes did not even see him there at all. This was unusual because Kimski never took off during the peak summer season. Riet rambled over to the vacant window.

"Yeah, what can I help you with?" snapped an older man who looked vaguely like the missing owner.

"We came to visit with Larry like we do every week."

"He's not here—and he won't be again."

"Boss, Larry and Riet were friends. He used to like to talk to her, and he always gave Van a vanilla cone," said Sally Jenkins, who had worked at the Carvel for three years.

"Well, they'll be no more free cones. Maybe that's why my brother left no money behind," said Paul Kimski in a rude and condescending voice.

"Left behind?" murmured Riet.

"Yeah, he left behind nothing but this heavily mortgaged cra-phole when he died." It suddenly hit Riet her friend had passed away, and there would be no more long talks with the old guy.

"And don't come around here looking for free stuff anymore. That ain't gonna happen—get it?"

"Mr. Kimski, you're being cruel," said Sally. "She was his friend, and he loved that little kid."

"If you want to keep your job, you'll watch how you talk to me, Miss Jenkins." Paul Kimski stared down his employee until she cowered in fear. He then turned back to the window to confront Riet, but she was gone. She and Van sat on a curb about ten feet from his window.

"It'll be OK, Van."

"Where is the nice man who's always here?" sobbed Van, crying because his mother was crying.

"He went away to a better place."

"So, no ice cream today?" murmured Van, and Riet was too upset to answer.

"Look at that pathetic girl trying to get free ice cream by shedding some crocodile tears in front of the store," said Kimski to Sally Jenkins, who had stopped listening and was going about her business at the adjoining service window with other customers—a middle-aged couple who shook their head in disgust at the owner.

"We'll have two chocolate milkshakes," said the husband and then nodded at his wife and added, and whatever, those two usually have." Sally Jenkins smiled at them and quickly filled the order.

"I heard the whole conversation," consoled the woman. "And I know you aren't crying about ice cream but about Larry. We loved him too. Maybe this will help calm your son down a little and put a smile on his face." Riet's tears evaporated, not because of ice cream but because of the kindness of these people. Seeing his mother smile and seeing a vanilla cone made Van break into an ear to ear grin.

"Thank you," was all Riet could say as she took the cones and hugged her son.

"Children should never have to cry. Their youth is too short as it is." The woman sighed. Riet smiled and turned to wipe some of the melted ice cream from her son's hand. By the time she looked up, the white couple was already ten feet away and merely waved at the young black mother and her child.

Gyp and Rosalie DeAngelis never realized, they had met their grandson, Van.

PART
3

"Summer of Love"
"Reach out your arms. Touch the moon, touch the sky."
- John Fogerty

Summer 1969

36

"Hey, Mr. Spaceman"
- *The Byrds*

Diary of DJ Spinelli

Entry #50– July 3, 1969

IBROUGHT BOBBY BRIGHT EYES INTO my songwriting, and we've produced some decent stuff. He's a great musician. The other night I showed him the rough outlines of "If You Live, I Could Love You," and he did magic with riffs that fleshed out the song. We got so involved in playing it that we missed a concert we were supposed to review. We're not going anywhere right now, but maybe someday.

Entry #51 July 10, 1969

I'm looking forward to this music festival upstate. Just me and some cows sitting in a field. Do they really expect to make money from this whole thing — oh, the sacrifices I make to be a music critic.

I found out Neil can't make it. He has to work. You can't ask the police department for time off for a festival of peace and love.

Entry #52– July 20, 1969

I ran into Dougie on campus. He is getting a lot of pressure from the draft board. I guess he trusts me because he told me he is considering running away to Canada. I told him to go. Hey, that would clear my path to Aylin.

Entry # 53 – July 21, 1969

A man walked on the moon today. I still can't believe it. We all cheered and jumped up and down and went crazy. Then I looked over at your mom, and she was crying. In all the excitement, no one seemed to notice. I went and sat next to her.

"Johnny?" I whispered. She said nothing but nodded. "Yeah, I imagine he would have loved this stuff."

"You mean, *he is* loving it."

Are you?

We had all gathered at your house to watch the moon landing. We felt we wanted to be together for it, and it would have been very tough for your dad to go anywhere else. So here we were crammed around the little TV in your living room.

It was Neil, Mary Lou, Alex, Mr. and Mrs. DeAngelis, Adele McAvoy, and her daughters Aylin, Maggie, and Sioban. Did you notice how I wrote that like Aylin is just another acquaintance? As I looked around, it occurred to me that this was the remnants of the family and friends of Those Born Free. Did anyone else notice? Somehow your unknown band has drawn us together as if by some all-knowing power.

I was taking this all in when I felt a tap on my shoulder. When I turned, I saw Adele McAvoy staring at me. While the scene on the TV shifted to a newsroom, everyone else dug into pizza.

"I know you care a little about Aylin," she mumbled, not knowing it was far more than a little. "I'm scared for her. I found some tickets to some kind of rock music thing upstate in August. She hasn't mentioned it to me, so I don't know what it all means."

But I did. Aylin and Dougie were going to go to the music festival—but that wasn't all. Piecing together the information

I had gleaned from Dougie, the two of them would then continue to Canada—a straight run up the New York interstate. *Douchbag* would escape the draft and a trip to Vietnam. But what about Aylin? With only Dougie for companionship, how long would it be before drugs became her only consideration? But what could I do? Damn, why did I encourage him to go?

"Look after her," pleaded Mrs. McAvoy desperately.

"I'll try," was all I could think to say. Even as I did, an idea hit me. I excused myself and worked my way over to Neil to discuss my quickly forming plan. I then approached Aylin. I wanted to tell her that *Dougie's a fuckin' scumbag who is just using her and that she is going to die from drugs or spend the rest of her life doing unmentionable things to pay for her habit.* At that point, Aylin would have said, "Fuck you," and walked away. So, I tried another tack.

Johnny, you would've been proud of how deceptive I was today.

"So is Bobby Bright Eyes going to use my ticket to that upstate music festival?" Damn, Neil nailed his line!

"Music festival?" questioned Aylin.

"Yeah, Bobby and I are going up there with comp tickets to review it for my paper."

"Comp tickets from whom?" Aylin asked skeptically. However, I knew two things about her that she didn't think I knew. First, she was going upstate. Second, she was a big fan of Chris Delaney.

"Chris Delaney sent me tickets. I'm meeting him backstage just before he goes on."

"You're fucking kidding me?" She looked to make sure none of the elders heard her language. My fishing expedition had her nibbling at the bait. Yet, she still hadn't admitted to me she was even going.

"Yeah, he's going to call me with the time to meet." I was drawing her in. I wasn't going to tell her I still had never met Chris and indeed didn't even know what he looked like.

"How could you possibly know him? I mean 'Heroes in the Night' is one of the absolute best songs ever written." Then she started singing (very well I might add).

There were heroes in the night,
One black and one white,
The night I almost died on Lispenard.

"Holy shit," I gushed excitedly but softly so as not to offend the elders. "You don't know? Do you?"

"What do you mean?"

"You do know it's a true story? That there actually is a black hero and a white hero?" "Yeah," she answered. I couldn't hold in my laugh anymore.

"Here's your real hero right there," I nodded toward Neil.

"Yeah, I know how he saved Mary Lou and didn't even take credit for it, but . . ."

Neil said nothing, amused at his anonymity.

"But he was also on Lispenard. That's how we met. I interviewed him." I preened at my own brush with fame.

"Holy shit!" Everyone heard that language!

"Neil is the white hero in the night."

"I never knew."

"Well, he is humble."

"Mr. White Hero at your service," agreed Neil bowing—and blushing.

"DJ, I've tickets to go too. Do you think I can meet you there? Can you introduce me to Chris Delaney?"

Boom, I had her hook, line, and sinker. At least, now I'd be able to keep an eye on her. I mean, how hard would it be to find her in a big open cow-shit field with a thousand people or so?

I noticed as the night went on, she spent more and more time with Neil. She wanted to be in the company of a star.

———◆———

Entry #54 - August 13, 1969

Chris Delaney found out that he is going on at 3 p.m. on Sunday. When he first told me this, I figured I'd meet up with him when I got there early Saturday morning. If that didn't work out, we would meet just before he was about to play. I told Aylin the same thing, thinking it would be easy to find them in an open field. OK, now the media is talking about 50,000 people being there. I believe that is impossible, but if so, I may never find her in the crowd.

———◆———

Entry #55 – August 15, 1969

Bobby is driving right now, but the reality is we are at a total standstill on the New York Thruway just past the tolls at Woodbury. I'm writing in the car because we aren't moving. The reporter on the radio just finished talking about upwards of a quarter-million people camped out on the fields of Yasgur's farm. I'm no longer worried about finding Aylin or Chris Delaney, both of whom have been there since Thursday. No, I'm concerned about not getting there at all. We may have to hunker down for the night in our car.

Entry #56 – August 16, 1969

What a jerk I've been. I'm looking back at my entries in this book, and I wrote about a thousand people in an open field. We are about to abandon our car and walk the final fifteen miles. Over half a million people are waiting for us there!

I'm leaving this book so that we can travel as light as possible. We have some water in old canteens and some non-perishable food—no extra clothes, no diary. I'll have to remember everything I see.

37

"Woodstock"

"We're going down to Yasgur's farm—
going to join in an uproar there."
- Crosby, Stills, and Nash version

TICKET COLLECTION SOON BECAME OBSOLETE as the deluge of people descended on Max Yasgur's 600-acre dairy near the town of Bethel in the Woodstock area of New York. Official estimates varied. Four hundred thousand to over 500,000 attendees found their way to the muddy fields of the festival area. Thirty-two acts performed. These ranged from the very famous to the soon to be forgotten. One scheduled performer never made it to the stage.

———◆———

DJ Spinelli and Bobby Bright Eyes arrived about noon on Saturday. Exhausted from a night of sleeping in an uncomfortable car and then plodding miles through mud, they arrived in time to see the obscure band Quill perform "They Live the Life." DJ looked over the sea of humanity and thought, *how true, how true.* He immediately realized that any hope of finding Aylin or Chris before their Sunday rendezvous was hopeless. He accepted he would simply have to relax and enjoy the performances on the stage. Using the press credentials Chris had obtained for them, they worked themselves into a relatively good location with which to view the performers. Careful to make their water and food last, they relaxed and enjoyed the music.

DJ never stopped looking out over the wave of humanity in hopes of spotting Aylin. Before leaving, he spoke to Mrs. Mac and knew she had taken her mother's car—without permission. Somewhere in this chaos sat the getaway car for a Canadian adventure. DJ had to find her. Life in Canada with "Douchebag Dougie" would not be good for Aylin.

Aylin and Dougie had been among the first group to arrive at the festival. They had prime seats in front of the stage. However, neither of them had heard very much of the music presented. Dougie brought enough drugs to last them through the three days of the festival and into his first week or two in Canada.

Assuming it would take at least a week to establish a dealer in his new homeland, the supply he brought would ensure an unbroken succession of highs on both sides of the border. However, at the rate they were both consuming his stash, they might not have that luxury. They'd already gone through the weekend's allotment and were well into the Canadian portion of his supply.

They did not seem to know or care about this fact.

Chris Delaney was scheduled to go on after Joe Cocker sometime Sunday afternoon. Because of weather and organizational problems, performance times became inconsistent. The first four acts had not arrived in time, and Richie Havens had been called upon to open the festival with a very long set. The New York Thruway was at a standstill. Because of this, Chris Delaney's journey to the concert had been cut short. Eventually, Air National Guard helicopters ferried musicians into the area, and he was able to find his way by Sunday morning. However, there had been no room for Trip—no matter how much Chris begged.

DJ and Bobby, and the rest of the wet and dirty crowd, listened to Santana, Credence Clearwater, Janis Joplin, The Who, and many more groups all through Saturday night. Jefferson

Airplane, who were supposed to close out the previous night's performances, actually took the stage at 8 a.m. Sunday morning. Though exhausted, DJ was content to enjoy the show and take sketchy notes in a tiny assignment pad he had brought with him. He and Bobby discussed all they had seen, including the fact that The Grateful Dead almost became *actually* dead by electrocution, standing in ankle-deep water and touching their electric guitars.

Yet as Joe Cocker took the stage at 2 p.m., DJ's only thoughts were that Chris Delaney was scheduled next. Midway through Cocker's performance of "Feelin' Alright," DJ and Bobby started to work their way toward the stage entrance where they had arranged to meet Chris. Dark Clouds consumed the skies, and a pending storm became obvious.

———◆———

Dougie Wilk had never intended to take Aylin McAvoy with him to Canada. Though she'd now passed her eighteenth birthday and was no longer jail bait, he was just not interested in her enough to make her part of his new life. Yet, he did need her car. He needed to leave while she was stoned. The scheduled meeting with Chris Delaney was a perfect opportunity to sneak away.

As they worked their way to the stage with the backstage passes, Dougie suggested a brief stop to take the edge off. As he injected Aylin's vein in her left arm with a high dose of heroin, he could not know she had had the same idea of taking the edge off. Only minutes before, she had injected her right arm. As the two of them approached the front of the stage, Aylin's body started to feel the effects of the double dose of drugs, and the world spun in her eyes as she continued to move toward her long-awaited meeting with Chris Delaney.

Dougie felt he could leave while she was distracted by the star. Although he liked the music, drugs, and the whole atmosphere of Woodstock, Dougie feared induction into the army and a trip to Vietnam. He would leave as soon as . . .

———◆———

Chris Delaney was the first one to witness the total physical collapse of Aylin. His first vision of this auburn hair beauty from the stage was as she plunged face-first into the mud ten yards away. Next to her stood a frightened young man, obviously in the throes of panic.

"I don't know her, but I just saw her take a lot of drugs," babbled Dougie as he started to flee the scene.

"Which drugs? What did she take?" yelled Chris as Dougie escaped through the crowd. By the time Chris reached Aylin, she was fading in and out of consciousness. Chris was confused. He knew this young girl needed help, but he also knew a doctor would need to know what she had taken. The answer to that question could only be answered by the guy who was now rapidly working his way through the crowd.

Chris pleaded with the crowd around him. He would chase the escaping bastard if someone else brought this girl to the clinic. Stoned faces stared at him blankly as his eyes kept rotating from Aylin to the fleeing Dougie. "A Little Help from My Friends" played out in the background as Joe Cocker's set came to an end.

That's just what I need right now—a little help from friends, fans, strangers, anyone! thought Delaney. "Please, I'm the only one who knows what he looks like," he pleaded to the crowd.

"We got her," shouted a voice from behind Chris's back. Not wishing to lose sight of his quarry, he did not even turn around but immediately took off after Dougie.

"You're on, Delaney," yelled the stage manager. Chris's entire future lay in his performance today, but this girl's life depended on him too. He weighed his choices, and with a grimace on his face, he waded into the crowd.

———◆———

Aylin's eyelids fluttered, and her breathing grew shallow. DJ and Bobby knelt over her. They had never seen who had pleaded for help before diving into the crowd. The stage manager's voice made them aware it was the man they had come to see. DJ was taken back by the irony. He had once again failed to meet the musical superstar. He then looked down and recognized that the victim was Aylin.

"Aylin! Aylin, no please!" DJ screamed at the still body in

front of him. He quickly picked her up in his two arms and started to run toward a clinic set up on the premises. They had passed it by on their way in the day before.

"You take her, and I'll follow him," declared Bobby pointing to the distant figure of Chris Delaney. "Either I'll lead him back to the clinic or come back and get you. We just have to make sure he knows where to go after he catches that bastard."

"OK," DJ answered as the tears rolled down his face, and he started his trek. At first, the microphones announced the upcoming performance of Chris Delaney. Soon, spoken sounds were drowned out by the ear-splitting noise of massive thunderclaps. The storm indefinitely put on hold any thoughts of music. Within minutes the already saturated ground became inches deep in mud. DJ struggled to see in front of him as the rain limited his vision.

"Hold on Aylin, please . . . please, Aylin, don't leave now," he whispered to her, but his words fell on deaf ears. He could not tell if she was even breathing. DJ soon found himself ankle-deep in mud. As he went to lift his left foot, it stayed mired deep in the muck. With his momentum moving forward and his foot planted, he lost his balance plummeted downward into the sludge. Streaks of lightning filled the sky, and crowds either hugged the ground or ran for what little shelter could be found.

With both their bodies encased in thick layers of mud, DJ pushed the dirt away from Aylin's face. He put his ear to her mouth to listen for any sounds of life. He found none. He knelt over her motionless body, not knowing what to do. In the distance, he heard one stoned concert goer screaming and ignoring the lightning strikes. What was he yelling?

"Don't worry, everyone! This is the age of Aquarius—the sign of water. Enjoy the storm. The gods have sent it to us. Yes, Yes, the Age of Aquarius—a time when we're all *born free*." He then promptly collapsed in the mud but continued to rant. DJ had heard enough.

Born free? Those Born Free? Johnny had first met Bracko when the kid was doing something called CPR on Tony. Johnny went into great detail about how he pushed on his chest and then counted and then pushed again and again. As if in a vision, the actions Johnny described to him came back in vivid detail. He put them in some kind of logical order in his mind and then proceeded to recreate what he remembered on the fallen Aylin.

"I'm not giving up on you. I love you, Aylin," DJ yelled as he pushed and pumped her lifeless body. "C'mon, you can do it." Thunder crashed overhead, and many around him screamed in fear. DJ, however, remained oblivious to his surroundings, concentrating solely on reviving Aylin. Suddenly he felt movement in her body. Her eyes opened briefly, then rolled back in her head. She had started breathing again, but it was weak, strained breathing. He knew he did not have long to get her real help. He rose from the ground to continue his journey toward the clinic.

The fields that only minutes before had been alive with crazed concert-goers were now a sea of bodies attempting to become one with the Earth to avoid being hit by the rapidly striking bolts of electricity from the sky. Only one figure now stood upright as he trudged forward, constantly moving his eyes between the path before him and Aylin's face. As he reached an incline in the ground, the going became more difficult. Every few steps, he would lose his footing and fall, always careful to protect Aylin from the impact. His legs weakened, and it was only his feeling for her that kept him going. Ten feet from the peak of the hill, he fell a final time. If he could just get up once more, the clinic was in eyesight. He could make it if he could stand, but he could not. His legs had not the strength to rise. He tried over and over again.

"Goddamit! Get up you piece of shit," he yelled at his own fatigued body. Yet, his body answered with only rejection. He knelt over Aylin. Her breathing was barely perceptible. She did not have long. He had not prayed lately, but he did now even as he made unsuccessful attempts to stand up.

"C'mon, man, we gotcha," said a voice next to him. DJ turned and saw a man who stood tall and straight over him. He would be hard-pressed later to describe anything else about him other than he had long hair and a beard, and every inch of him was covered in mud. He quickly lifted Aylin in his arms and yelled for some of his friends to help DJ up.

"We got him, Simon," assured another stranger, equally covered in mud. Once standing, DJ and the stranger with Aylin in his arms plodded toward the clinic. While being helped up, DJ looked back at the stage and was amazed at the distance he had covered. By the time they reached the door of the clinic, he had regained his strength. The stranger turned and handed Aylin to DJ.

"Thanks," whispered DJ after checking that Aylin was still breathing.

"Hey, isn't it all about love, man?" The stranger flashed him the peace sign.

DJ looked down at Aylin's face as he pushed through the door. By then, Simon had disappeared into the rain. DJ held Aylin in his arms until a nurse came forward to help him. He stood over her and wondered if he was too late.

"Can you help her?" DJ screamed to the nurse.

"What did she take?"

"I don't know."

"There's only so much I can do without that info. By her blood pressure, I'm guessing that it's either an opioid or a hypnotic. But it could be a barbiturate. A doctor might be able to tell better."

"And I'm guessing there is none here."

"You don't know how lucky your friend is. Dr. Lopez made a trip here to deliver a baby. Do you believe this shit? Coming here nine months pregnant? Anyway, I'll tell her to see your friend. . .?"

"Aylin, Aylin McAvoy"

"But it really would help her if we knew what and how much she took."

"I'll be back," yelled DJ as he ran out the door.

———◆———

Aylin and Dougie had been among the first to arrive at the festival. Because of this fact they had found parking not too far from the venue. As Chris started his quest to find the stranger, Bobby followed Chris. When DJ joined the chase, he realized that he knew exactly where to go. He had noticed Aylin's car, with its distinctive Mac's Candy Store logo, when he and Bobby arrived. Dougie must have always planned to steal the vehicle for his escape to Canada. The bastard had never even considered taking Aylin with him. He had used her. Yet this fact allowed DJ to know precisely which way to run, and he soon met up with Bobby, who had been on his way back to find him.

———◆———

"Hey, asshole, you're not going anywhere," screamed Chris Delaney so that he could be heard over the booming thunder and drenching rain.

"Who the hell are you?" answered the surprised Dougie Wilk. He had not even considered that he had been followed from the staging area to Aylin's car.

"It doesn't matter who I am. It matters that you abandoned that girl to die of an OD, and I need to know exactly what she took."

"I don't have any idea what you are talking about."

"Are you really going to play dumb while a girl's life hangs in the balance?"

"I'm just coming to my car to get out of the rain." Dougie fumbled with the keys he'd taken off Aylin as she lay unconscious. Chris lost his patience. He rushed the distance between them and pinned Dougie to the driver's side door.

"If that girl dies, you're going away for murder. I'll see to that." Chris immediately realized he had said precisely the wrong thing. If Dougie opened up now, he would be admitting to a crime. Chris took a step back and let go of his arms.

"I don't know what you are talking about. What do you want, man?"

Chris decided to change strategies. He would have to compromise if he was going to save her. "Tell me what she took, and I'll let you go."

"After you beat the crap out of me."

"No, I promise not to lay another finger on you." Dougie eyed Chris skeptically through the sheets of rain.

"You promise you won't touch me?"

"Promise."

"I gave her heroin, but after the fact, I figured out she'd taken some on her own. She'd just gotten some LSD tabs from the people around us."

"And you just left her—knowing that?" Chris's anger grew, but he now understood why no one else had bothered to help her besides the late arrival who promised to take her to the medical tent. His fists clenched, but he remembered his promise. He didn't have time to deal with this piece of shit.

"Remember . . . you promised," pleaded Dougie.

"Yeah, but I didn't," bellowed a voice from behind Chris. DJ arrived on the scene and immediately rushed past Chris. In one motion, he threw a devastating roundhouse punch that crushed Dougie's jaw. As the slightly built villain slid down the side of the car, DJ stepped forward and stood menacingly over him.

"DJ?" muttered Dougie.

"DJ?" echoed Chris.

"Yeah, Dougie, it's DJ, and *I'm* not in a mood to negotiate."

"I gave my word," said Chris Delaney though DJ had still not turned.

"We don't have time for this," interrupted Bobby, the least emotionally involved with Dougie's disposition. "You know what she took?" he asked Chris. "And you know where she is?" DJ pointed toward the medical tent. With that, Chris and Bobby raced off, but DJ faked one final blow to Dougie, who was returning to his feet.

"If you think you're fuckin' taking Mrs. Mac's car," DJ started to say, but instead of finishing the sentence, he shook his head. He quickly kicked Dougie in the balls, causing him to fall face forward in the mud. DJ then stepped on the wrist of his nearly unconscious victim, forcing Dougie's hand to release the car keys.

"Canada may hide you from the draft, but not from me if Aylin dies. You better hope Aylin makes it." He turned and ran to catch up with Bobby and Chris. All three jogged at the fastest pace the mud allowed. Noticing for the first time Chris Delaney was also his high school teacher, DJ was incredulous.

"Brother Christian? Are you kiddin' me? I've been talking to you on the phone all this time and didn't know that Chris Delaney is Brother Christian. Well, fuck me!"

"It's better than changing my name to 'Denny Spin.' What

the hell is that?" Though worried about Aylin's fate, they both allowed a small smile to flash on their faces.

The three of them arrived at the clinic ten minutes later. Though the rain had washed most of the mud from their bodies, they still resembled the disheveled dregs of society. His job done, Bobby decided to stay outside the clinic and rest. Chris and DJ entered.

"So, you found him," said the nurse assuming that Chris had been Aylin's supplier and therefore was responsible for her near-death condition. This prompted the doctor to want to lay into him immediately. However, the patient was her first priority.

"OK, what did she take?"

"A great deal of heroin and also some LSD," answered Chris.

"You shithead. What are you so high that you didn't think of what you were doing to this poor girl?" She didn't wait for an answer and instead immediately turned to the nurse and gave her instructions that would save Aylin's life. The doctor and nurse worked diligently and paid little heed to the two men who stood watching helplessly. Soon the doctor took a deep breath and turned to the nurse.

"I think she'll make it," the doctor said, and then turned sharply toward Chris, "No thanks to you."

"But, I . . ."

"Aren't you a bit old for her? Aren't you a bit old for this whole scene?" The doctor sneered at Chris with belligerence oozing from her tone.

"I'm just here for the music. I didn't even know her," answered Chris defensively.

"That's even worse. You take advantage of a young girl you don't even know? And what drugs did *you* take?"

"Nothing, I was . . ."

"Yeah, I know, just here for the music," mimicked the doctor.

"You're so wrong," yelled DJ, who finally looked away from Aylin long enough to pick up on the conversation. "He *is* here for the music—to play it. He saw her from the stage and jumped down to save her when everyone else ignored her situation. He even missed his chance to perform."

"Oh, then, who are *you*?" She now looked at DJ with suspicion.

"I'm her friend, and I was coming to meet her here when I saw him jump off the stage to help her. He then chased the guy who did give her the drugs while I brought her here."

"Oh, is that the truth?" relented the now humbled Doctor Lopez.

"Yeah, like I said. I was just here for the music," maintained Chris with forgiveness in his voice. Yet he couldn't resist one dig. "And what are you here for?"

The doctor answered, "I'm here for the music too. But I'm afraid I missed the one act I most wanted to see in my free time. On the way to the stage area, the woman in the next room decided to give birth. You know, duty calls."

"Who was the act?" questioned Chris.

"Chris Delaney," sighed Doctor Lopez.

DJ looked away from the healthier-looking Aylin and started to laugh. He whispered under his breath, "Oh, this is going to be good fun."

"You might be the only one of half a million people who would give that answer," insisted Chris. "Have you ever seen him before?"

"Nope, been too busy working, but I love his song 'Heroes in the Night.'" She stopped, looked down at Aylin and determined she was doing very well. Put in a better mood, the doctor began to sing.

"There were heroes in the night . . ." Chris joined her for the rest of the chorus.

One was black and one was white,
The night I almost died on Lispenard.

"You're . .

"As I said, I came for the music."

———◆———

Three hours later, Aylin opened her eyes for the first time, and the first sight she saw was DJ.

"Why are you crying?" asked Aylin.

"We almost lost you. Your mother couldn't take that."

"How about you?"

"I couldn't take that either."

"You know, I did have some moments of consciousness while you were carrying me. I heard some things. . ." She took DJ's hand.

———◆———

Confident that her patient was out of danger, Dr. Lopez walked outside into the fresh air. The rain had stopped. Strains of Country Joe and the Fish could be heard in the distance.

"What's that spell? What's that smell?" Joe McDonald screamed into the microphone before unleashing the anti-war message of "I-Feel-Like-I'm-Fixin'-To-Die."

"So, you finally got to hear some music," consoled Chris. He sat on the bench near the tent.

"Yeah, the lyrics are clever and make a statement—I just don't like the statement it's making."

"What do you mean?"

"The meaning of your song was uplifting and gave people hope. This just ridicules certain people."

"You're ex-military, aren't you?"

"Yeah, but not ex. I'm on a month's leave and decided to spend some of it here. It might've been a mistake. Does the military show?"

"I'm an ex-religious brother—does that show?" Chris realized this doctor was the first person he'd ever shared that information with besides his friend Trip.

"You're fuckin' kidding me. Oops, I guess I have to watch my language around you."

"I did say 'ex,' didn't I?"

"I saw so many brave men die over there. I hate the smug attitude that singers have about them. I mean, I understand the right to protest the war, but don't protest the warriors. Speech over."

"OK, let's start over. I'm Chris Delaney, formerly Brother Christian, a Marist teaching brother and one of DJ's teachers. But, that's a story for another time."

"Will there be another time?" she pondered, now staring into his eyes.

"I hope so," he answered.

"OK. I'm Doctor or Major Shyanne Lopez. Yeah, I know, weird name. My father came to America from Puerto Rico. He learned to speak English by going to all the John Wayne westerns that played in the movies. He named me after Chey-enne, Wyoming, but he only heard the word and never knew how to spell it, so my birth certificate reads S-h-y-a-n-n-e. For a while, kids in school thought that it was a description of me, you know shy–Anne. I quickly changed to a nickname that was a combination of my first and last name 'Shy' from Shyanne and 'Lo' from Lopez. So, my friends call me Shylo. Of course, my father thinks I took the name after the Civil War battlefield of Shiloh. He couldn't spell that either."

"Pleased to meet you, Shylo."

38

"After the Storm"
- Crosby, Stills, and Nash

Entry #57 – August 25, 1969

THERE IS SO MUCH I want to put down in this little book. However, some of it is too personal and I will have to think long and hard about what it all means before writing.

Woodstock (which is all they are calling it now) was musically fantastic. The parts I saw will be the subject of many of the articles for the *Queens Undies*. However, I missed so much that happened on the stage. Where do I begin?

Chris Delaney never performed because he was busy helping save the life of someone very special to me. That comes as no surprise when you consider that Chris is Brother Christian! Yes, *the* Brother Christian who taught you the bass and used to jam with us in the cafeteria. All he did was shorten Christian to Chris and use his real last name, but I never connected the two. Of course, I blame myself. My stupid, misguided adventure as Denny Spin kept him from knowing who *I was*. In light of that, Denny Spin is dead, long live DJ Spinelli.

To summarize: I came with a current friend, Bobby—met an old friend, Aylin—reconnected with an older friend, Chris—made a new friend, Shylo. I also dispatched an enemy, Dougie. Oh bullshit, I'm not going to play with words. I decked him, as in knocked the shit out of him with one punch. Johnny, you'd proudly laugh about that one. It was the first punch I've ever thrown. You used to mock me for being a softy. You liked to say, "Guys from the Heights had their first fight before they had grown any teeth to get knocked out." Damn, does my hand hurt. No guitar for a few days—can't hold a pick.

———◆———

I will never forget the feeling as we listened to the last notes on Monday morning. Bobby, Chris, Shylo, Aylin, and I commandeered a blanket and sat on the grass outside the medical tent.

"Now that's a song I can relate to," said Shylo as she held Chris's hand. They had known each other for less than two days, and yet they had connected.

"What do you mean?" Chris asked.

"The Star-Spangled Banner," said Shylo, "And played by Jimi Hendrix, no less."

"Yeah, that's a surprise."

"You know he's a veteran," Shylo stood a little taller. "I even served with him briefly in Fort Campbell in Kentucky. I was just starting out, and he was always in the doctor's office."

"Better not tell the crowd," joked Chris, and then he put his arm around her shoulder and softly squeezed her affectionately. I saw this relationship developing and only wished it would be the same for Aylin and me. There remain too many barriers to our happiness. Yet here we all were listening to the final strains of a festival we knew would go down in history. I know we'll savor that moment forever.

Hendrix had just stopped playing when I looked down into Aylin's eyes. Gone was the vacant look that had been so depressing to me. She was now lucid, but with that awareness came a sadness which seemed more profound than usual.

"I need to get help, DJ—real help."

"That's the first step, Aylin—knowing that you need it."

"When we get back, I am going to go away for treatment, and I'm going to stay for as long as it takes. And, DJ…"

"Yeah?"

"Will you be there when I get out?"

"Yeah, yes—if you want me there."

"I want you there."

For the first time in what seemed like months, I saw her smile.

We all waited one more day for the crowds to disperse and then went our separate ways with the promise to meet up soon after we arrived back in the city.

Entry #58 – September 21, 1969

Life seems to move at a dizzying pace. I haven't had time to write. First, it is the usual mundane stuff like school and the *Queens Undies*. I'm taking eighteen credits, which is bad enough while still doing the paper. Bobby has been a great help. We have grown closer as friends after our experiences at Woodstock. We have continued our symbiotic relationship where I teach him to write, and he teaches me the guitar.

Because of Woodstock and everything else going on in music and youth culture, they have called this past summer, "The Summer of Love." I don't know if I agree with that description as it applies to the world in general. I mean, there is the Vietnam War, civil rights protests (and the reactions to them), and riots in the streets. Yet on a more personal level, it truly was a summer of love.

Chris Delaney and I have talked about collaborating on some musical projects. Unfortunately for him, his relationship with Shylo has been put on hold as she finishes her last six months of military commitment. I have no doubt their relationship will continue once she musters out permanently. They write to each other continuously, and he tells me that he finds it hard to write anything but syrupy love songs.

Neil and Mary Lou are always together. He confided that when he is officially a cop, he is going to propose to her. He knows he'll only be 21 years old, but he doesn't seem to care. Meanwhile, Mary Lou and Alex continue to live with your parents and provide a great deal of physical and emotional support in these hard times.

And then there is Aylin and me. Well, not really. Aylin has been in a residential treatment facility since I brought her home from Woodstock. She isn't allowed visitors the first ninety days. I miss her, but for the first time, I don't see any roadblocks to our relationship besides her own emotions. I'll take it. It's more than I ever had with her.

So yeah, on this last official day of the summer of 1969, I believe it was a summer of love – at least in my world.

Entry #59 – October 10, 1969

Your parents asked if they could meet Chris. They were not like every other star-struck person who asks me. No, they wanted to thank him for all he had done for their son. Though I would do anything for these two beautiful people, I have to think about this.

Johnny, you were out of music. Your crippled hand seemed to negate any chance of ever playing again. Then Chris taught you to play the bass even with the weaknesses in your hand. The bass ended up being your therapy. You went on to regain full use of your hand. So, Chris, as Brother Christian, worked a miracle for you.

Yet it was the music that led to all the bad things. Whether you are dead or missing, music led you wherever you are today. Is Chris a hero—or a villain? I guess your parents would answer that it was better to have lived and lost than to have never lived.

Entry #60 – October 12, 1969

It's Columbus Day. College is closed, so I took this opportunity to drive Chris over to meet your parents. I knew this would be an emotional moment, but couldn't know it would be Chris to cry first.

Your mom walked over to a corner of the room and picked up a plastic bucket. She had caressed it as if the wealth of a thousand diamonds lay inside it. Yet it was empty. She then handed it to Chris, who looked at it in confusion.

"Each night, Johnny came home and filled that bucket with ice and water and stuck his damaged hand in it. He thought we didn't know about his ritual." Your mom sighed.

"I didn't until you told me," added your dad.

"Johnny was in excruciating pain every night after his hours of practice on the bass."

"I didn't mean to. . ." started Chris.

"No, it was good. When I would peek in and see my son's submerged hand, there was always a big smile on his face. He was happy. You had made him happy, and for that, we will always be grateful."

Chris tried to think of something to say after such an emotional story. He failed. He simply walked over to your mom and hugged her. Your dad reached from the bed and held his hand. When they both finally separated, Chris still held the bucket.

"Would you like to keep the bucket, Chris?" asked your mom.

"I would."

———

Chris told me later that whenever he played from that day on, the bucket would be on the stage with him. Johnny, it was there to commemorate you.

39

"Private Investigations"
- *Dire Straits*

NEIL CONNAUGHTON HAD ONLY A few months until his twenty-first birthday and immediate induction onto the New York City Police force—as long as he did not somehow screw up. Therefore, he worried when he received a note to report to his captain's office for questioning.

"What can you tell me about this Cippitelli family," asked the neatly dressed detective who sat opposite Neil in a room usually reserved for criminal interrogations.

"What do you mean?"

"You know exactly what I mean? Where is their son hiding out?"

"What?"

"We know that you've been seeing a girl that is living with them. Where do the letters from the son come from?"

"They don't get letters from him. They're not even sure he is alive. And why are you asking me all this?"

"I'll ask the questions. Do you understand that, *Cadet* Connaughton?" This detective hinted his status with the department was not secure—that his career could end with just one phone call.

"I really don't know anything, sir." He wanted to say, *and if I did, I wouldn't tell you.* He kept his mouth shut.

"Kid, if you're lying to me, you're done."

"Sir, if you'd sent me in there undercover, I couldn't tell you any more than I'm telling you now. God's-honest truth."

"Look at this and tell me if you have seen any of these guys hanging around," said the detective. He held out a photo of Those Born Free to show Neil. In reality, only one of the faces in the band picture *could be* hanging around. Detective Richie Shea knew for a fact that the other four were dead.

"Oh shit," said Neil recognizing a face he had not seen in years.

"So, you have seen Johnny," yelled the excited Shea.

"No, this one on the left—Bracko's his name. He saved my life when I was in high school. It is the first time I've seen his face since that day."

"Oh, OK," said Shea, and he took the picture back from Neil. As he opened his wallet to place the picture back in, Neil noticed his identification card and his name. He remembered the name. Shea was Guy Provenzano's cousin. He also realized his placement in Cambria Heights had been no accident.

40

"As Tears Go By"
- *Marianne Faithfull*

Diary of DJ Spinelli

Entry #61 – November 5, 1969

NEIL CAME OVER TO SEE me today. He decided you must be alive because the Provenzanos are still looking for you. That is good news and bad news. It means they didn't kill you. However, they're still looking for you. Neil and I vowed to find you first. Should we tell your mom our belief, or will that only frighten her more?

Entry #62 - November 11, 1969

Johnny, your dad died today. Your mom told me his last thoughts were of that weird story about the night in St. Albans Naval Hospital when an angel (or someone with a halo?) and two invisible men told him you were alive. I didn't tell her that he had told me all this when it happened. I didn't want to worry her. Now, I guess we'll never know.

It's Veterans Day today, a brutal reminder his cancer had been contracted during his stay in Hiroshima. He is a casualty of World War II that no one will ever recognize.

Entry #63 - November 14, 1969 – 7 a.m.

We are laying your father to rest today. Johnny, you should be here! But you aren't. Perhaps, someday you'll grieve.

THOSE BORN FREE Tape – undated

"Jimmy Mac, why do you have the tape recorder on now? Joey and Bracko aren't even here yet." (Johnny)

"Oops, I meant to press 'play' to let you hear the new Kinks song I taped off the radio." (Jimmy Mac)

"Those two are always late." (Gio)

"With their screwed-up fathers, they're lucky to get here at all." (Johnny)

"I don't know how Bracko survives the beatings. I don't know why he takes it." (Gio)

"He won't take it forever. This band is his way out, and if we aren't, he'll find another way after he is eighteen. The clock is ticking on this band." (Johnny)

"I'm just thankful for my parents—even my sisters. They're good people. They make me laugh." (Jimmy Mac)

"OK, we don't laugh that much in my house, but I wouldn't trade Gyp and Rosalie for anything. They're little old-fashioned Italians. You know Mass and pasta every Sunday and baccala on Christmas Eve— that's salted cod for you Irish. Anyway, they are good to me." (Gio)

"Yeah, the same for my parents. But I worry about my father. He just has never been healthy. As long as I can remember, he has never been right. Yet, he keeps working two jobs and never complains about it. I worry he is never going to get well." (Johnny)

"Nothing is gonna keep Big John down." (Gio)

"Yeah, but I know that I will have to be there for my mom if something does happen." (Johnny)

"Don't worry, I know you. You'll do the right thing." (Gio)

"Hey, Bracko, Joey, it's about time you got here. We were just talking about The Kinks." (Jimmy Mac)

Entry # 64 – November 14, 1969 –2:43 p.m.

I'm home now from the funeral. Death is so final, and it is so emotional. It has made me think of so many different thoughts—so many mixed feelings.

Your mom is going to spend the night with Adele McAvoy because she has no one else. You hear me, you asshole? I renewed my vow to stick this diary up your ass when I eventually find you—and I will! I'm coming for you, Johnny.

Anyway, Jerk-off, your mom encouraged "the young people" to do something together. So, later we are all going over to the now-famous Lispenard Street.

I know that the funeral I attended was for your father, but I couldn't help thinking of Those Born Free throughout the ceremony. Almost every person alive who knew the band was in the church. I take that back. Guy's two assholes, Sammy Crespo and Sal Timpani were in the rear. I know they weren't there to pay their respects. They were checking to see if *you* were there. I smiled at that. I don't know where you are, or even if you are alive, but I do know *they* didn't kill you!

41

"Come Alive"

Look deep inside, where there's no place to hide.
You'll find the answer, tears we have cried.
Now is the time for us all to come alive.
- Capt. Kirk Lloyd Douglas and Hundred Watt Heart

Entry #64 - November 15, 1969

L AST NIGHT CHANGED MY LIFE. I began my new future. Bobby Bright Eyes and I arrived at the Grand Lispenard around 7:30, just about the same time as Neil, Mary Lou, and Alex. For all of us, it was our first visit to the converted factory home of Chris and Trip. I wasn't surprised there wasn't any alcohol anywhere in sight. As I looked around, I understood. Many of the experiences that bound us together were the result of drug and alcohol abuse. Aylin's brush with death, Freddy Resch's drunken attack on Mary Lou, and we all knew the story of Bracko's abusive, drunken father. Yet, there was more behind this. I would find out later in the night just how much more.

Once we were all there, we ignored the sizeable cold room that was the central living area. Taking pillows from the couches, we moved to one of the abandoned sound rooms in the back. It made the whole night more intimate. It was Neil who proposed a moment of silence in honor of your dad. I found my eyes drifting around our little group and thinking about our connections.

We were inextricably tied to each other by you and the rest of Those Born Free. Neil, Chris, and I had had our lives changed by knowing you. But, so had Trip, Mary Lou, Alex, and Bobby in less direct and obvious ways. Even though she wasn't there, so had Aylin. Somehow, I feel there are probably others out there somewhere whose lives have been affected by you and the others. I don't know how I know this—I just do.

What word can I use to describe us? A diverse group that also includes the Cippitelli, McAvoy, DeAngelis family survivors? We're somehow bound together. Not a cult, that's too negative. Was it more like a mutual aid society or a fraternity? One word keeps coming to my mind (forget the male connotations)—we are a brotherhood, yes, a brotherhood—forever tied together by the impact of five lost individuals.

Chris and Trip ordered pizzas. The Grand Lispenard is ten feet from Little Italy, so we all were treated with some of the best pies we had ever tasted. As we were finishing up the last slices, I interrupted the many conversations to speak.

"To Mr. C, gone before his time and long to be remembered." I lifted my glass of Coke.

"To Mr. C," they all replied. A sudden silence overtook all of us. I noticed three guitars on music stands spread around the floor—Chris's weapons of choice. He picked one up. I don't think he intended to play; he was merely feeding a nervous habit of having his fingers running through the six strings. I remembered Johnny saying Bracko always did this. It must be a trait of great guitarists.

"It was such bad luck for him to die at such a young age," lamented Trip breaking the melancholy.

"It wasn't bad luck," shot back Neil with bitterness in his voice. Only Neil, Mary Lou, and I knew the circumstances that had led to your dad's death.

"Explain," demanded Chris. I nodded at Neil to affirm it was time to tell the others the story.

"Mr. C. first told Neil and me what happened to him a few

months ago. He often met with me to flesh out his story—to give me all the details of what happened to him and others. He said it needed to get out there—that I would be the one to do it."

"No one had been willing to listen. No one else seemed to care," added Neil.

"He seemed to be holding on to life for many reasons, the hope of Johnny's return, for Anna, and even to be there for Mary Lou and Alex. Yet, he resisted many of the pain killers offered to him so that he could maintain clarity of thought and memory. He finished telling the tale last week—the day before he died."

I took out the pieces of paper I had been carrying with me since I'd started taking down his story. This was the rough draft of the article I would publish in the *Queens Undies* and eventually circulate to a broader audience. I told them all the details about the life-saving mission that the navy had undertaken in Hiroshima—a task that ultimately cost your father his life. I gave them more information than I've even put in this diary. Perhaps, someday you'll read my whole article.

A hush fell over the group. What could be said? Nothing, but something could be sung. I picked up one of the acoustic guitars that lay nearby. Emotion often makes me act rather than think about consequences. I'm glad it did this time.

I'd been working on a poem/song about your dad, a tribute. I was nowhere near the guitarist that either Bobby Bright Eyes or Chris Delaney was, but I'd become fluent in the language of chords. And so, I played and sang.

When he passed, I cried
In the past, they had lied
When will the story be told?

I know the sorrow is real,
The good people all feel,
When will the story be told?

Unfortunately, it was all that I had, and to be honest, I didn't think that it was good. However, Chris quickly picked up on my tune and started to add poignant background notes. To my surprise, Bobby Bright Eyes grabbed the other electric guitar and complemented Chris' playing. The notes intertwined beautifully. After a few minutes of this, I returned to the same lines I had sung before. However, this time both Chris and Bobby harmonized with me. Just when I was kicking myself for not creating more lines to this ode, Chris began to sing. He sang most of my words; however, the changes were significant and accompanied by tears.

When he passed, I cried
In the past, I lied
When will the story be told?

He never was a man,
My lies cannot stand,
He deserved better from me.

Bobby immediately broke into an exceptional solo on his borrowed guitar as Chris wept uncontrollably. This had been your dad's eulogy and his farewell. Yet we all knew that something was eating at Chris's soul. His verses were about something else—someone else. I stopped playing, and Bobby soon followed suit. The room was again dead silent except for the faint hum of Trip's camera, which he promptly turned off.

"No, Trip, put it back on," sobbed Chris. "This isn't an honest documentary unless it tells the whole truth—and I'm finally ready for that."

It was then that Chris told us about his brother Andrew's death. He hadn't ever shared the story with anyone besides Trip. Even his brothers Kevin and Tommy were unaware of his deep dark secret. He was now ready to tell us, and soon he would tell the world. Perhaps then he would finally be free of guilt that had driven him from his carefree days with Delaney Brothers and into the religious life—and then to here.

"I know this story already, Chris," interrupted Trip. "You don't need to tell it again. You did nothing wrong."

"No, Trip, *all my friends* need to know the story."

He told us the story of his brother Andrew. I won't write that story down here, but I know that Trip will eventually tell the world in his film. To that end, Trip kept his camera running, as Chris requested. Mary Lou hugged him first, followed by Neil, Bobby, and me. Even Alex, woken by the commotion, joined in the group hug. We stayed like that for what seemed like forever until Chris looked up at us and smiled, a weight of a thousand pounds lifted from his shoulders.

I now understood why he couldn't play with his brothers. Why he never drank. Hell, I even think I understand why he dedicated himself to a brief religious life. He was continually seeking redemption. I guessed he had punished himself enough and had earned his way back into humanity. I don't know why, but something clicked in him last night. Perhaps, it was just sharing it with friends. We continued to talk to him, hoping even further to relieve his grief.

"You are a good person," I reassured him, "Nothing can change that."

"You saved Aylin's life," consoled Mary Lou.

"Your music has changed people's attitudes about the world," added Bobby.

"Not to mention making both of us famous," teased Trip, trying to break the somber mood with a smile.

Chris returned the grin.

"I'm thankful for your support, and actually, just getting it out has helped. I screwed up, and I own that. I will forever. I can't change what I did. But I think with all your help, I can live with it."

I realized sharing emotions brought all people together, and between your dad's last thoughts and Chris's confession, we had become bound together even tighter as a group.

Little Alex let out a loud yawn and mumbled, "Can we go home now? I'm tired." After one more hug from Mary Lou, the three of them left. Only Bobby and I remained in Trip and Chris's Lispenard apartment now. I realized we still held his guitars.

"Let's go through that song one more time. DJ, I think it has potential."

"I would be honored for you to use it."

"*I* wouldn't use it," Chris answered. Yet before I could ask why, he continued, "*We'll* use it. I'd like you and Bobby to join me permanently. I'm ready to be in a band again. I know where I can find drums and bass."

I think Chris's brothers, Kevin and Tommy, could hear my jaw drop in Connecticut. I was going to be in a band. Chris, Kevin, Tommy Delaney, Bobby Bright Eyes and me. The Delaney Brothers return.

"Of course, you know that we'll have to write a whole new tune to go with the words. You were singing the tune to 'Death of a Clown' by The Kinks."

"No wonder it sounded so damn familiar," chuckled Bobby.

"Oops." I grinned sheepishly.

"Can I stop filming yet?" questioned Trip.

Entry #65 - November 21, 1969

Chris Delaney went home. He had physically been in his parents' home since his brother Andrew's death, but this was different. He was going back to be honest with them about all of the circumstances and beg for forgiveness. Trip had met the Delaney clan and didn't doubt they would resolve every issue that had kept Chris from being a part of the family for so long. They were good people, he explained to me. (This also explained the thought behind the Chris Andrews' stage name.)

"You are going to enjoy working with Kevin and Tommy, too," Trip told me, "You'll get a kick out of them."

"Hell, I will be thrilled to play with anyone, no less the three Delaney brothers and Bobby. They are all so musically above me that it's crazy."

"Don't sell yourself short. As good as those four are, it's your songwriting that will make the group something special. Chris isn't just being good to you; he's being smart."

"Thanks."

"DJ, Chris explained to me that this is not going to be a cover band. You and he are going to write original songs. The band is going to make it on those songs, or not at all."

———◆———

Trip and I picked up Chris from the train. He looked happy, but a bit drained. I questioned him about what Trip and I had discussed—my role in the band.

"Trip explained your plan for the band. I just want you to know that whatever you want, I'm good. I'm just happy for this opportunity."

"DJ, you don't understand. *You* are my opportunity. I need you to be able to do this. I need you to be the heart and soul of this group."

"Damn, not too much pressure on the kid, Chris," interjected Trip.

"Here's the scoop. I play pretty good lead guitar."

"Chris, you're not just pretty good. You're great."

"But Bobby Bright Eyes is even better than me. Imagine the dueling solos? And sometimes, I'll switch over to keyboards and leave the leads to Bobby for some versatility."

"And I'll just play my mediocre guitar."

"DJ, I've heard you. You may not be ready for any leads, but your rhythm guitar work is solid. Your voice is good, and your songwriting exceptional. You'll carry your share of the load quite well. Do realize they'll be five of us who can sing?"

I thanked him for the compliments.

"We're not going to rush this thing. Understand? You go back to school. Graduate. Get your degree in case this whole thing falls apart. Tell Bobby to do the same thing. My brothers have to wrap up some work in Connecticut. We'll practice on weekends in the studio on Lispenard. We'll write songs—we'll create. Then next summer—boom, we come out with an album and a tour."

"How can you know that?"

"There are perks to being a one-hit-wonder—and an almost Woodstock performer."

He had no bitterness over not getting to perform at the now mythic festival. He had saved Aylin, thus reducing some of the internal self-loathing that had consumed him. Not playing at Woodstock had been the beginning of his recovery. I won't even mention that it led to his blossoming love affair with Shylo.

Yeah, things are all working out. College graduate, rock star? Could this really be my world? Now, if only Aylin can get well.

Entry #66 - November 23, 1969

I've been going over my diary trying to find lyrics and ideas for songs. Isn't this how I'm going to earn my keep? Johnny, it's hard to look back at the depression caused by you going missing, and I will keep my vow to find you.

Yet so much has changed in my life. I have a band of true friends with which to share my life. I looked back at what I wrote last week about being a brotherhood, and the term fits. But if our link is defined by those affected by the five lost souls of Those Born Free, then I just know there are others out there. Gio's secret girlfriend? Your dad's mystery visitors at the hospital?

Entry #67 – December 3. 1969

For the first time since she had been admitted to the rehabilitation center, Aylin was allowed non-family visitors. Mrs. Mac had given me regular updates, but it wasn't enough. I longed to know how she felt about me. Were her flirtatious comments just that, or did she have real feelings for me? More importantly, were her feelings overly influenced by a sense of gratitude?

We spent a great deal of my visit with small talk and silent stares, as if we were boxers in a ring trying to size up our opponent. At some point, our hands found each other and linked.

"DJ, they tell me I'm too fragile to develop any relationships right now. If I don't even know myself, how could I know another?"

"Aylin, if you only want me as a friend, I'll understand. No pressure. You don't have to make excuses."

"I'm not. The shrink told me to lay low. Otherwise . . . otherwise . . ."

"Otherwise, what?"

"Otherwise, I would be jumping your bones right here," she

teased with a seductive smile. Yet, even as she said it, she sank into a melancholy mood and looked down at the floor. The psychiatrists had dug deep into her mind, but they had not reached the core of her problem.

However, there is some good news. Aylin will be coming home for a trial run around Christmas.

42

"Come Together"
- *The Beatles*

Entry #68 – December 8, 1969

"I'M QUITTING SCHOOL," MUMBLED BOBBY as we drove to our new band's first practice. I was so excited about the coming day that the comment almost flew right over my head. I'd accelerated my academic pace so that I'd graduate after the next spring semester. Bobby, in turn, was a year younger than me and had gone at a slower pace. He still had two years more of college.

A lottery had been held the previous week to determine the order of induction into the army for those of us who were eligible. It was based on a person's date of birth. Luckily, both Bobby and I had received high numbers, which cleared one obstacle to quitting school.

"I wasn't going anywhere fast. Music is what I love, and now I have a chance to pursue it."

"But it's an education,"

"And it will still be there if this whole thing falls apart." He then surprised me with his next comment. "What about you?"

"What *about* me?"

"You do realize the whole band is waiting for us in order to hit the road."

"No."

"As we were leaving our first meeting, I heard something."

"What?"

"Chris told his brothers that his agent could get us work as early as February. DJ, as your former teacher, Chris feels an obligation that no other bandleader would ever feel."

I thought about this long and hard as we continued on our way to practice.

The practice itself was an indescribable experience. Yes, I realize my entire life has revolved around words, but now I'm at a loss.

Chris stood erect, his Stratocaster tuned to perfection. Kevin held his Fender Jazz bass and joked with his brother Tommy who sat behind his set of Slingerland drums. Bobby Bright Eyes looked up at me and smiled. He was as happy as a pig in shit. And so was I. And then I did something stupid.

Without any warning, I started to play three chords that could have been "Louie, Louie," but weren't. They had begun as that, in memory of Johnny's historic first three chords with Those Born Free. Yet, after I had repeated the A − D − E progression, I inexplicably sang into the microphone.

Wild Thing,
You make my thing ping.

After that brief outburst, I stopped—embarrassed. What the hell was I thinking? The looks on the three Delaney brothers seemed to be saying, *Are you kidding?*

Bobby's look said, *Are you trying to screw this up for us?*

"I don't know what I was thinking—sorry," I blurted out. However, I did know what I was thinking. Johnny had told me of the stupid things his bands had done with equal amounts of immaturity and silliness. In my excitement, I had tried to recreate the youthful exuberance of all your bad practices. I had failed. At least, that is what I thought until all three Delaneys started to laugh in unison.

"That's all ya got," sniggered Tommy from behind the drums. "A classic, but a bit dated." He proceeded to start singing Dionne Warwick's ballad, "Anyone Who Had a Heart," which from his mouth became "Anyone Who Has to Fart."

Kevin was next. He put down his bass and picked up one of the spare guitars and broke into Credence Clearwater Revival's "Bad Moon Rising." He didn't change the lyrics but merely sang the words while bent over *mooning* us.

Chris laughed through all this, but finally made a cut symbol to his brothers and turned to me.

"DJ, music should always be fun. When it stops being that—stop doing it."

"The Night He Died," would be our first single unless something better came along. We were reluctant to relive the sadness of Mr. C. However, nothing creative came to us. Yet, as we were about to leave the topic, Chris looked at me and smiled.

"DJ will come up with something better," declared Chris, "I know it."

Entry #69 - December 9, 1969

At practice today, Chris floated an idea. He wants us to perform a few gigs using a pseudonym.

"Until the band has enough original material to go public, we need to get some experience—without damaging our image. You and Bobby have never been before a crowd. Better to get it out of the way before the eyes of the press are on 'Chris Delaney's Group.' It would be better to make our mistakes in obscurity."

I volunteered a name—The Missing Spirits. I explained it to them.

"Mr. C saw two men at the hospital—two men we know weren't there—*missing spirits?*"

Weird but with some kind of meaning. I couldn't tell them I was also thinking of the missing spirits of Those Born Free. Perhaps, we would be inspired by you and the other four—that your spirits would be within us.

Entry #70 - December 19, 1969

It has only been weeks since the formation of the group. We

already have ten covers down pat. We know this is only a temporary gig. When we go public, it will be purely original stuff.

We redid "Heroes in the Night" with all kinds of instrumentation and changed its tempo. Chris set the ground rules. We will play this song at the beginning of our performances. Groups usually leave their best song until the end of a show. Chris wants everyone to know we are not a one-trick pony, that the best is yet to come.

We have perfected "The Night He Died" as a ballad, so we don't want it to be our first release. We all feel that our first release should be something up-tempo. With my help, Chris has written an autobiographical song, "It Brings Me Back," that hints at how music helped rescue him from the depths of depression about his brother's death.

"Where Do I Stand" is a lament for unspoken love. Yeah, it probably is inspired by my situation with Aylin. Write what you know. Another song I wrote was titled "I'm Number One." No, it is not a self-indulgent bragging song, but rather an attempt to read the mind of an anonymous young man who finds himself finally coming in first in something, but ironically, it's the draft lottery!

These songs are outstanding (if I do say so myself) for a band with less than two weeks' experience. Yet we are still searching for that blockbuster hit that will announce our existence to the world. I want to have a conversation with Aylin before telling the band about "I Could Love You, If You Live."

She comes home tomorrow.

43

"The Game of Love"
-Wayne Fontana and the Mindbenders

Diary of DJ Spinelli

Entry #71 – December 24, 1969

CHRISTMAS EVE. MOST OF US have families with whom we will spend tomorrow. However, we agreed that your mom, Mrs. Mac, and Gyp and Adele DeAngelis should not spend this night alone. Aylin and her sisters Maggie and Siobhan have spent the day helping decorate the Cippitelli home, while Neil and I were purchasing the food and beverages.

Aylin's looking pretty good, especially for someone who has been in detox for almost four months. When I say good, I mean healthy. Oh, bullshit! She looked g-ooo-d. Her reddish-brown hair almost touched her ass, and her green eyes sparkled on her beautiful facial features. Her body was perfect as a result of a concerted effort to eat well and exercise while away. To paraphrase The Troggs, "Wild Thing, you make my . . ." OK, Aylin is a wild thing, but I don't want to disrespect her by finishing my thoughts on that subject.

Initially, we had planned an intimate night. However, because of our closeness, the group swelled to include Chris, Bobby, and Trip. Bobby had told me that he could only stay a few minutes, but as the night wore on, I noticed he was still there—and attentive to Siobhan McAvoy. I guess I should have seen that coming. Aylin's younger sister is almost eighteen, and Bobby's only nineteen. Music and the *Queens Undies* had taken up much of his time, but not slowed down his libido. I might also mention that Siobhan is every bit as beautiful as her sister.

The night was punctuated by great conversation and a tremendous amount of laughter and joy–just what the doctor ordered for all of us.

Somewhere around nine, I noticed Neil nod to Trip, who immediately made an excuse to go out to his car. Neil went back to decorating the tree with Mary Lou and Alex. What happened next was amazing.

"Alex, give this one to your mother so she can put it high up on the tree," whispered Neil. The young boy complied. As Mary Lou took the richly painted globe, she remarked that it sounded like there was something in it.

"Nothing in my decorations that I know of," answered your mom, who was in on the plot. "Open it up," the rest of us yelled.

Mary Lou did just that.

"It's . . . it's a ring! Does this mean that you want to marry me?"

"Well, yes and no," answered Neil mysteriously. "I'm proposing to *both* of you. I love you and want you *both* to be my family. I want you to be my wife," pronounced Neil, and then he knelt to be eye level with Alex, "And you to be my son."

As three of them hugged, Trip popped the cork on the non-alcoholic champagne. Cups were filled and passed around. As they were ready to toast, Neil interrupted.

"Hey, you never answered me."

"What do you think, Alex?" asked Mary Lou.

"About what?"

"About having Neil as your daddy?" The boy immediately hugged Neil, who was still kneeling at his level."

"We're good," laughed Mary Lou and then turned serious and looked down at Neil. She took his face with both her hands. "And I will love you forever."

I was so excited for Neil and Mary Lou that I hardly noticed Aylin take my hand. However, I soon realized she wasn't tenderly interlocking fingers, but instead clutching them in a sort of desperation. I looked in her face and saw nothing but sheer terror.

"What is it?" I asked. Instead of answering immediately, she pulled me away from the crowd and into the kitchen. Tears were running down her face. It was only then that I noticed that we both still held the faux champagne. She now looked down at the glass.

"I'm not going to make it, DJ. I want this to be real champagne, and I want to drink it—as the first step toward getting blasted. I want to chug a bottle until it is empty." She looked at me for a reaction, and I had none. I could write prose, poetry, and lyrics for the world, but I couldn't think of a word to say to her. I tried to speak, but she cut me off.

"DJ, I understand it's not your problem."

"Yes, it is. I love you, and I have for a long time." She said nothing but held on to me as if her life depended upon it. And maybe it did.

Entry #72 – December 26, 1969

The band met today, the day after Christmas. The group has become our life. We practice every day, so our unique two-day break for a holiday brought more than the usual pre-practice banter. The Delaney brothers had gone home to Connecticut, and there were countless funny stories connected with the homecoming. They recreated all the jokes and pranks typical of a Delaney family reunion. Laughter healed many of the wounds that had kept Chris from his family for so long. It didn't hurt that the truth about Drew's death had finally come out. Chris turned a bit serious and described how they all had talked into the night. There is a saying going around, "The truth will set you free." I guess the Delaneys are free.

I had spent Christmas with Aylin. We had gone to an early mass at Sacred Heart Church in Cambria Heights. While walking in, I had a feeling of déjà vu—but it was not my déjà vu! I thought back to how you felt when you went to church with Maria. I remembered how proud you were to be seen with her. Was I unconsciously reliving your life? It's not the first time this thought crossed my mind. I'd become close with your parents. I was in a band. And I was now walking into *your* church with a beautiful girl on my arm. Too weird.

I spent the whole day with her. First, we went back to her house, and I took part in the Christmas morning joy that the three sisters and their mother created. There had been a great deal of sorrow for these four. They had lost their father and brother. They had also lost the store that had taken the lives of the Noel and Jimmy McAvoy. Adele had barely held on to the business since losing them, and then Aylin had gone into rehab. To pay for her stay, Adele McAvoy had sold Mac and Son Candy Store. Aylin felt guilty about this despite her mother's best efforts to convince her she sold it because it reminded her of her husband.

I took Aylin to my house for dinner. It was the first time my parents met the love of my life. They welcomed her with open arms. However, she was soon overwhelmed with the entire concept of a big Italian holiday dinner. After the antipasto, soup, and lasagna, she told me she thought this was too much food, even for the seventeen people who sat at the table. She had done her best to sample everything in an effort not to offend any of my relatives.

"I don't think that I even have room for dessert," Aylin told me.

"Aylin, we didn't even get to the main course yet," I said as my mother and her sisters brought in the turkey, ham, fish, and four thousand side dishes. I thought she would excuse herself and follow the ancient Roman custom of forced vomiting to make room for the food.

After the very long dinner, Aylin and I went off by ourselves and sat by my Christmas tree. Dinner had been in our finished basement as usual, and so the living room and its tree were a peaceful respite from the boisterous atmosphere a floor below.

"What do you think?" I asked her.

"I love it. They're all having so much fun. Except . . ."

"Except what, Aylin?"

"Except, I wish I got the jokes."

"Oh, that," I answered. "My uncles think that by telling the entire joke in English and then the punchline in Italian, that my cousins and I won't realize that it's an off-color joke."

She giggled at my explanation.

"They don't realize that, after all these years, we've come to understand the key phrases. I can't speak Italian, but I can curse in it thanks to those jokes!" Aylin laughed heartily before becoming serious.

"DJ, I have a little something for you."

"But we said we weren't going to do this," I objected. "I have nothing for you."

"DJ, you gave me my life. That's enough." I knew I had her gratitude. But did I have her love? I could wait. I knew she needed to get her head straight before she could think about that. She handed me a tiny box.

"It's not much," she said, hoping I wouldn't be disappointed with her gift. As I unwrapped the little green and red box and lifted the cover, I found a guitar pick. On the white pick, she had painstaking painted the letters A-Y-L-I-N very neatly.

"To remind you of me while doing the thing that you love most in this world," Aylin murmured with a big smile. I hugged her, but I held back from saying what I thought—*playing music was not what I loved most in this world.*

44

"I Love Rock and Roll"
- Joan Jett

Entry #73 - December 27, 1969

UNBELIEVABLE. BOBBY GIVES ME A call the two days after Christmas and tells me that he has a job for the band on New Year's Eve. First, I say we're not ready, but then I realize that it's not my decision. He should give Chris a call. The bottom line is that Bobby's cousin is in a spot. He is a social director for a large corporation, and a real quality band just bailed on the New Year's Eve gala. Every major local group of any talent was already working that night. He wanted to know if his cousin could help out. Bobby said yes, pending speaking to us. Bobby and I have never played in front of an audience. His cousin Paul said he had about two hours to wait for an answer.

I called Chris, and he said, "What the hell? Let's get our feet wet. Tell Bobby yes, and let's all meet at the Grand Lispenard tonight at six for rehearsal."

OK, so I was excited, but scared shitless when I arrived for our practice. Chris, Tommy, and Kevin (who have taken to renting rooms in the same place) were joking around as usual when I arrived. *Don't they ever feel any pressure?* When I actually asked them that question, Tommy drops his drumsticks, and Kevin carefully took off his bass, turned off his amp, and sat down.

"Here we go," Tommy whined.

"Damn, why didn't we warn him?" replied Kevin as if I wasn't even in the room.

"I thought you would, Kevin."

"Well, I thought you would, Tommy."

"Kevin, you are older."

"Only by eleven months."

"Still, you know what's going to happen now."

"Yup."

"Will you two stop," interrupted Chris. "I've got to calm DJ down by telling them the story of . . ."

"The Pi Epsilon Pi fraternity dance of New Year's Eve 1962," moaned Tommy and Kevin as they finished their older brother's sentence and rolled their eyes.

"I'm guessing that you two have heard the story before?" I offered.

"How many fingers and toes can you count on?" roared Tommy.

"And you can use mine when you run out," added Kevin.

They both walked out of the sound-proof studio. Kevin feigned sleeping on a couch, and Tommy went to the refrigerator and made himself a sandwich.

And Chris told his well-worn story.

I was a freshman at the University of Hartford. My friend Carl tells me he has a job for New Year's Eve. He could use another guitar to play as one of his guys had dropped out. I'm thrilled to get a paying job, and I ask about practice. He tells there is no time. Just show up at the frat house at eight with my guitar and amp.

I show up a half-hour early, and no one is there but Carl and his younger brother, Hal. Now I know that Hal also plays guitar, so where are the drummer and bass player? Notice, I said drummer and bass player—not drums and bass. That's because the actual instruments are set up and ready to go, but there are no musicians to go along with them. I ask Carl about this, and he tells me they aren't coming. Then I catch on.

"Carl, did you have a band when you accepted this job?" I ask.

"Well, not exactly," he says.

"How not exactly do you mean?"

"Well, I have Hal and you, and drums and a bass."

"But Carl, those instruments don't play themselves unless you know something I don't?"

"This isn't my first rodeo, or frat dance, my young fellow." I just stared at him incredulously.

"Chris, you have to understand what's going to happen here. These are frat guys. They are going to drink insane amounts of alcohol in a very short time period. By our second or third song, they will think that we are the greatest band on Earth."

I tried to argue but was interrupted by Carl. *"So, what do you want to play first?"*

"How about something by Everly Brothers?"

"No, numbnuts! What instrument do you want to play?"

"What the hell, I always wanted to try the drums," I answered.

Carl was right. *After fifteen minutes, we were asked by slurred voices why we weren't on tour somewhere. So, the moral of the story is, don't worry about drunken New Year's Eve audiences—they think everyone is great.*

Just as Chris finished his inspirational story, Bobby walked in the front door. The first words out of his mouth were, "I'm a little nervous."

"Did I ever tell you the story of the Pi Epsilon Pi frat party?" started Chris. Kevin rolled his eyes, and Tommy simply stuffed what remained of *his* sandwich into *Bobby's* mouth and whispered in his ear, "Shut up!"

Entry #74 - January 1, 1970

Holy shit! Every expectation that we (performing as the Missing Spirits) had of our first public performance was wrong. We went to the address given to us and found out it was a huge hall occupied by over three hundred well-dressed (and well-behaved) executives with their significant others. If they were going to get stinking drunk, it would probably take them a bit longer because they had to pretend to have a touch of class.

"You got this," Chris declared to Bobby and me as we hit our first notes. We played the twenty or so cover songs we knew well, and the audience seemed to enjoy us. We tried to discourage requests because our playlist was limited. However, in the middle of our third set, one of the big cheeses of the affair came up and asked us if we knew "Heroes in the Night" by Chris Delaney.

"Yeah, what the hell? Let's do it," spat Chris to the rest of us. We played a very different version than Chris had made famous, and it was received extremely well by the crowd. When we were done, the *biggest cheese* came over and spoke to us.

"So, Chris. . . Chris Delaney, right?" gushed the *biggest cheese* (who we found out was a record company's *biggest cheese*), "Come in my office on Monday, and we'll talk record contract and tour."

"What? How?"

"I would have recognized you anywhere. However, Dave Weissman, Bobby's adopted dad, gave me a head's up. Hiring you guys for tonight was a well-planned setup—an informal audition. We knew you would be great, but had to see about the backup band. I'm glad to tell you they were fantastic. You trained them well."

"I didn't train anyone. These guys were always great," rebuked Chris.

"OK, I'll buy that. How about you introduce yourself as Chris Delaney to these wonderful people?"

"I'm sorry. I can't do that. I'm not a solo act. We are a band— The Brotherhood Blues Band," insisted Chris smiling at us.

"Oh, I get it—because your two brothers are in the band," insisted *Mr. Biggest Cheese*.

"No, not even close," answered Chris as we took to the stage. However, Chris asked me if I could introduce this set. I'm guessing he was trying to take a back seat to point out the whole band concept. Little did he know that his brothers, Bobby, and I had discussed *the* band name when he wasn't in the room. We had all agreed that we liked the Brotherhood Blues Band for the implications it had to our conversation the week before. OK, the "Blues" part was Bobby's idea. We thought of all the shit that each of us had been through individually and decided that "blues" fit in a very non-traditional way.

So, as we got ready to perform, Chris honestly expected me to introduce us as the Brotherhood Blues Band. Instead, I stepped to the mic and clearly announced the official name that four of us had agreed on.

"I'd like to introduce you to *Chris Delaney and* The Brotherhood Blues Band."

45

"Wrote a Song for Everyone"
- John Fogerty

Entry #75 – January 14.1970

THIS IS MY FIRST ENTRY since my big New Year's Eve news. We have all temporarily taken rooms at the Grand Lispenard. We now rehearse for ten hours a day. Incredibly, we've come up with ten good original songs, so we'll be going into the studio sometime at the beginning of February, and then hitting the road in March for a tour of ten cities.

What goes unsaid is that both Bobby and I have dropped out of college. We can always go back if this whole thing flops, but it's not going to—we're too good. Kevin and Tommy continued to hone their skills even after Chris left them. If you ask them, they'll tell you they always knew he'd be back. Bobby Bright Eyes is my Bracko, my superstar guitarist. Having heard both, I couldn't tell you who was better. Of course, there is Chris, superb guitarist, keyboardist, lead singer, and co-songwriter. I just do my best.

Today, I went to see Aylin. What little free time I have, I spend with her. We have grown close—very close. I live for the moments when we can share a passionate kiss or simply hold hands. She still holds back. Her addiction counselors have told her to go slow. But is there still something—some emotion—some memory or feeling that keeps her from fully giving of herself? I can go slow. She's worth it.

THOSE BORN FREE Tape – June 14, 1967

"Johnny, get me another tape from the case. This one is almost full." (Jimmy Mac)

"Damn, Jimmy Mac, you have a shitload of these things full—and another shitload of blanks." (Johnny)

"You know, cassette tapes are very fragile. They can deteriorate over time." (Tinman)

"Thank you, Professor Tinman. Another damn lesson learned." (Jimmy Mac)

"He's right, Jimmy Mac." (Johnny)

"I know, numbnuts. You think I'm stupid?" (Jimmy Mac)

"Well, now that you mention it." (Gio)

"Every time we finish practice, I put the tape in my mother's cedar-lined hope chest. I'm not hiding them, but she hasn't used it in years." (Jimmy Mac)

"They do look in good shape." (Johnny)

"Yeah, just waiting to be converted to vinyl for our boxed set." (Jimmy Mac)

"Somebody please tell Bracko to stop playing 'You've Got to Hide Your Love Away.'" (Gio)

"Gio, do you even complain in your sleep?" (Bracko)

"Bracko—with a putdown? The world must be coming to an end." (Johnny)

Entry 76 – January 15, 1970

Aylin showed me something amazing today. Her mother decided to pack up the house so she can sell it. While packing, she came upon Jimmy Mac's treasure trove of Those Born Free tapes. They are perfectly preserved in her mother's hope chest. In the two-and-half years since the band ceased to exist, we only found a few tapes and wondered where the rest were.

Here is the motherlode—all Those Born Free's original songs. The labeling system is not great, so it will take time to go through them. I'm leaving soon for our tour, so the responsibility falls upon Aylin. Johnny, I have to tell you that I'm facing a moral dilemma here. There are at least seven great songs, and I'm tempted to use them with my band. Aylin and I talked long about what to do.

"DJ, you can use these for your recording session. You told me that there were great songs that the boys were ready to release."

"But, Aylin, they're not my songs."

"Well, some of them are."

"Yeah, maybe Words of Doubt, Enchanted Days, and parts of others."

"But there are so many other great ones. I should know. I was there when they were recorded right here in my basement. Use them, DJ, use them all."

"Aylin, you and I know that Jimmy Mac did very little of the writing."

"Yeah, I know, I don't own them. But this isn't a legal matter, DJ."

"Yeah, but I just don't feel right about the whole thing."

"DJ, that means the music is as dead as my brother Jimmy."

She started to cry.

Johnny, those are your songs, and now they are orphans. They will stay that way. I'll never use them—unless you tell me I can, or I know for sure that you can't.

Entry #77 - January 16, 1970

Chris, Neil, Mary Lou, and I went over to Aylin's after practice to listen to the tapes. I almost wrote down that this was a tape party. But, Johnny, nothing we do concerning Those Born Free is ever a party, but rather a memorial.

Because they were mine, we did pull out the ones labeled "Words of Doubt" and "Enchanted Days." Johnny, it brought me back to that day when I was part of the band—playing the harmonica on both tunes I'd written. You asked me to go into the studio when the band recorded them. At practice, you called them DJ's songs. This tape made it abundantly clear to me that songs like "Thief of My Forever" and "Gypsy Rose" are not "DJ songs"—reinforcing my decision never to use them. Chris and I even discussed it.

"From what I have heard, I know we could put out a whole Those Born Free album. But it just wouldn't be right."

"Yeah, I was thinking the same thing," I agreed.

"Well, we'll just keep looking for Johnny and Gio, and when we find them, we'll bring them into the band and do their songs."

"Chris, if the story that Mr. C told us is true about the two guys in the hospital—then, unfortunately, we are only looking for Johnny."

"Yeah, dammit," Chris agreed.

"They did an excellent cover of 'Catch the Wind.'"

"Johnny always said that song was special to them—that they would catch the wind to success. He used to tell Maria the same thing. Chris, you would have liked Maria.

"I'm sure."

"They never did catch that wind, and now they are . . ."

"What is it, DJ?"

"I'm not sure, but I just got an idea for some lyrics, and I want to write them down before I forget. I'm not sure how this is going to go, but start thinking of some riffs and hooks. I'll meet you back at your place in three hours or so."

"I don't get it, DJ."

"Well, we don't feel right doing one of Those Born Free's songs—but how about doing a song about Those Born Free?"

Yes, Johnny, we wrote a song about all of you.

46

"Dancing on the Other Side of the Wind"
- Chris Delaney and the Brotherhood Blues Band

"We were living lives of passion,
Never wanting to go slow,
Never worrying 'bout tomorrow
Never knowing where to go.

We were drifting on the winds,
Living for the day.
We kept asking each other,
Who knows the way?

We were dancing,
We were dancing,
On the other side of the wind.

We listened to our hearts,
Never thinking we had sinned.
We went down together,
Throwing caution to the wind.

We were brothers in the music,
Bonded in the song,
Us against the world
Nothing could go wrong

We were dancing,
We were dancing,
On the other side of the wind.

47

"We've Got Tonight"
- *Bob Seger and the Silver Bullet Band*

Entry #78 - February 1, 1970

HEARING THE BAND'S TAPES IS bringing so much of you—all of you—back to me. Should I feel guilty living the life that you were struggling so hard to attain? Next week we go into the studio to record an album. We are calling it *Dancing on the Other Side of the Wind* because that is the first single. If it's a hit, Johnny, in a sense, you will have made it. The song is all about you—all of you.

I don't have time to write anymore. Everyone is coming over here to the Grand Lispenard for a final get-together before we leave for two months. The whole Brotherhood will be there— almost. The entire band and their wives and girlfriends. This includes Kevin and Tommy's wives and surprise, Siobhan McA- voy, who was now getting pretty serious with Bobby Bright Eyes. Chris was alone; Shylo is still in the army. Neil came with Mary Lou, but they left Alex with your mom, who was invited but decided not to come. We know she is still grieving. How- ever, her time with Alex helps.

And of course, Aylin will be here. The goodbyes will be tough. She still needs support—spiritual, mental, emotional. She is so fragile. However, she gets angry with me if I even suggest not going on tour and staying with her.

"Johnny would kick your ass into next Tuesday if you passed up this opportunity to record and tour. Think about it, I'll be your top groupie. I want you to go and do whatever it is that you do in that band."

"Ouch, you know what I do—rhythm guitar and background vocals."

"And songwriter, you jackass! The band will go far because of what you write."

"I hope so."

"You don't get how good you are. I hear the lines to 'Dancing on Other Side of the Wind,' and I'm back there with them—all of them."

"Yeah, but most people who hear the song won't know what it's about."

"They don't need to—yet."

"Someday, we will tell everyone. Someday when we know for sure about Johnny and Gio."

"And when Mad Guy Provenzano isn't still around. It's not like he is going to figure out what this song is all about, but someone might, and then tell the dumb shithead."

"That's true."

"Now come here, my dumb shithead, and let me show you how much I'm going to miss you. Better yet, DJ, let's go up to your room."

"But, Aylin, it's a mess."

"Hey, you naïve numbnut, it's going to be a bigger mess after we're done."

"Oh."

Alone in my tiny cubicle in the Grand Lispenard, we shared passionate kisses.

"Aylin, I'm going to miss you."

"Yeah, me too, but shut up and kiss me again."

"But I'll be gone at least six weeks."

"And then we'll have the rest of our lives together."

"Really, Aylin?"

"Really."

"But how are we going to survive ten weeks apart?"

"Because we'll think of this."

Aylin stepped away from him and lifted the straps of her one-piece dress from her shoulders. It slowly fell to the floor. She moved closer.

"And DJ, we've got tonight."

48

"Memories"
- Elvis Presley

LISTENING TO THE TAPES REMINDED Aylin of the brother she lost. They made her laugh, and they made her cry. They made her remember and, for some reason, also helped her to forget. Mostly, they filled the lonely days while she waited for DJ's return.

———

THOSE BORN FREE Tape – Jan 1967

"DJ fuckin' Spinelli, what the hell are you staring at?" (Jimmy Mac)
"Nothing, Jimmy Mac, nothing." (DJ)
"Now, you're calling my sister Aylin's ass nothing?"(Jimmy Mac)
"Er, no, I mean, I wasn't looking at nothing." (DJ—stuttering)
"Anything." (Tinman)
"What?" (DJ and Jimmy Mac in unison)
"'I wasn't looking at nothing' is a double negative. You're supposed to say, 'I wasn't looking at anything.'" (Tinman)
"Shut the fuck up, Tinman. He's scoping out my kid sister's ass, and you're giving us a lesson in grammar?" (Jimmy Mac)
"You're right, Tinman. If I'm going to be a writer, I have to be more careful." (DJ)
"Shut the fuck up. My little sister's honor is at stake, and you two nerds are still talking grammar." (Jimmy Mac)

Aylin smiled as she sidled over to a mirror and looked at her ass.

"So, DJ, this is what first captured your attention."

Diary of DJ Spinelli

Entry # 79 – March 3, 1970

We've been working on the album for four weeks now and completed it a few minutes ago. These are the first moments I've had free to write.

I think that the album is goddamn great—and I'm not in the slightest bit prejudice. "Dancing on the Other Side of the Wind" is going to be the first single. If that works out well, "I Could Love You, If You Live" will follow. The rest of the album is flushed out by songs I have mentioned: "The Night He Died" (with new chords), "I'm Number One," "The Music Brings Me Back," "Where Do I Stand," "Words of Doubt," and "Heroes in the Night."

Aylin is getting a lot of support from her family and friends. She also spends a great deal of time listening to the tapes. Sometimes, she is alone. Other times, Neil and Mary Lou come by to listen. They leave Alex with your mom because the band's language was not for little kid consumption.

I called Aylin, and she told me she loved me again, and I answered her the same.

49

"So You Want To Be a Rock and Roll Star"
-The Byrds

Entry # 80 - April 29, 1970

IT'S BEEN SEVEN WEEKS SINCE I've had the time to write in this book. So much has happened.

Johnny, we are goddamn stars! "Dancing on the Other Side of the Wind" is number one, and "I Could Love You, If You Live" was released a week ago and is heading in the same direction. Our album is in the top ten on Billboard's charts. We even get interviewed.

"So, guys, 'Dancing on the Other Side of the Wind' seems to be referring to a specific musical group or just a group of people who come to a bad ending. Could you expand on this issue?"

"Sorry, the words are there for interpretation by the listener. I'll say no more," answered Chris.

"But Chris, this tragedy that you hint at—is it real?"

"It could be that the passage of time brings disappointment to everyone," interrupted Kevin.

"Yeah, that's it,' chimed in Tommy, wanting to be seen and heard on TV.

"Usa tu imaginación," whispered Bobby Bright Eyes.

"Does he speak English?" The interviewer eyed Bobby Bright Eyes and looked perplexed.

"Zent ir narish aun mshuge," replied Bobby and continued with a big smile—and in perfect English, "I'm guessing you don't speak 'Jewban?'"

"Huh?" was the very unprofessional reply of the interviewer.

"I am Cuban, raised by Jewish parents, so I speak Spanish, Yiddish, and English. It's a long story that I'm saving for my memoir."

This sidebar with Bobby had effectively ended any conversation about the meaning of our song. That was the way we wanted it. The story of Those Born Free would never be told until you and Gio are found.

50

"Riet in My Heart"
- *Those Born Free*

THOSE BORN FREE tape – May 1967

". . .yes, there's a Riet in my heart, and it's making me go wild— *forever." (Gio singing – fade out)*

"*Yo, mama, that was great!" (Jimmy Mac)*

"*Thanks." (Gio)*

"*Gio, I understand overpowering love causing your heart to explode, like a riot—and the tune is great, but…" (Tinman)*

"*Go ahead. You've wanted to say it all day." (Jimmy Mac)*

"*Riot is spelled r-i-o-t not r-i-e-t." (Tinman)*

"*Yeah, Gio, explain that!" (Johnny-facetiously)*

"*Yeah, Gio, you're making us public school guys look bad—like we can't spell. Johnny, fix the spelling on the tape." (Jimmy Mac)*

"*No! It stays!" (Gio)*

"*I agree." (Johnny)*

"*OK, no big deal—poetic license." (Tinman)*

"*What kind of license?" (Gio)*

"*He's saying you win. The title is 'R-i-e-t in My Heart.'" (Johnny)*

"*Damn right, I win. It's my song and she's. . ." (Gio)*

"*OK, Bracko, let's take 'Riet in My Heart' from the top again." (Johnny)*

———◆———

"What was that all about?" asked Mary Lou, trying to understand the conversation.

"Maybe, it was like the Guess Who song," added Neil.

"What'ya mean?"

"Well, Mary Lou, the group Guess Who released a song 'Undun,' which misspelled the title—'U-n-d-u-n' instead of 'U-n-d-o-n-e,'" explained Neil.

"No. 'Undun' only came out six months ago. That would mean that Gio dreamed up the misspelling idea first. That would never have happened, and. . ."

"And what, Aylin?" questioned Mary Lou.

"There is something in Gio's voice that tells me this is very important to him. Also, Johnny's tone tells me that he 'gets' the meaning of the misspelling."

"I guess we'll never know."

"No, Neil, we won't—unless we find Johnny."

Aylin was missing DJ, but the time spent with Neil and Mary Lou helped ease the loneliness. She wanted their meetings together to last at least until DJ returned, and so she very seldom listened to the tapes alone. However, as she was putting the tapes away that night, she noticed a tape in the box with the title "Guest-starring DJ Spinelli." Knowing the band, they had written that label sarcastically. However, it did mean that she would hear DJ on this tape—and she needed a little DJ time right then.

———◆———

THOSE BORN FREE Tape – June 15, 1967

"Hey, Johnny, you see those two assholes Timpani and Crespo hanging out at Tino's?" (Gio)

"I wouldn't be saying that too loud. They are still Mad Guy's main men." (Johnny)

"C'mon, ya gotta laugh at Crespo still having a pompadour and long sideburns here in 1967." (Gio)

"And wearing sunglasses, day and night." (Jimmy Mac)

"You don't know why he does that? His two eyes are different colors." (Johnny)

"Heterochromia iridium." (Tinman)

"What the fuck, Tinman? Another lesson? Are you normal?" (Gio)

"As a matter of fact—yes." (Tinman)

"In my opinion, you have a screw loose." (Gio)

"Hey, don't let the facts get in the way of your opinions." (Tinman)

"You keep talking, but I won't keep listening." (Gio)

"I'd insult you back, but I don't think you'd get it." (Tinman)

"Enough, you two. We don't have time for a rank-out session." (Johnny)

"But it was fun to watch. Right, Bracko?" (Jimmy Mac)

"Yeah." (Bracko)

"Thanks for that lengthy contribution to our conversation, Bracko." (Johnny)

"OK." (Bracko)

"Let's take it from the top with 'Words of Doubt' while we have DJ here to play the harmonica. We'll use that as one of the songs for our audition when Vinnie the Cat sets it up." (Johnny)

"If it's this week, I can't make it as a guest performer. I got some family stuff. Sorry. But tell me about these two thugs Crespo and Timpani? You know I like to hear Heights' stories." (DJ)

"DJ, we don't use the word thugs. We prefer assholes." (Johnny)

(laughs from the band)

"Well, Sammy Crespo, with his heterochromia something, sideburns, and pompadour looks and acts like a jerk. And get this, Timpani is now calling himself Salvatore Timpone to sound less like a wop." (Gio)

"Timpani or Timpone—he's an ass" (Johnny)

"But he is the smarter of the two jerks." (Gio)

"If a picture is worth a thousand words, in his case, they all spell 'u-g-l-y.'" (Jimmy Mac)

"Yeah, if that's not a mask he's wearing—he should get one." (Gio)

"Anyway, as I was saying before being interrupted—Crespo and Timpani or excuse me, Timpone, are Mad Guy's superstars." (Johnny)

"You forgot to mention the giant port-wine birthmark all over the left side of Timpani's face." (Gio)

"Probably the reason they're so mean is that they can't get girls to talk to them." (Jimmy Mac)

"Whatever it is, you don't want to be messing with them." (Johnny)

"Nope." (Bracko)

"Now, let's get back to work. DJ hit that harmonica." (Johnny)

Aylin turned off the tape. She now understood everything that happened to her brother—and to her. An explosion of emotions overcame her—remorse, fear, sadness, and decidedly, rage. She fell to her knees and pounded the floor with closed fists. Tears streamed from her eyes as she crawled over to her brother's dormant drum set and removed one long unused drumstick. Caressing it, she wept for Jimmy Mac as she had never done before. And she knew what she had to do.

Diary of DJ Spinelli

Entry #83 – April 30, 1970

I'm seeing Aylin tonight. Our tour returned to New York, and we will be playing at the Fillmore East. Can you believe it? We'll be on the same stage as all the greats like Hendrix, The Dead, and The Doors. Aylin is going to be in the front row. Kevin and Tommy's wives are coming, and Siobhan is coming to be with Bobby Bright Eyes.

The biggest surprise is that Shylo can make it now that she is out of the army. She's even bringing old army buddies to meet the band. We are all getting together at four for dinner and a reunion. The entire Brotherhood will be there except for Neil, who has to work. Mary Lou and Neil will catch up with us at the show. It's going to be great. Johnny, this one's for you.

51

"Foxy Lady"
- Jimi Hendrix

THE BLACK DRESS WAS SO tight that it appeared painted on, and five-inch 'do-me' stiletto heels accented her long legs. Her auburn hair was parted on one side and hung almost over one eye. The thick black eyeliner made her bright green eyes explode from her face and give a come-hither look. There was no doubt that she was desirable to any man she passed. It was what she wanted.

However, the entire costume was meant for one man and one man only—and it was not her boyfriend DJ Spinelli. Tonight, Aylin was dressed to kill.

———◆———

DJ had one eye on the door and one eye on the people around him. Aylin had not arrived yet, and that worried him. He kept telling himself she would make it, and they would finally be together.

However, part of him was distracted. Shylo's friends were both interesting and entertaining, an unusual pair who had suffered debilitating injuries in Vietnam. That was how Shylo had come to know them. She treated their wounds and saved their lives. Yet, Dr. Shyanne "Shylo" Lopez had saved many lives and not become friends with all of them. These two had such humor and personality that they had bonded with her immediately.

As soon as she mustered out of the service, Shylo made a beeline to New York City. Chris Delaney, the love of her life, would return from touring and come home to the big apple—and her. However, while she waited for him, she had renewed her friendship with Goody Barlow and Leo Leonardo. Of course, it had to be her initiative to find them because the two enlisted men had never even known her real name.

Goody and Leo were both attending college on the GI bill. They were inseparable because Goody was the "eyes" for his blind friend, and Leo, in turn, was more mobile than the one-legged Goody.

"Hey, Goody, point me toward Chris Delaney. I don't want to be seen talking to the second string." Before anyone could take offense, Goody cut in and whispered.

"When he gets rude like that, I face him toward a wall and make him look stupid."

"Hey, I'm not deaf! I heard that, Goody. You know, sometimes the wall is more interesting than you." Then both vets broke into boisterous laughter.

"OK, which one is DJ?" Goody turned him toward DJ, and they both shook his hand.

"Next, the twins, Kevin and Tommy," said Leo.

"But we're not twins," responded Tommy.

"You look the same to me," said Leo. "Get it? Just a little blind humor." The entire group laughed.

Next, it was Bobby Bright Eyes' turn.

"Y dónde está el gran guitarrista?" started Leo.

"Leo, stop showing off," interrupted Goody.

"Hablas Espanol?" returned Bobby.

"Sí," answered Leo.

"OK, what he said was, 'Where is the great guitarist?'" translated Goody

"So, you speak it too?" responded an amazed Bobby.

"Yeah, if we are going to be lawyers in this city, we figured it would be a good skill to have," declared Goody, and Leo nodded agreement.

"It is amazing to meet two buddies who went through all of this together," said DJ, fascinated by the two.

"There were four of us."

———◆———

Happy hour had just begun at the Top Cat Bar. Aylin had done some research and knew this was where she would find who she was looking for. She surveyed the entire scene and spotted him. There was no doubt—the out of style pompadour and the sideburns and the mixed color eyes—Sammy Crespo. She had to be alluring, but not too obvious.

———◆———

Bobby Milano and Artie Simmons sat at the bar. Just turning 18, the two were finally able to drink legally in New York State, an ability they had taken to the extreme by downing a half a dozen drinks before the happy hour had begun. They were the first to notice the arrival of a stunning woman who had just taken a seat at the bar.

"Look at that! Holy shit, you don't see *that* in this kinda place too often," gushed Simmons.

"I agree," babbled Milano.

"I'd like a piece of that."

"You and everyone else."

"Bobby, what the hell does that mean?"

"She's easy, Artie, very easy—young and very easy."

"You know her?"

"Aylin something or other. McKay, McCarthy. One of those mick names."

"If I wasn't so drunk. . ."

"You wouldn't do shit with her. I'm sure she has some standards, Artie."

"Oh yeah, watch me." With that, Artie Simmons stood up and proceeded to fall flat on his face.

Giggling, Bobby Milano picked his friend up and shook his head.

"Time to leave?" snorted Artie.

"Time to leave." agreed Bobby as he helped his friend out the door. Maybe your mom won't notice you're drunk when I bring you home. They both laughed.

———◆———

"McAvoy, Aylin McAvoy?" murmured Sammy to the bartender Vic.

"Could be. Do you know her?" The bartender's answer was noncommittal.

"I know *of her*. And I think I will get to know her a little bit better right now."

Sammy winked at her and was not surprised when she winked back. After all, he was the top dog in this place. The object of his attention was in the process of deciding what drink to order when Sammy, with a slight wave of his hand, indicated to the bartender to put it on his tab and moved to the stool next to Aylin.

"What are you having, little lady?"

"Oh, I don't know. What's good?" Aylin had to hide her repulsion to everything about Sammy Crespo. This would take the greatest acting job of her life.

"I prefer Jack Daniels on the rocks."

"Then that's what I'll have," tittered Aylin, knowing full well that every time Crespo turned away, she would pour her drink into his. She had to have all her senses to do this right. She would have him drunk and alone as soon as possible.

"Here you go, young lady," snapped the bartender handing her the drink and looking at Sammy with veiled disgust.

"Keep them coming, Vic." Crespo moved his hand to the small of Aylin's back.

Aylin had been with many men in her life, something she had come to regret. However, she would play the part of the slut one last time. It would not be easy because of all that he was— and all that he had done.

As the Jack Daniels readily flowed, Aylin consumed none of it, but continued to play the part of an inebriated bimbo that she knew so well from her past life. Crespo didn't notice because he was busy pawing her.

"Have you got a cozier place where we can take this to the next level?" Aylin suggested.

As they entered Sammy's car for the short ride to his apartment, Aylin was torn between the fear of being in a car with someone who was blind drunk and her total loathing for what she was doing. She placed her hand on his thigh and seductively stroked it, always moving closer to his blossoming crotch. She could only continue if she remembered why she was here.

For three years, Aylin McAvoy's life had been hell. There had been drinking, and there had been more drugs than she could remember. There had been men—bad men who had shared a bed with her and treated her like dirt. There had been the near-death experience at Woodstock.

And then there had been DJ. Like a bright light shining through clouds, he had come into her life and loved her. Yet as much as she thought she loved him, her mind had been torn apart by something she could never understand—until she heard the tape. The description of Sal Timpani and Sammy Crespo had brought it all back—brought back that night.

On August 15, 1967, Aylin had exited out her bedroom window on the second floor. She used an old clothesline to let herself down to street level. It was then a short walk to her family's candy store. If she got there a few minutes after closing, her dad would be in the back doing paperwork, and her brother would slip her some of the teen magazines that she so loved. Her dad scolded her about the loss of profit, and so she depended on her brother Jimmy Mac to provide her with the contraband pages. Sometimes she blackmailed him about something she knew he had done—but most of the time, it was just a loving bond between brother and sister that motivated the exchange.

Aylin had arrived at the store at 9:10 p.m. At first, she thought there were some lingering customers still milking the last sips of their egg cream. She crossed the threshold of the store and peered above the stand that held the magazines.

She saw the first shots.

The reality of that night had finally come back to her. There were two of them. Her brother had hit one masked man with a baseball bat, but then the other had shot him in the chest. The victim of Jimmy Mac's bat had then ripped off his mask to breathe. She had seen his face—the pompadour, the sideburns, the different colored eyes—the same ones that now stared at her—Sammy Crespo.

Her father leaped over the counter to save his son and tore the mask off the shooter. She remembered seeing briefly the port-wine stain that Those Born Free had joked about on the tape now revealed him to be Sal Timpani. Her father pummeled the bastard, but the forgotten Sammy Crespo had taken aim at her father's head and blown a hole in it.

There had been silence while her brother and father lay dying. She looked at the faces of the murderers—and walked away. She hadn't called the police. She hadn't gone home to her mother. Instead, she had roamed the streets of the Heights filled with fear and horror. When she did finally return home hours later, her mind was blank. All that she had witnessed had been lost. The terror had bored itself into the inner recesses of her mind. There it festered until it destroyed its host and created three years of insanity.

But now everything was clear. The burdens had been lifted. Now was the time to make things right.

———◆———

It was almost 5 o'clock when DJ started to get nervous because Aylin had not yet made it to their pre-concert dinner in Manhattan. He drifted off from the group and found a payphone. He knew that Neil would be home from work and was hoping to get in touch with him before he left to pick up Mary Lou.

"Neil? How ya doing buddy?"

"Hey, DJ, can't wait to see you guys perform tonight."

"Yeah, Neil. I got a big favor to ask."

"Anything for you, star."

"Aylin isn't here yet, and I'm worried. Can you find her?"

"I'll get right on it. Don't worry about a thing."

———◆———

Neil Connaughton hit the streets. He prided himself on investigative skills. Someday he would be a detective on the NYPD. He started at Aylin's house and ascertained she had borrowed her mother's car. She wouldn't do that if she were going to meet DJ in Manhattan. She was a relatively new driver, and Manhattan was not an easy place to maneuver. No, she must be someplace local. He would scour the Heights for the distinctive family station wagon of the McAvoys that still had "Mac's Candy Store" painted on the side.

Periodically, he stopped kids playing in the street and asked if they had seen her car pass. He followed a path from her home on 114th Ave to Linden Blvd. There he found a few girls playing double-Dutch in front of A - Z Hardware, who had seen her turn onto Linden and head west. He knew she would not cross over Springfield Boulevard. Though there were very few fights any more, Cambria Heights was still a town in upheaval, and west of the line was not a place Aylin would go.

Then he spied it—the Top Cat Bar, the last bar in the white section of the Heights. He hoped he was wrong. This was a hangout of the Provenzano gang. Answers were not going to come easily in this place.

"I'm looking for my sister," he lied and then described Aylin. It seemed as if everyone in the bar was laughing at this, and then went back to billiards and warm beers.

"Get the hell out of here—we have no use for your kind," screamed the bartender. Neil suspected he was putting on a show for the patrons. This act was confirmed when the bartender winked at him but simultaneously announced he was putting out the garbage. The crowd laughed, taking it as an insult to Neil.

As he escorted Neil toward the door, the bartender spoke fast and under his breath. "That dirtbag Sammy Crespo took her to his apartment."

"Was she drunk?"

"No, I served her quite a few drinks, but I noticed she disposed of them in various ways when Sammy wasn't looking. The jerk probably drank twice as much as he thought he did."

"Was she having fun?"

"No, she was coming on to him—like she was trying to seduce him, but damn that girl looked mean." They exited the bar and stood on the quieter street.

"You know where Sammy lives?" Neil asked, lowering his voice.

"Corner of 114th Avenue and 224th Street," answered Vic.

"Thanks, but why are you doing this?"

"Hasn't that McAvoy family had enough pain?"

"Wait a minute! You knew who she was?"

"Aylin McAvoy."

"Did anyone else know?"

"Only one other person—Sammy."

"Oh shit!"

Neil started back to his car but turned one last time. He wondered why a Provenzano employee would be so helpful.

"Why—" he started, but Vic already knew the question.

"I hate the bastards. You remember that band that played at the Driftwood three years ago when it got raided, and later they all either died or went missing?"

"Yeah."

"Well, I never bought into the whole story of coincidences. I only pretended so I could feed my family—and maybe stay close enough to find the truth. I do *own* the Top Cat, and I need the gang's business. But what happened to those guys bothered me."

"That's very noble of you," sneered Neil sarcastically.

"No, it isn't. There was one other victim of that whole fiasco."

"Yeah, the bartender, Vinnie something-or-other. Did you know him?"

"Vinnie 'The Cat' Catalano, or as I called him Vincent—my son."

5:21 p.m.

"DJ, where the hell were you all this time?"

"Oh, just making a phone call, Kevin."

"Wait until you hear this, DJ?" Tommy interrupted.

"These two guys are from Cambria Heights."

"Maybe they knew Johnny and the guys," said Chris, suddenly interested in the conversation.

"Johnny who?" said Goody.

"Johnny Cipp."

"John Cippitelli?"

"Well, yeah, but everyone called him Johnny Cipp back in high school."

DJ was now interested.

"Oh, you must mean the son," said Leo.

"Yeah, we met the father when we had a one night stay at St. Albans Naval Hospital."

"Wait, weren't you guys in the army?" asked DJ.

"Yeah, but Shylo snuck us in for a night so our families could visit. It was all hush-hush. Records were fudged and stuff," said Goody.

"Yeah, Thanks again, Shylo," said Leo, and he waved to her. Unfortunately, she was not where he thought she was, and he waved at a blank wall. The table laughed only after he admitted that he did it on purpose.

"Wait a minute. *Two soldiers who were there and not there because of Shylo.* Could Mr. Cippitelli in his drugged state have meant 'Shylo' when he said 'Halo?'" It was all coming together for DJ.

"Yes," said Chris, who was the only other one there who knew the story.

"Did you tell Mr. C anything about his son?" DJ could not get the words out fast enough.

"You mean, you don't know? Did the message die with him? Oh, Goody, we didn't do right by Chinx." Leo now looked depressed.

"Chinx?"

"Chinx, aka Greg Cincotta, made a death bed confession that Guy Provenzano had wanted him to kill the two remaining members of some band called Those Born Free. Provenzano said he had the juice to keep Chinx out of the army and jail. Chinx turned him down, and he paid the price with his life— he died in 'Nam, saving *our* lives."

"What did you tell Johnny's father?" blurted out DJ who grew impatient.

"That Provenzano had murdered this other kid Gio and that his son Johnny was alive and on the run. In fact, Chinx—or Greg as Johnny knew him—had secretly helped Johnny get a ride to the Jersey Turnpike."

"Holy shit!" was the only comment from DJ as he ran from the room.

"DJ, The Fillmore!" yelled Chris, but DJ hadn't heard. He was busy getting in a cab. He had to get to Aylin and tell her what he knew."

5:46 p.m.

Inside the second floor apartment of Sammy Crespo, Aylin felt her time to act approaching. She could only take so much garlic and beer breath kisses and slobbering hands. Pushed against a wall, she started to reach for the gun she had removed from her late father's security box. Slowly she tried to lift it daintily from her purse. She moved ever so carefully so as not to alert the bastard. As it had just started to crest the rim of her purse, Crespo moved suddenly in an act of unbridled lust and pumped his groin into her already trapped body. The gun fell to the floor.

"I should have expected this," sneered Sammy

"You know that a girl has to protect herself, you know with all these *moulies* around." Aylin was not racist, but she suspected that Sammy was and that her explanation would hold up.

"Nice try, Aylin."

"Oh shit!"

"Did you think I didn't know who you were?"

"No, I just didn't think that any of you assholes were smart enough to remember me." With her deception uncovered, she chose to bare her real feelings. Her intense anger had now subjugated her fear. Venom dripped from her every pour.

"You want to kill me, don't you?" Sammy teased, holding the gun in his left hand.

"You and all of your fuckin' friends."

"Yeah, but I have your gun—and mine." Tucking her gun in his belt, he pulled out his Glock and waved it toward her.

"So, now what?"

"Well, first, we are going to have some fun. Then depending upon how good you are to me, I'll decide if your death will be quick or slow. Then you can join your brother and all his goddamn band friends in hell."

"All of them?" Aylin was now startled.

"Well, almost all of them. We're still looking for that Cipp asshole."

"Johnny's alive?"

"Not for long."

"Hey, numbnuts, it's been three years. If you could've found Johnny, you would have." She smiled.

"If that's what you want to believe, that's fine. OK, you little whore, let's get down to business."

"If I wanted you, I'd be more than you could handle," Aylin hissed.

"Well, let's just find out about that."

"Now, why the hell would I fuck you if you are going to kill me anyway?"

"Because if you don't, I'll kill you and then fuck Siobhan and Maggie before I kill them. Do you think I don't know about your sisters? Hell, maybe I'll even do your mom."

"You bastard," she yelled and charged him. Aylin reached into her bra and pulled out a four-inch kitchen knife that she had hidden there. Caught by surprise, Crespo did not react until she had plunged the weapon into his left shoulder. His right arm, however, was uninjured. He delivered a powerful uppercut to her abdomen, followed by a crushing blow to her face. Aylin fell to the floor into a rapidly forming puddle of her own blood.

"I hope that mess doesn't interfere with my fun," roared Crespo. As he stepped toward her prone body, she kicked at him with her stiletto heels. He caught both her feet in his hands and removed each of the erstwhile weapons. He then lowered himself to the floor and pulled up her dress.

As Crespo's body pressed against hers, she resisted losing consciousness. She pushed him away until his two powerful arms pinned her to the floor. She tried to think. Reeling from pain, Aylin searched for something, anything to ward off the attack. As Crespo held her down, she looked him in the eyes and spat blood into his face. Furious, he released her right arm so that he could deliver another crushing blow to her face.

Now that Aylin lay motionless, feigning a blackout, Sammy moved to unbuckle his pants. As he allowed her right arm to go free, she stealthily probed for a weapon. As Crespo's attempted to lower his pants, she found one. Tightening her grip around the toe of her stiletto, she lifted it and, in one swift motion, plunged it into Crespo's right eye.

"You bitch, you bitch," he screamed. Aylin laughed out loud.

"I got the good one, you know, the blue one."

"You bitch, you bitch!" In severe pain, he rolled off her and onto the floor, clutching his damaged eye.

"You ain't seen nothing yet," she answered as she pulled his abandoned Glock. She fired the first shot into his chest. "Isn't that where your asshole buddy shot my brother?"

"Aylin!" A voice in the distance called her name, but it did not register with her crazed mind.

"And these are for Gio and Tinman." She shot out both his kneecaps.

"Aylin." The voice seemed closer.

"And this one is for Bracko. I loved his guitar playing." She lifted the right hand of the helpless thug fired into his palm.

"Aylin."

"I won't put a bullet in you for Johnny because you were kind enough to let me know that he is still out there."

Thinking he had survived the worst of it, Crespo revealed a slight smirk. He lay helpless. He had lost an eye, and he had four bullets and a knife in him. However, nothing yet was fatal. *She doesn't have the guts to kill me* were his last thoughts.

"What am I forgetting? What am I forgetting?" teased Aylin as she circled Crespo. "Oh yeah, I know. Where was it that you shot my father? Now I remember." She placed the gun firmly against the back of Sammy Crespo's skull and pulled the trigger. She continued to pull it over and over until the Glock ran out of bullets.

PART
4

"Broken Dreams"
"One more shattered illusion, one more broken dream."
Oh, that the morning brings the sunlight."
- Justin Hayward

December 1989

52

"Bridge Over Troubled Waters"
-Simon and Garfunkel

Diary of DJ Spinelli

Entry #84 - December 20, 1989

MY SON WOULD HAVE BEEN eighteen this year—just a little younger than I was the last time I picked up this journal. Johnny, he never lived. He was never born. Instead, he was murdered in the womb by Sammy Crespo's cruel blow.

It has taken me almost two decades to write that paragraph. It hurt to go on and my quest to find you had died. Johnny, I hope that you've found happiness. At least now, I know you are alive. Aylin and I both found out that fact that fateful night almost nineteen years ago. You did not die in that bloodbath that took all the other members of Those Born Free.

Before I renew my search for you, I guess I should catch you up with all that happened—all the tragedies that befell our group. I remember when I was going to document every moment of my life. I was then going to create great works of literature based on my experiences. I guess John Lennon had it right when he wrote the words, "Life is what happens while you are busy making plans." For better or worse, my life happened.

———◆———

I never did play at the Fillmore East that night back in 1970. I never played with the band ever again. I did continue to write songs for them, and they continued to accumulate gold records and fame. "Dancing on the Other Side of the Wind" sold millions, and the album won a Grammy. The members of the band have grown wealthy. I was happy with the royalties on all the songs I wrote. It allowed me to take good care of my family. Yes, my family—have I been stalling in telling that story?

———◆———

When we found Aylin, gun in hand standing above Crespo's bullet-ridden body, I was paralyzed. Neil was a cop, and his duty should have been to report a homicide. However, we both knew what *that* meant—Guy Provenzano would know. The embarrassment of Sammy taken down by a woman would eat him up. How tough could his right-hand man be if this girl got the jump on him? We had to get Aylin out of there. While I stood stunned, Neil took charge.

"Are you sure?" I looked at Neil, who had sworn an oath. I should've realized he had a more pragmatic morality. Aylin's arrest would mean almost certain death. A jury might understand that Crespo had murdered Aylin's brother, father, and friends—and that he had tried to rape her. They might let her off. Mad Guy never would.

As an aspiring detective, Neil knew how to scoop up the evidence of Aylin's presence (including her father's gun and her stiletto heels). Aylin's shots to Crespo's head obliterated any indication of his initial eye wound. As police sirens filled the night air, Aylin and I exited the building through a rear entrance while Neil held up his badge and claimed to be protecting the crime scene. We found our way to the McAvoy home.

Mrs. Mac was surprisingly calm. She immediately called her parish priest, Father Hanratty. Adele McAvoy did not think that her daughter needed to make an immediate confession for breaking the Fifth Commandment. Instead, she insisted the priest would have a good idea what to do next—and he had connections. Father Hanratty sent for a doctor who realized that Aylin was bleeding internally and needed hospitalization immediately. Quietly, an ambulance took her to Franklin General in Nassau County. Emergency surgery was required because Aylin's internal damages included a hemorrhaging uterus. They saved her life. However, the devastating effects of that surgery left her unable to bear children. The two-month-old fetus she was carrying would have been my son—our son.

As devastating as that was, it was not an end to our misery. Aylin was unresponsive when we found her—only one small step away from a complete nervous breakdown. She took that step. She hadn't known she was pregnant. The loss of our child now compounded her guilt over her brother's death. If she had not sought revenge against Crespo, the baby wouldn't have died. Aylin's physical recovery would take months—her mental recovery years.

Father Hanratty announced to the outside world that Aylin had entered the novitiate as a prelude to becoming a nun. He pre-dated his lie so that she couldn't have been around when Sammy died. While he said she was gone studying, she was actually away in an institution receiving therapy—both mental and physical.

I visited her night and day. I loved her, but I also felt guilty. In January, I left with the band, knowing she was fragile. I'd gone to follow my dreams of fame and fortune with little thought of how much she needed me. Johnny, you once told me that every-thing you did with the band was for the sake of Maria. I wish that I'd been that noble. I believe that I loved Aylin with the same passion. However, I left for selfish reasons. But never again. It took that tragedy to understand what Aylin meant to me.

After almost a year, Aylin was released. She moved to a little cottage on the grounds of the Sisters of Charity Convent on Springfield Blvd. Her mother and sisters moved in with her when they lost the house to foreclosure. I visited every day.

On April 29, 1972, Aylin and I were married at Our Lady of the Skies Chapel at Kennedy Airport. Her childhood vision of walking down the aisle of Sacred Heart Church in Cambria Heights became only another broken dream. The rest of the world believed she had become Sister Adele James. Because nuns used pseudonyms in those days, there was no way to track her down—in case Mad Guy had any spies among the Sisters of Charity. OK, Johnny, that last part was a joke. In reality, no one ever suspected anything. Victor Catalano, the bartender at the Top Cat Bar, told Mad Guy that Crespo had left the bar with a short mousy blonde. The rest of the patrons were so drunk they couldn't dispute this fact.

With the gobs of money coming in from my songwriting and the success of Chris's band, Aylin and I moved far away—60 miles out on Long Island. There we lived in a little apartment while I finished up the credits I needed to get my degree in English and certification as a teacher. By 1975, you couldn't have picked us out from the hundreds of thousands of city-folks who had moved out to cookie-cutter developments in the suburbs.

Johnny, I forgot about you. I justified my lack of interest by telling myself that I knew you were alive and probably leading a wonderful life. Hey, maybe you and Maria found each other—stranger things have happened in this world. I mean, I know you're OK. You never were the kind of person to drink or take drugs, so I knew you would land on your feet somewhere.

Entry #85 - December 21, 1989

I have to tell you that most of us—the group that we call The Brotherhood do think about you. We meet every year around Christmas to see each other and relive all that we went through. We marvel at the strange chain of events that brought us together. We also realize that you and the rest of Those Born Free link us together. At least, those of us who are still around.

Johnny, there have been some casualties in the past two decades—your parents, who were more to us than just your parents—they were our friends. If you have been reading this, Johnny, you know that. But could you know that Gio's parents were murdered? Or that Aylin's sister Siobhan and my friend Bobby Bright Eyes have passed?

In a few days, we will all meet at our house. I want to remember as much as I can about you, and all of those who are gone. We will meet to toast those we have lost and talk about the one we could never find—you.

However, the reason that this diary is out now is that we are going to make Mad Guy Provenzano finally pay for his crimes. Neil and I and a few others are going to make our plans when the group gets together. Neil got information three weeks ago that has set us on our journey. It may take a few more months, but revenge will be sweet.

Johnny, until then, let me tell you our stories—the bad and the good.

53

"The Needle and the Damage Done" (Reprise)
- Neil Young

Diary of DJ Spinelli

Entry #86 - December 21, 1989

READING THIS DIARY, I CAN'T help think back to the loss of Bobby Bright Eyes and his wife, Siobhan. Bobby and I had shared the *Queens Undies*, Woodstock, and the Brotherhood Blues Band. We continued to be great friends even after I left the group. We would see each other whenever the band was in town. We then became family when Bobby married Siobhan McAvoy. I was proud to be his best man and to welcome him as a brother-in-law. However, the story of Bobby and Siobhan didn't have a happy ending.

Bobby Bright Eyes was one of the all-time great guitarists. In my eyes, he ranked up there with Clapton, Beck, and Page. The trouble was that *he* simply didn't believe it. He always thought he needed to be better—to prove himself to the band and the world.

Bobby wanted to know how to be the best. He heard stories about guitarists who claimed to play better while high on drugs. Bobby didn't take into account that many like Jimi Hendrix had died following that path. He experimented, and it cost him his life. However, Bobby didn't die from an overdose. In his final days, he wished he had suffered that fate. Instead, his addiction also caused his wife Siobhan's death.

He never wanted anyone to know of his need, so he snuck off to the dark underbelly of every city. He would leave shortly before each performance and find a fix to get him through the show. After the group left the stage, he would sneak off and not return until he could fool those who knew him best with an act of total sobriety.

No, Bobby never died of an overdose. Instead, his addiction led to his sharing of needles. Unfortunately, one of those lapses led to a disease that none of us had ever heard of at the time, AIDS. He didn't know what was wrong with his health for far too long—long enough for the happily married Bobby to spread his misfortune to his loving wife, Siobhan.

They both suffered greatly—never knowing until the very end, what was killing them. Bobby died in 1981—Siobhan a year later. Aylin and I couldn't allow ourselves the luxury of grieving. We were too busy fulfilling their final wish—that we raise their son.

When we adopted Roberto McAvoy Weissman, we had already been caring for him for years. He loved us, and we loved him, but I personally always felt a tinge of guilt about how we finally had come to have a child. Why hadn't I seen what was going on with my friend?

Roberto was seven when we took him in and nine when we adopted him. The social worker wanted him to use the surname of Spinelli, but we thought he was old enough to have a say in the matter. Roberto was a McAvoy through his biological mother *and* his adopted mother. Weissman was the proud name of the man and woman who had made his father Bobby's life in America possible. Spinelli was the family he was in now, but we made no claims on him to take our name.

He was his father's son in every sense of the word. At age nine, he was already an excellent guitarist. He was a professional musician in the making, and we encouraged him.

"Mom, Dad, (he easily transitioned into calling us that), can I pick my name—first and last?"

"Sure," we answered readily.

"Well, I always heard about my *two* moms' brother, Jimmy Mac."

Amazing, Those Born Free found its way to another generation.

"And he was a great musician, right?"

"Yeah."

"And my dad was the famous Roberto "Bobby Bright Eyes" Weissman—right?"

"Right again," I answered.

"So how about I choose Roberto Mac?"

Was anyone surprised last year when Roberto Mac nee Roberto Gonzalez McAvoy Weissman Spinelli, at age 18, became the lead guitar of Chris Delaney and The Brotherhood Blues Band? We are very proud of our son.

54

"Murder in My Heart for the Judge"
- *Moby Grape*

December 5, 1989

DETECTIVE NEIL CONNAUGHTON HAD HAD a long day. He had testified in a murder case that had sent away a local gang leader for life. Not satisfied with that accomplishment, Neil went out into the field to chase down some promising leads on another homicide case. By the end of his shift, all he wanted to do was go home to his family. Mary Lou has promised him a thick juicy steak smothered in onions. She had hinted that she would provide mouthwash to cover the onion breath for some "dessert" later on that evening. Before he went home, he would catch his son Jake's varsity basketball game. He might even have time then to call stepson Alex, who was away at Stony Brook University.

Neil's after-work activities were important to him, and he wouldn't give them up for anything—until he got a call from his borough commander and former partner, Cliff Collins.

"Something of particular interest to you came across my desk today."

"Can it wait until tomorrow?"

"Neil, we nailed a member of the Provenzano gang, his cousin Nicky Toto. We've got him cold for a hit he did for Mad Guy. We think we can get him to flip."

"Nobody would ever give up Mad Guy, and you know that."

"What I know, Neil, is that this little worm will do anything to avoid the electric chair."

"So, what makes you think that he is credible?"

"He's admitting to a two-decades-old murder that we previously couldn't even prove was a murder."

"What does that mean?"

"On July 5, 1967, he claims to have carried out a job for Mad Guy."

"July 5, 1967?"

"Yeah, he admits to burning down the Brackowski house."

"Bracko."

"I thought that would get you. I was listening all those times you talked about Bracko in the patrol car."

"Holy shit. Bracko's murderer."

"Yeah, and he claims that in 1984 Mad Guy approached him about doing another hit for him. However, Mad Guy later changed his mind and wanted the satisfaction of doing it himself."

"1984?"

"Yeah, the murder of Gyp and Rosalie DeAngelis, the parents of Gio DeAngelis. We've got him! We've got Mad Guy Provenzano!"

———◆———

Neil Connaughton did not go see his son's basketball game, and he did not call his stepson Alex. He did not go home for his waiting steak dinner or the promised "dessert" that would follow. Instead, midnight found him in an interrogation room with Nicky Toto, the murderer of Bracko.

"My lawyer says that you can give me a few decades of cushy time if I cooperate. So, do we have a deal?"

"Did you kill Bracko?"

"Who the hell is this Bracko character?"

"Rocco Brackowski and his father, Stanley."

"Do we have a deal on this—and my latest adventure?"

"It's not an adventure! It's goddam murder that we are talking about."

"Calm down, Detective Connaughton," said both Commander Collins and Toto's court-appointed lawyer David Cooperman almost simultaneously. Typically, all cases for members of the Provenzano gang were defended by Richie Shea, cousin to both Nicky Toto and Guy Provenzano. However, if they wanted Nicky Toto testifying, instead of in a coffin, the entire affair would need to remain extremely quiet.

The wheels of justice moved slowly. At the courthouse the next day, a judge decided that Toto would appear before a special grand jury. The FBI would work the case along with NYPD, and the entire investigation would now take months to develop. That was the way the judge wanted it. However, this turn of events did not sit well with Detective Neil Connaughton. He wanted Toto sent away tomorrow, and Mad Guy Provenzano dead yesterday.

55

"You've Got a Friend"
- James Taylor

THOSE BORN FREE Tape - December 20, 1966

"Rockin' Around the Christmas Tree? Really?" (Jimmy Mac)

"C'mon, it'll be fun." (Johnny)

"OK." (Jimmy Mac)

"Hey, what are you guys doing for Christmas?" (Tinman)

"With the size of my family, there are just too many of us to buy presents for everyone. So we each pick a name out of a hat and give to that one." (Jimmy Mac)

"Yeah, my parents take care of me. That's how I got my first guitar." (Johnny)

"What about you, Tinman?" (Jimmy Mac)

"Some gifts, mostly piano related. For my parents, it's all about church. Which is OK. What about you, Bracko?" (Tinman)

"Just a black eye—if I'm lucky. Christmas? Just another day for my father to get drunk."

"Bracko, Christmas is about many things—or at least it should be. But to me, it's being with people you care about." (Johnny)

"But what if you have no one who cares." (Bracko)

"Whoa! Stop right there. You have a room full of people right here who care. You know what? You're coming to my house on Christmas Day." (Johnny)

"I couldn't do that." (Bracko)

"My parents will welcome you. At worst, the other two dozen members of my extended family won't even notice you in the crowd."

"Yeah, like they won't notice a giant Nordic-looking guy among all you short, dark Italian types." (Jimmy Mac)

"True. Well, Bracko, you coming?" (Johnny)

"Yeah, and thanks." (Bracko)

"Now, let's practice." (Johnny)

"OK, what song next?" (Tinman)

"No, no, guys, I don't mean the band. If Bracko truly wants to fit in at my place, he has to learn to say 'pasta," not 'paster' like he did the first time I brought him home." (Johnny)

"Huh?" (Bracko)

"P-ah-sta. Now repeat after me—P-ah-sta." (Johnny)

"You're a nice guy, Johnny." (Gio)

"Wait! Is the tape running? Did you get that? Gio said something nice about me?" (Johnny)

"Consider it your Christmas gift." (Gio)

"You know what? Why don't you all come over around six? You know, after you finished whatever you're doing. Bracko and I will be there—it will be good to share Christmas. You know some cannoli, some pizzelle." (Johnny)

"OK, enough wasting time. Bracko, start us off." (Jimmy Mac)

Bracko hit the first notes of the Rolling Stones' "Satisfaction," but then abruptly stopped and spoke one word . . .

"P-ah-sta." (Bracko)

DJ Spinelli pressed the stop button on the tape recorder. He and Aylin had listened to every minute of the Those Born Free tapes in the years following their discovery. Many times, they listened to hear the musical genius that had come forth from five underage and overambitious kids. It would have been so easy to work with Chris Delaney and make them hits. But they didn't.

They also listened to the tapes over and over again for the conversations. They realized that the words spoken were not pearls of wisdom that would forever be remembered in the halls of academia. Instead, these were words of friends—real friends who understood and cared for each other despite the snarky and sarcastic comments. The fact they had this permanent window into their existence helped to keep them alive. DJ even philosophized more than once that it was not the real people that they were remembering, but rather the idea of who those people had been. They were models of friendship and loyalty. Someday, DJ wanted to tell their story in writing. Someday.

Once a year, the idea of a reunion of friends at Christmas had come from that tape—in remembrance, they always had "P-ah-sta."

———————

This 1989 Christmas gathering at DJ and Aylin's suburban home was one of the best attended so far. The three Delaney Brothers were on hiatus from touring for the holidays. Chris and Shylo had come out from the city, and Kevin and Tommy Delaney and their families had come across the Long Island Sound on the Port Jefferson Ferry. Trip Grimes, who was often on the road filming documentaries, was in between projects. Neil and Mary Lou came with their younger son, Jake. Alex, now a young adult, would be coming out later.

Leo Leonardo and Goody Barlow and their families had long ago become part of the group and would not miss out on one of these get-togethers. In the years following their return from Vietnam, they had finished law school together and simultaneously entered the District Attorney's office in New York City. Their long-ago revelation of speaking to John Cippitelli, Sr. in the St Albans Naval Hospital, had made for an instant connection with the group. Besides that, they were Heights guys and shared a love of the neighborhood and a hatred for Mad Guy Provenzano. That hatred was now assuaged by their impending investigation and hopeful conviction of the long-time gang leader. They could not share this information with the group yet.

Pandemonium reigned while all of the children created havoc in the Spinelli home. Some of the older ones sat and watched TV, but the younger ones became involved in a two-hour game of indoor hide-and-seek. By midnight all of the children were out cold in every nook and cranny of the Spinelli home. Some of them still in their last hiding spot.

The adults joked about it but looked forward to the quiet time. Everyone was staying the night, and sleeping bags eventually covered every square inch of the second floor of the colonial-style house. When calm finally prevailed, the adults found their way to the den. Guitars appeared. There was singing, and there was laughing. And there was crying.

——————◆——————

One by one, most of the adults found places in which to catch a brief repose before the chaos of the morning when the children arose. DJ took Aylin aside and told her to get some rest. He would see to the final night birds still sitting by the fire. It was his duty as a host. As the clock was just approaching 3 a.m., he sat with the last stragglers, Neil, Leo, and Goody. It was not an accident. The three had been waiting to talk to DJ alone. What they told him blew his mind.

Mad Guy is going down.

56

"Wild World"
- Cat Stevens

Diary of DJ Spinelli

Six months later

Entry # 87 - June 5, 1990

GIO DEANGELIS HAS A SON! More than that, the kid is a baseball phenom. Johnny, I remember you telling me how Gio was not a great stickball player and not much competition. Laughs on you, loser. Johnny, I don't know if you have read about him wherever you are, but Gio DeAngelis Jr, known as Van the Angel, is a stud. What have you got to say to that?

Of course, I'm a selfish prick, so I'm only thinking of how this helps me find you. Yes, you stupid bastard, I'm still looking for you. I can write this now because the secret will be out soon. Since last Christmas, I've been interviewing Nicky Toto, cousin of Mad Guy and confessed killer of Bracko. Yes, your guitarist and your friend, Bracko. You are probably asking how the hell I know this? It's a long story.

Around Christmas, the police busted Nicky Toto for the execution-style murder of Desiderio Gomez. The Hispanic gangs aren't as powerful as the Mafia yet, but they are trying to be. Mad Guy decided to send a message the old-fashioned way and entrusted his cousin with the hit—Gomez died, but Nicky got caught. Nicky isn't prepared to die for his crazy cousin, so he is blabbing. He's been testifying to a secret grand jury for most of the spring. Any day now warrants will be issued, and Mad Guy Provenzano will go down. Perhaps when they finally arrest the prick, I'll have a better idea where you are. How's that sound, buddy?

So, Johnny, you are probably asking if this is so hush-hush, how do I know about it? Neil has become one of my best friends, and it was his idea to have me document all of these events for the eventual publicity releases—and a book when it is all over. Why me? Well, Johnny, that's where ego comes in, and I don't mean mine. (Well, maybe a little).

You know that I didn't write in this diary from the time I married Aylin almost twenty years ago. That does not mean I wasn't writing! Chris Delaney and I share a few Grammies for songs we wrote for his band's first album, and we have been nominated half a dozen times since then (last winning again in 1986). But I write songs for fun. I make my living as a serious writer of fiction and non-fiction. In 1987, I won the Pulitzer Prize for my expose of the MTV payoff scandals. I have also written five novels and regularly contribute to *Rolling Stone, Creem*, and *WWD*. Yes, Johnny, I *am* a big shit. However, it's not *my* ego that got me this crime scene gig.

Robert Morgenthau is the district attorney for New York City, and he hopes to become governor of the state. Get the picture? He wants his name out there, and who better to do it? Therefore, when Neil suggested last Christmas that I sit in and take notes, Morgenthau jumped at the idea. Unprecedented? Yeah. But political ambition knows no bounds. It didn't hurt that Leo Leonardo and Goody Barlow are on the prosecution team and put in a good word for me. They are about to bust Mad Guy. I'm taking this opportunity to put my notes together and get ready to tell the story.

57

"Human Wheels"
- John Mellencamp

Diary of DJ Spinelli

Entry # 88 - June 6, 1990

I KNOW THAT THE BUST IS coming down on Mad Guy any minute now—or at least any day now. However, I can't pass up the opportunity to speak to Gio's son, Van DeAngelis. I think back to 1967, twenty-three years ago.

Johnny, you kept telling me that in the days leading up to the band's last performance, something was off about Gio. You never figured it out, but now the world knows. The investigative reporter in me has to see this through for you. Maybe this person Riet has an idea where you are, or possibly your location will be revealed by Mad Guy after his arrest. That seems unlikely. If he knew anything about you, you would be dead. Sorry to put that so coldly. Anyway, I'm pursuing every angle.

———◆———

It was a funny feeling returning to the Heights. Aylin and I moved away after she killed Sammy Crespo. Meanwhile, Chris and Trip were on the road. After your parents passed away, Neil and Mary Lou saw no reason to stay, and they headed out to Nassau County.

But yesterday, I found myself standing on the doorstep of Riet and Van's house. How could I convince them that I could be trusted? They didn't know me—I'm not *that* famous. And even if they knew my reputation as a writer, they might think I was trying to use them. I had to get to the point that I knew Gio quickly. That never happened. And it's your fault!

I knocked firmly on the door. While waiting for an answer, my eye caught something out of place. A white man in an old Toyota with Florida plates was parked at the curb. Johnny, it was you—I am sure of it!

However, I hesitated because I'd already rung the bell and feared I would lose out meeting Riet if I ding-dong dashed them. While I was wrought with indecision, a tall, athletically built black man answered the door. Lost in thought, I just couldn't get out the words that I'd practiced. He looked at me dismissively and turned to a woman who must have been Riet. I could swear I heard her say something about a journal. He promptly slammed the door in my face—a loss. But if I could run to the car where I believed you to be, I would have something. The car was gone.

So, I ask again, "Was that you?"

58

"Desperado"
- The Eagles

"OK, PRESS THE RECORD BUTTON and then proceed with your final interview, Detective Connaughton. Now that the grand jury has indicted Mr. Toto, I want his testimony clear and concise before we make the arrest."

"So, Nicky, tell us about the crimes of 1967."

"Mad Guy—can I call him Mad Guy?"

"Nicky, your testimony is going to tie Provenzano to at least seven murders, and you're worried about calling him a name? You made a left turn at crazy and went straight to bat shit."

"OK, Detective Connaughton, back on track."

"Nicky, tell us about your immediate involvement in the deaths of Rocco and Stanley Brackowski."

"Mad Guy was pissed off royally at these kids for screwing him up with the capos. So he says to me, 'Nicky, you're the only one I trust to take care of these fuckers.'"

"Aren't you all that, Nicky?"

"Detective! Let him speak."

"So, I sneak in the house while both them Brackowskis are out, and I spike all the drinks in the frig."

"But the kid didn't drink anything."

"So, he's wide awake in the basement when the fire started?"

"Yeah, I had to lock the kid in. But he does the weirdest thing when he can't get out. He keeps playing the guitar down that basement until. . ."

"He dies."

"Yeah"

"So, if you were the only one Mad Guy trusted, how come he sent two others to take care of Noel and James McAvoy?"

"Umm, ah, he thought it was a job for two, and I only worked solo."

"Stop, bullshitting, Nicky. You screwed up by first not making sure that Bracko was out cold and then by getting in the news as a so-called hero. When you were seen coming out of the house, you told the police you were trying to save them. That didn't go over well with your boss."

"No, it didn't."

"And that's why someone else did the hit on Noel and James McAvoy—right?"

"Yeah."

"So, who killed the McAvoys and the young Montgomery girl who was hiding in the back?"

"I've got a deal, right?"

"Why? Are you afraid of Crespo and Timpani coming to get you?"

"No detective, you and I know they're both dead."

"Yes, but for the record, Provenzano ordered the hit—correct?"

"Yeah."

"OK, who killed the Tinley boy up in Boston?"

"Some WASPY-faced hitman—I never caught his name."

"But, you did hear Provenzano order the hit?"

"Yeah."

"And Gio DeAngelis?"

"They talked about it in hushed tones, but my best guess is that Guy did that one himself—with Crespo and Timpani there."

"Now we've got all your testimony straight, I only have one final question. Which one of you bastards killed Johnny Cipp?"

"What are you talking about?"

"Detective, you are out of line. You know that we are not charging Provenzano with that one."

"With all due respect, Mr. Morganthau, we should get to the bottom of this whole thing now."

"OK, Detective Connaughton, but make it brief."

"Once and for all, Nicky, you are going to answer my question. No deal unless you tell us who killed Johnny."

"Mr. DA, can he do that?"

"No, but I would like an answer to that question."

"It's not that I won't tell you. It's just that no one *did* kill the Cipp kid. As far as Provenzano knows, he is still alive."

"How can you be sure?"

"Because he had our other cousin, Richie Shea, looking for him for almost two decades—with no luck I might add. You can ask Richie if you don't believe me."

"Shit, Johnny *is* alive?"

"Detective Connaughton, please act more professional."

"Now, just so we are clear. Are you prepared to testify in court?"

"OK, Detective Connaughton, you have permission to make the arrest as soon as possible. Guy Provenzano is going down."

59

"Paint It Black"
- Rolling Stones

Diary of DJ Spinelli

Entry #89 - June 10, 1990

I GOT THE CALL AT SIX in the morning that there would be no bust of Guy Provenzano. He's missing. He went out on his boat, the *Fun Ghoul* last night, and never came back. All that work and anticipation for nothing—he escaped.

Entry #90 - June 12, 1990

Neil, Leo, and Goody asked me to meet them this morning. Mad Guy Provenzano is dead. His body washed up on shore in Connecticut. He drowned. However, there are so many questions surrounding his demise, and they wanted my opinion.

Tony Provenzano was also found dead—his body riddled with bullets. How could that be? Why would he be the one shot and his evil brother not? The bullets found in the body of Tony matched those taken by the medical examiner from the bodies of Gyp and Rosalie DeAngelis six years ago. What was the connection there?

The police found Tony's blood on the flybridge of the boat.

However, they also found blood all over the main deck, the rear seating area, on the cabin wall, and a ladder leading to the upper deck. It wasn't Tony's blood. It didn't match anyone known. It was type AB positive, a rare blood type found in less than 4% of all people. Therefore, there was at least one other person on the boat that night when the Provenzano brothers died. Although Neil is a great detective, he is stumped. I wasn't.

Johnny, you have AB positive blood. We did blood tests in freshmen biology, and you squealed like a baby when we had to poke our fingers and take blood to test. I remember Br. Patrick explaining how rare your type was. Now I know that it was you in that car in the Heights a few days ago—and it was you on that boat. But where are you now? I have to face the reality that no one came back from that boat.

Entry #91 – June 19, 1990

It has been nine days since the recovery of the Provenzano brothers' bodies, and the investigation is at a standstill. In reality, it's all over. Leo and Goody don't have a stake in the case because their suspect is dead, and to be honest, they don't care who killed him.

Neil, as usual, is doing the right thing and vigorously trying to figure this whole mess out. Without my little secret, however, he is lost. Should I tell him? As I sit here, my path becomes clear. June 19 is the date I just wrote down at the top of this entry. It was precisely 23 years ago today that the world went in the crapper for Those Born Free. I have listened to their tapes, and I searched all this time to find their story. It's time to shit or get off the pot. There is only one person alive who can give me answers—Richie Shea.

Entry # 92 – June 20, 1990

This diary entry is the last time I will write to you, Johnny. I will search no more. If I ever write words in this diary, it will be *about* you, not *to* you. Every bone in my body tells me that you are dead. However, because I'm a coward and don't wish to join you, I'm done. Only Aylin knows the truth.

Last night I drove to Richie Shea's social club. It is so stereo-typical of the places seen in cheap mafia movies. The storefront has the words "Southeast Queens Social Club" clearly painted on the glass. However, there were no dances, meetings, or other social events held there. It was the hang out for the still pros-pering Provenzano gang—minus anyone named Provenzano.

When I entered, more than twenty pairs of eyes stared at me with looks that could kill. Either these guys all shopped in the same menswear shop, or somewhere out there, a few dozen black leather jackets "fell off a truck." I summoned the nerve to make it known that I wished to see Richie Shea. After the laughter died down, a guy with a scar across his left cheek spoke, "And who the fuck are you?"

"DJ Spinelli," I answered with a false sense of bravado. More laughter.

"He's famous," volunteered an anonymous voice in the crowd.

"A famous pussy," added Scarface. (Am I again stereotyping with the nickname?)

"No, he wrote that song 'Dancing on the Other Side of the Wind' and some books," added a skinny guy in the back, obvi-ously trying to impress the others.

"And since when could you read?" joked another voice from the crowd (more laughter).

"Well, Spinelli, at least you are Italian, so we aren't going to mess you up too bad," mocked Scarface taking control of the room. With that, a door to the back room swung open.

"What do we have here?" Unlike all of his minions, Shea didn't wear black leather, but rather an Armani suit. His graying red hair was neatly coiffed, and he was the epitome of style and class—the opposite of his outer room employees.

"This guy—" started Scarface.

Shea cut him off. "*This guy* is DJ Spinelli, the world-ac-claimed songwriter and author. You slugs need to get out more or maybe read a little."

"See, I told you so," interjected Skinny from the back, only to get looks from the rest of the group.

"Come in, Mr. Spinelli."

Richie was not the gangster I expected, but rather a polite, sophisticated gentleman. I thought this would go well—until it didn't. He offered me drinks, and we had polite conversations about my career. He avoided talking about himself. I knew he'd been a beat cop in Queens before becoming a detective at a very young age. (A payoff to the right people by his cousin Mad Guy?). He then had gone to law school at night and emerged as the legal face for the Provenzano gang. Guy Provenzano had died without ever having a single arrest or even a parking ticket. Shea was damn good, and now he had inherited the leadership of his cousin's gang.

"So, what do I owe the honor of your visit?"

I thought long and hard about how to broach the subject of Johnny, the boat, and everything else that had gnawed at me for over two decades. I couldn't expect any kind of confession of crimes from him. However, I hoped for some tidbit that would help me in my quest.

"Do you know who else was on the boat with your cousins Guy and Tony?"

"No."

"Did you know Guy was about to be arrested that very morning he died?"

I could see that he didn't. He was stunned, and he pumped me for information. I stupidly started to fill in the blanks. Mistake. He was using me without reciprocating. It soon occurred to me that he might have ordered the hit on his cousin. If he had done that, Johnny, you were just collateral damage. Perhaps soon, I would be too. I pulled back a bit—a decision that might have saved my life.

"Do you know anything about Johnny Cipp?"

"Who?" was his quick response, but his body language told me he was lying.

"Johnny was my friend, and I have been trying to find him since his disappearance over twenty years ago. . . and I think he may have been on the boat with your cousin ten days ago." He came toward me, and I thought he was simply going to respond that he knew nothing, but with more emphasis. Instead, his left hook caught me by surprise and sent me staggering into the wall behind. Like a cat, he was on me. He rifled through my pockets and patted me down. I assumed he was looking for a weapon but was surprised when he took out my portable tape recorder and smashed on the ground. It had not been running, but it was apparent that he did not want any proof of what he was going to say next to me. As he held me pinned to the wall with his hand around my neck, he spoke the words I will never, ever forget.

"Listen, and listen well—your life depends upon it. Those shitheads out there are the dumbest, but toughest motherfuckers you will ever meet. But they are *my* motherfuckers and will do anything I ask."

"Yes, sir," I answered like a scared puppy.

"If you ever, and I repeat, ever, ask about my cousin again—in person or print, you're dead. If you try to come after me, you're dead. Unless you have something that will put every one of those two dozen idiots behind bars, you're dead. Not only that but your lovely wife, Aylin. . ."

"What about Aylin?" I whispered, terrified. He now stepped back and regained an air of composure.

"Aylin *McAvoy*. . . right? Well, she might just want to visit her brother Jimmy Mac and her father—get it?"

"You wouldn't."

"No, no, I wouldn't, but. . ." Richie nodded to the outer room.

"One of them would. And I would permit them to have a good time before they finalize the deed."

"You goddam motherfucker," I said with fury in my voice. He answered with another gut punch.

"Yes, I am a motherfucker—and don't you ever forget it."

I got the message. And as he started to open the door to throw me out, Shea whispered one final warning in my ear.

"Also, if you write or talk in public about Johnny Cipp. . . ever. . .well, you know the drill. Oh, and say hello to Roberto Mac. While you're at it—even say hello to Detective Neil, Mary Lou, and the kids. You get my gist?"

When I got home, I went right to the little office where I do all my writing and pulled out this diary. I went to the framed pictures on the wall and removed two. One was of the whole Brotherhood group that I took at the last Christmas party. The other was a family portrait of Aylin, Robby, and me. I took both pictures out of the frames, and I placed them next to these final words. I want them there to remind me what would be at stake if I continued to search for you.

Goodbye, Johnny.

60

"The End of the World as We Know It"
- REM

11 years later

NEIL CONNAUGHTON HAD BEEN A member of the NYPD for over three decades. At fifty years old, he could have retired long ago. However, he loved his job. His dedication and intelligence had helped him rise to the level of borough commander. However, he dreaded what he had to do today more than anything he had ever done on the force. As he dressed in his finest blue uniform, his wife Mary Lou eyed him with loving devotion. She knew how hard today would be.

"Neil, he's a good man—and he's been a good friend to you for all these years."

"Mary Lou, how could I not see what was going on? Cliff was my training officer. He even went out on a limb to warn me about the Provenzanos back when I had just got on the job. And he never took that bastard's money. But he did get dirty later on. I keep asking myself why?"

"Kids in college, that new boat. Who knows? Neil, you're still a good friend for introducing him to our big shot lawyer friends, Leo and Goody."

"Yeah, if anyone can get him a deal, it's those two."

"At least after that messy business, the rest of your day will be great."

"It will be good to see the guys again. DJ's driving in from God's country out in Suffolk County to meet Trip and me after I introduce Cliff to Leo and Goody. Then we're all going to join up with Chris at lunch."

"Oh, a good old boys club get-together."

"Actually, Mary Lou, no. Shylo might join us later after our meeting."

"You make it sound so official."

"Well, I was going to surprise you and the kids when it was a done deal. Trip has been talking about doing a documentary, and DJ, Chris, and I are going to be involved."

"You know I love Trip, but what's new? He is always filming documentaries—damn good ones too."

"Oh, he's not filming this one. He's in it. And so are Chris and me. DJ is writing the soundtrack."

"About?"

"When did Chris, Trip, and I all meet?"

"'There were heroes in the night, one black and one white'— the night that Chris almost died on Lispenard."

"Not a bad voice on you, old lady."

"You weren't calling me an old lady last night around midnight."

"No, I wasn't. You've still got it, Mary Lou."

"I've got an idea. Why don't you invite DJ, Chris, Shylo, and Trip back here for pizzas? I'll call Aylin and see if she wants to drive in and join us. Ask Goody and Leo if they want to come too."

"You know that's a great idea. We haven't all been together since last Christmas."

———◆———

Cliff Collins was not in uniform when they met downtown. In reality, Collins might never again be in uniform. If he was lucky, the commissioner might take into account his forty years of service, and let him retire quietly with his pension. The alternative was not just losing his pension, but losing his freedom. That's where Neil's lawyer friends came in. Since leaving the district attorney's office, the named partners of the Barlow and Leonardo Law firm were the most sought after and respected lawyers a defendant could hire. Collins was lucky Neil knew them well enough to set up this meeting.

"I'm always amazed at the size of the skyscrapers here in Manhattan. How does the ground hold them all up?"

"Don't ask me, Cliff. I'm just some kid from Queens. I can't wrap my head around it either."

"Neil, do you think these guys can keep me out of jail?"

"Hey, internal affairs has you dead to rights. Yet, you never know how these things will go. Cliff, what were you thinking?"

"When I took the bribes? I wasn't thinking. That's the problem."

"You ready?"

"As ready as I'll ever be."

"OK, I take the ride up with you in the elevator and introduce you to my friends, but then I have to leave. It would be a conflict for me to stay."

———◆———

After introducing Cliff Collins to Goody Barlow and Leo Leonardo, Neil returned to the elevator bank and breathed a sigh of relief. His part was over. When he reached the ground floor, he waved off the driver provided by the department and decided to walk the ten blocks to the little café where he was meeting Trip. He was in good shape, perhaps better shape than most of the men he commanded. It was a beautiful day. He should be able to make his appointment at nine with Trip. Chris and DJ would arrive later.

———◆———

First, he heard a loud rumble that seemed familiar, but so out of place in downtown New York City. As the booming roar continued, he found himself looking up for its source. Something wasn't right. It was then that he saw the American Airlines flight 11 crash into the North Tower of the World Trade Center—the building he had just left.

———◆———

While tremors shook the entire tower, the destruction of floors 93 to 99 was immediate. There was no time for a reaction from Goody and Leo before the debris from the stories above crashed down upon them. There were some immediate deaths, but many in their office on the 91st floor survived the initial impact. However, flames surrounded them, and sections of concrete blocked their egress. Goody lay trapped under an interior wall that had collapsed, and Leo lay stunned a few feet from him.

"There's no way out," whispered Cliff Collins, sitting in what appeared to be the only undamaged chair in the entire office.

"Are you there, Collins?" Leo tried to get his attention above the din.

"Yeah, I'm here."

"Where is my partner? I need you to help me find him."

"Why?"

"Goddamit! You have noticed that I'm blind—right?"

"He's over there. He might be dead. There's an awful lot of wall on top of him."

"Take me to him. C'mon, you asshole. I need help."

"Why bother? None of us are getting out of here alive."

They then heard the panicked sounds of the first jumper—followed by others who had given up hope. Leo could not see the look in Collins' eyes as he debated joining the forsaken.

"Help me. . . please."

Collins forgot his despair for the moment and led Leo over to Goody, who seemed to be regaining consciousness. He placed Leo's hands on the section that needed moving and then instructed him to lift when he counted to three. Goody crawled from the debris.

"You OK, Goody?"

"Look for yourself."

"But he can't. . ."

"See? Yeah, Collins, we all know that. But that's his idea of humor. That means he's doing alright."

"Well, Leo, buddy old pal, not exactly *completely* alright."

"Did he used to have two legs?"

"Goody, what does Collins mean?"

"You know how I was going to be a pirate next month for Halloween?"

"Yeah."

"Well, I'm going to need a new peg leg."

"Oh shit!"

"Collins, grab him under one armpit, and locate me under the other—then let's get the hell out of here."

"There *is* no way out."

"Collins, what are you doing?"

"Goody, what the hell is he doing?"

"Collins, don't do it. . . no, dammit."

"Even if I get out of here, what's ahead for me? Jail? Disgrace? This way, I die a hero, and my family gets my pension. It's a win/win."

"It's not win/win if you're dead."

"I don't see it that way."

"No, Collins. . ."

"Goody, what the hell?"

"Leo . . . he jumped."

"Asshole. I mean him, not you, Goody. I guess that's one less client we have."

"Leo, does the humor ever end?"

"I guess it will end when we. . ."

"End?"

"Yeah, that's what I was thinking. So, let's get the hell out of here."

"Yeah, but now I have to carry you out of this building alone."

"It brings back such sweet memories of Vietnam."

"Is there a way out?"

"I think I see some guys breaking through to the hallway."

"OK, let's go for it."

"I hope you put on deodorant this morning. You're going to be on my back for 91 floors, and you tend to stink."

"Just like the good old days. Your legs and my eyes."

———◆———

Neil Connaughton knew it was his job to run toward trouble, not away from it. He broke into a jog and retraced the route he had just taken away from the towers. As he started to approach the damaged skyscraper, he noticed Trip Grimes coming toward him.

"What the hell are you doing here?"

"Well, obviously, we're not still meeting for breakfast."

"Trip, I'm going in."

"Well, then, so am I."

"Trip, this is my job, not yours."

"Sorry, you don't get to be a hero alone this time. When Chris writes another song about heroes, you're not going to hog all the glory."

"You're nuts, Trip."

"Remember. . . *what would Bracko do?*"

"That's my line."

"Neil, you taught me well. Now let's do this."

As they were working their way up to the fifth floor, they heard the second plane hit the South Tower.

———◆———

Chris and Shylo Delaney left their hotel room at 69th Street and 2nd Avenue in the early morning. Chris had a quick meeting with his agent, and Shylo paid a social visit to some of the doctors at Memorial Sloan-Kettering Cancer Center. They met up and caught the subway downtown. When they exited the underground, they were met by thousands of confused and running people. They could see the flames and smoke surrounding the upper floors of the North Tower, and chaos filled the streets below.

Instinctively, Shylo headed toward the danger, and Chris followed. Ironically, they stood very near the Belle Terre Restaurant, their planned rendezvous point with Trip and Neil, when United Airlines Flight 175 hit the South Tower. It was evident that these two crashes had not been accidents. Panic enveloped the entire area.

It was not long before the first injured victims came into view. Without asking permission, Shylo intercepted them and set up a makeshift triage station in the restaurant. Chris immediately acted to recruit patients to their impromptu medical facility. Many just kept running, but those who stopped had their wounds tended to by Shylo. The Belle Terre Restaurant had been a frequent meeting place of many of their friends, and the owner knew them by name.

"We were supposed to meet Neil Connaughton and Trip Grimes here. Did you see them today?" With tears in his eyes, owner Jose Santos simply pointed toward the damaged towers.

"Dammit, Shylo, I know those two—they went in there to help."

"Chris, I hope not."

"Trip and Neil, my 'Heroes of the Night,' please don't do anything stupid," whispered Chris to himself.

"Meanwhile, Hon, don't you even think about joining them. You can do more good here helping me."

Chris looked at the buildings one last time and rolled up his sleeves and started to shift tables to create a temporary emergency room.

DJ and Aylin Spinelli were still at their home more than sixty miles away from the unfolding tragedy. Yet, they lived every moment emotionally through the minute-to-minute coverage on their TV. Aylin sat crying. DJ was too stunned to react.

"We've got to go, Aylin."

"Where?"

"To see Mary Lou. Neil could be in there."

"Oh, God, no!"

"Neil was meeting with Leo and Goody in the North Tower."

"She must be frantic."

"Cell towers are down. There is no way for Neil to contact her if he left before all this happened."

"And if he didn't get out? If they didn't get out?"

"Leo and Goody's offices were pretty high up."

"Oh shit."

"We better get to Mary Lou. Hurry up, North Bellmore is an hour away on a good day. Who knows what chaos is going on out there now?"

"Who knows anything at this point?"

Leo had carried Goody down the crowded stairs. By the time

they reached the landing of the 49th floor, his legs had started to give out. They both were in their early fifties and kept themselves in decent shape. However, the two fit young men who had survived the jungles of Vietnam had long since accumulated a bit of middle age flab. They sat side by side, resting.

"We'll get out, Goody. We're way below the damage now. They made these buildings to last forever."

"Leo, I don't know if anything is made to last forever."

"Some friendships are."

"Yeah, I guess they are. But, Leo, you have a much better chance of getting out of here if you don't have me on your back." He thought Leo would come back with some kind of remark to make him laugh, but instead, he started singing. He immediately recognized the Billy Joel classic about Vietnam, "Goodnight, Saigon."

Goody was amazed that his friend knew every verse verbatim, and he listened intently even though Leo only had a mediocre singing voice.

And we held onto each other,
Like brother to brother,
We promised our mothers we'd write.

And we would all go down together,
We said we'd all go down together.

Goody then joined in, and they sang one more time.

Yes, we all would go down together.

———◆———

Trip and Neil had worked their way up to the 43rd floor. Neil's uniform screamed of his rank, and dozens of police and firefighters followed his directions to clear debris from the staircases and help the escaping crowds. Trip helped those trapped behind physical barriers. Yet even while accomplishing salvation for many, they continued to ascend the stairs. Now the human traffic had disappeared. All those who were going to make it down from higher floors had already passed them. Their job appeared done.

"Trip, Goody, and Leo are still up there."

"I'm afraid so."

"You can go down. This is my job. You're a civilian.'

"Heroes in the Night, man. Heroes in the Night," responded Trip. "One black," he continued pointing to himself. "One white," he snapped with strength and emotion pointing to Neil.

They smiled and fist-bumped and started up the stairs. It was then that they heard singing.

◆

"Stop that racket, you two. We're here."

"Leo, you can't see their sorry faces, but it's Neil and Trip."

"Are you shittin' me, Goody?"

"I shit you not, Leo."

"OK, we were asked to get you the hell out of here by the music police. They've heard enough lousy singing," teased Neil.

"Very funny, Neil. Very funny."

"Put Goody on your back, Trip. I'll help Leo walk down."

"Why is that, Neil? Why is Goody going with Trip and not you?"

"Leo, have you ever seen Trip?"

"Actually, no. Neil, in case you didn't notice, I'm blind."

"Trip is 6'6" and built like a brick shithouse."

"Oh, OK, I just thought that this was a racially segregated rescue operation. You know white with white and black with black."

"Yeah, Leo, that's what I was thinking too." Goody chuckled.

"Do you guys ever stop joking?" questioned Neil.

"Neil, it's what's gets us through. It's what gets us through all the shit that the world has thrown at us. Right, Leo?"

"Right."

◆

At 9:29, they heard the loudest rumble and crashing sound that humanity has ever known. The South Tower had collapsed. In minutes over a hundred stories of concrete and steel lay on the ground only yards away from the building they were trying to exit.

"That can't be good," whispered Neil to Trip.

"I'm not deaf, guys. I heard that."

"Leo, I can't speak any louder. The dust is choking my throat."

"I didn't think anything could bring these towers down. The fact that one came down means that so can this one, right?"

"Yeah, Goody. I'm afraid it probably increases the chances of it happening."

"Wow, Neil, Thanks for making it real."

Trip wanted to change the subject. "What were you guys singing when we rescued your asses?"

"Good Night Saigon—Billy Joel's song about Vietnam. You know, 'We said we'd all go down together.'"

"Will you two stop for a second? Please."

"OK, it's your rescue operation."

"When you sing, 'We'd all go down together,' did you mean down the stairs, or down as in . . ."

"Yeah, the second one."

Neil coughed deeply. It came out a faint whisper, his words caught by the dirt, dust, and phlegm in his throat. "We said. . ." He coughed again, but continued and was soon joined by Trip, Goody, and Leo.

"We said we'd all go down together."

They heard an all-consuming and enveloping rumble around them. All four nodded at each other, instinctively knowing what this sound meant. They sang as loud as they possibly could. It was their final futile act of defiance.

"We said we'd all go down . . ."

At 10:38 a.m., as they were approaching the 26th floor on the downward journey, the North Tower came down.

PART
5

**"If We Don't Die Young,
We Might Just Live Forever"**
- Little Big Town

February 2013

61

"Time Is Here and Gone"
- *The Doobie Brothers*

JOHNNY CIPP HAD NOT DIED in 1967. DJ Spinelli knew that. However, in his heart, DJ believed Johnny *had* been killed in a showdown with Mad Guy Provenzano on the Long Island Sound in 1990. If he hadn't died, why hadn't he returned home now that the threat of Mad Guy was no longer there?

DJ Spinelli couldn't know that Johnny had made a deal with the devil. While in the hospital recovering from three bullet wounds, Johnny had been offered a proposition by the new leader of the Provenzano gang. Richie Shea had spared Johnny's life on the condition he never return to New York.

"Johnny Fuckin' Cipp, let's get this straight. I'm not letting you go because I'm a nice guy. Your disappearing helps me. However, if you ever step foot in New York again, you *are* dead. Just in case you ever think of reneging on our deal, I want you to remember that I will not only kill you but also enjoy doing it."

In turn, Johnny Cipp could not know that only ten days later, the same Richie Shea would threaten the life of DJ Spinelli and everyone around him. If DJ continued to ask questions about Mad Guy Provenzano, Johnny Cipp, or anyone vaguely connected to the newly ascended crime lord, it would be the last thing he ever did.

For 23 years, DJ Spinelli and Johnny Cipp had lived their lives without any knowledge of each other. That situation might have continued if it had not been for the death of Riet Carver. That tragedy had brought Johnny back to Queens, New York, for the first time since 1990.

DJ Spinelli never realized that Johnny Cipp, the object of his lifetime search, had been within reach.

Richie Shea did.

62

"Tears in Heaven"
- Eric Clapton

Diary of DJ Spinelli

Entry #93 - March 20, 2013

JOHNNY'S DEAD. I FOUND THAT out today. This time I wasn't guessing based on bloodstains on a boat drifting in the Long Island Sound—or any other circumstantial evidence that had accumulated over the 46 years since I last saw him. I went to the source—his executioner.

Now I know the final truth. When I stopped writing in this diary in 1990, I tried to stop thinking about Johnny. Would we even recognize each other if we passed on the street? What was he to me after all? Was he merely a remnant of my past life—an idealized memory of my youth?

I've reread all the entries of this diary and followed my progression of feelings. Do I know the source of my loyalty? Was it all about Johnny? Or was it the band and the role it played in catapulting me to wealth and fame? Or was it just that Johnny and I had such damn great times together, and he was such a good person that I couldn't give up on him.

But as of today, I will never write *to* Johnny. If I did, my final message to him would simply be a quote from an Eric Clapton

song, "Would you know my name if I saw you in heaven?"
It all started yesterday.

63

"Too Old to Rock and Roll, Too Young to Die"
- Jethro Tull

Diary of DJ Spinelli

Entry #94 – March 21, 2013

YESTERDAY, CHRIS AND SHYLO FLEW into Islip McArthur Airport from Myrtle Beach. When Chris had turned 70, he and his brothers had decided to give up touring. It seemed inconceivable that "old men" could rock, but weren't the Rolling Stones still filling up stadiums?

However, for the brothers, there had been no sense of urgency to perform. They had had a lifetime of success and more than enough money to live comfortably. Therefore, it was surprising when Chris called me and proposed we meet to talk about producing a new album. Why would Chris leave his beautiful beachfront home in Murrell's Inlet to spend hours in a stuffy studio working on an album? He had nothing to prove. Though he was a bit disappointed that the Rock and Roll Hall of Fame hadn't called their name, Chris was more philosophical about it than angry. For all these reasons, I wasn't prepared for his proposition when the four of us sat down at Grumpy Jack's for chicken wings and burgers.

"We just can't find wings like this," slurred Chris as the unique-flavored sauce dripped from his mouth and down his chin.

"Then you should move back up here to Long Island, and we can be together all the time. Shylo, you know that we do have beaches up here," prodded Aylin.

"And cold winters," replied Shylo.

"How's Robby doing?" Chris abruptly changed the subject.

"His band, Roberto Mac and the Attack, is knocking them dead," I boasted.

However, both Chris and I knew that Roberto would make no commitments until Chris officially retired.

"Yeah, I miss him. All those years of playing together, I began to think of him as my son."

"Whoa, Chris, we're not giving him up," I replied, and we all had a good laugh. Then I asked the question that hung over our heads, "So, Chris, what brings you up here to the Island?"

"Those Born Free. I think it's time to do their music," he answered quickly.

"Chris, we've talked about this—endlessly. You know Aylin and I aren't comfortable with that yet."

"DJ, it's been almost half a century. If we don't do it now, it will disappear forever."

"Maybe it should." Aylin and I had come to that conclusion long ago.

"DJ, the lyrics were timeless, and the music could be tweaked a bit to make it up to date."

"It's not that, Chris. We agreed that until the story was over, it just wasn't right to use their songs."

"And by 'story over' you mean Johnny is found—or proven dead?"

"Yeah."

"Give it up, DJ. He's gone."

"There's no proof of that," I answered.

"DJ," interrupted Aylin, "That's not entirely true."

"Aylin!" I rarely spoke in anger. No one else knew of the significance of the blood found on the boat in 1990. Only Aylin knew of my belief that Johnny had died on the *Fun Ghoul*.

"But," was all that Chris could get out before I lost it.

"No, it's not time," I screamed. The patrons at the adjoining tables turned to look. "Now, let's talk about something else."

Chris looked dejected and tried to smile.

"To friendship," said Shylo raising her glass, hoping a toast would ease the tension.

"Nature calls," mumbled Chris in a neutral tone. He rose from his seat and headed away from the table. However, he headed in the direction of a door labeled *Kitchen*. When he saw the printed word, he turned and headed back passed the table where we sat. He looked embarrassed. He had been in this bar at least a dozen times.

"Were you going to find the secret recipe for the wings?" quipped Aylin to Chris. He didn't respond at first, but then spoke, "When I get back, you'll have to tell me how Robby's doing." With those parting words, Chris made his way through the crowd.

Shylo broke into tears. Aylin quickly put her arm around her and held her tight.

"Vascular Dementia," whispered Shylo as she heaved in waves of emotion. "It's minor now, but the doctors say that it will gradually get worse. They can't predict how fast it will progress, but it's possible that he won't even recognize me within a few years."

Saying nothing, Aylin held Shylo even tighter.

"You know we're there for you. Anything you need or want… just let us know."

"DJ, that's why we're here. In his better moments, Chris knows what is happening to him. He knows that the window to producing a final album is closing—that's why he wants to do the Those Born Free material. He's always wanted to do those songs."

"But would he be capable of working on it?"

"He is doing pretty well—now. You didn't notice anything until he asked about Robby a second time and couldn't find a men's room in a restaurant he's been in many times. Additionally, the music you guys used to play in the quiet rooms of the Grand Lispenard is fresher in his mind than anything he has done in the last ten years. With his condition, his long-time memory will always be much better than his short-term memory."

"I just don't know."

"Listen, DJ, I know you feel bound not to use the music until . . ."

"Until I *know* Johnny is dead."

"And there is no way of doing that."

"There is one way," I conceded.

"DJ, if you are thinking what I think you are thinking. That's a big no."

"Aylin, some things just are worth the risk. We wouldn't have had the life we've had if it weren't for Chris. And you wouldn't even have a life at all if Shylo hadn't saved you back at Woodstock."

"But, DJ, I'm not ready to lose you."

"Sometimes, friendship requires sacrifice—and Chris is more like a brother than a friend."

"Will you two tell me what you are talking about?"

"Aylin and I know of someone who can give me answers. Once and for all, I'm going to find out what happened to Johnny—or die trying."

64

"Devil in Disguise"
- Elvis Presley

Diary of DJ Spinelli

Entry #95 – March 23, 2013

THE LAST TIME I APPROACHED Richie Shea in 1990, he had threatened to kill me. According to the newspapers, he was now in the hospital and didn't have long to live. I did some research to find exactly where. Maybe now he would give me the truth.

Two massive guards stood by his door, barring my entry as I approached. Yet, when I told them why I was there, Shea overheard and beckoned me into the room. I was shocked by the sight of the emaciated and sickly gangster. The intimidating gang leader I had known had now been replaced by a fragile, old man on death's door. Perhaps, that is what encouraged me to speak bluntly.

"There was blood found on the *Fun Ghoul*, and it was AB positive blood, Johnny Cipp's very rare type. I think he died on that boat in 1990."

Richie Shea's laugh was boisterous until it transformed into a hacking cough that seemed to disrupt every internal organ in his body.

"You're a fuckin' idiot."

"Why?"

"Because Johnny Cipp never died on that boat."

"Are you saying that wasn't his blood?"

"Oh, it was his blood, alright. He just didn't die."

"So, you want me to believe that your cousin Guy didn't kill him?"

"I don't care what you believe—but it's true."

"You're just saying that to protect him."

"Protect him! Guy's been dead for over two decades, you stupid asshole—and I didn't like him that much when he was alive."

"And why should I believe you?"

"You don't have to believe me. You're the idiot who came to me even though I told you I would kill you if you ever approached me again."

"About that . . ."

"Relax, you're not worth the bullet. Besides, it's fun rehashing old times."

"So, Johnny's alive?"

"Well, now, I didn't say that."

"What are you saying?"

"You just missed him—literally. He died last month."

"Died?"

"Well, to be more exact, he was murdered."

"Do you know who did it?

"Well, yeah—me."

"What are you saying? Johnny's dead, and you're confessing."

"Yeah, I thought I made that pretty clear. Before you get any ideas, I could be dead before the cops even got here to put the cuffs on. You were a good boy for twenty-three years by not following up on your theories and creating havoc for me. This knowledge is your reward."

"Fuck your reward!" I shouted and lunged at him, but Shea's bodyguards tackled me and pinned me to the ground. I lay helpless.

"All these years, he was alive, and I could've found him."

"Well, I don't know about all these years. I only found Johnny by following him from Riet's funeral. You could've done that, and maybe saved him. I told him never to come back to New York, or I would kill him. He came back, and so. . ."

"You son of a bitch."

"You have to understand. In 1990, I told Johnny to stay away. I was being nice—my mistake. It was assumed that the Gomez gang killed Mad Guy. I was quickly made boss so that there was no void in leadership. Johnny's blood was found on the boat. As long as it couldn't be matched to anyone, the story of how Mad Guy died was whatever I said it was."

"And you let Johnny live out of the kindness of your heart?"

"No, if I killed Johnny, then I would have to kill Riet and Van too because they knew the story. I couldn't do that because Van was a celebrity. But Johnny's blood was all over the place. My solution was to smuggle him out of the hospital to Riet's house. There he could recover."

"So, what changed?"

"Johnny came back."

"After twenty-three years, who cared?"

"I did. If the story of Johnny ever came out, my credibility and leadership would be questioned."

"By who?"

"I'm not giving you an inside scoop on my organization. I may have already said too much. Let me just say I was being pressured recently about events in 1990."

"And so, you killed a man."

"The last thing I ever said to Johnny Fuckin' Cipp, twenty-three-years ago, was that if it came down to him or me—he was dead."

"And that was it?"

"Now, now, I made you the same promise, and you're still here. Besides, who the hell are you? A big shot writer? But in 1990, and even now, how do I know you weren't looking to kill him yourself?"

"Why would I do that?"

"I don't know. Maybe it was to keep all the royalties to yourself? Maybe, you made a deal with D-mon. Who knows?"

"Whose D-mon?"

"It's a long story that I don't need to tell you. Because even dying, I don't trust you."

"You don't trust me? That's a good one."

"From where I sit, er, lie, you're feeling a bit guilty. First, you let me scare you off in 1990. Second, you didn't go to Riet's funeral and see Johnny yourself. What's the matter, enjoying the good life too much to worry about your old friend Johnny?"

"How?"

"Do you really want to know?"

"I need an end to the story—his story."

"I had my guys follow him from the funeral to his home and then to a secluded beach. Then I came. It was a beautiful sunset for me, but not for him. Though I admit, it was nice of him to provide for the easy disposal of his body—the ocean being right there."

"You bastard!"

"I swear on my soon-to-be-filled grave that I put a bullet in his head."

"You're lying!"

"Think about it—why would I lie now?"

"Where and when was this?"

"None of your goddam business. If you'd followed Johnny from the funeral, you would know."

"How can you be so calm talking about the death of a human being?"

"Because they tell me that *this* human being very shortly will be joining Johnny in the hereafter."

"No, I don't think you'll be seeing Johnny. You'll be in two different zip codes."

"Good one. Nice play on words. Now I see why you're a writer."

My hands had not unclenched, and Shea had taken note of it. I wanted to take his feeble neck in my hands and strangle the last breaths from his body. However, his goons still had me pinned to the floor.

"You do realize that if my guys let you go and you try anything in here, you're dead."

"That doesn't stop me from wanting to do it."

"Discretion is the better part of valor." With that, he started to uncontrollably cough, blood spewing from his mouth. His breathing grew strained. Machines began to beep and buzz, signifying severe distress for the patient. Nurses ushered me from the room. I waited outside to return to finish our discussion.

I had all kinds of thoughts—anger, guilt, remorse. I didn't want to admit to relief. It was over. After all these years, I had an answer—though not the answer I wanted. As I stood dazed, I heard Shea regain some composure. He yelled at the nurses to get out of the room. I heard struggling as Shea's bodyguards pulled the nurses off of him.

There were a few seconds of calm, interrupted by Shea pressing the buttons of his cell phone. After a few seconds, I heard just two words, "Do it."

This was followed almost simultaneously by the sound of a cellphone falling to the floor, and Richie Shea's heart monitor flat-lining.

65

"Last Chance"
- John Mellencamp

Diary of DJ Spinelli

One Year Later

Entry #96 – April 9, 2014

IT HAS BEEN A LONG year. The creation of our last album was filled with blood, sweat, and tears—and love. This music was something I had anticipated for over four decades but had hesitated to do because of Johnny. Now that I knew the truth, we began to work immediately.

The first step had been listening to the tapes that had been preserved by Aylin and me. They proved a treasure-trove of material as we always knew they would. It took us three months to produce the album. I was a taskmaster in pushing us to work hard, but as quickly as possible. I knew that it was only a matter of time before Chris might not be able to function.

We released the album, *For Those Born Free* in July of 2013— only five months after I learned of Johnny's demise. When it was released, most listeners did not catch on to the theme. They thought the title, *For Those Born Free*, was a general concept. They didn't get that it was a dedication. Even without the public understanding its real meaning, the album zoomed to the top of the rock charts—with three of the songs making Billboard's top ten list and "Thief of My Forever" winning Song of the Year last December.

I won't go into all the details. They are there on the album for all to see. However, the process of creation opened our eyes even further to the world of its authors. Yet, we had to make each song relevant to the 21st century.

We worked hard on "Gypsy Rose," "The Piano," "Words of Doubt," "Enchanted Days," and three other excellent songs I had never heard. The guys must have been busy in that last month before their end.

Of course, the biggest hit was the Those Born Free song about themselves—"Thief of My Forever." This song was made all the more poignant by the real-life events that took place and the group's final demise. I believe this was the song that kept me from pursuing the album. Admitting that a thief had finally stolen all their forevers was too much for me. Therefore, singing this song had the cathartic effect of releasing my ghosts. Johnny was gone. They all were gone, and I had to accept it.

The last song on the album was the only one on the whole disc not written by Those Born Free, but rather about them. We remastered "Dancing on the Other Side of the Wind." We'd had a gigantic hit with this tune in 1971, and it had catapulted us to stardom. We knew what we were singing about, but had always been vague on the topic when asked. Our *new* version was much longer than the original. We added five verses. The song became a hit all over.

The public never really understood the meaning of the song. Tomorrow night I will tell them.

66

"Tonight's the Night"
- Neil Young

DJ LOOKED INTO THE MIRROR and evaluated his appearance. He had been going for the "cool with a touch of class" look. Though not usually vain, he realized that tonight millions of people would hear him. Talk about pressure. He had to do this right. It was important to him. It was important to them—all of them—the living and the dead.

One last look at his notes was in order. He had to make sure he gave credit to everyone who deserved it before he went into the core of his speech. He would tell the story that had never been told before. He had to do it right.

"You almost ready?" Aylin asked from the next room.

He did not immediately answer. He looked down at the iPod that sat in the Bose speaker in his bedroom. DJ had long ago converted the fossilized Those Born Free tapes to digital form. In remembrance, he still labeled each of the "songs" on the playlist as a "cassette message" with the date copied from the original. Sometimes that information had not been available, and the fading tapes only listed a month and year, or maybe the title of a song. He was so mesmerized by the list that he hardly heard the soft feminine voice now right next to him.

"One last listen before the big night?"

"Yeah," was his only reply.

"I think this one is the most fitting," Aylin said as she reached over and pressed the iPod icon title that simply said, "June 3,

1967."

"Yeah, that one says it all."

"If . . . if only Johnny were still alive, he would get it."

"But he's not, and *we* have to learn to live with that."

She cried and hugged her husband tightly.

THOSE BORN FREE Tape - June 3, 1967

"Let's start at the beginning." (Johnny Cipp)

"Where else would we start, asshole?" (Laughing—Gio DeAngelis)

"This song is a story, so, of course, we'll start at the beginning. Well, actually, all songs are stories." (Joey "Tinman" Tinley)

"Are you done with the philosophy lesson, Tinman?" (Gio)

"I'm just saying that it is good to start a story at the beginning." (Tinman)

"Are you ready, Bracko? Jimmy Mac?" (Johnny)

"Yup." (Bracko)

"Hold on a sec. I need to see if the tape recorder is on. Oops! It's already on." (Jimmy Mac)

"You and those damn tapes." (Johnny)

"You're just jealous because you aren't singing on them. Or maybe we should just do 'Louie, Louie' a few times?" (laugh—Gio)

"We all have our strengths and weaknesses. You wanna go a few innings of stickball, Gio?" (Johnny)

"Tooch, Touch, tootsie, . . . whatever the hell that word is for 'You got me back.'" (Gio)

"You mean, touché? Obviously, vocabulary is another challenge for you." (Johnny)

"Ha, ha, ha, and fuck you." (Gio)

"Ha, ha, ha, and fuck you and the horse you rode in on too!" (Johnny)

"Hey, you two, my sisters are here!" (Jimmy Mac)

"Oops" (Johnny)

"Maggie and Sioban are upstairs. And you think I don't know that word? Well, then fuck you, brother dear, I'm sixteen, you know." (Aylin McAvoy)

"Aylin!" (Jimmy Mac)

"Little sis is all grown up, Jimmy Mac" (Johnny)

"Brother dear, what are you going to do? Tell Mom when she gets

home from the store?" (Aylin)

"Aylin!" (Jimmy Mac)

"Someday, some guy is going to have his hands full with that girl." (Johnny)

"Hey, someone had to inherit the crazy gene in the family." (Jimmy Mac)

"Jimmy Mac, good thing mom figured out parenting by the time she got to me." (Aylin)

"Enough, you two! Jimmy Mac, are you ready yet?" (Johnny)

"Wait, let's take a step back here. Johnny, what do you mean, 'some guy's going to have his hands full with that girl?'" (Jimmy Mac)

"I stand by what I said." (Johnny)

"I know one person who might disagree with you. Did you ever see the way DJ Spinelli looks at her?" (Gio)

"Our songwriter and my friend, DJ Spinelli?" (Johnny)

"Well yeah, our songwriter and our friend can't take his eyes off her." (Gio)

"If he wasn't such a vital part of our success—and a helluva nice guy, I'd beat the crap out of him." (Jimmy Mac)

"Who is good enough for your sister? Or do you picture her a nun in that convent down on Springfield Boulevard?" (Johnny)

"You do know that I'm standing right here?" (Aylin)

"How could we forget?" (Gio)

"DJ interested? Let me think about that one." (Aylin)

"This tape is recording." (Tinman)

"It's OK. I've got plenty of blanks." (Jimmy Mac)

"Since your uncle gave you all those blank tapes, it seems like you're taping every moment we practice—why?" (Tinman)

"I want us, the five of us, Those Born Free, to be remembered—forever." (Jimmy Mac)

"Forever?" (Johnny)

"Yeah, forever." (Jimmy Mac)

"Then, forever, it is." (Gio)

"Forever." (Tinman)

"Forever." (Johnny)

"Bracko, ready to start us off?" (Johnny)

"Yup—and, oh yeah—forever!" (Bracko)

"Well said, Bracko, well said." (Gio)

67

"In the Air Tonight"
- *Phil Collins*

Diary of DJ Spinelli

Entry #97 – April 11, 2014

IT WAS A NIGHT I'LL never forget. Chris, Kevin, Tommy, and Roberto Mac had designated me to speak for the group at our induction into the Rock and Roll Hall Fame. It should have been Chris. He was the heart and soul of the band, and this induction had been his lifelong dream. We tried to convince him to be our spokesperson even though we had all come to realize that he might not be up to it. However, Chris had enough awareness of his condition to be terrified of speaking in public. It didn't matter. He was happy. Chris Delaney, my Brother Christian, my brother, had finally achieved the one goal in life that had eluded him.

By default, it fell to me to be the speaker. As Kevin put it, "You wrote most of the other words that came out of our mouths for over forty years." Though it was our induction into the Hall, it was also all about Those Born Free. It was their music that had finally put us over the top with the voters. It was their songs and their story that had brought us here. And so, I spoke.

This has been way too long in coming. Though we thank all those responsible for getting us into the Rock and Roll Hall of Fame, that's not what I'm talking about. Most people now realize that our album, For Those Born Free, has a story behind it—they just don't know what that story is.

Our band was formed in 1970 by a group of guys joined together by a common interest and friendship. However, it was more than that. It was a bond of love for a group of people that some in the band had never met. It was a respect for the memory of those who actually danced on the other side of the wind.

People have asked us, "What is the story behind 'For Those Born Free?' These songs were written by five young guys who never got the chance to perform them. They never got their chance to grab the gold ring and be in the spotlight. Tonight is not the time, and this is not the place to tell their complete story, but that will happen—soon.

This performance is for Bracko, Jimmy Mac, Tinman, Gio, and Johnny—Those Born Free—rest in peace.

The audience cheered. Though I'm not sure the people knew what they were cheering for. Roberto Mac hit the first notes of the song that every man, woman, and child in attendance knew by heart. I looked over at Chris, worried he was not up for this—our final performance ever.

He smiled at me, and we were back in high school. He was Brother Christian, with Johnny, Tinman, and me, his loyal students. We were laughing and enjoying the complete joy of creating music. There were no thoughts of death or dementia.

Chris Delaney rocked last night—his last night in the public eye. He knew that he had hard years ahead of him as his incipient illness took charge of him. But last night Chris was brilliant. He played and sang with passion and purpose. The crowd roared as we played the music and sang the words they knew so well. If they had understood my speech, they would now know what it all meant. We had always sung the song in the first person, a ploy to hide the fact that we were talking about real people. Its appeal made people believe that any person might look at the world from the other side of the wind. However, to emphasize that these were particular victims that we were singing about, we changed all the "we's" to "they's."

> *They were living lives of passion,*
> *Never wanting to go slow,*
> *Never worrying 'bout tomorrow,*
> *Never knowing which way to go.*

The crowd sang along with us in a unified throng as we sang of "living for the day" and "not knowing the way." They knew these words intimately. As we approached what would have been the end of the song in 1971, the volume was tumultuous.

> *They were running with the music,*
> *They were dancing with a song*
> *They were living with the notes.*
> *And trying to get along.*

> *They were dancing,*
> *They were dancing,*
> *On the other side of the wind.*

But then the crowd's voices dropped off. We were now at the part of the song that we had added this year—a lesser-known part. It was here that we became more specific in our dedication. Our additional lyrics were a unique tribute. We had planned it that way. We softly spoke names into the microphones so quietly that only the recording engineers with a great deal of technical know-how were able to comprehend.

On cue, Roberto Mac stepped up to the microphone and whispered, "Bracko," the name of a guitarist who had perished long before he had ever been born, a guitarist loved for both his playing and the honorable life that he led.

> *Making the strings whine,*
> *Over the frets fast and smart.*
> *He played from his soul,*
> *He played from his heart.*

He then went into in awe-inspiring guitar solo that brought the crowd to its feet. He hit high notes, low notes, and harmonic notes with varied speeds and moods that left most of us breathless. When it was over, he again caressed the microphone and whispered, "Bracko."

He waited for crowd tumult of applause to die down and then continued, "and for my Dad, everyone's Bobby Bright Eyes." I winked at my son Roberto, knowing he still loved his long-gone father, the *original* guitarist of the Brotherhood Blues Band.

We played the chorus and sang harmony one more time before Roberto again stepped up to the mic and whispered. "Jimmy Mac." It was his uncle's name, an uncle he never got to meet because events had gone so wrong in 1967. Robby stepped from the limelight—making room for Chris to sing the next verse.

He was playing on the tom-tom,
He was making the cymbals ring,
Keeping those drums beating
And finding time to sing.

Tommy Delaney then broke into a drum solo that seemed impossible for a man his age. However, he had been preparing for months, all the while knowing he would never play again. He was OK with that idea; he would never want to play without his brother Chris anyway. Using athletic jargon, he left it all on the field.

Chris Delaney smiled at his brother as the drum solo shattered the expectations of the listeners. As Tommy finished his performance, it was Chris' turn to whisper into the mic and take a solo on the organ.

As Brother Christian, he had known Johnny, Tinman, and me a lifetime ago. It was getting harder for him to remember the past, but our time in the McCarthy High auditorium was the exception. Some particular moments remained crystal clear. He whispered, "Tinman," and then started to sing in a voice of pure devotion.

In reality, Those Born Free and The Brotherhood Blues Band could both trace their origins back to those sessions. Chris Delaney, master of many instruments, had brought hope to Johnny by making him a masterful bass player. Likewise, he had lured Joey, who would later take on the "Tinman" moniker, away from classical music into the world of rock. Johnny and Tinman went on to form Those Born Free, and Chris and I, The Brotherhood Blues Band. I had cut my songwriting teeth by writing lyrics for the group. Chris knew that none of this would have happened if Joey Tinley had not chosen to spend his lunch period playing piano instead of eating.

Chris hesitated at the mic, and I knew that he was having difficulty. These were new lyrics, and his disability had made him freeze. Like it was a rehearsed part of the performance, I joined Chris at his mic, and as I sang beside him, the words came back to him. He gave me a wink and a smile. We sang together in our tribute to Tinman, a person we both had admired.

> *He was giving the music soul,*
> *Tickling the black and whites,*
> *Singing background harmony,*
> *Helping them to new heights.*

Chris slipped away, and I stayed center stage for the tribute to Gio. I was the natural choice to introduce his tribute stanza. No one ever considered either one of us more than rhythm guitarists. However, we were forever joined together by our friendship with Johnny. He had always been Johnny's absolute best friend, whereas I was his best friend, *not in the band*. I think I may have gained brownie points for my life-long quest to find our friend. However, even in death, we competed for Johnny's friendship.

The passing years have revealed that Gio was a much more complex personality than the fun-loving, foul-mouthed guy I thought I knew. I whispered "Gio" and sang his verse.

> *His right hand strummed the chords,*
> *The rhythm in his wrist strong.*
> *His voice, his other instrument,*
> *Told the story of each song*

Our presentation had all been rehearsed way in advance. Our tribute stanzas had followed a particular order—the order that they left this earth. Therefore, Johnny's verse came last. If Gio was the mouth of Those Born Free, Johnny was the heart. He had brought together his old bandmates Gio and Jimmy Mac with his classmate Tinman, and Bracko, who he found in the Garden of Eden. Five very different guys who, when put together, created magic. I whispered "Johnny" and sang his verse.

He was hitting the low notes smoothly,
Four strings carrying the beat,
Pounding out the runs,
Bringing the crowd to its feet.

We were dancing,
We were dancing,
On the other side of the wind.

As the only ones in the band who had known Those Born Free, Chris and I sang harmony for the final verses of the song— the new verses. The verses about their ultimate fate.

They were brothers in the music,
Bonded in the song,
Five against the world
Thinking nothing could go wrong.

Now there is no running to the music,
The dance has gone all wrong.
They play no more tunes,
Silence is their song.

They were dancing,
They were dancing,
On the other side of the wind.

68

"All Things Must Pass"
- *George Harrison*

THE MUSIC OF CHRIS DELANEY and The Brotherhood Blues Band ended forever that night seven months ago. Chris returned to his beachfront home in South Carolina. Under the watchful eye of his private doctor, his wife Shylo, he hoped to enjoy life to the fullest.

Kevin and Tommy Delaney had had a lifetime of playing together, and they knew when to quit. It wouldn't have been the same without Chris at their side. They were satisfied to go home to Connecticut and spoil the accumulating grandkids.

Roberto Mac started a solo career. We get to see our son when he plays anywhere near New York. When we miss him too much, we hop on a plane and catch up with him. His wife Kristin and son Gram keep a home locally, and we get to have some real quality time together even if Roberto is away.

And me? I finally wrote the book that has been in the making for almost fifty years. After our performance at the Hall of Fame ceremony, numerous publishing houses approached me. They wanted to know if I would be interested in writing a book about Those Born Free and my half-century quest for their story. I laughed because they thought they had an original idea. I had already been researching and writing this story in my diary my entire life.

One of the less impressive book reps even had a title: *The Stanley and Livingstone of Rock and Roll*. If anyone younger than sixty even knew who those two 19th century guys were, I would be astonished. Besides, I already had a title, and it had come naturally to me.

Their Story—our story is one of loyalty and admiration—and honor and righteousness. And it all started over four decades before in the cafeteria of a Queens high school. It was then that Brother Christian took three impressionable young musicians under his wing. It was the beginning of a group that *would* die for each other—and did. I have come to realize that death didn't end the legacy of Those Born Free, or the effect that they had on the world. Oh so many people's lives were changed by their brief time on this Earth.

A band tape that found its way from Tinman to Brother Christian changed the direction of Chris Delaney's life and led to his redemption.

Bracko's selfless defense of Neil Connaughton led Neil to be the man who would ultimately save the lives of Trip Grimes and Chris Delaney, and later die a hero on 9/11.

Gio's love of Riet allowed her to keep her faith in him when all others had turned against him.

Mary Lou Casali's strength in facing Freddy Resch had been bolstered by the words of "Thief of My Forever."

Johnny's parents transformed their grief over the loss of Johnny into love and charity toward Mary Lou Casali and her son Alex.

Leo and Goody's lives had been changed by their experiences with Greg "Chinx" Cincotta—Chinx's own existence altered by his interaction with the band and later listening to the words on a simple tape recording.

Aylin's tumultuous path in life had only been resolved after the truth came to her while hearing the group talk about Sammy Crespo.

And me, DJ Spinelli, whose entire existence seems to have been raised up by a brief moment of enlightenment in the 1960s.

And the list goes on and on. Our story is one of the lives intertwined with five young men who never made it to their 18th birthdays. So many of us knitted together in the fabric of life for so very, very long—almost to a *forever* that no thief could ever steal.

We were bound together like a family. No, the name that I had always used without even understanding, now fits best. And so, it is with great pride that I will now put the final touches of the book that has been my life's work—*The Brotherhood of Forever: Those Born Free and the Legacy They Left Behind.*

69

"The Last Time"
- *The Rolling Stones*

March 2, 2015

AYLIN THOUGHT SHE WOULD HEAR an exuberant scream when it happened, but instead, DJ just stood solemnly in the doorway to their den and spoke quietly, "Aylin, it's done. I'm finally ready to send it to the publisher."

"So, DJ, does that mean we can finally cash that big, fat advance check they gave you?"

"Yeah, and let's buy something nice."

"DJ, we've had more than enough money for quite a while now. This isn't going to change our lives."

"You're right. Perhaps, I could use it to set up scholarships for musicians who want to hone their skills in college?"

"Or maybe just buy equipment for kids who are talented and can't afford lessons, or instruments, or anything?"

"Sounds good. Aylin, really you should be the one to decide."

"Why?"

"Think about it, Aylin. You and Roberto Mac are the only living blood relatives of Those Born Free. Their songs, their story, are by all rights yours to do what you wish."

"DJ, that's just not true. You're forgetting. . ."

"Oh yeah, your sister Maggie," shot back DJ.

"You know she took off after my mother died in 2007, and I

have no idea where she is. I mean someone else…"

"Yeah, Gio's son, Van DeAngelis. He has refused to talk to me for so long that I put him out of my mind." DJ's bitter resentment of Van was evident.

"But he is still an heir to their life story, even if he never met his father or knew anything about Those Born Free," offered Aylin.

"So, what are you suggesting?"

"DJ, you have to bring him in on this—get his blessing. After all, you are writing a book that includes his father's life and death. The question is, how to do it?"

"How about I send him a proof copy of the book before publishing it and then ask if he will meet with me. If nothing else, he needs to hear what happened to his father before the rest of the world."

"And then?"

"Then, Aylin, you and I are going to go see him in person and see what he has to say."

"And what if he doesn't give you his blessing after all these years of your research and writing?"

"Then, the book dies in my drawer."

"DJ!"

"Aylin, it just wouldn't be right."

"DJ, you're a good man. An idiot, but a good man."

◆

The plane taxied into Marathon Airport on a warm afternoon in March. Aylin had discovered that Van DeAngelis worked as an instructor and baseball coach at a college near Miami. She had packaged DJ's book *Brotherhood of Forever* along with an extremely long letter explaining everything that had happened in her husband's life—and everything that they knew about Van's father.

Three weeks had passed, and DJ and Aylin had received no response. Desperate at this point, they called Van's employer and were told by the departmental secretary that Mr. DeAngelis had indeed received the package. Mrs. Garcia was a fan of DJ Spinelli's writing and gave more information than she probably should have under confidentiality laws. She even pointed out that the coach had taken his team down to the lower Florida Keys for their traditional spring break getaway. She also told DJ where and when Van could be found—practicing each morning at the Sugarloaf School field.

Not only had Aylin booked them flights to Marathon Airport, but had called Chris and Shylo and asked if they would like to join them for a vacation. She pointed out all the sites found in Key West: Hemingway's House, sunset on Mallory Square, and a dozen other hotspots. The highlight of the trip would be meeting the son of Gio DeAngelis—if he would talk to them.

After arriving on the morning of March 5, the two couples started their trek down the overseas highway in a rented car. After taking the views on the Seven-Mile Bridge, they almost forgot their mission. However, they knew that Van DeAngelis and his team only practiced mornings and so they hurried along to arrive before practice ended.

Once they parked, it was easy to pick out Van. His 6'5" body towered over even the largest of his players and he still retained the fitness that had propelled him to a shortened, but stellar major league baseball career.

"Are you sure that he's Gio son?" said DJ shaking his head in disbelief. "He certainly didn't inherit his height from Gio. That guy would have kicked Daddy Gio's ass ten ways to Friday by the time he was six years old."

"Yeah, I know," said Aylin. "But from what I understand, he had an uncle on his mother's side that was that big at least. I hear his Uncle Thad died in prison a few years ago."

"OK, let's do this before I get cold feet."

"Why?"

"This is the closest I've been to someone associated with Those Born Free in almost a half a century."

"Oh yeah, who was that in bed with you last night? You do know after four decades of marriage that I *am* Jimmy Mac's sister?"

"Yeah, but this is new."

"Are you calling me old?"

"I would quit now," interjected Shylo.

"He should have quit ten minutes ago," added Chris.

They watched a few minutes as the coach, and his assistant worked the team through some drills, and the team looked pretty good.

"Maybe we shouldn't interrupt them," whined DJ.

"You got me to get on a goddamn plane and fly down here." chastened Chris in fake anger. "You are going to talk to Van—you little chicken shit."

"But he's soooo big," replied DJ.

"Yes, he is," agreed Shylo, teasing a sexual innuendo.

"Sure is," added Aylin in an equally flirtatious manner. The two women then laughed.

"OK, let's go talk to him before our two old ladies try to seduce him—or something worse," said Chris.

"Who you calling old ladies?" snapped Shylo.

"Shylo, have you looked in a mirror lately. We are old . . . but not dead. So I think we'll just keep looking," teased Aylin, and both women laughed heartily.

They all moved toward the batting cage that held Van DeAngelis. When DJ balked for a split second, Aylin placed her thumb and index in her mouth and let out a whistle that could be heard for miles.

"That's how my father used to call us home when we were kids," chuckled Aylin. The whistle had the desired effect as Van DeAngelis noticed them and walked toward the group.

"Hi, I'm. . . I'm DJ Spinelli."

However, Van looked right past him as if he wasn't there and approached Chris Delaney with a broad smile and extended hand.

"I'm a big fan of yours. Have all the records."

"Thank goodness, I brought him along," whispered DJ aside to Shylo and Aylin.

"I guess so," chuckled Shylo.

"Does he know I wrote most of the words to those songs he loves so much?"

Immediately, Van turned toward DJ, who had not whispered soft enough.

"I know exactly who you are. I've known for quite a while."

"Then why have you never answered me all the times that I've contacted you?"

"I saw no good reason. You were just a stranger trying to make money writing something sensational about my father."

"I knew him. I liked him. I could have told you so much about his life. . . about his group."

"But you couldn't tell me anything about my mother and him, could you?"

"No, but that's why I tried to talk to you. I wanted to know more about them—about all of them."

"I didn't know if you could be trusted. How did I know that you wouldn't write bad things about my parents, or worse?"

"What do you mean?"

"The first time I met you, how could I know you were not working for Mad Guy—and out to hurt us."

"But this *is* the first time."

"1990—you knocked on our door. You were a stranger at just a time when we had been warned to beware of strangers."

"Warned by whom? Wait! The only person who knew you were in danger was. . ."

"Johnny Cipp. Yup, he told us there were people out to get us—and then presto, you are at our door."

"That means that you knew, or at least met, Johnny. Right?"

"Let's just say he saved our lives and leave it at that."

"Wait! Was it Johnny's blood on Mad Guy's boat?"

Silence.

"So, was he still alive after 1990? You've got to tell me. Last year, Richie Shea told me he had just killed Johnny on a beach. Wait! It was down here in the Keys—that's where Johnny has been all this time. And you knew him."

"And loved him like a father." Van lowered his head.

"You've got to tell me more. I may have to revise this book."

"Oh, I would just throw the whole damn thing in the crapper."

"Why? I've worked on it for over a year after researching for four decades. It's been my life's passion."

"Life's passion? Thanks a lot," interjected his wife, Aylin. DJ ignored her and stared into Van's eyes.

"What aren't you telling me?"

Without a word, Van walked passed them toward the parking lot and opened the door of his late-model Honda. He picked up what looked like an old composition book. He came back toward the group.

"This will tell you the true story. It's quite different from what you wrote."

Van handed DJ the "Journal of Johnny Cipp."

"I don't understand. What is this?"

"Just read it, and you'll understand."

"But where? Where did this come from?"

Stunned, DJ Spinelli didn't notice Van's assistant coach approaching and starting to speak, "I gave it to him."

Shylo looked confused, while DJ and Chris stood in shocked disbelief.

"Johnny!" screamed Aylin as she ran to him.

70

"With a Little Help from My Friends"
- *The Beatles*

Diary of DJ Spinelli

Entry #98 – March 5, 2015

SO MANY YEARS, SO MANY words, and this diary didn't even get the story right. Tonight, when we meet, I'll give Johnny my diary. Do I have the time to edit it? Can I go back and erase all the passages where I showed my anger toward him? Can I take back the fact that I wrote my diary passages *to him*, rather than *about him*, precisely because I told him I was going to stick the book up his ass?

Our meeting this afternoon was emotional. Van's secretary had warned Johnny that we would be coming, but it didn't smooth the meeting between us. I can't imagine what it was like for him, all those years of isolation and despair abruptly ended by our arrival. We bombarded him with questions, and he pulled back, definitely overwhelmed. Johnny stopped us in our tracks.

"Take my journal and read it. It will answer all your questions without me having to relive the events of my life all over again. When you have all your answers, we'll meet up tonight—at my club." Johnny smiled for the first time since we had found him. "Yup, my club, the Those Born Free Club. Just get into

Key West, and almost anyone can tell you where to find me."
He took a few steps toward the parking lot, and then turned
and ran back to Aylin and grabbed her in a bear hug. Still holding her, he pulled me and Chris and even Shylo into a massive
group hug.

Tears streamed down from his eyes, but his smile was conta-
gious. We all held each other tightly, but only Johnny spoke or
rather sang slowly.

> *Sometimes I sit for hours,*
> *Thinking of times past,*
> *All those years of innocence,*
> *that abandoned me so fast.*

"Tonight," he said and walked away.

We all recognized the line from the "Thief of My Forever."
Johnny had written that verse with his band, and we had sold
millions of copies of it when we released it. I think we ought to
talk about giving him (and Van) a hell of a lot of royalties.

Entry #99 – March 5, 2015 (later)

We read Johnny's journal together this afternoon. We took
turns reading aloud. Each of us would continue until emotion
choked our throats closed. The book was then passed around
to the next person. Now we understood—now we knew. I was
the one reading when we came to the end. The final journal
entries had been written about a year ago—just *before* I had
visited Richie Shea in the hospital. A scrap of paper acted as
a bookmark to the location, and Johnny had hastily scribbled
some words on it—probably this very morning.

"DJ, this will give you a hell of a climax to your damn book!"

71

"Still Crazy After All These Years"
-Paul Simon

Journal of Johnny Cipp

Entry #111- February 15, 2013 - 11:37 p.m. (my final entry)

THE BAND NOW FADES FROM the clouds, and there is a silence on the beach. The tingling sensation again tells me that the Music Doctor wants to speak to me. He wants to educate me. He wants me to know that I am right. I am the last vestige of something that was but is not anymore. When I go, the memories of us will truly "fade to never."

He's laughing at the irony that it has taken me forty-six years to come upon the one line of a song, a song whose release by The Youngbloods came on the very day of our demise and spoke to the truth of our existence.

"We were but a moment's sunlight. . . fading in the grass."

Feb. 16, 2013 12:03 a.m. (entry continued)

There are no words to explain what happened to me a few moments ago. But I'll try. I'd just finished being philosophical about no one remembering us. And then good old Karma gave me a gut punch. Oh yeah, I was remembered, but by the wrong person. After I wrote that last entry, I walked to the water's edge. I always do that to make myself remember how I almost foolishly took my life in 1990. My shoes were off, and I was calf-deep in the water when I heard my name called.

Was it the band beckoning me? I fell for that once. It could have been the wind. There I stood staring at the clouds—saying my nightly goodbyes to the guys when I heard my name again followed by footsteps, walking in the sand.

"Johnny," again. But it was not from the band. It was behind me. I turned. The voice had a body—Richie Shea. The man who said he would kill me if he ever saw me again—was seeing me again. Dammit, I should have expected this after I went to Riet's funeral. But why does he call my name? Why does he care?

"What the fuck were you doing? Trying to kill yourself?"

I don't answer. Could I tell Shea that I'd been there and done that more than twenty years ago? However, my life was good now. I wouldn't mess it up for anything. Would he care? From his point of view, I had messed it up. I'd gone to Riet's funeral.

I staggered on to the sand. I sat down in silent acceptance of my fate. He sat beside me as if we were old friends. I finally answered him.

"I once tried to do your job for you."

"What job is that, Johnny Fuckin' Cipp, as my cousin called you?"

"Killing me."

"Well, death isn't always the answer."

I remind him that he once hunted me to cause that death.

He didn't answer immediately. A huge cough enveloped him. It occurred to me that this man was not well. He struggled to breathe. "Take it from someone who knows."

"Because you caused so much of it?" I'm bold. Nothing I say or do is going to change why he is here.

"Believe it or not, I never killed anyone in my life. Sure, I covered it up for my crazy cousin, and I'll pay for that someday soon." He looks to the sky.

"So, when you threatened me with death if I ever came back to New York?"

"I would love to play poker with you. It was all a bluff."

"So, I almost missed Riet's funeral for no reason?"

"Well, not exactly. There is a good chance you are going to die because you went to that funeral."

"But I thought you said . . ."

"Not from me," His voice grew in volume from either anger or frustration. He then immediately went into a prolonged coughing spasm that seemed to tear apart his insides. He got back his composure and continued.

"When you killed Mad Guy Provenzano, his sons were little."

"Who me?" I interrupted.

"I don't have time to play games. But if you prefer, when you went on your cruise with my lunatic cousin, his kids were still just kids. But now . . ."

"Are you telling me that I now have two little 'Mad Guys' out to get me?"

"Well, one at least. Guy has two sons Dominick and Carmine. It turns out that Carmine is a little faggot. He moved to the East Village, changed his name to Carmen, and performs in a drag show called 'Good Bellas.' Get the play on words?" With that, a small smile crossed his face. "It would've killed Guy if someone hadn't already done that." He looked at me accusingly. He never did find out that it was Tony who actually committed the act.

"Yeah, someone," I sneered, being snarky.

"But his other son, Dominick, named after his violent grandfather, might be even crazier than Guy."

"Is that even possible?" He didn't hesitate a second to answer me.

"Yes, fucking yes. The apple didn't fall far from the tree. I've spent decades trying to keep *D-mon* in line. Yeah, that's what they call him." As if on cue, he let out a prolonged mucous filled cough. He continued, "And I won't be doing that much longer."

"You're sick?"

"I'm fucking dying, asshole. I would gladly trade places with you now."

"Sorry," I mumbled, and unbelievably, I think that I meant it.

"Dominick has been angry and confused about his father's abrupt passing. He was never satisfied with all the explanations I gave him. It built up inside of him. He had guys investigating for years, and he eventually got most of the story about his father and Those Born Free."

"Shit!"

"Shit is right. D-Mon sent guys to Riet's funeral. If they had seen you, well, that is why I told you that I saved your life by banning you from New York."

"But Mad Guy never did find me."

"Yeah, but I did! I simply had guys follow Van after the funeral. I was there when he left that stupid book at your club. Hell, I was at your club tonight. 'Fear the Reaper'? What was that all about? The soundtrack of your life?"

"Music Doctor," I mumbled and then just finished with, "Never mind."

"Get the hell out of here. Go somewhere else. D-mon's got a computer search and good old-fashioned privates eyes looking for you."

"I can't do that. This is my life now."

"Well, not for long."

"Yeah, but you just gave me a reason to live. Now I want to stick it to another Provenzano."

"You know that you are nuts, Johnny?"

"Yup." I took notice that his voice was more compassionate and that I had become "Johnny" instead of "Johnny Fuckin' Cipp."

"You gonna make it back to New York?"

"Yeah, I have to. Believe it or not, I'm going to do everything I can to protect you. Anybody asks me—you're dead. At least that's what I'll say."

"Not that I'm sorry, but why?"

"I don't know. Regret? Remorse? Restitution? I'm hoping the Big-Guy-Up-There takes notice and takes care of me in the end."

I didn't know what to say.

"Come here, kid," he said, and he pulled out a Glock. I didn't have time to be terrified before he took the clip out and removed one bullet. As I came closer, he reached up with a shaky hand and put the shell in my ear! He laughed so hard that he fell to the ground gasping for breath, but still smiling.

"What the hell was that?"

"Anyone—I mean anyone—asks me about you," Shea started laughing and wheezing—finding it harder and harder to breathe as he tried to stand up. He fell back to his knees. "I'm going to tell him that I put a bullet in your head. Get it? I mean, I don't want to be lying on my deathbed, right?" He laughed even louder, coughing ferociously.

I thought he was nuts, but he was now my protector. I helped him up. He started to walk away across the sand. I knew I would never see him again. When he turned back to wave, I had to speak.

"What's wrong with you?"

He looked at me and somehow suppressed a cough. He didn't answer right away. I guess that he was deciding if we were close enough buddies after our almost half-century, love/hate relationship.

"You know, I was a good cop. I loved it. I just couldn't say no to my cousin. Eventually, I bought into the lifestyle. I liked the money. But I never stopped being a damn good cop."

I didn't know what this had to do with anything, but he was opening up to me. Was I going to argue with someone who had just traveled 1500 miles to warn me of danger?

"Damn good cop," he mumbled again. I said nothing at first, but then gave in to my curiosity,

"So, what happened?"

"9/11 is what happened. I was twenty years off the force and the subject of more than one FBI investigation. I put everything aside and went down to be with my brothers at ground zero. I stayed there for six months. I have one of those cancers caused by breathing in all the fucking bad air."

I hadn't seen that coming.

"They gave me about eight months—eight months ago. But, hey, you think that you got bigger problems?"

How could I answer him? I didn't.

"Live, kid,"

I'm wondering what's with this kid stuff when he hit me with the final bombshell.

"Lotta funerals up there. I just went to one a couple of months ago."

I'm thinking Riet, but that was only last month. Maybe he was confused.

"While they were treating me at Memorial-Sloan Kettering, I struck a friendship with a guy about your age. He was suffering the same as me—only he was further along. We had the same oncologist. He was also NYPD, but I didn't know him. He had worked every day after his shift, combing through the rubble of Ground Zero."

I looked in his eyes. This story was not going to end well.

"We became friends before he died, sharing cop stories and stuff. I went to his funeral. You should have gone to that funeral too."

OK, now he had me confused.

"His wife grieved, but she had known that it was coming for a long, long time. I guess she had prepared herself. It was me who was thrown for a loop when I went up to give my condolences."

"Why?"

"The cop's name was Jason Carlson. His wife was that girl Maria Romano that you used to date. I knew her immediately. I mean, I had followed her for a very long time, waiting to see if you would contact her."

"Maria?"

He got up to leave, a little smirk on his face. "Still want to take that permanent swim now that the widow Carlson is available?"

I started to tell him again I never had any intention of repeating my 1990 plunge, but he was already leaving. Besides, my mind couldn't stop thinking of his last revelation.

I never saw Richie Shea again. I went on the computer every day to read the New York newspapers to see if I could find out what was going on with Richie and his heir apparent Dominick "D-Mon" Provenzano.

Richie Shea died quietly in his hospital bed a week later. The next day, the *Fun Ghoul* was found drifting in the Long Island

Sound with its lone passenger, Dominick "D-mon" Provenzano, dead of a bullet neatly placed in his forehead. Richie must have had someone do it for him. You were a bastard, but thanks, Richie.

72

"Gonna Live Like Tomorrow Never Comes"
- *Zac Brown*

Diary of DJ Spinelli

Entry #100 – March 5, 2015

IT MAY TAKE A WHILE, but with Johnny's permission, I will re-write my book. This time it will have the correct ending. I understand events much clearer now.

Shea was protecting Johnny when he lied to me. I can only guess that the cryptic phone call I heard outside his hospital room, "Do it," was the death order for Dominick "D-mon" Provenzano. Remorse for all he had done to Those Born Free, or one final act to reclaim his eternal salvation?

I don't know. There are far too many little details I need to clarify. I'll have to ask Johnny to elaborate on events. That means we'll be talking a great deal. We both look forward to that.

But that's in the future. Tonight, we partied. Unlike the confusion and chaos of our meeting this afternoon, our reunion at Johnny's club was a time of raucous celebration. Johnny introduced all of us to Padre, Cal, and Van's family. We laughed and told stories, and the years faded away. Music filled the Those

Born Free club, and even that was a surrealistic experience. The house band included two of Van's children—Harriet Callie and John Earl.

It did not take long for the audience to realize that there were two celebrities in attendance. Chanting, led by Van and his entire family, urged Chris and me to take the stage. Shylo was terrified until Chris whispered to her.

"I got this."

"You sure?"

"Yeah, but only if DJ and Johnny come with me."

What could we say?

Chris found his way to the keyboard, and Johnny picked up the bass. Van's son John stayed on the drums, and his daughter seamlessly moved from the keyboard to the guitar.

I could have picked up the other guitar, but I didn't. As I looked at Johnny, he smiled. After almost a half-century, I knew what he would do. As he hit the first four notes of a bass run, I retrieved a tambourine and once again became the swirling dervish of Mr. Tambourine Man that had so long ago inhabited our high school auditorium. It had not been planned, but Chris hit the organ intro, and the Spencer Davis Group's "Gimme Some a' Lovin'" filled the club. I twirled and struck a rhythmic beat on the tambourine that jangled throughout the house, and Chris sang his heart out. Suddenly, we were back at McCarthy High, and we were young and having fun. Yet we all knew that someone was missing. There was no attempt to give the macho pretense of hardness. The tears rolled down all of our cheeks, and Chris's voice cracked with emotion. Joey Tinman should have been here.

———◆———

At Midnight, we left the club. We asked all our friends to join us, but they all respectfully declined. They must have sensed this would be a special time when the remnants of another life needed to be together alone. We piled into our rental car and drove down to Zachary Taylor Beach. Because I had just read the final entry of Johnny's journal, the irony of the location wasn't lost on me. Though the beach was closed, Johnny knew a secret hole in the fence just like he did into the Garden of

Eden.

As we sat in the sand, it was if we had been together for all these decades. Chris and Shylo cuddled under a blanket, while Johnny, Aylin, and I built an illegal bonfire. We had brought a few guitars with us and spent some time singing some classic songs. It was here that we played the songs written by Those Born Free and recorded by Brotherhood Blues Band. Johnny and I even got up the balls to sing some of the bad ones we had written in high school.

We laughed a lot—and we cried even more. Randomly throughout the night, there were deep enduring hugs. No one wanted the night to end. No one wanted to break the magic spell that so enthralled us. As the red and yellow clouds of night framed the moon, I thought the significance of the moment would be lost—but we had all read Johnny's journal before coming to the club.

"Well, are they out there?" I questioned as I looked at him and pointed out to the clouds."

"They're always out there for me."

"Your band in the wind," I said, looking away from the sky and into Johnny's eyes. The rest of the gang understood.

"Did you almost . . ." mumbled an upset Chris.

"Yeah, I almost did."

There was an awkward silence until Aylin spoke. "I think I see them out there—your Band in the Wind. There's my brother. Those sticks of his are banging away just like I remember."

"Yes, Joey Tinman, play those keyboards," added Chris.

"So that's Bracko," said Shylo, "I remember Neil talking about him."

"Yeah, and there's Gio," shouted Aylin, and then imitated *her* mother to perfection, "The mouth on you, Gio DeAngelis."

We all laughed.

"Thanks for humoring my insanity. You know this is just my way of honoring the memories of those who are gone. For so many years, they were all I had," sobbed Johnny.

"Not anymore," I insisted as I put my arm on his shoulder.

"Not anymore," repeated Aylin and hugged his other shoulder. Chris and Shylo joined us.

What had once been Johnny's alone, would now forever be shared with us. Our five embracing bodies stared at the clouds as if they were a cathedral to the lost.

73

"Grow Old with Me"
- John Lennon

SHYLO COULD SEE THAT CHRIS was exhausted. His rapidly deteriorating medical condition had been pushed to its limits by the night's events. As they rose to leave, Aylin and DJ knew it was time to drive them back to their hotel.

"C'mon, Johnny, we'll give you a ride back to your place."

"Naw, I'm going to stay here a while. I'm meeting someone."

"What? Who?" asked DJ but then remembered from the journal that Padre did his nightly rounds picking up the Key-wasted on this beach.

"Don't worry. This is my home. I'll be fine."

"OK. See you tomorrow."

"Wouldn't miss it."

Johnny sat for another hour, strumming his guitar before he heard the expected footsteps walking in the sand.

She sat next to him.

"So how are the grandkids? And how was your flight from New York?"

"Good and good. I'll tell you the details later. I have to know how today went."

"Fantastic, I have so much to share with you."

"And what did DJ say when he heard about me?"

"I didn't tell them about you—yet. I didn't want to blow his mind completely the first time I saw him."

She took his right hand in her left, the silver band on her

index finger shining brightly in the moonlight. They lovingly peered into each other's eyes.

"Johnny, play for me."

"Don't I always? I think a little John Lennon to start."

"Yeah, you know I love that one."

> *Grow old along with me,*
> *The best is yet to be.*
> *When our time has come,*
> *We will be as one.*

> *God bless our love,*
> *God bless our love,*

Johnny played and sang the entire song, never taking his eyes off her face—a face that smiled back at him with an undying love. When he had finished, he could see that she was working hard to keep her eyes from closing.

"You look tired. Let me get you home."

He started to put his guitar in its case, but she put her hand on his wrist to stop him.

"Not until you do our song. You promised me that you would sing it to me every night of my life."

"For all those years, it was only a vision of a life. . . Gio and I in a make-believe world singing to you and . . ."

Johnny looked away at the clouds that were streaked with glowing moonlight, unable to finish the sentence.

"Do you see them?" murmured Johnny.

"Yes, of course," was her answer.

"It's Gio and Riet."

"Yeah."

"Johnny, somehow, I know they are happy that you became a father to Van."

"Hear that, Gio? She thinks you're happy with me. Think you'll ever admit that to me?"

"Don't get off track. Johnny, my song."

He hit the chords and sang as best he could the words to "Wonderful Tonight" by Eric Clapton. He remembered the despair of all the years that he had lost in a fog of drugs and alcohol. He also recalled that while in that haze, a single dream kept him going—a vision of a different life. It was a life where Gio had lived, and they had grown old and enjoyed times where they sang to their wives—and this was the song that they sang.

After the first two stanzas were completed, he again gazed in her eyes with a look of eternal love. A smile came over his face as he sang the words of the bridge...

I feel wonderful because
I see the love light in your eyes.
And the wonder of it all,
Is that you just don't realize,
How much I love you.

Maria lay her head on Johnny's shoulder and hugged him tightly.

EPILOGUE
to
Band in the Wind
Trilogy

"I'm Not Afraid of Getting Older, I'm One Less Day from Dying Young"
- Rob Thomas

June 19, 2037

"The End of the Line"

"Even if you're old and grey,
You still got something to say."
- The Traveling Wilburys

Diary of DJ Spinelli

Entry #327 – June 19, 2037

JOHNNY, THIS WILL BE THE final entry in my diary. You will notice I'm again writing *to* you, not *about* you. That is because I've reached the end of the line—or "The End of the Line." As you know, I started to use your Music Doctor's method of labeling my diary entries with a song. I think this one is fitting.

I've handed off my completed diary to my son Robby Mac. What he does with it is up to him. However, I wanted to send you my final thoughts in this email.

I know in the last two decades we have discussed my almost half-century quest to find you and the guilt you felt about it. Johnny, I want you to know once and for all that I didn't waste my time. The diary I wrote and the journal you wrote were the basis of the book that told the entire story of you and the rest of the band. That story needed to get out there. However, I don't want you to think that I lost all those years. I had a wonderful life. It was tough at the beginning with all the turmoil that Aylin went through, and I won't rehash that here.

I wouldn't do anything differently. I had my ups and downs, but it was never dull. I had friends who were everything to me and still are, even if they are now all gone. Most of all, I've had the love of a woman, a son, and a grandson. I miss Aylin, but I will be joining her very, very soon. I guess I will finally be able to answer that age-old rock n' roll question. Why is there a "Highway to Hell" and only a "Stairway to Heaven?"

I guess the best way to explain what I'm trying to say is to call upon our friend, the Music Doctor again. I wrote the song "Dancing on the Other Side of the Wind" to tell your story, a story of a group of guys who never got to live in the turmoil and excitement of this world—who never really got to live at all. Instead, they (and you) existed on the other side of the wind—a place devoid of the happiness and fulfillment you deserved.

Johnny, that wasn't me. You can shitcan the guilt once and for all. I did live. I did love. I did dance *in* the wind.

Farewell, my friend,

DJ

Knockin' on Heaven's Door
- *Eric Clapton version*

HIS ANCIENT EYES LOOKED UP from DJ's letter and peered at the TV in front of him. He ignored the sounds coming from the Those Born Free Club that lay on the first floor of his building.

Johnny had long since given over control of the club to Van DeAngelis and his family. In reality, it was his family. Johnny had long ago taken over the role of the patriarch—a position that should have belonged to his best friend, Gio. In his life, he had been called Johnny, Jack, Captain Jack, Just Jack, and Jackass. He now cherished being called J by his friends and acquaintances and Uncle J by his family.

A soft tap on the door of his apartment announced the arrival of the nightly visit of his "great-grandson."

"Come on in, Gio. I just want to see the nightly news before we go."

"Uncle J, you know I don't like being called Gio. I prefer Giovanni," answered the 17-year-old.

"Ha, your great-grandfather would roll over in his grave if he heard you say that." There was a slight smile in the older man's manner, but an undercurrent of sadness lay below the surface.

"I'm proud to be Giovanni DeAngelis IV—but you know that all the nicknames have been used up. My great-grandfather, your buddy, was the 'Gio' in Giovanni. And then, my grandfather was the 'Van,' and then my father got stuck with the last syllable and became 'Ni' and eventually 'Nico.' It's about time that someone used the whole damn name."

"OK, Giovanni, it is."

"Besides, it's interesting to meet people who try to figure out how a black kid got an Italian name."

As Uncle J looked at Giovanni, he had to smile. The kid was very obviously a young black man with an Italian name. Less than 10% of Giovanni's genetics came from his great-grandfather Gio. Yet, whenever Johnny looked in his face, he could not help seeing the mischievous glint in his eye that was so reminiscent of his best friend. The news anchor's voice from the TV interrupted his nostalgic thoughts...

We are all saddened to learn of the death of DJ Spinelli today at age 88. He is best known for winning a Pulitzer Prize, a Grammy, and for being inducted into the Rock and Roll Hall of Fame. His long and illustrious career began as a member of the successful Chris Delaney and the Brotherhood Blues Band, where he played rhythm guitar and wrote or co-wrote most of the group's hit songs. Even after he left the group, he continued to work with the band as a songwriter.

He then published decades of popular fiction and non-fiction works that sold over ten million copies. In 2015, he won the Pulitzer Prize for his non-fiction tome, Brotherhood of Forever, which chronicled the tale of a 1960s garage band whose members were murdered by the late mob boss, Gaetano "Mad Guy" Provenzano. Spinelli was able to document the story due to the contributions of John Cippitelli, the lone survivor of what the author referred to as the "Holocaust in the Heights," referring to the location of the murders—Cambria Heights in Queens, New York.

Johnny Cipp, as he is better known, has only appeared in public once, and his present location is a well-kept secret.

"It's not a secret to me! You're sitting right here," yelled Giovanni at the TV.

"Shhhh!" reacted Johnny.

Johnny Cipp's only known appearance in public came when he per-

formed with DJ Spinelli, at a memorial service for Chris Delaney. Delaney, along with his wife Shylo, had succumbed to the Covid-19 virus of 2020.

Dennis James "DJ" Spinelli will be buried on Thursday. He is survived by his son, superstar guitarist, Roberto Mac and grandson Gram Spinelli. His wife Aylin McAvoy Spinelli pre-deceased him in 2035

Thank you for being with us for this edition of the Nightly News.

"You OK, Uncle J?" Giovanni had noticed the formation of tears in the older man's eyes.

"Yeah, I'll deal with it. What choice do I have? But he was the last. They're all gone. The band, Padre, Cal, Riet, and Maria—everyone but me."

"Yeah, I loved to visit Aunt Maria and you. Especially when we stayed over, and you babysat us."

"Those were fun times."

"Yeah, she used to sing us to sleep. While she sang, she told us that it was to keep you from singing to us."

"Not very funny."

"I think her favorite comment to you was that 'Louie, Louie' was not a lullaby."

"Still not funny, Giovanni."

"You still want to go? You know, to the beach? I mean, are you still up for it after hearing this," said Giovanni nodding toward the TV.

"I want to go, especially after this."

"C'mon, I'll help you get down the stairs."

"Don't forget the journal and my guitar too."

"Why do you take these old things? The pages of this book aren't even attached to the binding anymore. I know you have trouble playing the guitar with your arthritis."

"They're my oldest friends—at least now they are. They give me comfort. And sometimes I even write in the book, or play the guitar."

"OK, I got them. Now, let's get you down the stairs and to the beach before you miss the sunset."

As they slowly made their way down the narrow and winding staircase, the music grew louder. Van and his three children came into view. Johnny saw them almost every day of his life now. Although Van officially ran Those Born Free Club, he handed off day-to-day operations to his eldest son Nico DeAngelis after he hit his 65th birthday. After retiring from a successful baseball career with the Yankees, Nico built a small empire around the concept that Johnny had started. He had Those Born Free clubs in Orlando and Miami and was in the process of expanding the franchise to Las Vegas, Los Angeles, and New York. Van was very proud of Nico and had become satisfied with his limited management role. He liked spending a quiet retirement with his wife, Kim.

As Uncle J was giving an affectionate hug to both Van and Nico, he heard music from the main stage area.

"Gio. . . ah, Giovanni, I'll be ready in a minute. Let's go say hello to your aunt and uncle."

Lead singer Harriet DeAngelis, only daughter of Van De Angelis, sang soulfully while playing the keyboard with skills obtained at Berklee College of Music. Her brother John-Earl was considered one of the best drummers in all of the Florida Keys. As their Uncle J entered the room, they immediately broke into their version of "Dancing on the Other Side of the Wind." They had gotten through the first verse when they saw their nephew Giovanni emphatically motioning for them to stop. Harriet and John-Earl signaled the rest of the band to stop playing. The song abruptly ended.

"Bad timing," whispered Giovanni as he made his way over to his aunt and uncle to explain the death of DJ Spinelli, author of the song. However, Uncle J saw what was happening and interrupted in the loudest volume his feeble voice box could muster.

"Play the damn song. That's how we remember people. I think the Music Doctor would think this just the right choice. Play it for DJ. Play for your grandfather Gio and your grandmother Riet. Play it for all of them. . . and for Maria and me."

We were living lives of passion,
Never wanting to go slow,
Never worryin' about tomorrow,

Never knowing which way to go.

We were dancing,
We were dancing,
On the other side of the wind.

A smile crossed Johnny's face, and he saluted the band as he and Giovanni made their way to the door. As he took one final look at the stage, his eyes focused on the bass drum, which held the band's name.

"Love that name."

"You should," said Giovanni. "It's a tribute to our whole family—and that includes you. We were all brought up to know the story of our great-grandfather Gio and our great-grandmother Riet—and you and Aunt Maria. And Bracko, and Tinman and Aunt Aylin's brother Jimmy Mac—and the story of Those Born Free."

"Yeah, but I didn't know that the Music Doctor even knew how to name a band."

"Think about it. Your journal was required reading in our family. It was the *Journal of Johnny Cipp* and the Bible—and I think that was the order of priority. We read every word. We know the story—and we *are* the DeAngelis Family, you know "of the angels." So I think that Harriet and John-Earl got it just right."

Johnny turned again to look at the bass drum and the writing that said, "Angels of the Wind."

———◆———

Giovanni started up his car as he turned to his Uncle J.

"You know, I remember him."

"Who?"

"DJ Spinelli—Uncle DJ." I know he hasn't been down here since he got too old to travel, but I do remember his visits. He used to drive down with Aunt Aylin in his 1949 Buick Sedanet. Sometimes he brought his son Roberto.

"You remember that? But you were so little."

"Well. Roberto Mac played the guitar in the club and brought down the house—and the Buick was dark green."

"How?"

"When someone tells me that he is in a car that was built the year that he was born and he's ancient, well, that's something you just don't forget."

"Gio—excuse me, Giovanni—you are amazing. His voice drifted off, and he sat silent until they arrived at the beach.

———◆———

"You sure that you don't want me to bring the folding chair I have in the car?"

"Nope, I want my toes in the water and my ass in the sand."

"Huh?"

"It's before your time—Zac Brown Band."

"Huh, I don't get it."

"Music Doctor, what am I going to do with these kids?"

"Oh, I get it. It's an old song."

"Yeah, real old, maybe 2010."

"Are you sure you don't want me to stay?"

"No, No, I enjoy being here alone."

"You're not alone," laughed Giovanni as he nodded toward the western sky and the setting sun. "We all understand that."

"Still crazy after all these years."

"You're not crazy. You just have a place to remember your friends—your Band in the Wind."

"Like I said, 'Still crazy after all these years.'"

"I'll be back while there is still enough light to get you off this beach and home in bed."

"Good enough."

"You know, Uncle J, I love you. We all love you."

"Yeah, I'm a damn lucky man."

Giovanni walked away. Left alone, Johnny took a pen from his shirt pocket, opened his journal, and began writing.

Journal of Johnny Cipp

"Thief of My Forever"

"In time, time takes everything."
- *Those Born Free and Chris Delaney and the Brotherhood Blues Band*

Entry #236 June 19, 2037

AGAIN, I SIT ON THIS moonlit beach. I do this almost every night. It's here that I find peace. It is here in the clouds that I can see my long-departed friends. It's on this beach that I can hear them play. I'm not crazy. I know they long ago left this mortal earth. However, most of them have graves in places I can never visit—and my best friend Gio has no grave at all. And so, this has to be the place where I can reminisce—where I can talk to them and be with them.

This particular beach had been so much a part of my life for so long. If these grains of sand could talk, they would tell the story of most of my adult life. It was here that I frequently found myself during a two-decade-long struggle with drugs and alcohol. It was here that Padre found me and started me on a path to sobriety. And it was here that I tried to take my life in 1990. It was here that I had my final encounter with Richie Shea. It was here that Maria and I spent our golden years finally being together until she finally. . .

I still remember that night with DJ, Chris, Aylin, and Shylo even though it was over two decades ago. They were so surprised to see that Maria and I had finally found each other—and it was Richie Shea who was responsible. When he told me that

Maria had been widowed, I lived out the moment that had been my fantasy for over thirty years. I drove the length of the East Coast—but I wasn't alone. The Music Doctor took the trip with me. He worked overtime coming up with songs that made the 1300 miles seem like nothing. "I Know You're Out There Somewhere" started my journey. And I couldn't help repeating "If We Don't Die Young, We Might Just Live Forever" by Little Big Town. And of course, "Grow Old with Me" and "Wonderful Tonight."

It was like a Hollywood movie. When I reached her door, no words were spoken—we just fell into each other's arms. We finally lived the life we had both had imagined so many years before. Each morning, Maria made sure that the two plastic flamingos on our lawn faced each other so that their heads and necks formed a heart—a reminder of all of the obstacles we had to overcome before finally being together. We had twenty-three beautiful years before I lost her.

Now DJ is gone too—the last link to the past. I had always felt that I was alone—apart from the real world. Now I really am. For a while, it seemed as if the universe spun forward, and people lived their lives—leaving me behind. I was on the outside—on the other side of the wind, a wind we had tried to catch in 1967. Decades ago, DJ wrote the words to "Dancing on the Other Side of the Wind" to express what had happened to me—to all of Those Born Free. *They* never got to live in this world. But I eventually did.

Strangely, I am the only one who understands the real irony of DJ dying today—70 years exactly after my hell began. June 19, 1967, was the day the raid on the Driftwood Club took everything from me. What did you write, Bracko? "In time, time takes everything." Yes, everything. Music Doctor, are you with me for this last trip? Will you take this journey with me?

I'm so tired. I just need to write one last entry—one final verse to our song. Perhaps, I can play it on my guitar. I'm straining to see all of my friends one last time. My eyes grow so weary I think that I will close them and rest awhile . . .

DJ, I haven't seen you in so long. Are you ready to do this? Maria and Aylin wait for us.

I can hear the music more clearly now.

Sure, guys, let's play, "Louie, Louie."

Maria, I love you. . . and, of course, you look wonderful tonight. Yeah, I know I have said that every night to you since I found you in my arms again in 2013. I've missed you. Now I will whisper them to you every night again—in person.

Slowly, his body eased down to the sand. His left hand stretched to touch the strings of his guitar one last time. His right hand lost its grip on the pen he had clutched, and his journal fell from his lap. The cardboard of its cover had long ago lost cohesive control of the pages held within. Those pages and half a lifetime of words written on them were lifted by the sea breezes and blown along the sand until they reached the water's edge. The incoming tide consumed them—except for its one final page of writing, which miraculously withstood the onslaught of seawater. These words were the last vestiges of the Journal of Johnny Cipp—its thoughts the last thoughts of his mortal being—a final verse to a song written so long ago.

> *Sometimes I sit for hours,*
> *Mourning times before.*
> *A kiss, a touch, my happiness,*
> *Lie just beyond the door.*

In time, the powerful surf took even that single page to a watery grave.

And the Band in the Wind welcomed Johnny to the stage.

Author's Note: In My Real World

"It's All Over Now"
- *Rolling Stones*

I T REALLY IS ALL OVER now. I've come to an end of my life-long journey to tell the fictional/nonfictional story of Johnny Cipp. As I have written many times and revealed on TV interviews—some of this story is true. I have made a careful effort to intertwine that which is real with that which is not. Hopefully, readers cannot tell the difference. However, as an act of closure, I don't want to leave you guessing.

I initially wrote a list of all the actual events that influenced this story. However, if I mentioned all of them, this section could have been another book. Therefore, I have culled it down to those I deemed most essential to telling my tale. I will eventually tell the rest of my background story on my website.

———◆———

The idea of the "lost" Those Born Free tapes came late to the party. I had already written the first two books when I found tapes from 1969. They were not from any band that I had ever been in, but rather just some of the many jam sessions that I periodically engaged in while in college. The guitarist, Bob Cappuccio was the basis of all the guitarists that appeared in these books. He did not suffer the abuse of Bracko or the addiction of Bobby Bright Eyes, but his playing was the model for both of them. More than that, the tapes revealed the humorous byplay before, after, and sometimes even during songs. It gave me the inspiration to include and expand these to remembered and misremembered conversations of the bands with whom I had played. I then came upon the idea that these tapes would be found by DJ and Aylin in *the Brotherhood of Forever*. I then had to go back and include mention of the recordings in the first two novels.

My house did have an ugly Rheingold clock down the basement. My father had a habit of collecting ugly neon signs.

A friend of mine became a New York City police cadet at age 18. I barely had taken my first credits in college and he was out in the streets.

The story of Chris Delaney's experience playing at a fraternity party happened exactly as described in 1968.

The Cambria neighborhood was rife with stories of girls who closely mirrored the life of Mary Lou Casali. Teen pregnancy was usually met with marriage at age 15 or 16.

Fred's Place did exist in Southington, Connecticut. My step-grandfather Fred and my grandmother Robina owned the place, and they did have the Connecticut State Horseshoe Championships there in the 1950s and 1960s.

There was a "Dougie Douchebag." Though he was a nice guy, he was in Queens College for seven years. He never went to class and never got any credits.

Johnny Cipp's bedroom, as described, *was* my attic bedroom on 217th street in Cambria Heights. It was accessed by eighteen winding steps complete with sheet music and other debris on the first four steps. Once in my cross-shaped room, the clutter was incalculable with dirty clothes and various guitars, and other instruments that I attempted to teach myself. Until the day I left home, there were comic books and a Hall of Monsters.

—◆—

St. Albans Naval Hospital was only three miles from my house, and my father was a nurse on the staff before leaving the Navy.

—◆—

My daughter, Brittany, did live in the building I named the Grand Lispenard. Its physical description, as well as its location, are precisely as depicted. It had the defunct music studio rooms described and was definitely a fire hazard. In the book, I left out the part about the trapeze artist swings that hung from the high ceiling and were used for a resident's practice circus sessions. With gentrification, the building is now an art gallery.

—◆—

Though not as violent as many cities in America, there were riots in New York City following the assassination of Dr. Martin Luther King. Due to the mayor and black leaders' cooperation at the time, they were held to the minimum. Weeks later, there was a riot on the campus of Queens College. In a secluded music lab most of the afternoon, my girlfriend (future wife) and I found ourselves trapped between the violent crowd and the massive angry police presence sent to quell them. Unbelievably, we found ourselves unable to get off the campus because every gate was locked—trapping us. Unlike the emotional Aylin, my future wife, Marilyn was able to scale the ten-foot fence as we barely escaped.

—◆—

Though the story of the Weissmans and Bobby Bright Eyes is fictional, it is a story based on some reality. It is part of our family legacy, how my maternal grandparents, Tony and Lola, got caught up in the revolution of Fidel Castro. While visiting Cuba, they barely made it onto the last ship out of Havana. I simply added a little stowaway to the story.

—◆—

DJ Spinelli is based on a friend I met more than a half-century ago in my freshmen year of Archbishop Molloy High School. While the rest of my friends were jocks, Jimmy (James Spina) talked about writing. We stayed friends through high school and college, and he stayed true to his writing interests. He wrote about music for decades and still is involved in publishing magazines. He, along with his brother Dennis and the aforementioned Bob Cappuccio, have been with me every step of the way in the publication of these books.

———◆———

From the remembrances of Nazi concentration camps of the fictional David Weissman to the deaths of DJ Spinelli and Johnny Cipp (not accidentally) is precisely 100 years. In a sense, *Brotherhood of Forever* is meant to be a view of the times (1937 – 2037) through the eyes of typical people. What else could you expect of someone who taught a Western Civilization college course?

———◆———

I have saved the two most important stories for the end. Perhaps, it is because once they are written, it *really* will all be over. However, I know that is not true. I have been holding off because I know these will be very emotional moments for me. But here goes. . .

———◆———

I lost my father in 1982. Most of his life he was not in good health, and I attributed it to bad luck or perhaps poor health habits. It was only a casual comment by older members of the family that clued me in to the real reason for his illnesses and premature death. William John Rostron, Sr. had been in the United States Navy before World War II, and also long after the peace celebrations in the states. He was in Japan. . . in Hiroshima, ministering to the sick of both the victorious Americans and the defeated Japanese. The world understood little about the long-term effects of radiation. Ironically, he never mentioned this to me even though I went on to obtain a master's degree in Japanese History. He never regretted that part of his life, but he never spoke of it.

———◆———

When I set out on my journey to write this trilogy of books, I never intended to publish them. My original intention had been to amuse my friends who had experienced some or all the events described with my tale. During writing, I had visions of what specific individuals would think of seeing their lives revealed with a tone of fiction. In at least one case, I was too late.

I have often written that my characters are a combination of many real people. However, one person was there for all of the moments of Those Born Free—Central Park, the Café Wha, and the raid on the Driftwood Club. He claimed my bass as his instrument, thus saving me from arrest. Artie does not have the foul mouth of Gio, nor did he have an African-American girlfriend. However, in many senses of the word, he was Gio. His humor was a constant amusement to me in every band we shared. Though for half a century, we lived 1200 miles apart, we were in continuous contact. Therefore, when *Band in the Wind* was published, I mailed him one of the first copies.

Three months later, we finally met in Florida. We laughed as usual and reconnected. However, when the conversation came down to the book, reality set in. He had indeed enjoyed the first twenty pages—every time he read them. We had suspected, and his wife confirmed that he was in the early stages of vascular dementia. Each day, the same pages were new to him.

He and his wife now live back in New York, and we see them more often. Sometimes, we laugh like old times, and sometimes it is tough. He still mentions reading and liking the book though he doesn't remember what he liked.

With this in mind, I wrote the sections about Chris Delaney and his affliction as a tribute. In a sense, Gio morphed into Chris, and Those Born Free morphed into the Brotherhood Blues Band. As long as we can, Artie and I will still remember and still joke about the old times. However, Artie's plight makes me realize that no matter how much we talk and no matter how many books I write, someday we will all be forgotten. It's sad, but it's true.

Over two decades ago, my daughter Brittany wrote the words that would become a "hit song" for both Those Born Free and Chris Delaney and the Brotherhood Blues Band. I borrowed her lines to use in my books. As I finish this final book of the trilogy, I can't think of a more universal truth with which to end.

In time, time takes everything,
As memories fade to never.
How long will you steal from me?
This thief of my forever.

ACKNOWLEDGMENTS

Special Thanks to **The Killion Group**

Kim Killion – cover design

Jenn Jakes – formatting and so much more

E.M Effingham, "The Word Chopper" – editing

———————

And thanks to my Proofreaders:

Marilyn Rostron, Robert Cappuccio, Mike Burduck

———————

The Other Side of the Wind
Band in the Wind - Book 4

Now available from Amazon and Ingram in paperback, hardcover, digital, Amazon audible, and Kindle Unlimited

Made in the USA
Monee, IL
05 November 2024

69432214R00222